Chapter One

Fresh shoe prints in the dirt outside the abandoned Sterling homestead confirmed that Deputy US Marshal Colin McKenzie's hunch was likely right—the arsonist who'd nearly destroyed Colin's life a decade ago was back. And once again, Colin was going to put Brian Sterling right where he belonged—in prison.

But he had to catch him first.

He drew his Glock 22 and scanned the thick woods that surrounded this remote mountain property half an hour southwest of Gatlinburg, Tennessee. Late-afternoon sun slanted across the one-story craftsman-style house, casting shadows along the sagging porch. The once proud structure sported peeling yellowed paint that had started out white, railings missing most of their spindles and a cracked picture window that he remembered had an amazing view of the Smoky Mountains.

Back when the Sterling siblings and the McKenzie brothers had gone to Gatlinburg–Pittman High School together, a split three-rail fence had marked the line where a manicured lawn ended and wilderness began. Now, half the posts were tipping like drunks desperately trying to catch their balance. The rest littered the ground, having surrendered to the high winds and violent storms that often blew through the area. This decaying family home was a sad

reminder of what the Sterlings had lost, all because of the
selfish son who'd destroyed everyone's plans for the future.

Including Colin's.

He tightened his grip on his gun and crouched down to
make himself less of a target as he crept from the gravel
driveway to the house. Most of the windows didn't have
curtains or even blinds anymore, giving him a decent view
of the rooms. They were surprisingly neat and tidy. Maybe
the Sterlings paid someone to come up from town every
few months to clean the place. Too bad they weren't paying equal attention to the outside.

After a full circuit around the structure, he was confident his nemesis wasn't inside waiting to take a shot at him.
A tour of the cobweb-filled shed and the sadly empty horse
barn out back confirmed that no one had been in them for
quite some time, probably years.

Cursing the summer heat, he wiped a bead of sweat from
his forehead and returned to the front yard. All the while,
he kept his pistol trained on the trees that surrounded the
property. Was Brian out there right now, watching him? Or
had someone else left that shoe print?

It wasn't like a hiker would accidentally stumble across
this place. The Great Smoky Mountains National Park and
the Appalachian Trail were several rugged miles east. And
the steep winding road up here only led to the Sterling
homestead and one other house, Colin's, two miles farther
up the mountain. But Brian didn't know that. Colin had
purchased the land and built his home several years after
the Sterlings left Gatlinburg for Memphis.

From what Colin had heard, the move cost Brian's father over half his client list. Had he been able to rehabilitate
his once successful financial-advisor career in Memphis?
Did his wife find a church community that she enjoyed
as much as the one here? Was their daughter happy? Had

she managed to forget everyone here she'd once loved, or who'd once loved her?

Colin tightened his grip on his pistol.

He didn't have the answers to any of those questions. All he knew for sure was that the family had sacrificed everything to move six hours away so they could be closer to FCI, the Federal Correctional Institution, where Brian was serving his fifteen-year sentence.

Until he'd decided to give himself a get-out-of-jail-early card less than twenty-four hours ago.

Colin hadn't seriously expected that the escaped convict would risk the long drive to Gatlinburg with his face plastered all over the news. But Brian wasn't known for being a deep thinker. He wasn't known for thinking much about his actions at all, or their impact on others. At nineteen he'd nearly burned two people alive. Now, at twenty-nine, while escaping a prison transport van that was taking him to the courthouse, he'd murdered a police officer. He'd made a wife a widow, a young son fatherless and put a target on his back for the entire Tennessee law-enforcement community.

Without noticing any movement near the tree line, and hearing only the sound of his own boots crunching on dry weeds and gravel, Colin eased back to his pickup. A few minutes later, he concealed his truck behind a stand of basswood trees about thirty feet from the roadway. Hoofing it from there, he selected a heavily canopied oak that would offer a clear view of the house while providing him with shade and concealment. After settling onto a thick branch a third of the way up the tree, he leaned back against the trunk and stretched out his long legs in front of him. Now, all he had to do was wait.

Chapter Two

Peyton Sterling coaxed her aging SUV up the long bumpy driveway that was more dirt than gravel. Her home loomed ahead and she immediately averted her gaze.

Focus on the garage. Don't look at the rest of the house. Don't look at the house.

But, of course, she did, and winced. Even though it had been over three months since she'd returned to Gatlinburg, the sight of her mom's weed-choked flower beds and the dilapidated family home still made her heart ache.

The life insurance money and small inheritance that she'd received had gotten her through so far. She'd paid a repairman to do the bare minimum to make it functional, like install a new garage door opener because she could barely lift the door otherwise. And she'd had no choice but to use a chunk of the money to renovate the kitchen. That was a necessity for her fledgling business, an investment in her future. Unfortunately, fixing everything else that was wrong with the house wasn't an expense that she could justify, or afford. Fixing them herself wasn't feasible either. She was far from handy in the home improvement department. If she tried to repair a leaky faucet she'd probably end up flooding the entire house.

Of course, even if she'd been handy, by the time she got home every evening, she was too tired to do much more than grab a bite to eat before collapsing into bed. Then she had to be up before dawn to bake fresh delicacies for the café and start the whole cycle all over again. There wasn't enough time, energy or money to make a dent in her long to-do list at home.

Thankfully, tomorrow was Saturday, the one day of the week when she had two full-time helpers at the shop instead of just one. With Joan and Melissa taking care of things, she could sleep in. But it wasn't like she could relax and do nothing all day. She had to use her day off to catch up on laundry, clean the house, work on the books for the store, order new supplies. In some ways, she worked harder on her "day off" than during the rest of the week.

Blowing out a deep breath, she parked inside the garage and then forced her tired body out of the SUV. If an aching back and bruised-feeling feet were what it took to make a business profitable, Peyton's Place should have been a roaring success by now. Unfortunately, success was coming much more slowly than she'd hoped. Sometimes the only thing keeping her from quitting was the worry over where Melissa and Joan would end up if she had to close the shop's doors.

After slapping her palm on the garage door button on the wall, she headed into the mudroom. As always, when she continued into the kitchen, the creamy yellow walls and white shaker-style cabinets embraced her like a hug, helping to ease the tension that had built up in her shoulders all day. This was her domain. This was where she felt most at home. And it was one of the few things that could always make her smile.

She hung her purse on a peg beside the door. But instead of heading through the cased opening on the left into the family room, she smoothed her hand over the cool marble island. If she was honest with herself, renovating the kitchen and bringing it into the current century wasn't just to enable her to supply her café with fresh baked goods. It fed her soul as well.

The sinfully luxurious stainless-steel Sub-Zero refrigerator, the double ovens built into the wall, the high-end finishes helped make this room her happy place. The treasured memories within these walls were priceless. Especially now.

I miss you so much, Mom.

Her father had labeled her and her mother obsessed. Maybe they had been. But there was no denying that her happiest memories revolved around cooking. Either they'd been making s'mores in the family room fireplace or she and her mom had been in here baking cakes, cookies and pastries. Somehow, kneading dough or making frosting from scratch could help Peyton forget the arguments, the trouble her brother kept getting into, even her mother's eccentric tendencies and unpredictable mood swings. When Peyton was working in the kitchen, all her troubles seemed to melt away.

Even now, just smelling a loaf of bread baking in the oven could transport her back to her high school days, when she was young and in love, happier than she'd ever been and probably ever would be again. To a time when her family was relatively whole, when *she* was still whole. But those days were gone and could never be recaptured. One horrific event had fragmented their lives forever. She'd lost everything that mattered that night. Or, at least, that's what she'd thought, until a slippery, rainy road just a few months ago proved she'd still had more to lose.

I love you, Mom. Wish you were here.

Her shoulders slumped as she reluctantly turned from her homey, comforting kitchen toward the opening to the family room. She needed to head to her bedroom, shower, change into her pajamas. But just looking at the cave-like gloom beyond the doorway was already making her feel down. Had it always been that dark? Or did it just seem that way now that the family who'd once lived in this place no longer existed? The only warm body around here at the moment was Peyton. Unless she counted the rats and squirrels that had taken up residence after she and her parents moved to Memphis.

She'd lost count of how many critters she'd either chased out or carried out after setting traps. Based on the scratching sounds she sometimes still heard in the walls, there were a few stubborn holdouts she'd yet to evict. Squeezing her eyes shut, she tried to recapture her earlier contentment. Remember the scent of all those candles her mom used to set around the house on evenings when it was too hot to light a fire in the fireplace. She could almost picture it, see her mom's sweet smile, hear the rustle of fabric as her mom put on a crisp white apron.

"Hey, Peyton."

Her eyes flew open. She automatically grabbed the broom that she always kept propped against the wall just in case another rat made an appearance. But she froze when a painfully thin man with strawberry blond hair a shade darker than hers emerged from the shadows to stand in the kitchen opening. Her jaw dropped open in shock as he watched her, his sheepish grin not quite reaching his haunted eyes.

"Long time, no see, huh, sis?"

"B… Brian?" Her voice came out a choked whisper as she struggled to make sense of what she was seeing. Of *who* she was seeing. "I don't understand. Is that really you?"

A sound behind her had her whirling around to see another man emerge from the laundry room. She pressed a shaking hand to her throat as she drank in the achingly familiar short dark hair, shoulders that had broadened and filled out since she'd last seen him. He was taller now too, towering over her, making the kitchen seem much smaller than it had moments ago.

He was dressed in light gray pants, a white button-up shirt and a tie. His sleeves were long in spite of the warm temperatures outside. Little white scars on the backs of his hands left no doubt about the reason for those long sleeves. Her heart seemed to stutter in her chest and her throat tightened.

"Colin?" The once treasured name that she hadn't allowed past her lips in years tumbled from them in a whisper that was a dash of pain and a huge dollop of guilt.

He didn't even glance at her.

He slid a pistol out of the holster on his hip and leveled it at her brother. "Brian Sterling, you're under arrest for felony escape and the murder of Officer Owen Jennings."

Peyton drew in a sharp breath. What was Colin talking about? He was arresting her brother? Dear God, no. This couldn't be happening. Not again.

The blood seemed to drain from her brother's face, leaving him a gaunt, frightened shadow of the person he used to be. His haunted gray eyes, the same ones that Peyton saw every time she looked in a mirror, pleaded with her to help him. The same eyes that had stared at her in bewilderment from the back seat of a squad car as a barn burned to the ground in the distance. The same ones that had blurred with tears on the other side of a thick glass partition in the prison's visiting room when Peyton broke the news about their mother's death.

She stood frozen, the broom clutched in her hand. It was ten years ago all over again. And just like then, she was forced to make a choice that no one should ever have to make—the choice between the man she loved and her own flesh and blood.

She slammed the broom against Colin's forearm, knocking the pistol out of his hand.

"Run, Brian! Run!" she choked out.

He whirled around and took off toward the front door.

Colin swiped his pistol up off the hardwood floor and gave her a furious, searing look that burned right through her heart. Then he sprinted through the house after her brother.

Chapter Three

Peyton twisted her hands together in her lap as she sat beside one of the desks in the squad room, waiting to discover her fate. The police officer who'd ordered her to sit there was talking to a handful of other men and women at the far end of the vast, open room. It seemed like every cop in Gatlinburg was here. The place was buzzing with anger and excitement as they studied maps and gathered flashlights, preparing to hunt her brother down like a rabid dog.

She wanted to scream, shake them, somehow make them realize what she couldn't all those years ago: *her brother was innocent.* The only thing stopping her was that there was no denying what she'd seen with her own eyes—Brian, standing in her kitchen five years before his sentence was up. They were right that he'd broken out of prison. But they were wrong about the horrible, evil thing they also claimed that he'd done—killed a Memphis police officer after the escape.

Brian had always been headstrong and rebellious, with anger and impulse-control issues that had had him seeing a therapist from the time he was ten years old. But he was also sweet and sensitive. Never a bully, he was the kid who got picked on by his classmates because he was so awkward and shy. He adored animals and had gotten in trouble countless times for bringing home strays. The brother who cried after watching a sad commercial could never have set fire to a building with two people inside. That was the reason she could never, ever believe in his guilt. And that was the reason she knew that he hadn't shot that police officer in Memphis.

"Is that why you came back to Gatlinburg? Because you knew your brother was planning to escape and you wanted to be here to help him?"

She jerked around to meet Colin McKenzie's accusing stare as he stood beside the desk. It pained her that his deep voice, angry or not, sent the same jolt of longing through her that it had since they'd both turned fifteen and discovered their friendship had blossomed into something more. The cute boy who'd made all the girls' hearts flutter in high school had matured into a mouth-wateringly gorgeous man. But all that physical perfection was spoiled by the look of hate blazing from his stormy blue eyes.

The hate was definitely new.

"I suppose from your viewpoint I deserve that. But, no. Why I came back has nothing to do with my brother. Even though he was wrongfully convicted, I would never help him escape from prison."

"You'd just help him escape from your kitchen when a law-enforcement officer placed him under arrest. Is that the line you've drawn in the sand?"

She curled her fingers against her palms. "Okay, I *definitely* deserved that. And I completely understand that it looked that way to you. But from my viewpoint, my *innocent* brother was being threatened with a gun. I was protecting him."

He jerked his shirt sleeve up a few inches on his left arm, revealing a smattering of puckered burn scars. "I pulled two people out of a burning barn after your brother set the fire. *Innocent* isn't a word I'd use to describe him."

Threatening tears burned her eyes but she viciously held them back. "I'm sorry, Colin. About everything. I truly am. I hate that you were hurt. But the truth hasn't changed. Brian didn't set that fire."

He jerked his sleeve back down. "Do you *want* to go to prison?"

She stared at him in surprise. "What?"

"You're in a precarious position, Peyton. If I officially arrest you and the DA decides to press charges, you could end up in prison for aiding and abetting a felon."

"But, I didn't mean—"

"Why did you do it? Why did you help him?"

She spread her hands in a helpless gesture. "I told you. I was protecting him. It was instinct. A choice—family or…" She chewed her lip.

"Or me. And once again, you didn't choose me."

The bitterness in his voice made her ache. But there was nothing she could do, nothing she could say that could ever fix what she'd destroyed so many years ago.

Because he was right.

"Give me a reason *not* to arrest you."

She slowly shook her head, no longer able to hold back the tears. "I can't. What I did today was wrong. I know that. But it was automatic, without any rational thought behind it. I'd probably do the same thing again if I had a do-over. Protecting my family is as ingrained in me as breathing. Can't you understand that?"

Every muscle in his body seemed to tense, as if he was debating what to say but didn't trust himself to speak.

She brushed the tears from her cheeks.

He swore softly and turned away, his ground-eating stride quickly taking him across the room to one of the groups of officers talking by a window.

Sniffing, she breathed deeply, willing the tears to stop. And all the while, she watched him, unable to look away. Her gaze caressed his profile the way her fingers once had. She knew every angle of his chiseled face, had traced the stubble across his jaw to his hairline, had kissed the barely there mustache. He still maintained that same look, like a man who hadn't shaved in three days. But where she'd loved and adored the boy, she didn't know what to make of the man. He was a stranger, with the power to destroy the fragile new world she'd created. And she couldn't even give him a reason not to.

He nodded at something one of the men said, then strode back to the desk. "Get up."

Her face flushed hot with embarrassment. She stood and smoothed her jeans and blouse into place before holding her wrists out in front of her.

He frowned. "What are you doing?"

"Hoping you won't make me put my hands behind my back to put the handcuffs on. This is humiliating enough as it is." When he only stared at her, she lowered her arms. "Aren't you arresting me?"

"That depends on whether you'll give me what I want."

She drew in a sharp breath, his words awakening memories of the two of them together. His mouth, hot against her neck. His tongue tracing the valley between her breasts. His teasing smile as he slid down her body and hooked his fingers into the top of her jeans.

His breath hitched. "Don't look at me that way, Peyton."

She shivered and ruthlessly fought back the erotic images that had goose bumps breaking out all over her suddenly hypersensitive skin. Trying to pretend ignorance, she asked, "What do you mean?"

His eyes narrowed. "Like you're remembering how good it was between us."

She swallowed, remembering exactly how good it had been.

His blue eyes darkened, but not with passion. "The past, what you and I shared, died the day you left Gatlinburg without so much as a goodbye. A lifetime of growing up together, four years of dating, of sharing everything two people supposedly in love can share, and you couldn't bring yourself to answer any of my calls, respond to even one of my texts. Well I got the message from you, loud and clear. And nothing could ever make me go down that road again.'

Her face flamed at his cruel, unnecessary rejection. She cast a surreptitious glance around the room before sinking back down into the chair so she could put some space between the two of them. Thankfully, no one seemed to be paying any attention to her and Colin at the moment. They were all too busy making plans to go after her only sibling.

Wait. Phone calls? Texts? What was he talking about? He'd never called her, not once. "Colin, I don't understand. What are you—"

"What I want is to make a deal with you. Your cooperation in exchange for your brother's life."

She pressed a hand against her throat, unable to reconcile his shocking words with the man standing before her. This wasn't the Colin she remembered, not even close. Had she ever really known him at all? Or was this hard, unyielding man the result of what *she'd* done?

"You're seriously threatening to kill him if I don't cooperate? How could you be so heartless and cruel?"

His eyes narrowed again, his brow wrinkling with anger. "Don't accuse me of contemplating murder as if you have some moral high ground to stand on."

She gasped with outrage. But before she could respond, he leaned toward her, arms braced on the desk, crowding her back against her chair.

"Unlike your cop-killing brother," he said in a furious whisper, "I'm not a murderer. I wasn't saying that I was going to harm Brian. Look around you, Peyton. *I'm* not the threat. *Everyone else* is. They're all fired up to hunt him down. Once the trackers get here, his chances plummet to near zero."

Alarm skittered up her spine. "Trackers? Chances? What are you saying?"

"Your brother murdered a law-enforcement officer. He—"

"No. He didn't. He wouldn't."

Colin made a frustrated sound in his throat before grabbing a chair from beside a nearby desk and rolling it in front of her. He plopped down and moved close, his knees almost touching hers.

"They're bringing in bloodhounds to hunt down your brother and the other escapees." He kept his voice low, barely above a whisper. "Police officers and federal agents are lining up in neighboring counties, demanding a chance to help with the search. They're going to find them, Peyton. A cop killer isn't going to escape, not around here."

"Stop saying that. My brother's not a killer." She let out a ragged breath. "Please, Colin. Stop."

Something shifted behind his eyes, like clouds tumbling through a darkening sky. He drew a slow, deep breath and glanced around the room as if to get himself under control. When he looked at her again, some of the anger seemed to have drained out of him. In its place was a sense of urgency and frustration, visible in the tense set of his shoulders, the firm line of his jaw.

"What I'm trying to tell you is that Brian's life is in danger. Not because anyone is going to purposely try to kill him. But because everyone is hyperaware that someone who's shot one police officer won't hesitate to pull the trigger on another."

"But—"

He held a hand up to stop her. "What you don't seem to understand is that whether or not Brian's the one who pulled the trigger doesn't matter. The officer was killed when Brian and three other criminals escaped. Under the law, all four of them are guilty of felony murder."

Muscle memory had her reaching for his hand before she even thought about what she was doing. To her surprise, he took it, and entwined their fingers together. In spite of his anger, in spite of everything that had happened, or maybe because of it, Colin McKenzie was holding her hand. And just like that, she was able to pick up the pieces of her crumbling world and glue them back together.

It had always been that way between them. A simple look, or the warmth of his touch, grounded her, calmed her when things were going wrong. How odd that it would work today when he was part of the reason that her world was falling apart.

"What does felony murder mean exactly?" she whispered, barely able to force the words past her tight throat. "Does it mean...does it mean Brian could face the death penalty?"

He nodded, his hand tightening around hers.

"Oh, dear Lord. What am I going to do?"

"All you *can* do for now is help me try to save his life. Worry about the trial, about possible penalties, later. The entire law-enforcement community is on edge. They feel like their uniforms make them a target for a man who's already killed one of their own. They'll be quicker than normal to pull the trigger, out of self-preservation. That makes for an exceedingly dangerous situation, all the way around."

His words rang true. The room was bursting with anger, nervous energy. Soon they'd be searching for her brother with that dangerous mix of emotions fueled by fear and adrenaline, while heavily armed. Brian was in a world of trouble, even worse than she'd realized.

"What kind of a deal are you offering?"

"I won't lie and pretend that I can guarantee your brother's safety. But he has a better chance of making it out of the mountains alive if I'm the one who catches him."

She blinked. "You? But you..."

"Have more reason than most to want to catch him? You've got that right. But out of respect for your parents, whom I once thought of as my own family, I'd like to capture their son alive and give him a chance in the courts instead of against a hail of bullets. If you cooperate fully, help me figure out where he might be hiding, then I'll hold off on arresting you for now."

His implied threat had her tugging her hand free. "Hold off? For now? What does that mean?"

He flexed his fingers and sat back, his face an unreadable mask. "I reserve the right to arrest you and charge you with a felony for that stunt you pulled at your family's house today. If you don't legitimately help me figure out where he is, I *will* put you in jail and bring you up on charges."

"You're forcing me to choose again? Between you and my brother?"

He arched a brow. "What would be the point? We both know how that would turn out."

She jerked back, his words stabbing her like a hundred daggers straight to the heart. But it wasn't the words that hurt the most. It was the pain that leached through his tone, pain he was obviously trying to hide beneath a veil of rage. His pain was so much worse to bear than his fury, because she was the one who'd caused it. She'd taken a sweet, kind young man and twisted him into this bitter, angry person in front of her.

She wrapped her arms around her middle and closed her eyes, shutting out the ugliness of everything that had happened, everything that was still happening. Somehow, she had to get a handle on her swirling emotions, without relying on her former childhood sweetheart to help her. She had to find the inner strength to do this on her own. If she gave in to her emotions, she'd slide onto the floor in a boneless puddle of anguish and self-disgust. And that wouldn't help anyone.

"Peyton?" His voice was laced with impatience now.

Breathe. Just breathe. Pull yourself together.

"Peyton? Are you okay? Do I need to call an EMT?"

The genuine concern underlying his tone had her eyes fluttering open. The truth was there, in the way he was watching her so intently. In spite of everything, he still cared. Maybe she hadn't destroyed him after all. Maybe there was still some goodness left inside. Maybe, just maybe, she could trust him to help Brian.

She straightened, drew a bracing breath. "No, I'm... I'll be okay. Thank you."

He frowned, seemingly unconvinced. But he gave her a curt nod and motioned toward the groups of officers scattered around the room. "You can play the odds and wait and see if the makeshift posse shoots first and asks questions later. Or you can work with me to increase his odds of being brought in alive. That's the offer that I'm making. It's your choice. But you have to make a decision. Right now."

"What happens if I say yes, that I'll try to help you?"

"Since your house is still being processed as a crime scene, we go back to my place and you answer my questions there. You tell me everything he's told you through the years, in every visit you made to the prison or every letter or email you exchanged. We make lists of places he mentioned, places he talked about visiting again one day, any people still in this area whom he might turn to for help. And we make a plan to lure him into a trap."

A trap for Brian, just like the trap closing in around her. She shivered even though the air-conditioning wasn't all that successful in keeping out the brutal summer heat.

"If I don't help you, my brother could be killed and I go to jail. If I do help you, he could still be killed, but you'll do your best not to kill him. And even then, he faces the possibility of the death penalty. In return, I have no guarantees that I won't go to jail at some point too. Do I have it right? That's the so-called deal you're offering?"

The fight seemed to drain out of him, leaving him looking tired, almost defeated. "That's the deal. I know it's not much. But it's the best I can offer."

"Okay."

His eyes widened. "Okay? Just like that?"

"I'm not an idiot, Colin. I can see for myself that you're right about the danger that Brian's in. And I can't help him while sitting in a jail cell. I'm going to have to trust that the Colin I once knew is still inside you somewhere—the man with honor, integrity and mercy. I'm putting my faith, and my brother's life, in your hands. We have a deal."

Chapter Four

After conferring again with some other officers, Colin returned to the desk. "The police are gathering in the main conference room to ask you some questions," he told her. "They'll let us know when they're ready."

Peyton followed his gaze to a door on the other side of the room. "The police? You make it sound like you aren't one of them."

"I'm not." His eyes hardened like brittle chips of ice. "Guess I neglected to formally introduce myself given our past…association." He pulled an ID badge out of his pants pocket and held it up. "Deputy US Marshal Colin McKenzie. At your service."

She ignored the gibe about their past, and his sarcasm, even though it was hard to keep absorbing his barbs without lashing out. That wouldn't do her or her brother any good. Still, she secretly admitted that the shiny silver circle with a five-point star in the middle that said United States Marshal made her proud. He'd followed his dream, kept his family legacy alive by going into law enforcement like his prosecutor mother and federal judge father. The Mighty McKenzie must be very proud of his third-born son. She wondered if his brothers had pursued similar careers.

"I didn't realize there was a US Marshals office in Gatlinburg."

"There isn't." He slid his badge back into his pocket.

"Knoxville's the nearest field office. But that's not where I work most of the time. Usually, I'm on taskforces throughout the state. Last week I started a new assignment here, working out of the Gatlinburg police station as a liaison, tracking down fugitives with outstanding warrants. Cold cases, basically."

That explained why she hadn't seen him around town since she'd gotten back. She'd both hoped for and dreaded bumping into him at some point.

"And you've been assigned to hunt down Brian?"

"No. A team of marshals was assembled out of Memphis to recapture him and the others immediately after the escape. The only reason I'm involved is because when I heard Brian was spotted heading toward this area, I decided to check out your place, just in case he went home. I was surprised to find that he had."

"No more surprised than I was."

His jaw tightened. "Your interference allowed him to get away."

"I'm—"

"Sorry. Yes. I know."

An uncomfortable silence settled between them until an officer opened the conference room door and waved at them.

"That's our cue. Chief Landry is ready to talk to you." Colin motioned for her to precede him. "It's a full house. Given the need to pass along any useful information to the search teams as quickly as possible, the team leads are all in there, as well as detectives. That's why they're in a conference room instead of one of the smaller interview rooms."

She wiped her suddenly sweaty palms against her jeans and headed toward the open door. But ten feet away, he stopped her with a hand on her shoulder.

"Do you know where Brian's hiding?"

"No. I don't. I swear."

He nodded. "All right. We'll talk later, in private, and try to figure out where he might be holed up. But if you do have any ideas and are asked about him in that room, tell the truth. Deal or not. Lying will only get you in more trouble."

"But I don't want Brian hurt. Won't telling them put his life in jeopardy?"

"Tell the truth," he repeated. "The second you feel like you know where he might be, I'll be the first one out the door trying to find him. I'll do everything I can to protect him. You have my word."

"Why? Why do you even want to help him, or me? And don't tell me it's because of my parents."

His brows raised. "You and I may be over, but I loved you once. If nothing else, for the sake of what we once were to each other, I feel obligated to keep you both safe. Is that so difficult to understand?"

"After everything that's happened, yes. It is. You're a far better person than me, Colin. In your place, I don't know that I could be so accommodating."

He frowned and started to say something but the officer who'd waved at them earlier motioned at them again.

Peyton didn't move. "Should I be asking for a lawyer?" she whispered.

He turned his back to the officer. "Probably. Are you asking for one?"

She considered her meager finances and the staggering cost of Brian's continued legal bills that had crippled her entire family financially. It would take her years to pay off her portion of his lawyer fees. Adding more legal costs on top of that would be devastating. "No. I'll just wing it, I guess."

He frowned. "If you can't afford one, I can take care of—"

"No." She cleared her throat and lowered her voice. "No, but thank you for offering. That's very…nice of you, especially considering…" Her voice trailed off. The air between them seemed to thicken with tension. She glanced at the white lines on his hands. How he could have gone through what he had and offer to help her was beyond her comprehension, in spite of his insistence that he felt obligated because of their past.

It felt a thousand ways wrong.

She could never take his money, even though she knew he'd never miss it. Money had never been a concern for any of the McKenzies. They'd become wealthy the old-fashioned way. They'd inherited it. Colin didn't work because he had to. He worked because he wanted to. But that wouldn't make it right for her to take advantage of his generosity.

He studied her, as if deciding whether or not to argue the point. Then he shrugged and led her to the conference room.

It took a supreme effort of will not to turn around and run when she saw the people waiting for her inside. A dozen men and women went silent at her approach. Each of them had a legal pad or an electronic tablet on the table in front of them. And every one of them was watching her like a scientist observing a particularly nasty insect through a microscope.

"Over there." A lean, middle-aged man with skin the color of an old saddle waved toward two empty chairs directly across the table from him.

She took one of the chairs. Colin took the other.

The man who'd motioned them to sit down gave her a smile that was polite, but far from warm. "I'm Chief Landry. Obviously, you already know Deputy US Marshal McKenzie. Everyone else in this room is either a regular police officer or a detective working for me. Miss Sterling, I want to make it clear that you're not under arrest. I'm going to ask you some questions and, hopefully, you'll do me the courtesy of answering them. You're free to go at any time. Do you understand?"

She glanced longingly at the door but nodded. She understood more than he realized. The legal system wasn't exactly a stranger to her given her family's history fighting the charges against her brother. By not arresting her, the chief didn't have to tell her about her legal rights or remind her that she could have an attorney present. She probably should go ahead and ask for a lawyer, in spite of the cost. But she didn't want to prolong this any more than necessary. She'd just see how things went. Although how they could look worse than they did right now was beyond her.

A stack of folders sat to Landry's right. He took the top one and set it on the table in front of him. He flipped it open, revealing an ugly window into the past, half a dozen color photographs that he methodically lined up in the middle of the table.

The burned-out hull of a building, smoke rising as fire fighters doused the embers.

The dance hall with scores of students clustered in small groups, being questioned by the police.

The ambulance taking Colin away.

Beside her, Colin tensed in his chair.

"Brief history for those in the room unfamiliar with Brian Sterling's case." Landry pulled a sheet of paper from the thick folder and ran a finger across a bulleted list. "The only son of Molly and Benjamin Sterling, Brian was suspected of setting five separate fires as a juvenile but was never convicted, mainly because no one was hurt, the damage was minimal and his parents agreed to make restitution to the property owners as well as take their son to a therapist. That all changed when, at the age of nineteen..." He frowned and flipped the page as if looking for something else. "This doesn't look right. He was a senior in high school? At nineteen?"

Peyton's chest tightened. She hadn't known about the fires. That hadn't come out at the trial. It must have been part of a sealed juvenile record that the chief had convinced some judge to let him access. Her parents, and her brother, had hidden that information from her. Why? To keep her from doubting her brother's innocence? If whatever had happened in his past was relevant in any way to the accusations against him when he was nineteen, the judge at his arson trial would have unsealed the records. Her parents should have trusted her to understand that, and to know that she would continue her support and faith in her brother. She knew him better than anyone. She loved him. Unsealed records thrown at her in a room full of police who wanted to hurt him didn't change that. She drew a shaky breath and forced herself to answer the chief's question.

"Brian had...difficulties in school. He was held back a year, so he was a senior the same time I was even though he's a year older than me."

"Thank you, Miss Sterling. Says here that a few weeks before graduation, Gatlinburg–Pittman High School held a dance at a place called The Barn, a combination restaurant and dance hall on a nature preserve just inside the Great Smoky Mountains National Park. Toward the end of the evening, Brian poured accelerant on the dilapidated original barn that was no longer used for dances, and set it on fire."

"Wrong."

He glanced up at Peyton. "Excuse me?"

"My brother didn't set the fire."

"Twelve jurors disagree with you and sentenced him to fifteen years in prison."

"Juries wrongly convict innocent people all the time. I'm sure you've heard of DNA exonerating people after they've spent years in prison for crimes someone else committed."

He sat back and glanced at Colin before continuing. "I can only deal with the facts as they stand right now. Your brother is a convicted arsonist. There were two people in that barn—"

"No one was supposed to be inside. No Trespassing and Danger signs were posted outside."

"Yes, well, that doesn't change the fact that a pair of randy teenagers snuck away from the chaperones at the dance and hid inside the barn for a make-out session."

Her mother had been one of those chaperones. *Why couldn't you have kept a better eye on them, Mom?*

"When your brother set the fire—" He held up his hands to stop the denial she'd been ready to make. "When the structure went up in flames and the couple was overcome by smoke and trapped by those flames, Deputy US Marshal McKenzie, at the time a senior at the same high school, rescued those people at no small cost to himself, as I'm sure you're aware."

"Yes." She swallowed hard. "I'm well aware."

Colin rested his forearms on the table. "Thank you for that history lesson, chief." His droll tone said that he was anything but thankful. "What you all need to know is that Brian Sterling is a convicted arsonist with a complete disregard for human life."

Peyton stiffened.

"You should consider him armed and dangerous. Approach with extreme caution. And be aware that if cornered, he could resort to setting a fire in order to escape. Now, Chief Landry, I believe you had some questions for Miss Sterling that might assist your teams in narrowing the search area?"

Landry seemed to take Colin's interruption in stride and readily moved on to discuss her brother's escape, along with three other convicts, grilling her with questions as he did so. At one point, he announced that marshals had questioned her father at his Memphis home, immediately after the escape, due to his close proximity to the site. Benjamin Sterling had denied any involvement, not that Peyton would have expected otherwise. Her father had always been one of Brian's harshest critics. It was always she, and her mom, who stood up for him. The fact that the marshals had even considered that her father would help Brian was ludicrous.

"Your father claimed not to know where you were or how to contact you," the chief said. "Do you know why he'd do that? He didn't tell the marshals that you'd moved back to Gatlinburg."

She clutched the edge of her seat beneath the table. "I imagine he thought he was protecting me. Having police at my business or home would have stirred up all the old gossip. It could hurt my café, the life I'm trying to build here." And more important to her father, smear the precious Sterling name once again. Reputation was everything to her dad, far more important than his family.

The chief gave her a skeptical look then studied the notes in front of him. "Says here your mother passed away several months ago."

She could feel Colin's stare beside her. He'd seemed surprised to hear that she owned a café. And at the mention of her mom's death, he seemed genuinely shocked. She regretted that he'd found out this way. But that didn't mean that she was prepared to discuss the details. She was barely holding herself together. Discussing her mom right now would destroy her.

"My mother's death has nothing to do with what's going on with Brian. I'm not going to talk about her."

To her surprise, Landry nodded and moved to other questions. She began to wonder whether talking about her mom would have been easier than hearing the details of her brother's escape. Landry's account of what had happened had nausea coiling in her stomach.

Brian was being transported along with three other convicts to the courthouse in downtown Memphis. Apparently, his lawyer had gotten him a hearing about alleged inhumane conditions at the prison. Since Peyton was well versed in the lawyer's tactics, having worked many an odd job to help her parents pay for all those billable hours, she highly doubted that Brian was being treated unfairly. This latest complaint was likely based on Brian's desire to get some time out of his cell. And he'd apparently taken advantage of the situation by escaping from the prison transport van.

"—and you claim you didn't know anything about your brother's plan?"

She clasped her hands in her lap. "Again, no, Chief Landry. As I've said repeatedly, I didn't even know that he was out of prison until I saw him in my kitchen. Even then, it didn't quite register. I thought his lawyer must have finally managed to get his sentence shortened and Brian wanted to surprise me. Before today, I hadn't seen him in a little over three months."

"Then you didn't know that shortly after he and three other men got away, they were confronted by Memphis police officer Owen Jennings and one of them shot and killed him?"

She drew a shaky breath. "My heart goes out to Officer Jennings and his family. But, no, I didn't know anything about it. I still don't. How did they escape? How did the man who shot Officer Jennings get a gun?"

"You mean how did *your brother* get the gun? Deputy Marshal McKenzie has told me he used to take you and your brother target practicing when you were teenagers. So we know your brother's more than capable of handling a weapon."

She glanced at Colin, then back at Landry. "Are you saying that you know that Brian is the one who shot Officer Jennings? Not one of the others?"

"No. He's not." Colin sat forward in his chair, his gaze riveted on the police chief. "Dash cam video from the officer's patrol car shows him getting shot and the four prisoners running from the scene. Which man shot him is still to be determined."

The chief sighed. "Marshal McKenzie, you're here as a courtesy due to your close ties to the original arson case, and because you located Mr. Sterling earlier today in an unfortunately failed attempt to apprehend him. I'd appreciate you not interfering in my questioning of Miss Sterling."

"Stick to what's relevant and I won't interfere."

The chief smiled, seeming to shrug off Colin's admonition. Peyton figured the two must have a solid friendship, or at least mutual respect, for Landry not to be upset.

"I'm okay moving on to the question of an alibi. Miss Sterling, where were you yesterday morning between the hours of ten and eleven?"

"Alibi? For what?"

"We need to know who might have, and might still be, helping the four convicts who escaped during transport from the Federal Correctional Institution in Memphis yesterday morning. So, again, can you please account for your whereabouts?"

"You seriously think I would have helped them?"

"Peyton." Colin spoke softly beside her. "Just answer the question."

"No," she said. "No, I wasn't six hours away in Memphis while simultaneously at my shop here in Gatlinburg."

"Your shop? I believe you mentioned a café earlier?" Landry asked.

"Yes. I own a café and gift shop combination called Peyton's Place. It's in The Village, off Parkway. It's new, not far from The Hofbrauhaus restaurant."

"Can someone there vouch for where you were yesterday?"

"Joan—she works for me—she can tell you I was there all day, as I am most days. But she's not there right now.

The shop closed at six. It will open again in the morning, at nine."

"I'm sure you understand the urgency of verifying your alibi as quickly as possible. Waiting until morning isn't an option. Joan's last name? Her address?"

"Fairmont, Joan Fairmont. I should call her first and let her know that—"

"If you do, that will destroy the credibility of her as an alibi witness. One of my men will head over there now and speak to her. The address?"

She hesitated. "I don't want them frightened by a policeman knocking on their door."

"Them?"

"I have two employees. Joan is full-time, Melissa's part-time. They're roommates."

He motioned to one of the detectives who then wrote something down on the legal pad in front of him. Apparently he was making notes about her alibi.

"And why would they be frightened if a detective knocks on their door? Do they have something to hide?"

Her face heated. "Of course not. But they…they both have criminal records." She could practically feel Colin's gaze burning into her. "Nothing dangerous or anything. They were both homeless and became friends while trying to survive on the streets. They were hungry and got caught shoplifting at a grocery store. Both did a few months in the local jail."

"Are there any other criminals working at your shop that we need to know about?"

She had to count to ten before she could speak without yelling. "I don't consider Joan and Melissa to be *criminals*. Being poor and hungry are hardly crimes. They made restitution for what little food they took when they were practically starving. And they're working hard to turn their lives around."

"No doubt. My apologies if I seemed insensitive."

His sincere tone went a long way toward defusing her anger. She gave him a crisp nod, accepting his apology.

"Any other employees?"

She hesitated.

"Miss Sterling?"

She glanced at Colin, but his stormy eyes gave her no indication of what he was thinking. "Technically, no. But Mr. Hardy comes by to perform odd jobs for food. He… I believe he may have had some scrapes with the law as well."

Colin focused his gaze on a spot on the far wall.

"Do you have Mr. Hardy's address so we can speak to him too?" Landry asked.

"I don't think he has an address. I've offered to let him sleep in our storage room. But he always declines, says something about the stars being his roof."

"How often does he come around?"

"Pretty much every day. But there's no need to bother him. Joan will corroborate what I told you about being at the shop." She rattled off Joan and Melissa's address at the halfway house where they lived. "Please be polite and non-judgmental when you speak to them. They've had a hard time of it and have been wonderful friends and workers."

"I'm sure we can figure out how to ask them a few questions without traumatizing or insulting them."

Since she was feeling a bit traumatized herself, she had little faith in his statement. She wrapped her arms around her middle. How much more of this interrogation was she going to have to endure?

The detective who'd been taking notes about Joan and Melissa picked up his legal pad and left the room.

"Last question, Miss Sterling."

Thank God.

"You said you haven't seen your brother in three months, prior to him showing up in your home yesterday. Do you have any ideas about where he might hide given that we've got roadblocks and checkpoints all throughout the county?"

She shook her head. "No. I honestly don't. It's not like he has any friends left around here. Our house is the only place I'd expect him to go."

"If you think of something, you'll let me know?"

"Of course." Would she? She had no idea. If Brian had indeed killed a police officer, she'd be the first one to turn him in. But he'd been falsely convicted of one crime already. Trusting the police and the judicial system not to pin something else on him wasn't likely to happen. And she really hadn't had time to consider where he might hide. Where *would* he go if he was hunkering down, trying to keep someone from finding him?

The chief motioned to one of the detectives a few seats down, who then got up and handed him the tablet he'd been using during the meeting. Landry studied it a few moments, then turned it around and slid it across the table to Peyton. "Officer Redding typed up your statement, everything you said during our chat."

Chat? If this was a chat, she couldn't imagine how awful a real interrogation would have been.

He tapped the screen, scrolling to the top of the form. "Read through that. If you agree that it's accurate, sign at the bottom. If anything needs correction, have Marshal McKenzie get Detective Redding back in here. Make yourself comfortable while we confirm your alibi. You don't have your phone do you? I don't want you calling your employees."

She automatically felt her jeans pockets. "No. Actually, I don't. I think it's in my purse. But I'm not even sure where I left my purse." A feeling of panic settled in her stomach as she tried to remember where it might be. Her credit cards and pretty much her entire life was in there.

"It's locked in my desk," Colin said. "I think your phone was in the side pocket."

She smiled in relief. "Thank you."

He nodded.

"That's settled then." Landry shoved his chair back and stood. The other people in the room began filing out the door.

"Chief Landry?" she asked.

He paused. "Yes?"

"You seem to be focused entirely on my brother in regards to the escape and the death of Officer Jennings. Is there a reason for that? There were three other convicts involved, based on what you said earlier."

He smiled. "I assure you that we're looking into all four men and speaking to anyone who knows them. Perhaps I should have asked just to be sure—have you ever met Damon Patterson, Vincent Snyder or Tyler King?"

"None of those names sound familiar, no. Are they the convicts from the van? Do you think they're still with my brother or did they split up?"

He smiled. "Thank you again for your cooperation." He left the room, closing the door behind him.

Peyton clutched the tablet in front of her, painfully aware that the chief hadn't answered her questions. "What happens next?" she asked, without looking at Colin beside her.

"We wait. And hope that your alibi checks out."

"It will. I wasn't in Memphis yesterday. You believe me, right?" This time she turned to look at him.

He stared at her a long moment, then stood and crossed to the door.

"Colin? You do believe me, don't you?"

"I'm getting a bottle of water. Want anything?"

She slowly shook her head and he left the room.

Chapter Five

It was bad enough that crime scene investigators were combing through every inch of Peyton's family home, having obtained a search warrant based on Brian being inside earlier today. What was even more humiliating was standing in her own bedroom while a police woman rifled through the bag that Peyton had just packed.

Peyton crossed her arms, frowning at the woman's profile as she wadded up shirts and pants that Peyton had painstakingly rolled to avoid wrinkles. The woman pulled out yet another pair of Peyton's underwear, letting the red thong dangle in the air. What did she think? That Peyton was going to smuggle a gun in her undies and attack Colin in his sleep?

"I don't think they're your size," she snapped, unable to put up with the farce any longer.

Unruffled, the officer smiled politely, underwear still suspended in the air. "I'm just doing my job, Miss Sterling."

"Is there a problem in here?" Colin stepped into the room.

Peyton snatched the thong and tossed it into the overnight bag. "Not at all. Officer…"

"Simmons," the policewoman supplied, sounding infuriatingly amused.

"Right. Officer Simmons was just complimenting me on my fabric choices. Isn't that right?"

Simmons rolled her eyes. "You have a nice evening, ma'am." She stepped past Peyton, nodding at Colin before exiting the room.

"Did I miss something?" Colin asked.

She straightened the contents of the bag as best she could without dumping everything out and starting over. "I'm fairly certain that Officer Simmons was wrinkling my clothes and going as slowly as humanly possible just because—"

"Because you knocked a gun out of a marshal's hand and let a suspected cop killer get away?"

She stood frozen, his words sinking in. Shame made her face heat. "You're right. I'm so used to being on the defensive about Brian being innocent that I didn't look at it from her perspective."

He stepped to the bed and zipped her bag closed, then hefted it in his hand. "Maybe she was suspicious because you've packed half your bedroom in here. I bet this would require extra baggage fees at the airport."

"It's not *that* heavy. I know I packed more than I need for one night. But I always worry that I'll want something else after I've left the house."

"It's a good thing you did. I don't expect you'll be able to come back here for several days." He motioned toward the doorway. "Let's go."

"I can carry my own...wait. What do you mean *several days*? I have to do laundry, clean the house, work on the store's books, and a hundred other things. I can't put my life on hold."

"Why not? Think of it as a vacation. Don't worry about anything except helping me figure out where your brother might be hiding."

"I don't know what you were expecting but I can't ignore my responsibilities. I have to be back at the store Sunday and Monday. Those are Joan's days off. Melissa can't run the store by herself. This is the busy summer tourist season. Besides, my customers expect fresh baked goods Sunday through Friday. If I don't have new product in the display cases, I lose business. I'm still operating in the red, struggling to make this work as it is."

"If money's your worry, I can—"

"No. We've already had that conversation. I appreciate your generous offer, truly. But come early Sunday morning, I need to be in my own kitchen baking. Then I'm going to the shop."

He set the bag back on the bed. "Unless your brother and the other escapees are either caught or known to be in an area far from here by Sunday, you're not coming back. And you definitely aren't going into town."

"Colin—"

"Your brother showed up here once already. Odds are, he'll try again. The reports my fellow marshals have been sharing with me indicate that all four men were spotted traveling together at their last verified sighting. One of them is a convicted murderer with ties to gangs. Until I know it's safe, you aren't coming back here. Period."

Her throat went dry. Her brother was traveling with a convicted murderer? Brian wasn't exactly street-smart. Even after years in prison, he still seemed like a scared, naive kid every time she visited him.

Please be careful. Don't get yourself killed, Brian.

Since Colin was watching her, she forced a smile. "When you put it that way, I understand your concerns. I'll need to check whether Joan and Melissa can take on additional shifts for a few days." Not that she could afford the extra pay. And she didn't know if her employees could change their schedules last minute. "Since my alibi was verified, it's okay to call them, right?"

"Of course. Tomorrow."

"Right." The dark glass of her bedroom window clearly

showed it was too late to call anyone tonight. "I'll need to grab my baking supplies and take them to your place so I can bake things for the shop. I can ask Joan to come pick them up. Is that okay? Me using your kitchen?"

"You're welcome to use my kitchen. But let's head over there first and see if I already have what you need instead of hauling half your things over there."

"Why can't we just grab my stuff while we're still here?"

He blew out a breath. "Because the crime scene unit is still collecting evidence. Allowing you to take clothes and toiletries is one thing. Hauling out pots and pans and who knows what else is completely different." He motioned her toward the hallway and hefted her bag again.

The warrant. It all came down to that. She shook her head and headed down the hallway, Colin's boots echoing against the hardwood behind her. Just inside the family room, she had to stop to let a tech pass by with a laptop in a clear plastic bag.

"Hey, wait. That's mine. My business records are on that computer. I'll need that to work on invoices tomorrow." She reached for the bag. Colin pulled her against his side, nodding at the other man to continue out the propped-open front door.

"What are you doing?" She shook his arm off her shoulders.

"Keeping you from getting arrested for interfering with the execution of a search warrant. Come on. We need to get out of here."

She mumbled beneath her breath just what she thought of the search warrant but dutifully started toward the front door. When she saw Officer Simmons lounging on her couch like a plant taking root, she stopped again. "Shouldn't you be rifling through my underwear drawer or something?"

Simmons's eyes widened.

Colin coughed, then cleared his throat. "Sorry," he told Simmons.

"What are you apologizing to her for? Why is she—"

He took a firm grip on her arm and steered her out of the house, not slowing down until they were standing beside the open passenger door of his ridiculously tall pickup. White vans surrounded them, several parked right on the pitiful patch of weeds and dirt that used to be her mama's front lawn.

She gasped when another tech passed her carrying a precious family photo album. "Hey! Give that back. What are you doing with—oh!"

Colin lifted her up and deposited her onto the passenger seat and then reached for the seat belt as if she was a toddler. She snatched it from him and clicked it into place.

"I can fasten my own seat belt. And I could have climbed up into this monster truck of yours without help."

"No. You couldn't. You're so short you could pass for a hobbit."

She gasped in outrage.

He shut the door with more force than was necessary.

She crossed her arms, jaw clenched as she watched the vultures hauling out more of her things. A few seconds later, Colin hopped up on the driver's seat without a bit of trouble, making her resent him for his long legs. He tossed her bag onto the bench seat between them and sat there, as if waiting for something.

She clenched her jaw tighter, determined not to say another word.

Thunder rumbled overhead. In the distance, a flash of lightning lit up the sky for a few brief seconds. Yet another summer storm was moving into the area.

"I hope the rain turns the road into a river and those stupid vans slide into a ditch," she grumbled.

"There it is." He sounded almost cheerful as he started the engine. "*Now* we can go."

She crossed her arms. "You think you know me so well."

The almost smile that had accompanied his announcement faded and once again the sullen stranger took his place. "No. I don't think I know you at all. Not anymore, if I ever did."

His words were like a punch in the gut, reminding her of just how much water had passed beneath the bridge since they'd last been together.

He backed out of the driveway, the wheels kicking up gravel when he headed up the road.

Up.

Not down.

Unfamiliar terrain passed by her window, what little she could see in the moonlight. When she'd lived here before, this road had dead-ended just past her house. She hadn't realized since coming back that it continued around the mountain.

"Is this a shortcut?" she asked.

"No." He rounded a curve, the grade getting steeper as they continued higher.

"Colin, where…" White wood fencing appeared off to their left, illuminated by spotlights and marching across the fields as far as she could see. Another curve revealed even more landscape lights, on either side of a long, paved driveway. And at the end sat a huge white two-story farmhouse with an enormous wraparound porch, complete with a porch swing. She smiled sadly at the swing. She'd always wanted one but never had one growing up. Her dad had said their porch was too small.

"Beautiful house. Adore the swing," she said, more to herself than to him. "Is this where we're going?"

He nodded.

"Who lives there? Another police officer? You're going to have someone else ask me questions about Brian?"

He shook his head and turned up the drive. When they reached the garage, he pressed a button in the roof of his truck and the door began to rise.

"This is *your* house?"

"I built it a handful of years ago."

He pulled into the three-car garage. An expensive-looking black sports car of some type was parked two spaces away.

"I thought you had a chalet on Skyline Drive?"

He shot her a surprised glance. "I used to. How did you know about the chalet? I bought it a year after you left." He cut the engine.

She shrugged, unwilling to admit that she'd ruthlessly grilled an old friend for information about Colin after being forced to move to Memphis. "One of dad's clients or mom's old church friends probably mentioned it on the phone after we first left. But I never knew you built a new home a few miles up the road from mine. Why did you? Why here?"

He hesitated. "The land was available, the area familiar. No neighbors to worry about."

"And you just happened to build a white two-story farmhouse surrounded by acres of white fencing? With a porch swing? Like we talked about building together one day?"

His hands gripped the steering wheel so hard that his knuckles turned white. "I've always liked this style of home. Don't read anything into it."

She jerked back, and hated that she had. He'd hurt her, again, and she seemed helpless to hide it every time one of his barbs hit the bullseye.

His expression softened with regret. "Peyton—"

"I'll get the door myself this time." She grabbed her purse and overnight bag and hopped out of the truck before he could get out and help her. She stumbled but considered it a victory that she didn't do a face-plant on the pristine gray-painted floor of the garage. In comparison, her garage had cracks and oil stains all over the place from her constantly leaking SUV. She'd be afraid to park her car in something this clean.

Both of them were silent as he led the way into the house.

Similar to her home, the garage led into a laundry/mudroom. But that was where the similarities ended. They walked down a wide back hall with several doors, all closed. A cased opening led them toward the front of the house, around a concrete-and-metal staircase into a massive vaulted family room. They finally stopped in the kitchen in the back-left corner of the house.

Her mouth dropped open. She nearly drooled. What she'd considered to be a high-end redesign of her own kitchen seemed like a joke compared to Colin's. It was completely open to the main room with a massive island the only separation. Four saddle-style bar stools covered in black leather with matching black iron legs were snugged up beneath the overhang of the island on the side facing the family room. There wasn't a table and chairs anywhere that she saw. And she hadn't seen a dining room on their quick trip through the house. She wondered if he ate all his meals at the island or off trays in front of the television like she tended to do.

The ceilings soared up two stories high with skylights that allowed a breathtaking view of the stars. During the day, it would be awash with sunlight. Just like they'd imagined when they'd talked about their future together and the house where they one day hoped to live.

He opened a door and flipped on the light switch. "I wanted to show you the pantry since you were worried about baking supplies. My mom insists on keeping it stocked for when she comes over for family gatherings.

She enjoys baking too, like you and your mom. I imagine most of what you need is in here."

She ducked inside the enormous walk-in that was larger than her bedroom back home. Flour, sugar, spices of every kind lined one side, a much better variety than she had in her own pantry. It was a baker's dream. Even if her business started booming, she could never afford something like this. She stepped back, feeling like the poor relation. Which was odd, considering that the McKenzie wealth had never bothered her in the past. Now it seemed like a looming barrier between them.

"Nice. *Really* nice. I'll be sure to reimburse you for any ingredients I use."

"That's not necessa—"

"I'll pay you back or I can't do my baking here. And I really need to have product ready Sunday morning."

His jaw tightened but he didn't argue. "Are you hungry? And don't tell me you won't eat my groceries. You're my guest. I insist."

Guest. What a sad, lonely word. At eighteen, she and Colin had been ready to take on the world together. She'd expected that by twenty-eight she'd be working alongside him, fighting for justice. Coming home every night to a couple of kids, preferably boys with their father's deep blue eyes and blue-black hair. Every night, she'd fall into his arms in the king-size bed and make love until dawn.

"Thanks." Her voice came out barely a whisper. She cleared her throat and tried again. "I couldn't eat anything right now. Actually, I'm kind of exhausted. It's been a rough day all around."

He studied her a moment, as if he wanted to say something. But then he turned and led her back into the family room. He didn't stop until they reached the stairs on the far right side. "The guest bedrooms are upstairs. Pick whichever one you like."

She admired the industrial black metal handrail, smoothed her fingers over the iron cables. Modern farmhouse. A little more masculine and contemporary than she'd have wanted. But gorgeous, just the same. Seeing their dream brought to life—without her—somehow hurt worse than if their dream had never been realized.

"It's beautiful, Colin. Your home is…perfect." She smiled wistfully. "I don't suppose you have a horse barn out back with a palomino mare?"

He shook his head, a faraway look in his eyes. Was he remembering all the times they'd ridden trail ponies through the foothills? Or taken turns on the palomino her father got her for her sixteenth birthday? The same horse she'd had to sell when Brian was arrested and they scraped for every penny to pay for his defense.

"I've got a workshop out back, that's it. You were the one crazy about horses when we were young. Not me."

Her hand tightened on the railing. "I see." She took a deep breath, then another, struggling against the urge to cry. She'd rather die than let loose with another onslaught of tears in front of him when he was being so cold.

"Make yourself at home." His voice sounded strained. "I'm going to bed." He opened a door to the right of the stairs, a few feet from the main entrance to the house.

He needn't have bothered shutting the door behind him. He'd already shut her out just fine without one.

Chapter Six

Colin slowly lowered himself to his bed and dropped his head into his hands. Bringing Peyton here had seemed like a good idea when he'd originally thought of it. He'd been intent on getting the truth out of her, figuring if they were holed up together he'd wear her down, get her to tell him where her brother was hiding.

At the same time, he had a security system, something he'd noticed she didn't have at her house. She was safer here, especially if her brother had rejoined the other escaped convicts. But until he'd seen the truth dawn in her eyes when she realized he'd built their dream house—without her—he hadn't recognized the real reason that he'd brought her here.

Revenge.

The truth sickened him. He'd hurt her today, over and over. And all it had done was make him disgusted with himself. Not that he'd originally set out to build this house hoping to rub her face in it. His motivations had been even more pathetic. He'd loved her so much that he'd convinced himself that if he built their dream house, he'd be able to bridge the gap between them. He would talk her into coming back to Gatlinburg to recapture what they'd once had. But, of course, that hadn't happened.

He'd gone to Memphis, the day after the house was finished, and knocked on her father's door asking to see her.

Mr. Sterling had shaken his head and told him he was too late, that Peyton had gotten married. Colin had gone to a hotel and dived into a case of whiskey. He'd probably still be there if his brothers hadn't tracked him down and forced him to go home and sober up.

A few months later, he'd gone back, determined to man up, congratulate her on her marriage and wish her a happy life. But he hadn't even known her new last name. And when he'd turned onto the street where her father lived, he couldn't work up the nerve to get out of his truck and ask about Peyton.

Once again, he'd hit the whiskey. Once again, his interfering brothers wouldn't let him wallow in self-pity. Slowly, painstakingly, he'd pulled himself out of the gutter and figured out how to build a reasonably contented life without her. And he had, eventually. Or so he'd thought. Until he'd stepped into her kitchen today and she'd chosen her brother over him. Again.

Just like that day at the barn, when the police had Brian in their squad car and Colin was in the back of an ambulance. She could either have gone with Brian to the station or with Colin to the hospital. She'd chosen Brian. And other than at the trial, surrounded by a room full of other people, Colin had never seen her again until today. She'd opened all the old wounds by choosing an arsonist, a cop killer, over the man she'd once planned to spend the rest of her life with.

All the old resentments and memories had bubbled to the surface, leaving him stewing in frustration and anger and pain. He'd selfishly wanted her to feel the same pain. So he'd made that stupid deal with her to get her out here.

After seeing her eyes widen when his house appeared over the hill, hearing the joy in her voice when she'd mentioned the porch swing that Colin knew she'd always wanted, he'd realized what a horrible jerk he was being.

He never should have built the house. And he certainly never should have brought Peyton here.

That wasn't all he'd realized tonight.

He'd realized something far worse—that she still had the power to set his blood on fire. In spite of all the years, all the progress he'd thought he'd made, he still cared about her. And he wanted her, oh how he wanted her. He wanted her naked skin heating his, her silky hair fanned across his pillow. He wanted his name on her lips when she climaxed beneath him. He shuddered and squeezed his hands into fists, drawing deep breaths.

Not that it helped.

Thunder rumbled overhead. He stood, crossed to the front bedroom window and looked down the road, at the line of trees at the end of the driveway. Lightning flashed. Wind and rain whipped the trees as if they were no more substantial than blades of grass. But the storm outside was nothing compared to the storm raging inside him.

He was a coward. Running in here had been a spineless act of desperation. He'd wanted to escape, put some distance between himself and Peyton before he did something even more foolish than he'd already done.

Like kiss her.

If Peyton was still downstairs, if she hadn't gone up to bed yet, he should go back out there and beg her forgiveness. He should take her somewhere else. She shouldn't have to stay in this house with him, where everywhere she looked was a reminder of the plans they'd once made together.

He cursed and stalked to the door. But when he put his hand on the doorknob, he couldn't bring himself to turn it. He needed one more minute, maybe ten, to stop the flood of images that seeing her again had unleashed.

What he really needed was a bottle of whiskey.

He squeezed his eyes shut and rested his forehead

against the door. But closing his eyes did nothing to block out the memories.

Peyton's sixteenth birthday, her silver-gray eyes alight with excitement as she sat atop the palomino mare that she'd been begging her parents to buy for months.

Peyton smiling at Colin while wearing a figure-hugging black sequined dress that had him choking on his own tongue.

Peyton, a few weeks before graduation, lying on a blanket covered in nothing but her strawberry blond hair—and Colin—letting him warm her after they'd skinny-dipped beneath a waterfall.

Peyton, Peyton, Peyton. Nearly every treasured memory from his past began and ended with her.

Until one horrible night had ripped them apart.

The barn had burned long ago. But the scars on his arms, and in his heart, throbbed anew as if it had happened yesterday. He curled his fingers against the door and wondered what in the world he was going to do.

Chapter Seven

Thunder boomed outside, storm clouds darkening the sky as if it was still the middle of the night instead of morning. Colin had taken a shower, in spite of all the times his mother had warned him that it was too dangerous during a thunderstorm. But if he followed her advice, it would be the middle of next week before he got clean again. This storm showed no signs of letting up.

As he buttoned his shirt, it dawned on him that the low rumble he was hearing now wasn't thunder. He moved to his front bedroom window and saw a white Jeep barreling up the road, windshield wipers making little progress against the sheets of rain whipping against the glass.

Green stripes and a National Park Service emblem on the door told him it was probably one of his brothers. He groaned in frustration as more lightning cracked overhead. Hopefully Peyton was still asleep. He didn't want his family to know she was here. That would open up a whole new round of intrusion into his life that he didn't want to deal with right now. They'd probably start an intervention and take all the whiskey again.

A knock sounded on the bedroom door. "Colin?"

So much for Peyton being asleep.

The knock sounded again. "Someone's coming up the—"

He opened the door. "Morning, Peyton." She was sexy

as hell in a white tank top and matching capris that bared too much smooth, golden skin for his comfort. His mouth went dry as he tried not to let his traitorous gaze dip to that tempting valley between her breasts.

She backed up a step, smoothing her hands on her pants in the nervous gesture he remembered so well. "Good morning. Sorry to bother you. I just wanted to make sure you know that you're about to have company. It looks like some kind of official vehicle from the Park Service. Do you think…" She cleared her throat. "Do you think someone found Brian already?"

Thunder rumbled overhead.

"Not likely. The search in this area was halted last night because of the storm. They won't be able to risk going out again until the lightning stops. Which probably won't be any time soon."

A horn honked out front.

He motioned toward the back hallway. "Do you mind? I need to open the garage—"

"Oh, sorry." She moved out of his way.

He strode past the stairs and called over his shoulder. "Whoever it is, I'll try to get rid of them. It's ridiculously early for a visit."

"It's nine o'clock. How late do you normally sleep?"

He checked his watch. She was right. It was so dark outside that he hadn't awakened with the sun coming through the windows like he usually did. "Back in a few." He turned down the hall.

The horn honked again. He jogged the rest of the way to the garage. After disabling the alarm, he pressed the button on the wall and waited to see which brother he was about to battle.

When the door cleared the windshield, he groaned. Duncan. His second-oldest brother was even more stubborn than Colin. If he even suspected that Peyton might be here,

Duncan wouldn't leave short of a physical threat. Maybe he should go back inside and grab his Glock.

As soon as the Jeep pulled into the middle spot between Colin's truck and car, his brother cut the engine and hopped out, a look of concern on his face.

"I heard our resident arsonist graduated to cop-killer and is back in town. You need my help catching the bastard?"

"Good morning to you too. And, no. Thanks, but half the state is looking for him already. There's no need for you to take off work to help. Speaking of work…" He glanced at his watch and winced. "I'm running really late today. You should probably head back out. I need to get out of here."

Duncan narrowed his eyes. "It's Saturday."

"I work Saturdays. Sometimes."

"Since when?"

"Since whenever I need to." He motioned toward Duncan's Jeep. "Do you mind? Your little Special Agent car is dripping all over my garage."

Duncan rolled his eyes and stopped in front of Colin. He looked him up and down, skepticism heavy in his expression. "You Deputy US Marshal guys are getting sloppy these days. You normally wear jeans to work?"

"On Saturdays."

"Right. Where's your vest? And gun?"

Colin made a show of surprise, patting his shirt and then looking down at his hip. "Son of a…well, I'll have to grab those. Too much going on these days. I'm not thinking clearly."

"Like what? What *exactly* is going on?"

"Felons on the loose, like you said. Kind of my specialty so I need to get on it." He motioned toward the Jeep. "If you don't mind backing out—"

"Because you're on your way to work."

"Yep."

"On a Saturday."

"Mm-hmm."

"At nine in the morning, in jeans, without your Kevlar or sidearm. Yeah, I'm not buying that. Try for something more believable."

Colin crossed his arms. "Do you always have to be so difficult?"

"Remi says I'm charming."

"Remi's blinded by love. She'll find out the truth after you get married. Poor girl."

"Speaking of the truth—"

Colin lifted his hands in exasperation. "Okay, fine. I overslept and didn't want you ribbing me about it. I'm on my way to the office to look over some notes in my files so I can make a game plan. I figured I could dress down since not many people will be there."

"Whatever you say. What about the other guys who escaped? Have any of them been caught?"

Colin settled back against the wall, crossing his arms again. "Not so far. Have you been getting alerts?"

"Nothing useful. We were told the day of the escape that all four were seen a few hours west of here. Since then we heard someone had sighted Brian close by, but no details. We've got extra patrols out, when we can with this storm. The park's closed, of course. Adam's been running the evacuation. He got the last of the campers out a few hours before the storm hit. Have you heard anything specific about Brian?"

"Not since I saw him yesterday morning." Colin winced.

Duncan pounced on his mistake. "I *knew* it. I figured that little twerp would come after you. Where'd you see him? What happened?"

"Don't you have somewhere else to be?"

"My boss is flexible. I've got nothing but time. Tell me what happened."

Colin shook his head. "Nothing much to tell. After I

heard about the escape, I figured I'd check the old Sterling homestead, just in case Brian headed back somewhere familiar. I didn't really expect him to be there. We both pretty much surprised each other and he ended up giving me the slip."

"That sucks. So, you're working the case?"

"Officially, the conflict of interest because Brian set the fire that injured me makes me ineligible."

"So, you're working the case."

"Of course. I took some vacation time. It's not exactly a secret as to why. Chief Landry and the marshal in charge of finding the escapees are both being accommodating. They're willing to share information with me about the status of the search as long as I answer their questions about Brian's personality and history."

"If he's still in the area, there's nowhere he can go. Every main road I've been on this morning has a road block set up, even with the storm. No one's taking any chances. His only choice will be to head into the mountains, hunker down and hope he can outwait law enforcement. From what I remember, he was never the outdoorsy type. I can't imagine him lasting long without breaking into someone's cabin for supplies. That'll make it easy to track him down." He arched a brow. "Unless the guys he's with are better at living off the land and were smart enough to take supplies with them."

"Doubtful, according to the files I read. They're all city slickers."

"I wonder why they came this way."

Colin shrugged as if he had no clue. But he was pretty sure that he knew why. Peyton. In spite of being a year older than his sister, Brian had always relied on her to protect him. Either he'd intended to ask her for help, or she'd known he was coming and was waiting for him already when Colin interfered with their plans.

Lightning cracked outside, creating a strobe-like effect through the garage.

Duncan glanced toward the windows. "Don't get me wrong. This is a nice garage and all. But are you ever gonna ask me inside? The weather's nasty out there."

"You national parks guys can handle it. Although, that road out front does turn into a river sometimes. You really ought to head back down the mountain before it gets any worse."

"I've got a four-wheel drive that sticks to the road like a mountain goat. You aren't worried about me sliding into a ditch. Cut the crap and tell me why you're really trying to get rid of me."

"I think he doesn't want you to know about me."

Colin sighed and turned around. Peyton stood in the doorway, her curly blond hair tousled around her shoulders. Silvery eyes laced with pain pinned him with an accusing stare before she turned around and disappeared into the house.

Duncan's mouth fell open. "Was that who I think it was?"

"Would you believe me if I said no?"

"She's seen the farmhouse, the porch swing?"

"Since she's *in* the farmhouse, I'm guessing that's a yes."

Duncan put his hand on Colin's shoulder. "Where's your whiskey? I need to pour it all out."

"Not. Funny." Colin shoved his brother's arm off his shoulder.

Duncan pulled out his cell phone.

"What are you doing?"

"Calling for reinforcements. Ian, as usual, is incommunicado. What's it been, six months since we saw our prodigal baby brother?" He shrugged. "Adam, however, now there's the typical first-born reliable brother if ever I saw one. He'll drop everything to head over. Maybe I should ask him to bring Mom and Dad too. I bet they'd love to catch up on whatever the hell is going on here."

Colin yanked the phone out of his hand. "Fine. You can come in. But try to behave for once. Keep it professional."

Duncan pressed a hand to his chest. "You wound me, brother. I always behave." He grinned and strode past Colin into the house.

Colin swore and hurried after him.

Chapter Eight

Eavesdropping on Colin and Duncan's conversation in the garage wasn't Peyton's proudest moment. But no one was telling her anything and she was desperate for news about her brother. All she'd learned was that Colin was so ashamed to be seen with her that he was willing to lie to his own brother.

She was in the kitchen setting up the coffee maker when she heard them come in. She could feel them watching her but she focused on getting things ready instead of turning around. After starting the coffee brewing, she opened the cabinet above it to search for mugs. No searching required. They were right there, above the coffee maker where she kept them in her own kitchen. It made sense. Apparently, Colin thought so too.

The sound of whispering had her tensing. She imagined that Colin was bringing Duncan up to speed about what had happened over the past twenty-four hours. And why he'd dared to bring the dreaded ex into his home.

She grabbed some milk out of the refrigerator and added it to one of the cups—the one for Duncan. She put sugar in hers and left Colin's black. Enough coffee was already in the carafe for her to pour some, so she filled the three mugs before setting the carafe back into place. She drew a bracing breath, then turned around and set the mugs on the white quartz island. Both men stood on the other side, silent now, watching her.

She slid a cup toward each of them, then cradled her own between her hands. "I'm assuming you both take your coffee the same way you did when we were in high school." She blew on hers to cool it, then took a sip.

Duncan shot a look at Colin. They both stepped forward and took their cups.

"Thanks," Duncan said. "Smells great."

Colin took a sip. The corner of his mouth lifted. He nodded his approval and she hated that her stomach jumped with pleasure.

Duncan's smile after taking a sip of his own coffee was kind and generous, but didn't make her stomach flip like Colin's had.

"Perfect for a rainy morning. Thanks, Peyton," Duncan said.

"Is anyone hungry? I haven't had a chance to prepare dough and let it rise. But if Colin has any canned biscuits in the fridge, I can add my special touches and bake us some croissants that will taste great."

"Croissants?" Duncan looked like he was ready to drool. "Like your mom used to make?"

Colin glanced sharply at her, reminding her that she still hadn't discussed with him what had happened to her mom. That was a conversation she hoped to avoid as long as possible.

She smiled, working hard to keep the grief from her expression. "Almost. Like I said, I don't have my special recipe dough ready. But I can get it pretty close." She finally met Colin's probing gaze again. "Do you have bacon and eggs? Cheese?"

He slowly nodded, concern apparent in his gaze as he studied her, as if he was worried that she might fall apart at any moment. But, thankfully, he didn't press for more information. Not yet anyway.

"Then let's get this party started," she said. "We'll have bacon, egg and cheese croissants. I'll make enough croissants so that you can also have some with butter and honey if you want."

"You don't need to cook for us," Colin said.

"I *want* to cook for us. It won't take long." And baking was a great way to avoid things she didn't want to talk about.

His sigh could have felled a tree. "Fine. Then we'll help. Duncan, make yourself useful. Get whatever ingredients she needs from the pantry. I'll get the cookie sheets and mixer."

She turned around in surprise, a wooden spoon in her hand. "You want to help?"

"I insist on it." Colin pulled two stainless-steel cookie sheets from the bottom drawer in the island.

"What do you need from the pantry?" Duncan asked.

She rattled off ingredients and he rushed off to get them.

Colin opened another drawer in the island, pulled a full, white apron out and held it up. "Turn around."

She blinked, then turned, holding her hair up as he lifted the ties around her neck. She hoped he didn't notice the shiver of pleasure when his warm hands touched her skin. "I'm surprised you'd have any aprons around here."

He finished tying the strings and moved his hands to her waist, pulling those strings back behind her. He was far too close for her peace of mind.

His deep voice rumbled next to her ear when he answered. "I keep them here for my mom."

Mom. There was that word again. She had to breathe through the urge to cry. Thankfully, she had her emotions under control when he finished tying the apron and she turned around.

"Thank you."

"My pleasure."

She stared up into his eyes, admiring how his blue-green shirt deepened the color. And she wished, for just a moment, that she could feel his strong arms wrap around her and pull her in for a hug. She could really use a hug right now, especially from Colin.

"Here you go." Duncan strode in from the pantry, his arms full.

Peyton cleared her throat and stepped back. Then she directed Duncan to set everything down while she got what she needed from the refrigerator.

Colin moved to the island. "Tell us what you want us to do."

Both men looked at her expectantly. The idea of cooking with them was bittersweet and brought back so many good memories from when they were growing up and spending more time at each other's houses than their own. Until that summer when Colin's voice had deepened and her body gained curves she'd never had before, the summer when she and Colin began to look at each other differently and everything changed.

"Okay. Well, do you have a rolling pin?"

Both men started opening drawers in the island on a quest to find one.

By the time they'd finished cooking, eating and restoring the kitchen to its former glory, Peyton had laughed so much her stomach hurt. Duncan's sense of humor was contagious. His fake British accent was awful. His Irish one was much better, which made sense in theory since he was a McKenzie. But she knew none of the brothers had ever been to Ireland. Or, at least, they hadn't before she'd left.

Colin had grinned and laughed right along with his brother, although he was more inclined to elbow him in the ribs or purposely spoil the punchline of one of Duncan's jokes. That was one of the things that Peyton had always loved about the McKenzie brothers—the strong bond between them and how much fun they could have together. Her own brother was quiet and moody, almost fragile. She loved him dearly but could never imagine him horsing around like the McKenzies.

Duncan wiped his hands on a paper towel and tossed it into the trash. "We've talked about my fiancée, our family, Adam's job as a law-enforcement ranger and his new bride. But you haven't told us anything about you. How's your family?" His eyes widened. "I mean, aside from your brother of course."

She glanced at Colin, seeing the unasked questions brimming in his eyes. "Shouldn't we start brainstorming how to find Brian before some trigger-happy searcher gets to him first?"

He exchanged a surprised look with Duncan, she assumed over her less than subtle attempt at changing the subject.

"Sure. We can start right now. I'll get my tablet and we can sit in the family room."

"I think that's my cue to hit the road," Duncan said.

Colin shook his head. "That cue came a long time ago but you chose to ignore it."

Duncan grinned and the brothers pounded each other on the back. He stepped to Peyton and offered her his arm with a wink. "Walk me to my Jeep, pretty lady?"

"What are you doing?" Colin asked, sounding wary.

"Saying goodbye to an old friend. Come on, Peyton. Don't let that ornery bear ruin our fun." He pulled her hand through his arm and tugged her into the family room.

She smiled at Colin and shrugged helplessly. He'd crossed his arms and was watching them intently.

Duncan didn't slow down until they were standing by his SUV. He surprised her again by giving her a quick hug.

"It was good seeing you again, sweet colleen, even if the circumstances aren't exactly the best."

"You too. Thanks for being so nice to me. It was…unexpected."

He smiled and turned her hands in his, looking down. "I don't see a wedding ring. You're single?"

She tugged her hands free. "Yes, not that it matters. You're already taken," she teased. "Congratulations on your engagement."

He grinned. "Remi would love you. I think you'll find that everyone in my family still loves you, no matter what."

She blinked, not sure what to say to that.

His gaze flicked toward the door to the mudroom, then back to her. "I can't pretend to understand the choices you made ten years ago. I tell myself that you don't have any idea what all he went through, how much he needed you, or you'd have been there for him."

"Duncan—"

"You hurt him, more than you'll ever know. But I'll tell you something else. I can't remember the last time he laughed and smiled like he did this morning." He pressed his hand to his chest. "Granted, I'm a charming fellow. But it wasn't because of me that he was smiling." He sobered and took her hands in his again. "There's something special there, between you two, always has been. I, for one, am hopeful that it works out this time. He deserves some happiness in his life."

She stared at him in shock. "You've misunderstood why I'm here. It's all about helping Brian, trying to save his life. That's it."

He slowly shook his head. "Dear, sweet lass, my brother's a great guy. But if you think he'd help anyone else in your situation, try to save the man he holds responsible for everything he lost, you're fooling yourself." He kissed her on the cheek, then got into his Jeep.

Peyton wrapped her arms around her waist as he turned the car around on the back-up pad out front, then ventured into the heart of the storm. She didn't know what to think of his little speech. What had he meant when he said that she didn't understand what Colin had gone through, or how much he'd needed her?

Had everything her father told her been a lie?

The garage door started to close. She turned to see Colin leaning against the doorframe behind her.

"Everything okay out here?"

No. She wanted to run to him, throw her arms around him. Tell him how deeply she loved him, that she'd never stopped. The only thing holding her back was that she wasn't sure what he'd do, whether he'd welcome her embrace, or turn away. She didn't think she could bear it if he rejected her. Not as fragile as her emotions were right now. And he'd certainly made it clear at the police station that a future between them would never happen. Was that the truth? Or had he just said that as a defense mechanism, not wanting to open himself up to her again?

He straightened. "Peyton? Did Duncan upset you?"

Yes. "No, of course not. The past twenty-four hours have upset me. I can't seem to find my balance." She tried to smile, wasn't sure that she'd succeeded. "Would it be okay with you if we put off the questions until later?" Thunder boomed, making her wince. "A few hours won't make much of a difference, will they? It's not like anyone can head out searching in this weather, right?"

He hesitated, then nodded. "Of course. A few hours shouldn't hurt. But the storm is supposed to ease later this evening. The trackers will be out looking again. We don't want to wait too long."

"Okay. Thank you." She hurried past him into the house, suddenly in desperate need of some space.

Chapter Nine

The easy camaraderie Peyton had experienced with Colin this morning evaporated as the day wore on, probably because she was still mulling over what Duncan had said. Colin knew something was bothering her. But since she kept denying it, he was becoming more and more reserved. She hated that she was bringing out the stranger again, after having a precious glimpse of the old Colin earlier. But this was something she had to work out for herself.

How could she help her brother and love Colin too? Without hurting either of them?

After an awkward lunch with stilted conversation, Colin shut himself in his office down the back hallway. Peyton had been left to her own devices, which meant that she'd been baking. She'd made so much that she'd called Joan to come take the goods to the shop as soon as there was a break in the storm, rather than let them go to waste. She wouldn't even have to worry about baking more in the morning. The café was set for a while.

But even before calling Joan, Peyton had called her father to check on him and update him on the search for Brian. That had led to her admitting that she'd gotten the information from Colin and that she was temporarily staying at his new house. The ensuing argument had her belatedly wishing that she hadn't even called him. So, when she'd called Joan right after that, it had been a blessing to have that conversation go much better.

Joan had jumped at the chance to work extra shifts and had assured Peyton that Melissa would too, because she was in a tight spot and some extra money would really help out right now. Peyton felt guilty for not offering them the opportunity in the past. She decided that she'd have to give them raises, maybe even a small bonus once she was back at the shop, even if it meant dipping into her meager savings to cover the expense.

When Joan showed up for the baked goods, Colin disabled the alarm and stood guard, making her so nervous that she didn't stay any longer than it took to load her car. Peyton didn't want to speak to him in his current mood either, let alone suffer through another agonizing interview like the one with Landry. But the storm was definitely ending, as Colin had predicted. Putting off his questions was no longer an option. She reluctantly told him she was ready. Several hours later, she was convinced that Landry had been a prince. Colin, on the other hand, was a sadist.

He grilled her over and over with the same questions, rephrasing them, going off on tangents that didn't seem relevant in any way, circling back and asking the same things all over again. He took copious notes, asking her about things Brian had said, texted, emailed, any people he'd ever mentioned that he associated with at the prison. He asked for a list of anyone Brian had ever visited, talked to, or even fought with from the time they were little kids. She'd had to tell Colin all the places her brother loved to go, how often he went there, who went with him. And on and on and on.

Occasionally he'd retreat to his office to call Chief Landry or the marshals assigned to find Brian. She didn't like the idea of them sharing information back and forth. After all, if she and Colin did figure out where Brian was, she wanted Colin to capture him, not some over-anxious police officer. But she had to trust him, and put faith in his years of experience that he'd somehow manage to keep her brother safe.

Even with her fears, she welcomed the times Colin would close himself up in his office. It gave her a break. She came up with her own tactic to stop the questioning every now and then, asking for trips to the bathroom—so many that he'd sarcastically offered to take her to a doctor.

That was the end of her bathroom breaks.

The sun had set long ago by the time they stopped for a late dinner of soup and sandwiches that they prepared together. Working with him in the kitchen to make the food and clean up afterwards was easy, fun. They made a good team. She didn't even mind that they ate without talking. It was better than being endlessly questioned. But, of course, the respite didn't last long. Soon they were back at it again. The Spanish Inquisition had nothing on Deputy US Marshal Colin McKenzie.

She crossed her arms and shifted into a more comfortable position on the couch while she waited for his next question.

He scrolled through the screen on his tablet, checking his notes. "Let's see. You said when Brian began his prison sentence, you visited him once a week. But about a year ago, the visits stopped. Why did you stop visiting him?"

"We argued. He didn't want to see me anymore."

"That's not an answer."

"It's private. It has nothing to do with the escape. I promise. We never discussed him getting out except through legal means—appeals mainly, since parole isn't an option at a federal prison. That's it." She held her hands out. "How did he escape anyway? I don't understand. Shouldn't it be nearly impossible to do that?"

"It should be. But the government sometimes hires out

prisoner transportation to private firms to save money. The employees can be overworked, overtired and undertrained. And the vans aren't always maintained as well as they should be. The investigation is ongoing, but it appears that all of those factors contributed to the prisoners being able to pry open a faulty lock and sneak out the back of the van at a fuel stop."

"Wow. That's crazy—scary too. Please tell me that's rare, that people don't escape prison transports every day."

"They don't. But it does happen. This isn't a one-off. Luckily there was no one else around, so no one was hurt at the gas station. They took off on foot, later stole a car that someone had left unlocked with the keys inside."

"Is that how the police officer, Jennings, got involved? He saw them in a stolen car and tried to arrest them?"

"Yes, he…" Colin sighed. "How did we turn the tables here? You're supposed to be answering my questions, not the other way around."

"No one has told me anything. It's really frustrating."

"It's frustrating for all of us. There are a lot of things we still don't know. Like how the prisoners got the gun they used to shoot Officer Jennings."

"I don't have any guns. I can probably shoot better than most people I know because you taught me back when we were dating. But I don't own one, never have. And before you ask, no, I did not somehow provide Brian with a gun."

"Then we're back to the argument you had with him. Maybe it matters, maybe it doesn't. But I'd like to be the judge of that. What did you argue about?"

"You're not going to drop this, are you?"

"No. I'm not."

She shoved her hair back from her face. "You, okay? We argued about you."

He stared at her. "Me?"

"Brian thinks you're the devil, that everything that's happened to him is your fault."

He looked down at the white lines on his hands, his mouth tightening. "What do you think?"

"I think that you're the most honorable person I know. Do I wish that you hadn't testified against him? Yes. But I don't hold it against you. You promised to tell the truth. And I have no doubt that you told the truth as you see it. I don't blame you for anything, Colin."

His gaze flicked to hers. "I appreciate that."

"It's true." She clasped her hands tightly together. "Anyway, I couldn't take Brian's drama anymore. I've tried for years to get him to continue his education behind bars so he'd have a skill when he got out. I'd had a tough week, was struggling to find a new job after getting laid off at my previous one. I guess I kind of exploded. It shocked him. He must have felt betrayed, like he'd lost his biggest ally."

She shrugged. "Maybe our argument did play a role in the escape. Maybe he felt he had nothing left to lose and no one else to trust. I do know that prison was exceptionally hard on him. I mean, he'd have these mental breakdowns, end up in psychiatric treatment for months. You mentioned he had only five more years to serve. To Brian, five more years was an eternity. He was miserable. The whole time. He never adjusted in any way."

"You were his biggest ally? What about your parents?"

She wrapped her arms around her middle. "In the beginning, they saw him weekly, along with me. But something happened a couple of years ago. Dad and Mom had a fight, not that fighting was new for them. They've seen a marriage counselor for as long as I can remember. But this was worse, really bad. Things…changed. Between my parents, and between them and Brian. Dad went to see him one more time, by himself, and never went back. Mom started visiting him on her own, without me. I never understood why. She never told me."

"This blowup happened, your dad stopped seeing his son, your mom started seeing him alone, but no one ever explained what it was all about?"

"It was about Brian. That's a given. Mom always took up for him. Dad was always putting him down, since he was a little boy. Brian's shenanigans while growing up were an embarrassment to him. To my dad, reputation was everything. That's why he fought so hard for Brian, trying to keep him from going to prison. He wanted his son proven innocent so he could salvage the family name. All I can figure is that whatever their recent argument was about, it had to be about something that would embarrass my father even more if it got out."

"Like maybe Brian admitted he really had set the fire?"

She hesitated, then shrugged. "I can't imagine that happening. But, yes, if that was the case, my father would be ashamed and forced to admit he'd been wrong all this time. He can hold his head up now and insist the Sterlings are good, solid people and our family has suffered a tragic injustice. If he was proven wrong, he'd be devasted, bitter, ashamed." She shook her head. "Whatever it was, it tore my parents apart. Mom wouldn't go to marriage counseling anymore unless my dad would visit Brian. He refused. They were at an impasse."

The questions continued. Like any good son of a judge and a prosecutor, he covered the same ground again and again until she wanted to beg for mercy. After answering yet another question that she'd answered many times before, she dropped her head back against the cushy leather couch and closed her eyes. "Couldn't you just waterboard me or something? That would be less torture than this."

"What do you mean?" He sounded genuinely surprised.

She lifted her head. "You're kidding, right?"

He arched a brow.

"You're not kidding. Wow. Okay, we've been going around and around for hours. You keep asking me the same questions. I keep giving you the same answers. How is this getting us anywhere?"

He glanced at the darkened windows outside, checked his watch. "You're right. I may have overdone it."

"You think?"

"How about one more question?"

"Does the one you just asked count?"

He smiled. "No."

"Fine. One more. Then I turn into a pumpkin. A non-talking pumpkin."

"Some of them talk?"

"Obviously, you go to the wrong pumpkin patches."

"I'll have to remember that. Okay. Final question."

"Final answer. Drumroll, folks." She tapped her hands on her thighs, mimicking a drummer.

"You explained why you stopped visiting Brian. But then, three months ago, you went to see him one more time. Why?"

She closed her eyes. "Last question? Promise?"

"Promise. Unless I have a follow-up related to the original question, of course."

"Of course." She sighed. "It was because of my mom." She gave him a watery smile. "The subject I've been avoiding ever since the police station. I had to tell Brian about Mom. She…there was an accident, a car accident. It was raining. She lost control on a curve and slammed into a tree. The coroner said she died instantly. Thank God. She never felt the flames." She sucked in a breath and glanced at his hands. "I'm sorry. I shouldn't have—"

"It's okay. I'm sorry about your mom, Peyton. I really am."

She blinked furiously, then nodded.

"What about your dad?" he asked, his voice gentle. "Was he hurt in the accident?"

She blew out a deep breath, still feeling awful for bringing up the fire—even though it was in response to his questions. She just wished she'd measured her words more carefully.

"Dad wasn't with her. He's fine. As well as he can be."

"He lives in Memphis? Alone?"

"He does now."

"What do you mean, now? Was someone else living with him until recently?"

"I'm guessing this is one of those follow-up questions?"

He smiled again. "If you don't mind."

"I do mind. But I'll answer anyway. I'd moved out of my dad's place years ago, but…circumstances changed and I moved back. Then, after Mom died, he said he needed some time to figure things out. He needed his space."

"He kicked you out?"

Her stomach churned. She didn't have to ask what he was thinking. She'd practically grown up with the McKenzie family. The idea that their mother or father would turn away one of their four sons was ludicrous. Even amid all the stunts their youngest son, Ian, had pulled, they showed nothing but patience and love for him.

She lifted her chin. "I gave my father the space he needed in order to get over a terrible tragedy."

"You suffered the same tragedy."

"Don't," she warned. "Don't judge my father, or my family."

"I can't pretend to understand your father's actions. But I *am* sorry for your loss. I know you and your mom were close. She was…different. We didn't exactly click. But I respected her, because she loved you."

Was that what he thought? That her mother loved her? Peyton wasn't so sure. She'd always loved her mom and desperately tried to make her mom love her in return. But Peyton was never quite sure whether there was enough room in her mother's heart for anyone besides her beloved son. She forced a smile. "Thank you."

"You're welcome."

"Since you're being so nice, I'll give you a bonus answer without you having to ask another follow-up question. When Dad…asked me to leave, it's not like I didn't have resources. He knew I'd be okay. I have a small inheritance, an investment fund that my parents set up years ago in case anything ever happened to either of them. Plus a small life insurance payout. The house here in Gatlinburg is paid off. It's pretty much the only asset Dad hasn't sold. He's keeping it for after he retires. The point is, I can live here rent free, which helped me allocate my funds towards starting my own business. I figured it would be nice to be my own boss for a change instead of being at the mercy of corporations and budget cuts."

"Corporations? Where did you work?"

"Here and there. Whatever I could do to make ends meet."

"You wanted to work in the criminal justice field the last I knew. What happened to that dream?"

"When everyone in the family is working to pay a lawyer, that kind of nixes any plans to pay for college. Not that I'm complaining. It was my choice to start working right out of high school to help with Brian's legal bills."

He stared at her. "You were eighteen. Too young to throw away your dreams."

She shrugged. "You do what you have to do. Besides, I didn't throw away my dreams. I made new ones. That's why I started my shop. Although I'd give anything to have my mom back, the money she left me was a gift. That's what allowed me a fresh start. It's a struggle, but if I can make the café profitable, I'll have some stability in my life again, something long term. And we both know I love to bake."

"Do you? Are you sure about that?"

"Excuse me?"

"All your life, you've sacrificed for others. You were Brian's protector, his second mom, for as long as I can remember. You didn't go to college because you wanted to help your parents with the legal bills. Now you've started a small business that allows you to employ a couple of women who were unemployable by everyone else."

She fisted her hands in her lap. "You make it sound like helping others is a bad thing."

"It is when you're sacrificing yourself along the way. You talk about money being tight. But according to the investigation Landry has been leading, your shop is extremely successful. You should be in the black, not losing money. After seeing the enormous amount of bread you baked and gave to Joan, I can see why. That wasn't all for the café was it? I'll bet if I call the homeless shelter, I'll find that Peyton's Place is making huge donations of food every single day."

She gritted her teeth. "The soup kitchen," she admitted. "Not the homeless shelter."

"Soup kitchen. So they can feed the homeless and poor. Like I said. That's wonderful, Peyton. It truly is. The rest of us could learn a thing or two from all the good that you do. But what I want to know is—why?"

"Why do I want to help people?"

"Not just why do you want to help people. Why do you help them to the exclusion of yourself? You aren't living your life, Peyton. You're in servitude to others. I bet you're working more now than you did when you worked for corporate America. Why are you killing yourself for everyone else?"

She stared at his hands, at the white lines, before forcing herself to meet his probing gaze. "You wouldn't understand."

"I want to. Explain it to me."

She spread her hands in a helpless gesture. "Someone else starts a fire and you, Colin McKenzie, run into that burning building and save lives. Do you know how rare that is? For someone to be that selfless?"

"Peyton, I'm not—"

"Selfless? Yes. You are. You're so good, Colin. You're why I wanted to go into the criminal justice field all those years ago, you and your amazing family. Every one of you has made a career out of helping others. And then—" she shook her head "—then there's *my* family. I grew up watching my father pay people off to clean up Brian's messes." She grimaced. "Fights, graffiti, things like that. From what Chief Landry said at the station, it appears Brian did a lot more than I'd ever realized as a child. My mom, God love her, she wasn't just eccentric. She was a space cadet. And she played favorites with her children. It's one of the reasons that she and Dad fought so much. He loved me. She loved Brian. With no in between." A tear slid down her cheek. She furiously wiped it away.

"Everything for her was about Brian. There was never any time for me. That's why I started baking. Not because I wanted to, but because Mom loved to bake. That was the only time she seemed proud of me, happy with me. It was the only time she loved *me*."

"Peyton, stop. You don't have to—"

She held up her hands. "No. Let me finish. I'm not trying to play a blame game here and paint my parents in a bad light. We all made mistakes, huge mistakes. I was probably the worst offender, always protecting my brother when I should have been making him stand on his own two feet. He's always been different, eccentric, I guess, like you said about my mom. They were so alike. But I was an enabler, just as much as my dad every time he used money to make one of Brian's problems go away. You're like your father, William, The Mighty McKenzie, fighting for truth and justice. That's your legacy. What's mine? I'm a Sterling, with a dysfunctional family and an escaped convict for a brother. And, and…"

Colin moved to the couch beside her, taking one of her hands in his. She clutched it, unable to refuse the lifeline he offered.

She wiped at her tears again. "The more you ask me questions, the more I'm learning about this case, the more I'm scared to death that Brian may have started that damn fire after all." She clutched his hand harder. "You ask me why I'm using every penny I can to employ two women who wouldn't have jobs otherwise. Or why I make up repair work so I can feed a homeless man without him feeling like it's charity." She pressed her fist against her heart. "Because I'm scared to death that I'm like my father, my mother, my brother. I'm a Sterling by name. But not here." She pounded her chest. "Not in my heart. I don't want *their* legacy to be *my* legacy. I want to be a good person, Colin." She tapped her fist against her heart with each word she said. "I need to be a good person."

He gently brushed her hair back from her face. "Peyton. You are a good person. You always have been."

She shook her head. "No. I'm not. I should have been there for you, after the fire. No matter what my dad told me. Even if he did lock my door, take away my stupid phone. I should have been there."

His eyes widened.

"I should have found a way," she continued, the words feeling as if they were being ripped from her soul. "Duncan said you needed me, but I wasn't there. I wasn't there."

She collapsed against him, sobbing so hard she could barely draw a breath.

He swore and scooped her up, cradling her against his chest. He carried her upstairs and tucked her into the guest bed, whispering soothing words the whole time. The day's emotional toll had her so exhausted she struggled to open her eyes.

"Shh," he whispered. "It's okay, Peyton. Don't worry about anything. It's all going to be okay."

She fell asleep to the gentle pressure of his kiss against her forehead.

Chapter Ten

Drowning in guilt and self-loathing, Colin fisted his hands and paced back and forth in his bedroom downstairs. He couldn't shake the image of Peyton's beautiful, pixie-like face wet with tears. Her sweet, gentle voice choked with raw, gut-wrenching pain.

I don't want their legacy to be my legacy. I want to be a good person.

A good person? She was the *epitome* of good. The entire time he'd known her, she'd done things for other people, always putting them first. It was one of the reasons he'd fallen in love with her. She was the kindest, most caring person he'd ever met. And it had never occurred to him, until tonight, that her gentle, selfless nature hid a sea of pain.

I should have been there for you, after the fire.

Yes. But he should have been there for her too. He should have fought for her, realized something was keeping her from being at his side. Instead, he'd been so hurt, so consumed by his own pain and the giant-sized chip on his shoulder that he'd never once considered that she might be hurting. That maybe she needed him too.

What lies had her father told to keep them apart? She'd mentioned him locking her up, taking away her phone. Had his goal been specifically to isolate her from Colin? Had he told her Colin's injuries weren't significant or that he didn't want to see her? She'd been young, naive in many ways. They both had. Colin could easily imagine her being manipulated by her father, using her fierce protectiveness toward her brother as a means to control her.

As she'd said tonight, the fact that her father hadn't been close to his son didn't mean he wouldn't fight for Brian. Benjamin Sterling's reputation, his family's reputation, his business reputation as a trusted financial advisor, had all been at stake. If he'd seen Colin as the enemy, because his testimony could send Brian to prison and hurt his business, Colin could easily imagine him doing everything he could to stop him—including using his own daughter. The elder Sterling had wanted a united family front behind Brian. And he'd probably hoped, planned, that Colin would be so distraught over not being able to see Peyton, and worried about hurting her, that he might not testify.

His plan had almost worked.

At eighteen, Colin's entire life had been centered around the beautiful strawberry blonde with the sexy smile and silver-gray eyes that made promises his body was only too willing to take her up on. When she cut him out of her life, it had nearly destroyed him. Only the love and support of his tight-knit family had gotten him through. Ultimately, a stern lecture about civic responsibility from his father, William—known in legal circles as The Mighty McKenzie—had been the only reason that he'd persevered and kept it together long enough to testify. He'd done his duty, sitting upright in the witness stand, his face carefully blank, pretending that he wasn't in excruciating pain. After walking out of the courtroom, he'd collapsed, and ended up in the hospital for another month.

The combination of his injuries and the belief that Peyton had willingly dumped him had sent him on a downward spiral. But he'd never considered that Brian's treachery, and her father's duplicity, had done the same to her.

Even later, after finding out that she'd gotten married,

he'd assumed life was great for her. Well she didn't seem to have a husband now and wasn't wearing a ring. But he'd never bothered to ask if she was okay, if she'd suffered through a divorce or went through the trauma of losing her husband in some kind of accident or illness. Instead, he'd chosen to assume her life was all roses, that she was doing whatever she wanted, making friends, living a carefree life. In reality, she'd been working herself ragged going from job to job to help pay her brother's legal bills, while Colin had nursed his hurt feelings and congratulated himself on being the better person.

What an arrogant ass he'd been.

That wasn't his only sin against her. The supposed deal he'd made with her at the police station was a farce. Arresting her was never something he'd considered. The charges never would have stuck, as Landry knew, or he'd have arrested her himself. Then Colin had compounded his lies by exaggerating the danger to Brian.

His brothers in arms weren't a bunch of Mayberries who shot first and asked questions later. They were experienced professionals, intent on recapturing—not killing—four escaped convicts. He'd known the search for Brian and the others was in competent hands, which was why he'd been comfortable exchanging information with them. But he'd allowed Peyton to stew in worry, using that fear to make her answer his questions.

He shook his head in disgust and stopped pacing. All this self-recrimination wasn't doing him, or Peyton, any good. He owed her a heartfelt apology. But waking her up at midnight when she'd cried herself into an exhausted sleep would be one more selfish act to lay at his door. He wouldn't do it. But he had to do *something* with all this guilt and nervous energy or he was going to explode.

He moved to the window and looked out past the covered, wraparound porch. A gentle breeze rippled across the lawn, making the rain-wet blades of grass sparkle in the moonlight. The grass was a bit ragged and higher than he liked to keep it. His lawn tractor had broken down a couple of weeks ago and he hadn't had time to fix it. Sweating and struggling with that stubborn tractor engine was infinitely preferable to wrestling with his conscience. He could change the oil in the ATVs he kept in the workshop building too. Might as well do something productive if he wasn't going to sleep.

He figured the odds of Brian and his fellow thugs heading up the mountain and being anywhere near this place were low. Without knowing that Colin had a house here, or that Peyton was with him, there was no reason for her brother to risk being caught by remaining in the immediate area. Besides that, Officer Simmons was staying at the Sterling home for now. If she'd seen anything suspicious, she'd have called him. Still, it wouldn't hurt to take precautions.

He dressed as if he was going to work, making sure his gun was loaded and holstered at his hip with two extra magazines of ammunition in his pocket. It wasn't unusual for the occasional black bear to wander onto the property and it was best to be prepared. He grabbed a flashlight before heading out back.

Except for the well-used charcoal grill and a couple of lounge chairs, his back deck was empty. No muddy shoe prints marred the surface to indicate any recent visitors. He jogged down the steps into the yard, stopping at the tool shed fifty yards from the house. A circuit around the perimeter with his flashlight didn't reveal any tracks other than some paw prints that had likely been left by a hungry raccoon searching for its next meal. The padlock was securely in place on the door. The shed didn't have any windows.

He swept the beam of his flashlight back and forth along the trees that bordered two sides of the property. But aside from low-hanging branches gracefully moving in the steady, warm breeze, there wasn't any unexplained movement or shadows that didn't look like they belonged. Satisfied that all was well, he clicked off the flashlight and used the light of the moon to guide him toward his workshop. He was ten feet from his destination when the little hairs stood up on the back of his neck.

Chapter Eleven

Peyton bolted out of bed and fell to the floor, her legs tangled in the sheets. She batted at the stubborn material to free herself as she scanned the dark recesses of the bedroom. No bogeyman waited to pounce on her from the shadows. But something had startled her awake. What was it?

A small sliver of light leaked beneath the bedroom door. Was Colin still awake? She pushed herself up off the floor and checked the time on her phone, which was charging on the nightstand. A little past midnight. Maybe he was catching an old movie or watching a rerun of a favorite college basketball game. He'd always been a Tennessee Vols fan and had hoped to go to the University of Tennessee after high school. Had he gone? She hadn't thought to ask him.

Maybe he was having a late-night snack. Or, more likely after her humiliating outburst earlier tonight, he was regretting having his crazy ex-girlfriend around and was trying to think of a polite way to get rid of her. She certainly wouldn't blame him.

Bam!

She jerked back, swearing when her shin slammed against the wooden bedframe. *What was that?*

Bam! Bam!

She sucked in a breath. Gunshots. Coming from outside, behind the house.

She hesitated, not sure what to do, half-expecting Colin

to burst into the bedroom to check on her. When he didn't, a nagging sense of unease released a firestorm of butterflies in her stomach. She grabbed her phone, fingers poised to punch in his number—but she didn't *have* his number, or Duncan's or any of the McKenzies. Not anymore.

Clutching the phone, she ran to the closet to throw on some clothes. She yanked on a pair of jeans and a shirt, not bothering with a bra. After shoving her feet into some tennis shoes, she took off running. She practically flew down the stairs, hopping down them two at a time, a feat she'd never have thought possible before tonight, since she wasn't blessed with long legs like Colin.

The big-screen TV hanging on the far wall of the family room wasn't on. The light she'd seen from upstairs was coming from the back hallway. She hopped off the bottom step and circled around to the rear of the house. Her sense of unease intensified when she discovered that the lights in his office were on too, but the office was empty. A quick peek behind the other doors in the hall revealed a bathroom, a closet and the laundry room, but no sign of Colin.

"Colin? Colin? Are you here? Are you okay?" She yelled for him as she ran toward his bedroom at the front of the house. All the while she prayed that he'd yank open his door and look at her as if he thought she'd lost her mind. That would be infinitely better than the alternative, that he was outside where she'd heard those gunshots. But when she reached his door it was standing wide open. She didn't have to flip on the light to see that his bed was empty, looking as if it hadn't been slept in.

"Colin?" Her voice came out a hoarse whisper. The butterflies degenerated into full-blown panic as she ran through the house to the last place he could be, the kitchen. Just as she'd feared, it too was empty.

Boom! Boom!

She dropped to the floor, her pulse rushing in her ears. That had sounded so close!

Please, please don't let that be Brian out there shooting at Colin.

Her nerdy, insecure brother wasn't someone she'd ever thought could hurt someone. But as Landry had reminded her earlier, Brian did know how to shoot, almost as well as Peyton. Colin had taught both of them. Was Brian out there right now? Shooting at the man who'd been so patient with him when they were teenagers, and far kinder than most kids at school had been to her socially awkward brother?

Listening to Colin's theories and being forced to reevaluate every facet of her life—and Brian's—had opened jagged cracks in her confidence, letting the first stirrings of doubt creep in about his innocence—or guilt. Even if her long-held beliefs about Brian were still valid, she had no illusions about the men who'd escaped with him. One of them had murdered a police officer. They probably wouldn't think twice about killing a marshal.

Drawing a bracing breath, she forced herself to stop cowering and look out the window. A yellow bug light cast a warm glow across the deck. Beyond that, there was only darkness and the looming silhouette of a building that resembled a small barn. Had Colin taken his gun with him and gone outside to confront someone he'd seen sneaking around his property? Or had he already been outside, maybe without a gun at all, when the shooting started?

She yanked her phone out of her pocket, berating herself for not making this call as soon as she'd heard the first shot.

"Nine-one-one, what's your emergency?" a woman's voice came on the line.

"This is Peyton Sterling. I'm at Deputy US Marshal Colin McKenzie's home." She rattled off the address. "I can't find him. He was in the house earlier. But now he's gone. I heard gunshots out back. I think he's in trouble. It's possible that the escaped convicts everyone's been looking for are here and they're—"

"Ma'am, Ms. Sterling, hold it. I need you to slow down. You said you heard gunshots?"

"Get the police out here immediately, and an ambulance just in case. Send the marshals, send everyone. Colin needs help!" She tossed the phone on the counter, tuning out the operator's barrage of useless questions.

Bam! Boom! Boom!

Muzzle flashes appeared in the woods off to the left. There was no answering flash in the yard, but earlier she'd thought she heard return gunfire. If that had been Colin, then he was either inside the barn-like building firing from a window, or he was on the other side, possibly pinned down and unable to get to safety. He needed backup. Now. Not in twenty minutes, or however long it would take the police to climb up that crazy winding road out front. The only person around to be his backup was her. She swallowed and rubbed her palms against her jeans. What she really needed right now was a huge dose of courage.

And a gun.

Think, Peyton. Think. If you lived here, where would you keep an extra gun and ammunition? It would be some place easy to get to in case an intruder broke in. But not where a child or casual visitor would stumble across it.

She whirled around and her gaze locked on the pantry door. Colin put his coffee mugs where she kept hers. Would he put a gun and ammo where she'd keep hers too, easy to grab, close to an exit in case she had to run outside to either pursue or run from a bad guy?

She jogged into the pantry, throwing open the door so hard that it banged against the wall. Then she flipped the light switch and looked up. There—a wooden box on the top shelf. Just the right size to store a weapon. It was too high for small children to reach. Which meant it was too high for her too.

Bouncing on her tiptoes, she jumped up and down, desperately stretching her fingers up, up, up. She stumbled and fell against the shelving, barely managing to stay upright.

"Dang it, Colin. Why do you have to be so tall?"

She whirled around, looking for a ladder or a step stool, cursing herself for wasting time when she didn't find any. Colin wouldn't need them to reach the top shelf. So what could she use? A chair. But he didn't have a dining room where she could grab one. There wasn't even a table in the kitchen.

But there were bar stools.

She ran to the kitchen island and dragged one of the bar stools into the pantry, wincing at the sound of the metal legs scraping the hardwood floor.

Boom! Bam! Bam!

The sound of fresh gunfire sent her flying up on the bar stool like a monkey and grabbing the wooden box. She jumped down and tried to flip open the top. It wouldn't budge. The dang thing was locked!

She cried out in frustration. Of course it was locked. Colin was a marshal. He wouldn't take any chances that someone might get hold of one of his guns and hurt themselves. It looked sophisticated too, one of those fancy electronic boxes that required a fingerprint to open it.

Using curse words she hadn't realized were in her vocabulary, she scrambled to her feet and grabbed a large can off a nearby shelf. English peas. She hated peas. She raised the can and brought it crashing down. Again. Again. Again. Wood splintered and crunched. The lock held. The box didn't. She kissed the can, deciding she liked peas after all.

Lying on a bed of red velvet dusted by bits of ruined wood was the prettiest sight she'd ever seen. A Glock 22, the .40 caliber pistol framed by two full magazines. How many times had she complained when Colin insisted on taking her shooting in the mountains, sometimes with her brother tagging along? She'd assured him that her career path in the criminal justice field wouldn't be the same as his, that she'd be a victim's advocate or a defense attorney, not a cop. She didn't need to know how to fire a gun.

He would tell her it wasn't about her career. It was about making sure the woman he loved could protect herself in a world that too often was cruel and dangerous, especially for women. Well, tonight it was dangerous for men. One man in particular.

She shoved one of the magazines into the pistol and chambered a round. Pocketing the other magazine, she lunged to her feet.

"You've done everything you could to protect me, Colin. Now it's my turn to protect you."

Chapter Twelve

Colin crouched down, his left shoulder butted up against
the workshop building as he pointed his .40 caliber Glock
22 toward the woods to the south of his property. In spite
of there being no physical evidence that anyone was out
here when he'd reached the building, his instincts had told
him something was off. He'd cleared the inside, then made
a circuit around the perimeter. He'd just reached the far
side of the building when the first shot had kicked up the
dirt beside him. Since then, he'd been pinned down in this
same spot.

The solid wall on this side of the structure offered no access to the inside. And the shooter, or shooters, were having fun at his expense. They were aiming their shots at the
ground, or above his head, forcing him to stay where he
was. It was only a matter of time before they tired of their
sadistic game and made their shots count.

He had to get out of here.

He eased back toward the corner as he'd tried twice before. This time, he measured his stride in inches, going as
slowly as possible, hoping they wouldn't realize he was
backing up until it was too late to stop him. One inch,
two, three—

Boom! Boom!

He swore and jumped away from the rain of wood and
sawdust above and behind him. Laughter sounded from

the trees. Familiar laughter? Was that Brian, hiding like the coward he was? Once again playing God with other peoples' lives?

This cat-and-mouse game would end as soon as his tormentors got bored. He couldn't risk waiting any longer. He had to make a run for it, take his chances, lay some heavy cover fire so he could try to get to relative safety. And after that? If the gunmen decided to circle around, get him in their sights again? That was a worst-case scenario he didn't want to think about.

He popped out his empty magazine and shoved in another one. It was now or never. He aimed directly toward where he'd seen the last muzzle flash. *Bam, bam, bam, bam!* He squeezed the trigger over and over, never stopping, emptying the magazine as he backed up.

Boom!

A guttural scream sounded from the woods.

He slammed his last magazine of ammo into the gun and fired again, ducking and weaving, scrambling back toward the corner.

Boom!

The bullet slammed into him like a battering ram, stealing his breath, sending a shockwave of blinding pain through his entire body. He managed to squeeze off two more rounds then dove around the end of the building. He landed on his side and rolled onto his back, clutching at his chest, desperately struggling to get his lungs working again.

"Colin! Oh no, Colin!"

He jerked his head to the side. *Peyton! No!* She leaped from the back deck to the ground and started running toward him, ducking down but still an open, easy target if the gunmen noticed her.

Down! His mind screamed but he couldn't force any words past his constricted throat. *Get down!* He signaled for her to drop to the ground as he gasped like a fish on dry land, mouth open but no air getting in. Blackness hovered at the edge of his vision. No! He had to stay conscious. He had to get her to cover before the gunmen saw her.

Can't pass out. Breathe, damn it. Breathe!

He motioned again for her to get down. She hesitated, then started forward. He flipped onto his stomach and drove his fists against his belly. The impact loosened his diaphragm. Blessed air rushed into his lungs. He gulped it in, ruthlessly fighting back the darkness. He scrambled up, fell against the building, pushed himself upright. He took a wobbly step toward her, another.

She slowed again, then stopped thirty feet away. What was she doing?

"Run!" he rasped, still barely able to talk. He sucked in another lungful of air. "Run!"

Boom! Boom! Shots sounded from the woods again. But Colin couldn't tell where they were aiming.

He brought up his gun to fire back but she was already turning toward the woods, clasping a pistol he hadn't realized she was carrying. *Bam, bam, bam, bam, bam!* She kept squeezing off shots.

Colin holstered his pistol and sprinted toward her. When he reached her she stopped shooting, eyes wide with surprise. He scooped her up in his arms and raced back to the workshop building. As soon as they were behind the wall, he groaned at the painful throbbing in his chest and slid to the grass with her on his lap. The gunshots stopped and the woods went silent. He didn't know if that was good or bad.

"You crazy woman," he gritted out, drawing a shallow breath to try to ease the pain. "What were you thinking? You could have been killed."

"So could you! You shouldn't have left your cover to come get me."

He stared at her in disbelief. "I shouldn't have... I shouldn't have." He shook his head. "You scared ten years off my life, Peyton. If you ever do something like that again, I swear…" He yanked her against him, hugging her fiercely, not caring that it hurt like hell.

"Can't. Breathe. Colin," she choked out.

He let her go. "Sorry. Good grief, you scared me." He shook his head and scrubbed his face, then winced and rubbed his chest.

"Ditto." She put her left hand on his shoulder, the Glock still clutched in her right hand, finger on the frame instead of the trigger, the gun pointed away from him. Just as he'd taught her so many years ago. If he hadn't still been so rattled, he'd have told her he was proud of how well she'd handled the gun, was still handling it.

"What happened to you?" she asked. "I heard gunshots. Saw you leap around the corner of the building and then you were rolling on the ground."

"Had the wind knocked out of me. Took a bullet, dead center to the chest. The bastards."

She drew a sharp breath, eyes wide as she looked him up and down. "I don't see any blood. Where's the entrance wound?"

"The round hit me in the vest. I wasn't really expecting trouble, but came prepared, dressed just as I would for work, just in case." He shifted, then winced.

"A vest," she choked out. "You're wearing a vest. Thank God." She let out a shuddering breath. "When I heard the gunshots, saw you fall…" She shook her head.

"Why in the world would you run outside if you heard gunshots?" he demanded.

She looked at him as if she thought he'd lost his mind. "Because they were shooting at you! You needed backup."

"You're a civilian. Not backup. You shouldn't have risked your life like that."

"You're kidding, right? Colin, you were—"

"Where did you get the gun?"

"It's yours, from the pantry." She bit her bottom lip. "I had to smash the box it was in to get the pistol out. It looked nice, expensive."

"I don't care about a stupid box. I care about *you*." He pulled her against him again, less tightly this time, ignoring the fresh wave of pain in his bruised chest. Since she was hugging him back, the pain was well worth it.

Sirens sounded from down the mountain, coming up fast. He froze, then set her away from him and looked toward the house. Although he couldn't see the road out front, the lights from approaching emergency vehicles lit the night sky in hues of red, orange, and blue.

"You called the police?"

"Of course. I wasn't sure that you and I would be able to hold off whoever was shooting at you." Her eyes widened in dismay. "I should have called that officer at my house. It didn't even occur to me! She was much closer."

"You did great." He searched her gaze. "Did you realize your brother could be one of the shooters?"

She looked away, her chin wobbling, and gave him a sharp nod. He realized she was close to losing her composure. She'd known that Brian might be out there, in the woods. But she'd called the police anyway, and risked her own life, not to protect her brother this time, but to protect Colin.

She twisted her hands together, drew a ragged breath. "Did you see who was shooting at you? Do you…do you know if—"

"I didn't see anyone." He coaxed her hands apart, held them in his. "Try not to worry. We'll find out soon enough who was out there."

The sirens were louder now, probably a few hundred yards from the driveway. She turned the pistol around and offered it to him. "You'd better take this. If the cops see a Sterling with a gun, they'll probably shoot first and ask questions later."

"I think you're doing Gatlinburg PD a disservice in thinking that. But I understand where you're coming from." He shoved the pistol into his waistband, then cupped her face between his hands.

Her silver-gray eyes caught the moonlight as she stared at him in surprise.

He shouldn't kiss her. It would be a mistake on so many levels. But he also knew there was no way he could *not* kiss her at that moment. Her selfless act humbled him to the core and reminded him of the hundred different reasons he'd loved her. Still loved her. Maybe, just maybe, there could be a future between them again, once all of this was settled.

He pulled her to him, slowly, gently, giving her plenty of time to stop him if she wanted. But she didn't. Instead, her eyes fluttered closed, her breath tumbling out of her on a soft sigh. He knew he was lost the moment his lips touched hers. Electricity shot through every nerve ending, firing to life again as if reawakening after being in hibernation for a very, very long time. His hands shook as he molded her luscious body to his, drinking her into his starved senses. She trembled in his arms and kissed him back with an equally wild abandon, as if she too couldn't get enough of him.

All too soon, shouts and loud voices broke into the passionate haze that had wrapped around them. Bright lights flashed against his closed eyelids. He reluctantly broke the kiss and turned to see police officers and firefighters running around both sides of his house like ants pouring out of an anthill. Powerful flashlight beams danced across the ground, across the workshop building, across Peyton and him.

He sighed and looked back at Peyton. Her gorgeous eyes

were unfocused, passion warring with wonder and surprise. She licked her lips.

His body tightened with need.

"Colin." Her gaze dropped to his mouth. "I wish—"

"Over here!" someone yelled. "There's a body in the woods!"

Her eyes widened. "Brian!" She scrambled off his lap and ran toward one of the policemen approaching them.

Colin recognized him as Patrick Edwards, an excellent officer he'd worked with numerous times over the years whenever one of his taskforces partnered with the Gatlinburg police. Peyton didn't seem to notice that the officer's hand inched closer to his holster as she approached.

"It's okay, Patrick," Colin called out. "She's a witness. She saved my life."

Patrick's eyebrows rose in surprise but he nodded and relaxed his hand. He smiled at Peyton, giving her a polite nod when she stopped in front of him gesturing excitedly as she no doubt asked about her brother.

Now that his brief but pleasant interlude with Peyton was over, Colin's bruised chest decided it was time to remind him that it wasn't happy about being ignored. He closed his eyes and tried to take shallow breaths. Somehow the pain seemed worse now than when he'd first been hit. Probably because he'd been moving around too much.

"I can't believe you kissed her."

He sighed and opened his eyes. Duncan frowned down at him, hands on hips.

"You saw that, huh?"

"Half the police force did and a handful of firefighters."

Colin groaned. "Help me up."

Duncan shook his head and motioned toward some EMTs who'd just rounded the garage end of the house and seemed confused about where to go. "Since you're sitting on your butt instead of jumping into the fray with everyone else running around your property, I'm guessing you're hurt."

"Just bruised. Took a bullet in the vest."

"Let me guess. It only hurts when you breathe?"

"Pretty much." He held his hand out and this time Duncan hauled him to his feet.

The EMTs rushed up to him, two wide-eyed young kids who looked like they should be at home with their moms and dads, catching a few more hours of sleep before heading to school in the morning.

"Sir," the shorter one said. "Please sit down and let us check your injuries. Miss Sterling said you'd been shot and needed medical attention."

Colin arched a brow, looking around for her but she'd disappeared. "She did?"

"Yes, sir. Officer Edwards radioed us to come around back."

They both reached for him as if they thought he was about to fall down.

He shoved their hands away. "For the love of… I'm okay. I'm wearing a vest."

They exchanged a confused glance.

"Kevlar? Bullet resistant?"

"Oh," the same guy said. "Well, uh, you could have broken ribs or internal bleeding. We should still check it out, take you to the hospital."

"Hold that thought." He tugged Duncan a few yards away and turned his back to the overeager children. "Did you see where Peyton went?"

Duncan crossed his arms. "Landry was marching her toward your house when I walked up, no doubt to cross-examine her about whatever happened out here. What *did* happen?"

"I got in a gunfight with one or more cowards shooting at me from the woods. I didn't see them, so I'm not sure who—"

"Sir." The second EMT had found his voice. "We need you to sit—"

"Just a minute," he and Duncan both said at the same time.

Another commotion had them turning to see a group of men topping the small rise on the south side of his yard. Three were wearing white lab coats. The rest were police officers, escorting them toward a fifty-foot section of tree line that was being cordoned off with yellow crime scene tape that read DO NOT CROSS.

"The coroner's here. Must have already been close by," Colin said. "There's a body in the woods, one of the shooters. I need to know if it's Brian."

"Couldn't happen to a nicer guy."

"Duncan, I'm not the only one who fired a gun into those woods tonight. Peyton heard the gunshots when she was inside the house, got one of my pistols and ran out in the middle of a gunfight to help me. She not only put her own life on the line, she fired at the gunmen even though her brother could have been one of them."

Duncan paled. "Then she could have—"

"Killed her own brother. To save me. You and I both know that no one in charge is going to concern themselves with allaying her fears. It could be hours before she finds out the truth. I don't want her agonizing and wondering about her brother's fate if I can find out and save her some grief."

"What do you need me to do? Make Landry back off?"

"I need you to run interference with these guys." He motioned behind him, toward the EMTs.

"You got it."

"Thanks, man. I owe you."

Duncan grinned. "And I won't let you forget it." He

stepped around Colin. "Gentlemen, let's chat about Kevlar for a minute—"

Colin took off toward the woods. Each step jarred his aching ribs, making him wonder if the EMTs were right and he'd broken something. But finding out would have to wait.

Although Colin didn't have his badge handy, several of the officers recognized him. After explaining that he wanted to see whoever'd been trying to kill him tonight, they allowed him to step under the crime scene tape.

Battery-operated lights were being set up in this section of the woods, making it seem more like midday than a few hours before sunup. The coroner and his assistants were bending over the dead man's body. Colin's above-average height allowed him to see over most of the police standing around. But the dead man was facing away from him.

As he stepped back and moved around the outer perimeter to get a better vantage point, he noted the location of the body in relation to the workshop building. The man would have had a direct line of sight to where Colin had been pinned down. But close-set oaks formed a solid wall to his right, completely blocking the view of the rest of the yard. There was no way that Peyton could have shot him. Which meant that Colin had.

When he finally got a good look at the man's face, he sucked in a sharp breath. Hauntingly familiar silver-gray eyes stared sightlessly back at him. Any hope he'd had of rekindling the relationship between him and Peyton was as dead as the man on the ground.

There was no way Peyton would ever forgive him for this.

Chapter Thirteen

Peyton rested her elbow on the arm of the couch, only half-listening to Chief Landry's questions. The interrogation thing was becoming almost routine. At least this time he didn't intimidate her. After she'd endured hours of questioning by Colin, Landry seemed like a lightweight.

The man was definitely more aggressive in his questioning than he'd been before. She had to give him credit for that. But she still felt that Colin could teach him a thing or two about interviewing techniques. Landry was probably just trying to reassert his authority after she'd ignored his order to sit on the couch when they'd first come inside. Instead, she'd gone upstairs, put on her bra, and brushed her teeth and her hair before coming back down. No way was she going to sit there being stared at by half a dozen men while wondering if they were ogling her braless breasts through her thin white shirt.

"Miss Sterling?" Landry asked. "Do you need me to repeat the question? Maybe you could use a drink or something? I know you've been through an ordeal tonight."

She blinked and realized she'd zoned out again. Landry's face mirrored more concern than annoyance. Maybe he wasn't as bad as she'd thought. The men and women working for him seemed to like him. And he never raised his voice with them, not that she'd seen so far. He had a kind face, with character. He reminded her a little of her grandfather on her daddy's side when he'd still been alive.

As soon as she realized she was comparing the chief of police to her dearly departed grandpa, she realized just how exhausted she must be. She curled her legs beneath her and stared past the sea of detectives with their tablets and pads of paper toward the windows on the side of the house. Where was Colin? Was he still outside? Had he gone into the woods to figure out how many people had been shooting at him tonight?

Had he discovered the identity of the body that had been found?

No, she couldn't think about that. Every time she did, she started to shake and her throat tightened. It was humiliating enough already, being constantly treated like a criminal when she was just the sister of one. Crying in front of these men was *not* an option. She had to keep it together.

It wasn't Brian. The dead body in the woods wasn't her brother. She had to believe that.

Maybe Colin wasn't outside at all. She'd asked that nice police officer to get him medical help. Not being all that familiar with how bulletproof vests worked, she wasn't sure what kind of damage a shot could cause. But Colin had definitely seemed uncomfortable, to say the least. She imagined he'd be sporting a rainbow of colors on his chest for weeks as the bruises rose to the surface.

"Miss Sterling." The chief's voice broke through her musings again. "Did you hear my question?"

She cleared her throat. "No, sorry. I didn't. Can you tell me where Deputy US Marshal McKenzie is? He was hurt in the gunfight. He was wearing a bulletproof vest but I could tell he was in pain. Is he on the way to the hospital for X-rays or something?"

One of his bushy white eyebrows raised. "McKenzie? Seems like I remember Officer Edwards telling me that he'd sent some EMTs to check on him. I'm sure he's fine. You mentioned you took a pistol from the kitchen and—"

"You're *sure* Colin's fine?" She curled her fingers against the arm of the couch. "Does that mean you don't actually *know*?"

A flash of impatience crossed Landry's face as he turned to the detective beside him. "Get me a status on Deputy Marshal McKenzie. Edwards should be able to help you."

"And my brother." Her voice broke and she had to clear it before continuing. "I need to know whether Brian Sterling was...found on the property. I need to know whether anyone has seen him tonight."

"Peyton."

She turned to see Colin standing by the island that separated the kitchen from the family room.

"Colin!" She jumped up from the couch.

The chief grabbed her hand to keep her from leaving. "Miss Sterling. We aren't through here."

She shook him off. "Yes. We are." She jogged across the family room and would have thrown her arms around Colin in relief that he was okay, except that his chalky-looking face reminded her that he wasn't.

"Oh, Colin. You're so pale. You must be in terrible pain. What did the EMTs say was wrong? Shouldn't you be at the hospital? Where do you keep the medicine around here? I can get you some ibuprofen. If you don't have any, I should have some in my—"

"Peyton. We need to talk." He looked over the top of her head. "Alone. In my office." He took her hand and tugged her with him through the family room, around the couch grouping.

Landry stood and started toward them. "Marshal McKenzie, I'm in the middle of interviewing Miss Sterling. I need to ask you some questions as well."

"It can wait."

His tone brooked no argument. The chief stopped and fell silent as they passed. But the thunderous look on his face told Peyton just how furious he was. She didn't look forward to answering more of his questions.

Colin didn't seem to care one whit about Landry's anger. He completely ignored him as he turned down the back hall, his long strides forcing Peyton to jog to keep up with him.

She'd never seen him like this before. His profile looked etched in stone. His jaw was clamped so tight that the skin whitened along his jawline. Dread settled in her belly, making the earlier butterflies seem tame in comparison. Every instinct inside her told her to run, far away, that she didn't want to hear whatever it was that he was about to tell her.

He shoved the office door open and pulled her inside. A massive glass-and-wrought-iron desk sat in front of the window with two wing chairs across from it. A black leather love seat that matched the couches in the family room backed up against a wall of bookshelves on the left side of the room. He closed and locked the door, then pulled her to the love seat.

"Sit down, Peyton."

She stared up at him. "Colin, I don't—"

"Please."

She slowly lowered herself to the love seat and perched on the edge, her hands clasped together. He sat close beside her and covered her hands with his own. His thumb gently stroked across their fingers, his gaze downcast, his throat working as if he was struggling to find the right words to destroy her world.

In spite of her vow not to cry, a single tear escaped and traced down her cheek. "It's Brian, isn't it?" she said in a hoarse whisper. "Just say it, Colin. The wondering is driving me crazy."

He lifted his head.

She gasped at the raw pain in their stormy blue depths. "No. Oh, no. Brian."

His expression turned to anguish. "I went into the woods, saw the body myself. I had to be sure."

"Then Brian is—"

"No. The man who died tonight wasn't Brian. It was your father. And I'm the one who killed him."

Chapter Fourteen

Colin leaned against one of the posts on his front porch, watching the sun coming up over the mountains, and Peyton driving *down* the mountain in her banged-up white Ford Escape that had definitely seen better days.

A few minutes later, Duncan pulled his work Jeep to a halt in front of the garage. He hopped out and crossed to the porch, propping one of his boots against the bottom step. "Did I just pass Peyton?"

"You probably did. It's Wednesday, for goodness sakes. The middle of the week. Don't you ever work anymore?"

"I could say the same about you."

"I'm still on vacation."

"And I've been falling asleep at my desk with nothing to do since the park is still locked up tight. When are your fellow marshals going to do *their* jobs and catch Brian and his co-thugs so things can get back to normal?"

"I doubt they'll ever get back to normal," Colin mumbled.

"What did you say?"

"Nothing."

"Uh-huh." Duncan motioned down the road. "I don't recall seeing her SUV in your pristine garage when I stopped by the day after the shooting."

"Landry had to finally accept that Brian wasn't dumb enough to return to the Sterling household, so he sent Officer Simmons packing. He had a couple of his men bring Peyton's SUV up here so she could drive home when she was ready."

"I don't remember Landry being that accommodating in the past."

"He usually isn't," Colin agreed. "But after Peyton called 911 even though she knew her brother could have been the one shooting at me, and she risked her life trying to save me, she won over the hearts of a lot of law-enforcement guys around here, including the chief. Plus, I think he feels bad for her since she lost her father. He mentioned that she reminds him of his youngest granddaughter."

"Landry procreated. Who knew? Hey, speaking of dear old Dad, have you and Peyton worked through that?"

Colin shifted against the post, grimacing when his ribs sent up a jolt of pain in protest. At least they were only bruised, as the X-rays had confirmed. That was one thing to be thankful for. "Peyton claims she doesn't blame me for what happened."

"Claims? You don't believe her?"

They'd barely spoken to each other since he'd told her that he was responsible for her father's death. Her grief was too raw, too close to the surface. Nearly every time he'd said anything to her, she'd started crying and walked out of the room.

"I'm guessing that's a no," Duncan said. "Has anyone figured out why her father was in the woods behind your house?"

Colin shrugged. "Gun powder residue tests were negative, so he wasn't the shooter. Other than that, I have no idea."

"Shooter? Singular? There was only one?"

"That's the consensus, although I haven't been able to tell Peyton." It was difficult to have that kind of conversation with someone who left the room every time he brought up the subject of her family. "There were only two sets of shoe prints—Mr. Sterling and someone else." Colin swatted at a horsefly out looking for an easy meal. It took off, searching for another target.

"Meaning Sterling junior was our shooter."

"Most likely." Colin checked his watch and frowned.

"Well at least the ambush makes more sense now," Duncan said. "From what I've heard, Brian blames you for everything from him being in prison to the marshals having the gall to keep searching for him. I can imagine his warped mind wanting revenge against you. What I can't understand is why he'd shoot at Peyton. I thought they were close."

"He didn't. The CSU guys confirmed the bullet trajectories, that all the shots from the woods were fired at the other side of the building, where I was. When she shot towards the woods, he was probably ducking for cover, assuming that I was the one shooting. I don't think he ever saw her. I was his only target."

Duncan tapped his boot, slowly nodding as if he was mulling everything over and putting the pieces together. As a criminal investigator, he often brainstormed with Colin about things going on at either of their workplaces. He was seldom wrong in his conclusions.

"Okay, how about this for a scenario?" Duncan asked. "Little brother and the other numbskulls split up, each of them trying to find their own way out of the mountains around the roadblocks. But Brian can't get out. He's frustrated, breaks into a parked car or someone's cabin and steals a phone. Then he does what he's always done when things don't go his way—he calls Daddy to come rescue him. They both decide to enact a little vengeance on the man they feel is responsible for their woes and come up here to kill you."

"Pretty much what I came up with too. The part where Sterling senior wants to help his son kill me feels a bit off though. I have a hard time envisioning the father as a bloodthirsty criminal. But I haven't come up with a better explanation."

"Wait, you built this house long after the Sterlings moved away. And like most of us in law enforcement, you don't broadcast personal details like your home address on social media or anything. So how would Brian have known where you live?"

Colin started to cross his arms, then thought better of it when his ribs protested.

Duncan stared up at him, eyes widening. "Peyton told him, didn't she? I can't believe it. That little traitor. I should go arrest her right now. As a matter of fact, I think I will." He turned around and stalked toward his Jeep.

"Knock it off, Duncan. You can't arrest her for talking to her father on the phone. She admitted she called to check on him after she arrived, and that she told him where she was staying. She had no reason to expect that her father would come here. And no one would have predicted that he and his son would decide to join forces and cause trouble."

Duncan turned around. "Cause trouble? They tried to murder you."

"Let it go." Colin checked his watch again. "And stop blaming Peyton. You know she could never purposely hurt anyone."

Duncan gestured down the road. "She's leaving you again. So much for not hurting anyone."

"Knock it off. I'm a big boy and can take care of myself. Besides, you need to cut her some slack. It's not like her life is all puppies and rainbows right now. Her mother died three months ago. Her brother is on the run. And her father was just killed."

Duncan shook his head. "I want to hate her for not sticking around. But you're right. I can't. Heck, we all grew up together. Mom still reminisces sometimes about the old days and talks about how she wishes things could have been different, that Peyton was still around." He spread his hands out in a helpless gesture. "I guess I'll be there to support her along with you at her father's funeral. When is it?"

"There isn't going to be one. When the coroner releases the body, it will be shipped to Memphis. Peyton said she's going to have a private memorial, 'private' meaning just her. Anything else seems inappropriate after everything that's happened. Her words, not mine. When she left here, she said she was going to the Sterling house to clean out the refrigerator and pack her things. Then she's heading to Memphis to close up her father's house and find a new place to live."

Duncan stared up at him, then slowly mounted the steps. "Then it's really over between you two? She's not coming back to Gatlinburg?"

Colin shook his head.

"Well, that makes this really awkward." He pulled a small box out of his suit jacket pocket and tossed it to Colin.

Colin held it up, then shot his brother a glance. "Condoms? You brought me a box of condoms?"

Duncan shrugged. "When two ex-lovers experience a life-or-death situation, one would expect that would bring them closer together. Thus, you know, the need for…protection. I thought I was doing you a favor. My timing, and apparently my instincts in that department, are a bit off."

"Apparently." Colin shook his head and shoved the box into his pants pocket for lack of anywhere else to put it.

"Guess I should go inside and take the whiskey now," Duncan said.

"Do and you die."

Duncan smiled and leaned against the opposite post. "Man, I can't believe she's actually leaving Gatlinburg. Again. What about her shop downtown?"

"She's giving it to her employees, along with some seed

money to help them through until it's more profitable. She isn't sure what she's going to do but she wants a fresh start."

He arched a brow. "You sure I don't need to grab the whiskey?"

"I'm fine, Duncan. Knock it off." He wasn't fine of course. But he wasn't going to bare his soul to his brother out on his front porch. And this wasn't over, none of it, until he had Brian Sterling locked up again. Then he'd have to pick up the pieces and face whatever future he had—*somehow*.

"I imagine you'll be going back to work then, with Peyton out of the picture and the other marshals combing the mountains searching for our gang of fugitives."

"Nope. After the shooting, I have more incentive than ever to catch Brian. I haven't quit just yet."

"With all due respect for your great track record with locating fugitives, what makes you think you can do better than our law-enforcement brothers who are out looking for him right now?"

Colin glanced at his watch again. "I have something they don't."

"What would that be?"

"A GPS tracker on one of those fugitive's sister's SUV."

Duncan straightened. "I'm guessing that watch you keep checking isn't just a watch."

"Nope."

"Peyton didn't go to the Sterling homestead to clean out the refrigerator did she?"

"Didn't even slow down when she drove past the house. She's heading north toward town right now." Colin yanked his keys out of his pocket.

Duncan looked at him accusingly. "You thought she was innocent, that she wasn't helping her brother. So, why put a tracker on her car?"

"She *is* innocent. But she's also down to one family

member and is an emotional wreck. I figure she's desperate enough to try to find him on her own before heading out of town. She'll think she's saving his life. If she does find him, I want to be there."

Duncan nodded his agreement. "To put Brian away."

"To protect Peyton. I programmed my phone number into her phone and told her to call me if she needs me. But I'm not sure she'll even realize that she's in danger if she manages to stumble across her brother. She wouldn't in a million years expect Brian to hurt her. I'm not nearly as trusting." He headed down the steps, forced to go slowly because of his ribs. "I'll call you later, let you know how it plays out."

"I strongly suggest that you let Landry or your fellow marshals handle this."

Colin looked back over his shoulder. "And tell them what? That I put a GPS tracker on my ex-girlfriend's car without her knowledge? That I'd like them to follow her just in case she meets up with her fugitive brother instead of, say, a new boyfriend? Does that sound a little stalkerish to you?"

Duncan grinned. "When you put it that way, it's probably best that you don't mention it."

"Like I said, I'll call you later." He headed toward the garage.

Duncan hurried after him, pulling his phone out. "No way am I letting you do this alone. You need backup, just in case everything goes to hell again. And with the Sterlings, it usually does."

Colin entered a code on the keypad beside the garage and the door started up. He gestured toward the National Park Jeep. "That ugly monstrosity is in my way."

"You're just jealous that you don't have a green stripe down the side of your truck and a really cool arrowhead shaped emblem on your door."

"Yeah. That's it." Colin rolled his eyes.

"I'll move it. But don't even think about leaving without me." He raised his phone, then hesitated. "What am I going to tell my boss?"

Colin looked back. "Tell him the truth. You're going hunting."

"Oh, Peyton."

Chapter Fifteen

Peyton patted the front and back pockets of her jeans again, mentally inventorying their contents as she approached the football field.

Quit acting so jumpy and nervous. He could be watching.

She forced herself to drop her hands to her sides and took several slow, deep breaths before sitting on the bottom row of the concrete bleachers. They were harder and less forgiving than she remembered. Then again, at eighteen, she probably wouldn't have noticed things like that. She'd been too busy noticing Colin McKenzie.

She glanced up and down the chain-link fence separating the bleachers from the field and the thick woods circling the area. The fence was in sad disrepair. Rusty top rails had popped out of their brackets in several places. In others, the rails were bent into deep Vs in the middle, as if the entire football team had used them as springboards to hop over the fence. Maybe they had. But as far as she could tell, the section directly in front of her was intact, which was why she'd chosen this particular spot to sit.

Come on, Brian. You have to be here. Because I don't know where else to look.

Since deciding at the last minute to go searching for him, she'd spent the entire day driving around town checking restaurants, stores, movie theaters. She'd even wasted an hour in Ripley's Aquarium, convinced he'd be there, somewhere. After all, that was where she and Brian would often go to de-stress when the fighting at home was too intense. But she hadn't even caught a glimpse of that familiar spikey blond hair or those silver-gray eyes so like her own. And her father's.

Oh, Daddy.

She breathed through the pain, ruthlessly locking away her emotions. She had to keep it together. Her family of four was down by half. If something happened to Brian, her family would no longer exist. She couldn't bear that, which was why she'd ended up here.

When she hadn't found her brother at any of his favorite spots, it had dawned on her that it was probably because he'd seen the police checking those same places. If he was on the run, and needed to disappear, then he'd try to hide where no one would ever expect him to go, somewhere he hated. And she couldn't think of any place he hated more than where he'd been picked on and bullied for four years—Gatlinburg–Pittman High School.

For her, this had been a happy place, a magical place. Because this was where she and Colin had fallen in love. They'd first met in the second grade, when she'd been taller than him and had ruthlessly chased him around the playground. After that, they'd been inseparable, a tomboy and her best friend who just happened to be a boy. They'd explored the woods, climbed tall trees that swayed in the wind and gotten a week's worth of extra chores as punishment when their parents found out.

They caught lightning bugs and he'd put a frog down her shirt. She'd retaliated by dumping ice water down his pants. She became a regular fixture in their household, spending more time with the McKenzies than she did at home, while Brian had remained on the fringes.

Her brother had never felt comfortable around the McKenzie family. He was quiet and reserved where they were loud and boisterous. He didn't like the outdoors, preferring to veg out playing video games all day. But he didn't mind that she hung out with Colin, as long as she spent time with him too. So they played video games together, even though she didn't like them. They'd ride their bikes down the mountain to the closest neighbor's house and bum a ride into town. And when he was struggling in middle school and had to repeat seventh grade, she'd started tutoring him, filling in the gap left by a mother who loved her son but didn't always know how to show it. She'd rather bake him cookies or try out her newest scented candles around the house than teach him to multiply fractions.

Then, everything changed. The summer before their freshman year in high school, fifteen-year-old Colin McKenzie transformed. Gone was the thin, lanky boy who sometimes tripped over his too-big feet. In his place was a confident young man who was growing into his frame. Muscles rippled in his arms and powerful thighs. Dark stubble lined his strong jaw where other guys his age still sported peach fuzz. His lean waist, narrow hips and broad shoulders had all the girls swooning on the first day of school, and that female attention never waned.

Not that he noticed.

Colin was only interested in one girl at school: Peyton. His newly deep, rich voice would send shivers up and down her spine, making her blush and making him grin. They'd shared many kisses behind these very bleachers, although their very first, magical kiss had been next to a waterfall on some beautiful land on the other side of the mountain from Colin's current home. Caught up in a bubble of happiness, she'd thought she'd died and gone to heaven.

Meanwhile, her brother had been floundering. And she hadn't even noticed.

She'd wanted to spend every free minute with her boy

friend turned boyfriend. But Colin felt guilty taking her away from her brother so much. Especially since he was well aware of how rocky things were at the Sterling home. He insisted on including Brian in some of their outings, taking him with them to the occasional movie or dinner, even target practice. Brian might think of Colin as the devil now. But if it hadn't been for Colin's kindness in high school, Brian would have been even more lonely and miserable.

In his four years of high school, Brian had only made two friends. It would have been better if he hadn't. He'd managed to find the only kids in school more awkward and shy than himself. They looked up to him as their leader, which gave him confidence, but not in a good way. He'd acted out more than ever, leading the trio down a destructive path. Their petty thefts, graffiti and vandalism caused thousands of dollars in damage. And if Chief Landry was right, Brian had done far worse than that.

Did you really start fires as a kid, Brian? Are you the one who set the fire at the school dance, almost killing two people, hurting Colin, then blaming him for the choices you made?

If he had, she couldn't help but feel partly responsible.

"I'm so sorry, Brian," she whispered brokenly.

"For what?"

She jerked her head up.

Familiar gray eyes smiled back at her.

"Brian?"

She jumped up and threw herself against him. "I've been so scared. I'm so sorry. This is all my fault." She held on tight, moving her hands up and down his spine, hesitating when she felt the unmistakable outline of a gun shoved into the back pocket of his jeans. She squeezed her eyes shut against the tears that wanted to flow once again.

When he tried to step away, she hugged him fiercely, bumping hard against him and nearly knocking him over.

"Whoa, sis. Give a fella some air will ya?"

She let him go and straightened her blouse as she offered him a tight smile. "I've missed you so much. I'm so sorry."

He cocked his head. "What do you keep apologizing for?"

She gestured toward the bleachers, the field behind him, the school a hundred yards away. "This. All of it. It's where the worst of your problems started. I wasn't there for you. I was too wrapped up in—"

"Colin?" He gave her a lopsided grin. "Three's a crowd, sis. Colin was one handsome dude. But he wasn't my type."

She blinked, then laughed, then hated herself for laughing because it seemed so insensitive, so wrong with everything that had happened.

He caught her hand and pulled her to the bleachers where they both sat down. "School was never my thing. And there wasn't anything you could have done to stop my downward spiral. Your superpowers didn't extend that far. But you could bake an amazing chocolate chip cookie."

She tried to smile. But her heart wasn't in it. "I wish I could do it all over again. Like at the last school dance. The barn."

"Don't." His jaw tightened and he braced his forearms on his thighs, hands clasped together. "I don't want to talk about that."

"But we went there together. It was supposed to be a party and I promised I'd get some of my friends to dance with you. Colin was on a trip out of town with his family. I didn't expect him to get home early and come looking for me. But when he did, I should have told him no, that I was there with you."

"Trust me, sis. It wouldn't have changed a thing if you had."

She frowned. "But if we'd stayed together, or if I'd encouraged you to stay with Mom when she was chaperoning—"

He snorted. "Yeah. Mom the chaperone, keeping everyone safe. Wasn't that a joke."

"What do you mean?"

He gave her a sideways glance, shrugged. "She was a space cadet. Not tuned in to things going on around her. She'd rather roast those stupid s'mores in the fireplace than spend quality time with her kids." He shook his head. "How many s'mores can one person eat? And who uses their fireplace in the summer? Didn't you think she was weird?"

"I prefer to think of her as eccentric. But she's gone now. I don't see the point in disparaging her."

"To each his own."

"I thought you adored Mom. You were her favorite."

He scrubbed his hands against his jeans. Funny that she'd never noticed before that he had the same habit she did.

"Mom liked me because we liked the same things. She saw herself in me and didn't feel as weird, you know?"

She didn't know, but she nodded anyway.

"Now Dad, he and I had *nothing* in common. He couldn't stand me. But you were *his* favorite. I guess it evened out."

He sounded so cold speaking about their father. But she believed it was mostly bluster, a defense mechanism by a boy who'd always loved his dad, even if his dad seemed incapable of returning that love. The police had been able to keep the shooting out of the news so far, but that wouldn't last forever. She should tell him, now, but she wasn't ready.

She looked toward the trees on the far side of the field, back over her shoulder. "What happened to the guys you escaped with? Should I be worried that they're watching me from the woods?"

"I'm not going to let anything happen to you, sis. You were always there for me growing up. I owe you my protection, even if you are consorting with the enemy." He motioned toward the parking lot. "Where's your boyfriend hiding?"

Her stomach jumped. "Boyfriend? Hiding?"

"Tell the truth. Are you bait? He's hiding somewhere hoping to catch me?"

Her pulse leaped in her throat; his teasing tone had an underlying bitterness that sent a chill down her spine. "I'm all alone, Brian. He doesn't know I'm here."

His brows raised. "Snuck out, did you? Huh. Could it be you miss dear old bro after all? You just wanted to see me?"

Standing, she crossed her arms and moved to the fence, hoping he'd follow. "I did miss you, do miss you. I'm worried about you."

He pushed to his feet and joined her. "You always did worry about me." His smile seemed genuine, like the old Brian she'd once known. "But that's not your job anymore. It's time for me to take care of me, wrap up a few loose ends."

"L-loose ends?"

"Colin McKenzie, for one."

The bottom dropped out of her stomach. "But… I don't want you to do anything to Colin."

"Yeah, I know." He clucked his tongue. "But a guy's got to do what a guy's got to do. I'll protect you. You have my word on that. But I'm afraid you're going to have to live with at least one more tragic loss in your near future." He leaned against the top rail. It squeaked in protest.

His callous confession that he planned to hurt Colin had her wanting to throw up. And more committed than ever to her plan. She had to stop him, stop whatever he was planning. But she also wanted more information. She had so many questions, so many things she didn't understand. "Why do you hate him so much?"

His grin faded. "He testified against me. Fifteen years, Peyton. He and his fellow Mighty McKenzies put pressure on the judge and got me fifteen years."

"There were other kids roaming the property that night,

instead of staying inside the dance hall like we were supposed to. Colin wasn't the only one who testified that they saw you outside the barn, running away right before the fire. How do you explain that?"

"Explain it?" He leaned toward her, his mood changing lightning fast, anger blazing in his quicksilver eyes. "Fine. Truth. I *was* in that barn that night."

"Oh, Brian."

"But I didn't start the fire! Sure, I saw that stupid gas can. Some idiot had knocked it over, spilling gas all over a hay bale. I was worried someone would do something stupid, like sneak out of the dance and into the barn to smoke a couple of cigarettes without realizing the fumes could light the place up like a roman candle." He jabbed his thumb toward his chest. "I was being the responsible one. I was trying to *prevent* a fire. I ran the can outside, fully intending to warn people away from the place. When I came back, it was already going up in flames." He shook his head, his lips curling in a sneer. "And your *precious Colin* gets all the credit for being the good guy, for saving those stupid fools who never should have gone in there in the first place. There. Is that enough truth for you?"

"But Brian, if that's what happened, it changes everything. It explains why people said they saw you with a gas can. Did you tell your lawyer?"

He laughed, but didn't sound amused. "Dear old Mom and Dad told me not to."

She pressed her hand to her throat. "What are you saying? That doesn't make sense."

"Yeah, well, in hindsight, not being a green nineteen-year-old kid anymore, I agree with you. But they insisted that no one would believe me, that I'd be admitting I was at the scene of the crime. They said my best shot at an acquittal was for my lawyer to discredit the witnesses. There wasn't any forensic evidence that proved I started a fire.

Showing reasonable doubt would be a slam dunk." He wrapped his fingers around the pole, his knuckles turning white. "Not such a slam dunk after all, was it? And here we are, folks. Once again Brian goes down in flames for something he didn't do. I didn't plan the stupid jailbreak. And I didn't shoot that cop. But I'll still get the death penalty. Felony murder. Guilt by association. Which is why I need to get out of here before someone else figures out where I am."

"No, wait."

He frowned. "What?"

She had to keep him distracted, put her plan into motion. It was time to tell him about their father. "A couple of nights ago, there was a shooting, at Colin's house—"

He looked away. "Yeah. Heard about that."

"Then you know? About dad? He was…he was killed in the woods that night. Colin… Colin shot him while returning gunfire."

"Dear old dad tried to get payback for what your boyfriend did to me. Huh. Guess the old man did something good for his son for once in his life."

"Oh, Brian. How can you be so callous about our own father?"

He leaned against the fence, the top bar wobbling beneath his weight. "You're so naive, even now, aren't you? Daddy cared about Daddy—and the Sterling name. That's all he cared about. Why do you think he bought my way out of trouble all the time? It sure wasn't because he cared about me. He cared about how it would look. That's why I called him, told him to meet me."

"You called him? And he met with you at Colin's place? You were there?" Her voice broke on the last word.

Something flashed in his eyes. Confusion? Pain? Regret? Then he let out a deep breath. "I told him if he brought me enough money, I'd disappear. For good. He'd never have to worry about me dragging his precious name through the gutter again. But when he showed up, he didn't bring money. He brought a stupid lecture. The son of a gun must have finally developed a conscience after all."

She was starting to go numb inside, no longer processing the revelations he was making. Instead, she kept her focus on her plan. She slid her hand into her back pocket, then clasped both hands together and put them on top of the railing next to his. When he didn't look down, she moved her left hand oh so carefully, then put her right hand just slightly on top of his and leaned forward to cover what she was doing, looking down at the ground as if she'd seen something.

He frowned and leaned over the rail. "What are you looking at?"

One more slight adjustment. *Click. Click.*

She jumped back, stumbling and catching herself against the fence a few yards away. The whole thing wobbled, seeming much more unstable than she'd realized.

He frowned in confusion, then started toward her. He jerked up short, catching himself against the fence. "What the—" He looked down, confusion turning to fury when he saw the handcuff circling his wrist, the other end circling the top pole.

"I'm so sorry," she told him. "But I can't let you go. You have to stay and face what you've done."

He rattled the cuffs, his face turning red. "You conniving little…" He yanked his arm, straining against the railing. "Take them off. Now."

She backed up several more feet, his anger like a palpable force, thickening the air between them. "I took them from Colin's house. I don't have a key." She pulled her phone out of her front pocket.

His eyes narrowed. "Don't."

"I have to." She punched her favorites folder.

He cursed at her, saying things that pierced her heart like shards of glass.

Whirling to face the top rail, he grabbed it with both hands and pulled, his biceps bulging beneath the strain. The bar made a metallic screeching sound, then popped. The chain link fencing sagged away, leaving the top rail leaning toward the left, but still attached to both poles. Barely.

Peyton stared in horror as he slid the cuff along the rail toward the pole on the left. Using his free hand, he yanked and tugged on the bar some more. The bracket holding the pole creaked.

"Brian, stop. Please. I'm trying to help you." Her hands shook so hard she was having trouble pressing the preprogrammed number on her phone.

"Turns out you're as fake as everyone else," he sneered. "All you care about is dear old Colin." He spat the name at her like acid.

He moved back as far as his arm would allow, then slammed his shoe against the rail. It bent, but held. He moved back again, raised his foot.

Peyton desperately pushed the number and hit Send.

Brian slammed his shoe against the railing a second time. A piece of metal flew off the bracket, landing on the concrete with a metallic clang. The railing fell, jerking Brian to the ground as the handcuff caught on what was left of the broken bracket.

"US Marshal. Put your hands in the air, both of you!"

Peyton froze at the sound of Colin's voice behind her and slowly did as he'd said, her phone still clutched in her right hand.

Brian tugged and pulled at the cuffs.

"Don't move, Brian!" Colin yelled.

Brian jerked the cuffs loose from the broken bracket, but remained crouched on the ground with Peyton between him and Colin. He glanced up at her, one handcuff still attached to his wrist, the other dangling from the small chain. She'd never seen such a look of pure hate before.

He grabbed for his back pocket, then whirled around, looking at the ground, then up and down the perimeter of fence.

A bone deep cold crept through Peyton's body as she watched her brother searching for his gun so he could kill Colin, or her. Or both.

"Peyton," Colin yelled, his shoes thumping against the ground as he ran toward her. "Get down."

Brian cursed viciously and took off running.

Peyton tried to duck. She tried to obey his shouted command. But she couldn't move. Was this what it felt like to die? To have every organ in her body shut down at the same time? To have her heart shatter in her chest?

"Peyton!" Colin yelled again.

Brian disappeared behind the bleachers.

Colin stopped beside her, his gun pointed up toward the sky.

Duncan sprinted past them. She hadn't even realized he was there. Pistol in hand, he stopped at the end of the bleachers, peered around the concrete supports then disappeared.

Colin stared at her, his brows drawn down as he holstered his gun. "Why didn't you move out of the way? He could have shot you and there wasn't a thing I could do about it."

She shook her head. "He couldn't shoot me."

His jaw tightened. "After all he's done, how can you think he wouldn't—"

"I didn't say he *wouldn't*. I said he *couldn't*." She lifted the back of her shirt and pulled the pistol out of the waistband of her jeans and carefully handed it to him.

"He had that in his back pocket when he first got here," she explained, as Colin checked the loading before shoving the pistol in his own back pocket. "I took it when I hugged him. He didn't realize it until after I'd handcuffed him to the fence and he broke free. Actually, I'm still not sure he realized I took it. Maybe he thought he dropped it."

His face went pale. "You took a loaded gun from your brother? And handcuffed him to the fence?" He glanced behind her. "The fence that's falling down?"

"Yeah, well. I thought this section was solid enough to hold him. I was wrong." She shrugged and tried to smile. Then burst into tears and covered her face.

Colin's hands were shaking when he pulled her against his chest. His sharp intake of breath had her trying to push out of his arms.

"Your bruises. I don't want to hurt—"

"Forget the bruises. Come here, sweetheart."

The endearment, the first time he'd called her that in over ten years, had her throwing herself into his arms and soaking his shirt with her tears.

"Shh, it's okay. Everything's going to be okay." He rubbed her back and rested his cheek on the top of her head.

She clung to him, then gasped and scrambled out of his arms again. "Duncan. He needs backup. What if—"

"We came with backup. As soon as I realized you were going here, surrounded by woods that I couldn't secure, I called Landry and the marshals. Half a dozen of them are out there right now looking for Brian. More are on the way. Don't worry about Duncan. He'll be okay."

She swallowed and wiped her tears. "I don't understand. How could you get help so fast? I only just now called you."

He frowned and pulled his phone out. "So you did. It's on vibrate mode. I was too busy sneaking up behind you and Brian to notice it."

She stiffened. "Sneaking up behind me and Brian? Both of us? You, what? Thought I went over to the dark side and was helping my fugitive brother?"

"You know better than that."

She fisted her hands beside her. "Do I? You said you called the others once you realized where I was going. You were following me, admit it."

He shoved his phone into his pocket. "You told me you were going home to pack. You didn't even stop at your house and continued down the mountain."

She stared at him, trying to make sense of what he was saying. "How would you know that? What did you do, put some kind of tracking device on my car?"

He stared at her but didn't say anything.

"That was sarcasm," she told him. "This is the part where you say, no, of course I didn't put a freaking GPS tracker on your car." When he didn't say anything, her mouth dropped open. "You did! After everything we've been through, after I risked my life for you during the shooting, you still don't trust me."

"It's not about trusting you. It's about not trusting your brother, and understanding that a sister of course is going to try to help him. If you somehow figured out where he was, I wanted to make sure you were safe. I was going to—"

Duncan jogged back from behind the bleachers, breathing hard. He slowed to a stop a few yards away, glancing uncertainly back and forth between them. "What did I miss?"

Peyton narrowed her eyes. "Did you know that Colin had a tracking device on my car?"

He blinked. "I, uh—"

"Wait, you came here together didn't you? Of course you knew he was tracking me. Son of a—"

"Duncan, was there something you were going to tell me?" Colin asked, sounding exasperated.

Duncan gave Peyton an apologetic look before answering. "The marshals took over the chase. He's heading west through the woods. They've called for air support."

"Well," Peyton said. "Sounds like you boys have everything under control. Great. That's just great. Now, if you'll excuse me, I have to return to Memphis to settle my father's affairs."

Colin stepped toward her. "We need to talk."

"You put a *tracker* on my *car*."

"You lied about where you were going."

"You put the tracker on my car *before* I lied to you. And I didn't lie! I changed my mind!"

"Seriously? You changed your mind? That's your explanation?"

"My explanation is that I was trying to protect you. I decided at the last minute to try to find my brother before I left, to see if I could bring a peaceful conclusion to this ever-loving mess. And as you already know, I called you to tell you he was here."

His face reddened. "You were protecting me? You offered yourself up as bait to an arsonist!"

"Arsonist according to you."

"According to a jury. Did you forget that part? And the fifteen-year sentence?"

She crossed her arms.

He swore. "I can't believe you purposely put yourself in danger, again. Did you learn nothing the other night when you were nearly killed?"

She gasped, then whirled around and marched toward her car.

"Peyton, come back here."

She stopped, and looked over her shoulder. "Are you arresting me, Marshal McKenzie?"

His eyes narrowed. "You know damn well I'm not, *Miss Sterling*. But you need to give a formal statement about what happened here. And you and I need to talk."

"You and I have *nothing* to talk about. I'll phone my statement in to Chief Landry."

"Peyton—"

She stalked to her car and slammed the door, twice, just to make herself feel better. Then she gunned the engine and peeled out of the parking lot, mentally daring the uniformed cops who were just turning in to try to give her a ticket.

She'd only made it about five miles down the road before her flood of tears forced her to pull over. Hands shaking, she cut the engine and drew deep, even breaths, desperately trying to get a handle on her grief and pain. The way she'd treated Colin was unconscionable. Even while she was lashing out at him, she'd known it was wrong. That the hateful emotions spilling out of her weren't meant for him.

They were meant for Brian.

And her mom, for doting on her son one moment and ignoring him the next.

Her father, for the selfishness that had him so angry over being ignored by his obsessed-with-baking wife that he'd ignored the little boy who desperately needed his affection.

But mostly, she was to blame. Forever taking for granted the one truly good, honorable, decent person in her life. When had she ever been there for Colin when he'd needed her? And yet, every time life was imploding on her, he'd been there.

Movement in her rearview mirror had her looking up to see a familiar dark blue pickup truck pull onto the shoulder behind her. Colin. He looked in his mirrors before popping open his door and jumping down.

Peyton choked on a sob, then threw her door open and ran to him. But she stumbled to a halt a few feet away when she remembered his bruised chest. "Colin, I'm so sorry. What I said was—"

He stepped forward and pulled her against him, hugging her tight.

She clutched the back of his shirt. "Your bruises. You shouldn't—"

"Stop worrying about me. All right?" He gently rubbed his hand up and down her back as he held her against him.

He seemed content to stand there on the side of the road, holding her without any regard for the occasional car that drove by. She never wanted to let him go. Which was why she forced herself to drop her hands and step back.

She wrapped her arms around her middle and leaned against her SUV. "I can't believe you came to check on me after how horribly I acted back there."

"I wasn't exactly a saint myself at the school." His mouth crooked up in amusement. "And, actually, I came for this." He leaned past her and reached under the bumper, then straightened, holding up a metal disc with a blinking red light. "Tracker," he explained, before shoving it in his pants pocket. "I figured you'd think about it eventually, then realize it was still there and get even more upset."

He looked over the top of her head, toward the woods on either side of the highway, ever the alert marshal, always aware of his surroundings. When he looked down at her again, his eyes had darkened with concern, and something else.

"Peyton, I owe you a huge apology. I never should have—"

She pressed her hand against his mouth and shook her head. "Don't. It's okay. I understand why you did it. I destroyed your trust years ago. Then I compounded it by helping a convicted felon escape my house when you could have taken him into custody, right then and there." She feathered her fingers gently down the front of his shirt, careful not to press against his ribs. "You wouldn't have gotten shot. My daddy…my father would still be alive. And you wouldn't have put your life on the line yet again to save me from my own brother at the high school."

He cupped her face, forcing her to meet his gaze. "Let's stop with the self-recriminations and just agree that these are extraordinary circumstances and we're both imperfect. We've both made mistakes. We both have regrets." He searched her gaze. "What I need to know is that you're going to be okay. Are you sure you want to do this? Drive back to Memphis right now, alone? I could—"

She turned her head and kissed his palm before gently tugging his hands down. "I'm okay. Or, I will be. Really. Just seeing you again has made all the difference." She smiled up at him. "I need to do this, settle things, say goodbye to my father. Hopefully all of this—" she motioned in the air "—will be over soon, one way or the other. And then, maybe we can talk, like we should have years ago, and see where things end up."

He frowned. "Peyton—"

"You need to be extra careful. Brian's planning something. He blames you for everything, wants revenge."

"No surprise there."

"I mean it, Colin. Please, watch your back."

"I will. Promise." He smiled reassuringly.

She shoved her hair out of her face. "There are other things I need to tell you, for the investigation, things Brian said. A lot of it doesn't make sense. It's all so confusing. But I can't... I can't talk about it just yet. I'll call you, answer your questions over the phone. Maybe in a few hours, on the long drive to Memphis. Is that okay?"

"Of course. But you don't have to leave. You can stay—"

"Don't. I'm barely keeping myself together. There is so much grief and pain for me back here. So much." A sob escaped, but she breathed through it, held her grief in check. "In spite of what you may think, given our history, walking away from you isn't easy to do. And I don't..." She shook her head. "I need some time. I need to think." She stood on her tiptoes and kissed his cheek. "Take care of yourself, Colin McKenzie."

COLIN BRACED HIS hands behind him on the hood of his truck, using every ounce of his willpower to keep from chasing after Peyton as she drove away for the second time that day. He ached to take her in his arms, beg her not to leave. But it wouldn't be fair to her. She wanted time to think, whatever that meant. And he had to give it to her. But that didn't make it easy. As the sun began to set, he wondered if it was also setting on the last remaining hopes that the two of them could ever escape the echoes of their past.

His phone buzzed in his pocket. When he saw who was calling, he climbed in his truck and shut the door. "Hey Duncan. Tell me you found him. I'm ready for this to be over."

"Did you find *her*?"

He'd just started the engine, but hesitated at the urgency in his brother's voice. "I did. We talked. She's on her way to Memphis now. Why?"

"She was alone? No one could have been hiding in her car?"

He fisted his hand on the steering wheel, disappointment slamming through him at his brother's question. "You're telling me Brian got away? Don't worry about Peyton. I was standing by her back window while we were talking. No one could have hidden inside. I can't believe he escaped again. That guy is slipperier than a water moccasin and twice as deadly."

"You need to get back here, to the high school."

Duncan's voice was hoarse. Colin couldn't remember the last time he'd sounded so shaken.

"What's going on?"

"The police are pretty sure they found the other three escapees, a mile east of the school in a heavily wooded area."

"*Pretty* sure? What does that mean?" Colin checked his

mirrors, then turned around in the middle of the highway and headed toward the school.

"They were tied to the base of an oak tree. Someone had poured some kind of accelerant on them and lit them on fire. They're unrecognizable. The only reason the cops think it's them is because someone carved initials into the tree facing them—DP, VS, TK—Damon Patterson, Vincent Snyder, Tyler King." He let out a shuddering breath. "Colin, the police found them because they heard their screams."

"For the love of…" Colin let out a shaky breath of his own, his stomach roiling at the images his brother's words conjured in his mind. He flexed his hand on the steering wheel, the spiderweb of burn scars standing out in stark relief against his tan. "Brian's escalated from setting buildings on fire without worrying whether someone might be inside to deliberately setting *people* on fire. Honestly, I never imagined he was capable of something that heinous. Kind of makes me glad Peyton left. I don't even want her in the same state as her psychotic sibling."

"Psychotic sounds about right, someone out of touch with the normal world, for sure. But it gets worse. Remember I told you that after I chased Brian into the woods behind the bleachers, the marshals we'd called were already out there and took over the pursuit?"

"Yeah, go on."

"They couldn't fire any shots at him because some residences were close by. They lost him when he jumped into a vehicle he'd left strategically parked for a quick getaway—a stolen car, obviously. That car was a mile west of the school, *two miles* from where they found the bodies."

Colin tightened his grip on the steering wheel. "You said they were still screaming when they were found?"

"Yes. Any idea how long it would take someone's lungs

to incinerate and for them to lose the ability to scream in a situation like that?"

"I'm guessing not long. Is the medical examiner on the way?"

"ETA five minutes."

"I'll be there in two."

Chapter Sixteen

Peyton clutched the cell phone in her hand as she stared at the papers and photo albums covering the top of her father's dining room table. She had to make the call. She *would* make the call. But not yet. She needed a few more minutes alone with the horror that her life had become before she shared this latest batch of awful family secrets. Especially since the person she was going to share them with was the one person whose opinion of her and her family mattered—Colin.

Her hand shook as she straightened one of the stacks of medical bills before lowering herself to perch on an olive-green cushioned chair. In the week since her father's memorial service, she'd sorted through all of his belongings, setting aside items to donate to charity and others to be thrown out. And this, a handful of photo albums and several stacks of bills and paperwork, had painted a picture she'd never imagined she would see, even in her worst nightmares.

When she'd helped her father sort through her mother's things months earlier, he'd insisted on being the one to go up in the attic to bring down the boxes. Now she knew why. He hadn't wanted her to see these *particular* boxes. Because they contained bills and letters and photographs that laid bare a family history that would shred what little was left of the one thing that her father treasured above all else—the Sterling reputation.

Her hand started to ache and she realized she was gripping the phone too tightly. She set the phone down on the edge of the table, then slowly flipped through an old photo album that documented her mother's life from the time she was a child through the first years of her marriage to Peyton's father. The cardboard backing was brittle, the time-yellowed protective plastic covers crinkling each time she turned a page.

The baby pictures had been shocking enough, because Peyton and Brian had been told that there weren't any baby pictures of their mother, that she'd been an orphan, raised in foster care, and didn't have any knowledge of her birth family. Judging by the smiling faces of the many relatives surrounding baby Molly, that had been a lie.

Later pictures showed her mother with the same people, who were taking the happy toddler to a fair to ride ponies, pushing her on a swing at the park. She grew up on the pages in front of Peyton, learning to ride a bike, starting elementary school, holding up her fifth-grade report card while holding her nose, as if laughing at the bad grades she'd made. The transition from happy smiling baby to morose teenager in the second half of the album was startling to see. It reminded her so much of Brian that her heart ached.

The next-to-last page showed a two-story brick house with acres of rolling green hills behind it. No mountains, so it wasn't near Gatlinburg. Dozens of smiling, well-dressed people Peyton recognized from throughout the album— her mother's family—posed in front of the house. And in the middle, holding hands and smiling at the camera, was a blond woman with blue eyes in a bridal gown beside a thin man with silver-gray eyes in a business suit. Her mother and father, looking impossibly young and happier than she'd ever seen them. Obviously her mother hadn't aged out of the foster system with no relatives. Her entire history had been one big lie. And all Peyton had to do was turn the final page to discover why her parents had lied, why they didn't want anyone to know about her mother's real past.

Faded newsprint preserved behind plastic showed the article's title in big, bold letters.

Sorority House Fire Kills Three.

Below the headline was a group of six young sorority sisters from the house, clinging to each other in their nightgowns, tears running down their soot-streaked faces. Except one. Molly Andrews. She wasn't crying. She was smiling for the camera as the flames eerily reflected in her eyes and firemen struggled to bring the fire under control.

The story below the photograph was only two short paragraphs. Not much to tell in the early stages of the investigation. It simply said that the women pictured were the lucky survivors of the early morning house fire and that it was believed to have started in the kitchen. Molly Andrews of Chattanooga, Tennessee, mentioned that Sarah Engler—one of the girls who'd perished—had a habit of leaving the gas stove turned on. Molly openly wondered whether a dish towel may have been too close to the stove and caught on fire. Molly Andrews was a slightly younger version of the woman in the wedding picture in this same album. But there was no question that she was Peyton's mom, even though her mother's maiden name was supposed to be Tate and she was from Nashville, not Chattanooga.

Or so Brian and Peyton had been told. Yet another lie in a growing list of them.

She set the album aside and slid one of the stacks of bills toward herself. This was a stack that her father had also kept hidden in a box in the attic, and added even more details to her mother's story that she'd never known. The therapist her mother had been seeing for years wasn't a marriage counselor after all. He was a doctor who specialized in the treatment of addictive disorders, rage issues and impulse control problems. Exactly the kind of doctor who'd treated Brian when he'd gotten in trouble with the law and was forced to go to therapy.

But those weren't the only doctors her mother had been seeing.

A month before the car accident, she'd been diagnosed with stage four metastatic cancer, with tumors in her liver and her brain. Based on the doctor's notes in one of the folders that Peyton had found, her parents had decided not to take extraordinary measures. No chemotherapy. No radiation. Just pills to help control her mother's pain.

Oh, Mom. Why didn't you or Dad tell me? I would have been there for both of you. That's what families do.

Except, apparently, hers.

Once again, her parents had chosen to keep secrets from their children. But even that wasn't the final bombshell that had exploded in Peyton's life these past few days. There was one more box in the attic. A box of old-fashioned handwritten letters, possibly because the sender had given up on getting any replies to their electronic messages. All of the letters were neatly folded in their original envelopes. And all of them had been sent during that first year after Brian's arrest for the barn fire.

Half of them had been mailed to the Sterling home in Gatlinburg and the post office had forwarded them. The sender must have figured out their new address in Memphis after that, because the rest of them had been mailed directly here. But her father, claiming he wanted to protect the family from ugly, harassing letters people often sent about Brian as his trial loomed, had all of the family's mail forwarded to a post office box. Peyton had never seen any of these letters before.

Letters sent to *her*. By Colin McKenzie.

She picked up the phone again. It was time to face the past, to shine the light of truth on her family's secrets. She couldn't put the shame off any longer. Because somewhere out there were three families who'd lost their beloved daughters or sisters in a sorority house fire that Peyton's internet search had discovered was ruled accidental. Peyton didn't believe that for a second. And those families deserved to know the truth.

Colin answered on the first ring. "Peyton? Is everything okay?"

She smiled. His first words were concern about her. Why couldn't everyone be that decent, that wonderful? The world would be such a better place.

"Hi, Colin. No, unfortunately, everything is not okay. I need to see you. We need to talk. In person."

"Where are you? I'll get there as fast as I can."

"Still in Memphis, my dad's house. I'll come to you. The drive will help clear my mind. But obviously it's going to be late when I get there. Is that okay? Have you gone back to work yet? I don't want you showing up at the office unable to keep your eyes open because of me. I could stay at my house—"

"No. Don't. I asked Chief Landry to post someone on your property to keep an eye on things while you were gone. It would be better if you come here."

So he could keep her safe, no doubt. From her own brother. A tear slid down her cheek. She hadn't realized that she had any tears left. "Okay. Thanks. I'll go directly to your place."

"The curiosity and worry is going to eat me alive during your six-hour drive. Can you at least give me a hint what this is about? Maybe just the headlines?"

The picture of the sorority fire newspaper clipping flashed in her mind. "Headlines," she whispered brokenly. "Funny you would say that."

"Peyton?"

"Okay. The headlines. I know I've been a broken record over the years, claiming my brother didn't start the barn fire. Over the past few weeks, I'd pretty much decided I was wrong, that you and everyone else are right, in spite of what he said at the school, that I told you about over the phone on my drive here. But part of what he told me might be true. I've got a new theory about who started that fire. I believe this person probably started a lot of fires over the years, one in particular with deadly consequences."

He hesitated. "Do you have a name?"

"Molly Andrews of Chattanooga, also known as Molly Tate, aka Molly Sterling. My mother."

Chapter Seventeen

Colin set the photo album on top of the piles of papers that Peyton had spread out on his coffee table. She sat across from him on the other couch, her hands clasped together so hard that her knuckles had gone white. He waved to the newspaper clipping with its headline about the sorority house fire.

"I understand why that newspaper article would alarm you, especially considering everything that you've discovered and Brian's conviction. But while it raises suspicions, none of it is evidence of arson."

She motioned toward the album. "I didn't think cops—or marshals—believed in coincidences. That sorority fire is an awfully big one."

"Because your mom survived a fire as a young woman and her son was later convicted of arson?"

She nodded.

"Honestly, it doesn't raise any eyebrows for me, given that your mom doesn't have a criminal record. After our earlier phone call, I checked. Under all three names. The fire at her college is the only mention of her that I could find in any law-enforcement databases."

"Okay, well, how about the therapist she was seeing? Her and Dad lied about it, pretended it was marriage counseling." She spread out some of the papers, then extracted the stack of bills from the doctor and held them up. "I looked this guy up online. He's testified as an expert in two arson cases." She tossed the bills back onto the coffee table. "And there are other things—my mom's fascination with candles. She was always buying new scents. We always had lit candles in our house. And the fireplace. Even in the summer she'd have a fire going. Looking back, that seems like an unhealthy fascination with fire to me. And don't you dare start talking about how much you loved the s'mores she used to cook in the fireplace. You have to admit it's odd."

"Okay. I won't mention that I absolutely loved coming over to your house for s'mores in the summer."

She frowned.

"Or that my mom loves candles, too."

"Colin—"

"And that the vanilla-scented candles your mom was so fond of have a special place in my childhood memories. Your house always smelled great."

She spread her hands out. "Why are you fighting me on this?"

"I'm not fighting you. I'm saying that if you look at each thing by itself, it loses the sinister significance that you're attaching to it. If you want me to investigate your mom, I absolutely will. But are you sure you want that? As soon as anyone hears even a whiff of this, rumors will start running rampant. You won't be able to put that cat back in the bag. Your mother's reputation will be forever tarnished."

Rubbing her hands against her jeans, she seemed to consider everything, then nodded. "Yes. I want you to start an investigation on her. I understand the risks. But it's the right thing to do."

"Because you believe it could prove that Brian didn't start the barn fire?"

"No. I mean, it might. But that's not why I want you to look into this. It no longer matters whether he was innocent back then. He's changed. Maybe prison changed him or he fooled me all along and I'm only now seeing it. I'm telling you, Colin. He scared me at the high school. And his hate for you knows no bounds. He tried to kill you once already, and he'll try again if he's not caught. As far as I'm concerned, he needs to go back to prison for a very long time to keep everyone else safe. So, no, none of this is for him. It's for the families of those sorority girls. If that sorority fire wasn't an accident, if my mom was to blame, they deserve to know."

He shook his head in wonder. "I hope you can let go of all the guilt you carry around someday. Because you have a really good heart. You're a good person, Peyton. The very best."

She blinked several times, then pressed her fingers against her eyes. "You'd better stop. You're going to get me crying again. And I am so sick of crying." She dropped her hands and offered him a watery smile. "So you'll do it? You'll investigate?"

"I will. I'll talk to my boss, see if he'll make it official. That will make it easier to get the information I'll need, lend the investigation more authority with witnesses. Arson that causes deaths comes under federal purview. I should be able to take it on."

"Thank you. I really appreciate it."

"You bet. But there's one more thing I want to put out there, just in case it changes your mind. Statistics."

"Statistics?"

"On arson. Most arson is done for profit. With the barn fire, there was no insurance. There weren't any highway projects or real estate developments coming through that wanted the property and were trying to intimidate an owner who refused to sell. No matter who set the fire, profit wasn't the motive."

"Agreed. That makes sense."

"Another primary motive is to hide another crime, like

to cover up a murder. Fire destroys evidence. In this case, no one was killed—"

"Thanks to you."

He shrugged. "The kids I pulled out of there were just that, high school kids like you and me. They snuck in for a make-out session. They didn't have any enemies that the investigation could find. So, again, covering up a crime doesn't seem like the reason behind the fire either. Not from any evidence that I've seen. That pretty much leaves us the psychological reasons, which is what was presented at Brian's trial. The prosecution argued that he was a fire-bug, that starting fires for him was a compulsion, an impulse control problem."

"Impulse control is one of the specialties of the doctor who treated my mom."

"That's also a specialty of the doctor who treated Brian when your dad made a deal to keep him from being charged as a juvenile."

"The fires Chief Landry mentioned?"

He nodded.

She sat back, rubbing her arms as if to ward off a chill. "I knew he'd gotten in trouble, of course. But I never knew about those fires, and just how much trouble, until the chief mentioned it. I thought all this time that Brian was getting help for his anger issues, learning to channel his energy in more constructive ways. I had no idea it was this bad. Chalk that up to one more lie my parents told me."

"I imagine they were trying to protect you. You were young, with your whole life ahead of you. Maybe they wanted you to be happy and not be dragged down by all the worry they were going through."

"Maybe. It's dragging me down now, that's for sure."

"Then I'll get right to the point. Thrill-seekers, pyromaniacs, are extremely rare in the world of arson. Which makes having two in one family more unlikely than likely.

But it's the last statistic that's the most telling. Over ninety percent of arsonists are white males. The episodes are often driven by anger. And intelligence is generally lower than your average person. Not always, but the majority of the time. It seems to have to do with their ability to reason and think through the effects of their crimes. The lower intelligence contributes to their lack of impulse control. Be honest. Does that sound like your mother or your brother?"

She was quiet for a moment, then nodded. "Mom was more on an even keel, really calm—unless she was fighting with Dad. Then again, he was the one doing most of the yelling. Yeah, it sounds like Brian."

He rested his forearms on his thighs and clasped his hands together. "It's getting pretty late. I know you must be tired. Do you want to stop?"

She stifled a yawn, then smiled. "That was your fault, for reminding me how tired I am. But, no. If there's more that you can tell me, I want to hear it. If you can prove to me that my mom's innocent, I'll sleep a lot better tonight."

"I don't know that I can definitely prove she's innocent. But we can talk about the fire. We never have before. You sure you want me to go on?"

"I'm sure. But—" she motioned toward his hands "—I don't know that it's fair to ask you to do that after everything you suffered because of that night."

"It was a long time ago. I'm more than willing to discuss what happened in light of your questions about your mom. The night of the barn fire, she was a chaperone right? In the dance hall?"

"Yes. I think there were seven or eight chaperones. The dance hall was huge. Half the senior class was there. No one was supposed to leave the building, but of course a lot of people snuck out here and there. The setting was gorgeous, lots of paths through the woods, waterfalls and party lights throughout, strung on pergolas and buildings. A great place for couples."

He smiled at the memory. "It was beautiful. So were you. I seem to remember arriving late, getting a couple of dances, then sneaking you outside to steal some kisses by a waterfall."

She shook her head, but a smile played about her lips. "You were always stealing kisses by waterfalls. One of our favorite waterfalls was on the other side of the mountain from this place. I can't remember a more beautiful view in all of the Smokies."

Her smile turned sad and he understood why. They'd made a lot of promises when they were young. One of them was to buy that land one day, build their dream house and make babies beside that waterfall.

None of those promises had been kept.

"But you weren't supposed to be at the dance at all," she said.

"Our family trip out of town. Dad cut it short because of something that came up on one of his cases. As soon as we got home, I went to the dance looking for you."

"Right," she said, staring off as if picturing it in her head. "After the waterfall, we were heading back when one of my friends ran up to us, all excited about some guy asking her out. She wanted to tell me about it, so I promised I'd meet you back in the dance hall in a few minutes." She cleared her throat. "But that didn't happen. The next time I saw you, you were on a stretcher being taken into an ambulance. And my mother was yelling at me to come with her, that we had to go with Brian. The police were arresting him and she wanted us to follow him to the police station." Her haunted eyes met his. "I should have told her no. I'm so sorry, Colin. I made so many mistakes."

There was a lot they needed to discuss, one day, to clear the air between them. Their past, everything that had happened after the fire, was the elephant in the room that they'd never talked about. But late at night when they were both tired wasn't the time for that conversation.

"Let's get back to your mom. We were trying to see if she had an opportunity to start the fire."

She twisted her hands together. "Right. I'm guessing most of us could have gone to the barn during the dance if we'd wanted to. How do I prove whether my mom did or didn't go down there?"

He drummed his knuckles on his thigh, considering. "There's only one way I can think of that might prove where your mother was at the time of the fire. But you're not going to like it."

"Try me."

"Tell you what. I'm not even sure it's an option. Let me look into it first and see if I can work it out."

"Ah. One of those supersecret US Marshal types of things." She hid another yawn behind her hand. "If I weren't so tired, I'd argue with you to tell me right now. But honestly, even my curiosity isn't strong enough to keep me awake much longer." She stood and adjusted her shirt, which had ridden up around her hips. "Aren't you going to bed too?"

"You go ahead. I'll get the lights, have a quick look around to make sure things are secure."

She glanced at the windows behind him. "Oh. Okay. Well, good night, then." She started toward him, then stopped, looking uncertain. "Can I hug you? Your bruises—"

"Are pretty much gone. I'd hug you anyway." He stood and pulled her into his arms. It felt so good to hold her, especially since she'd been gone for over a week and he'd really never expected her to come back. He finally let her go only because he didn't trust himself to hold her any longer without kissing her. And kissing her would leave him aching for so much more.

Even if there had been no baggage between them, he didn't know if they'd ever be able to move past something far more tangible—his scars. The young man she'd made love with all those years ago wasn't the man standing before her today. And *that* was something they might never be able to overcome.

After she disappeared up the stairs, he pulled out his phone and sat down to call his father. Although Duncan had already broken the news to their parents that Peyton had come back—and had stirred up Colin's life again—Colin had put off making the same call. He knew there'd be no way to avoid telling them about getting shot once they started asking questions. Then he'd have to spend a good amount of time groveling for not telling them about it, even though he hadn't been seriously hurt and hadn't wanted to alarm them. Once he finished groveling, he'd have to answer even more personal questions, questions he wasn't prepared to answer. But if he was going to help Peyton get the answers that *she* needed about her mom, that conversation could no longer be avoided.

A quick look at his watch had him hesitating. His father was a night owl. But eleven thirty was late, even for him. Still, there was a chance he might still be up. Colin decided to risk it.

An hour later, he felt like he'd just gotten out of a boxing ring after twelve rounds and a knockout punch. Both of his parents had ended up on the call, tag-teaming each other in the interrogation like the pros they once were, when she'd been a prosecutor and he was a federal judge. In order to be forgiven for not keeping them in the loop about being shot, he'd had to promise to come up to their cabin for dinner for the next five consecutive Fridays, plus go to church with his mom on two Sundays of her choosing. The sacrifice had been worth it. Because in return, his father was giving him exactly what he'd asked for.

The part of the discussion about Brian's escape had been the easy part. His parents knew how law enforcement worked. They knew not to push for any nonpublic information—which was pretty much just that four escaped convicts had killed a Memphis police officer and were on the run in the Gatlinburg area.

As for the heinous killings of three of those fugitives, so far Landry had been able to keep that out of the media. He hoped to keep it quiet until after the killer was caught. Colin readily agreed. Peyton certainly didn't need to have that gruesome detail in her head, and he had no intention of telling her. Some burdens were better *not* shared.

He stood, stretched and was about to round the coffee table to head to his room when one of the papers caught his attention—the police report on the single-car accident that had claimed the life of Peyton's mother. Thinking about the irony that she'd been killed so soon after being diagnosed with terminal cancer, he picked up the report and skimmed it.

It had been a rainy night. The roads were wet. Her car had lost control on a curve and slammed into a tree. The gas tank had been punctured, and the vehicle burst into flames. The body was burned beyond recognition. Her father had had her remains cremated and Peyton said they'd sprinkled her ashes within sight of the prison walls where Brian was being held. It had been an unusual request in her mother's will and Peyton hadn't wanted to comply. But her father had insisted that they follow her wishes. She'd adored her son and that was her way of being close to him.

He scrubbed his jaw and slowly sat back down.

Cars bursting into flames were common in action movies. But in reality, even in severe crashes, it was rare. Thankfully, so were sorority house fires, especially fatal ones. What had Peyton said earlier tonight about her mom? That she'd always had candles lit around the house, and a fire in the fireplace, even in the middle of summer. Peyton had called it an unhealthy fascination with fire.

A terrible suspicion struck him. He immediately discarded it as ludicrous, the kind of fantastical scheme that might appear in a movie.

Like a car exploding into flames?

He scooted forward and rummaged through the papers on the coffee table until he found the life insurance policy he'd seen earlier. Mrs. Sterling's death certificate was stapled to the policy. Grabbing it, he jogged to his office down the back hallway.

Twenty minutes later, he had the autopsy report on Molly Sterling sitting on the computer screen in front of him—and even more questions. Dozens of internet searches later, and a promise to give his next Tennessee Vols basketball home game ticket to a police officer working the night desk in Memphis, he had the phone number that he needed. And he wasn't about to wait until morning to make the call. If this incredibly remote, insane theory panned out, he needed to get that information to the marshals and Chief Landry, immediately.

He pulled out his phone and made the call. After five rings, it went to voice mail. He didn't leave a message. He hung up and called again, and again, and again. On the fifth try, the phone was answered on the first ring.

"What the hell do you want?" the sleepy voice demanded.

"Dr. Afton, sorry to wake you at this ridiculous hour. But this is extremely important. My name is—"

"I'm going to hang up and you're not going to call me back. Instead, you're going to call the medical examiner who's on call, which is *not* me."

"If you hang up, I *will* call you back. Like I said, I'm—"

"And I'll call 911 and report that someone's harassing—"

"If someone has metastatic cancer with tumors in the

liver and brain, would that show up in an autopsy if the body was burned in a fire?"

The phone was silent for so long that Colin had to check to see whether the call had dropped. "Dr. Afton?"

"Who is this?"

Colin sighed. "I've been trying to tell you that I'm Deputy US Marshal Colin McKenzie. I'm assisting in the hunt for a wanted fugitive, Brian Sterling. While working that case, some questions came up that—"

"Wait, did you say Sterling?"

"I did."

"Any relation to Molly Sterling?"

"Brian is her son." Colin waited, but the line went silent again. "Dr. Afton?"

A loud sigh sounded through the phone. "I knew cutting corners would come back to bite me."

Colin straightened in his chair. "Cutting corners?"

"Give me five minutes. I'll call you back." The line clicked.

Chapter Eighteen

Peyton stepped off the bottom stair and paused when she saw her book bag sitting by the couch where she'd left it last night. Inside were the letters Colin had written her all those years ago. She'd meant to put the bag in her room until later, when the timing was better for a lengthy, extremely personal talk. Had he looked inside? Seen the letters?

"Morning." He rounded the corner from the hall behind the stairs holding a cup of coffee.

"Morning. I guess I owe you an apology for last night."

He stopped in front of her. "Why?"

"I shouldn't have left a mess in here. I should have picked up all my papers and photo albums." She glanced toward the coffee table—the now *empty* coffee table. "I guess you put them up for me somewhere?"

He followed her glance. "Oh. I took them to my office last night after you went to bed. I wanted to research a few things and didn't want to risk making too much noise out here." He motioned toward the book bag sitting in the floor. "I wasn't sure what you had in the bag and whether you wanted me to see it, so I left it alone."

Her cheeks heated. "Yes, well, it's nothing that I want to go into just yet. I'm guessing your research was about whatever you hinted at last night. Should we go to your office so you can show me what you found?" She stepped in that direction but he stopped her with a hand on her arm.

"That's not where you'll find what I was hinting at last night. We need to take a little drive."

"A drive?"

"About forty minutes, not far. I see you're showered and ready to start the day. Any objections to grabbing breakfast at a drive-through in town and hitting the road right now? Coffee's ready in the kitchen. You can take a mug with you."

"Have they…have they found Brian? Are we going to the police station?"

"Unfortunately, no. Let's get you some coffee and I'll explain on the way."

"Sounds like you're worried that I won't go if I know the destination ahead of time."

He gave her a crooked grin that made him look so young, her heart hurt.

"That's exactly what I'm afraid of. But you'll thank me later. Eventually. Maybe."

"Gee, you make it sound so appealing."

"Then you'll go?"

"Against my better judgment, I'll go."

"YOU'RE TAKING ME *WHERE*?"

Colin winced and glanced at a red-faced Peyton glaring at him from the passenger seat of his truck. Thankfully he'd waited until she finished her fast-food sandwich before he broke the news. Otherwise, she'd have probably thrown it at him.

Her jaw set, she stared out the window as if judging the speed of the truck.

He hit the automatic door locks.

She rolled her eyes. "Really? You think I'm stupid enough to jump?"

"Angry enough, maybe."

Her shoulders slumped. "*Angry* isn't the right word.

I'm...terrified. That they'll hate me. It's been ten years, Colin. After what my family has done to your family, after what I've done to you—"

"Hey, hey. You haven't done anything to me. Let that guilt go right now."

"You were burned. I wasn't there for—"

"Yeah, well. That's a discussion for another day, for you and me. Not you, me and my parents. It's none of their business. And this isn't a casual visit to reminisce and take a trip down memory lane either. It's a quest for the truth. So we can put all of this business behind us and get back to that conversation you and I need to have. Alone. All right?"

She leaned toward him and put her hand on his thigh. "All right. Thank you, Colin. I don't think I could have survived everything that's been happening if it weren't for you."

He swallowed and tried not to think about her warm hand sliding across his leg, or anywhere else. Out of desperation, he subtly shifted toward the door and she pulled her hand back.

"We'll get through this together," he said. "No worries."

She watched the trees passing by the window as he turned onto the narrow road that led up the last part of the mountain to his family home.

"I don't understand how going to see your parents is going to help with my quest for answers."

"People don't call Dad *the Mighty McKenzie* for nothing."

"I thought you didn't like that name. You felt it was derogatory."

He shrugged. "Depends on who's saying it, and their tone. It can be. On the other hand, it denotes a certain authority and respect within the legal community. During Brian's trial, your family resented my dad because even though he wasn't assigned to the case, he always seemed to know what was going on. Things pretty much went his way—which means my way, as a witness and, technically, a victim since I was burned."

Her glance flicked to his hands, then away. "Okay, and that will help us now, how?"

"Brian's case was important to Dad, for two reasons. Me. And you."

"Me? I don't understand."

He slowed for a particularly sharp curve. Once he was on a straightaway again, he glanced at her. "Don't you know, Peyton? I wasn't the only one who loved you back then. You were like a daughter to Mom and Dad. In the beginning, even with me telling them I saw Brian with that gas can, they did everything they could to prove he was innocent. Because he was your brother, because they wanted to help you."

She pressed a hand to her throat. "I never knew they tried to help."

"It wasn't like they were proud of it. In their eyes, they'd failed you. They felt there was nothing they could do for you after that, so they had to fully focus on getting me well and helping me through the ordeal of the trial."

She squeezed her eyes shut. "Getting you well. Colin, when you were burned, you actually wrote me sweet, wonderful, old-fashioned letters—"

"Stop."

She looked at him. "What?"

"We can talk about that later, okay? Let's focus on the case first."

She seemed like she wanted to argue, but she finally nodded. "Of course. Okay. I'm sorry."

He held out his hand toward her. She immediately threaded her fingers through his. He rested them on the seat between them.

"What I was trying to explain in my own clumsy way is

that Dad maintained a thick file on Brian's case. It's obviously not the official case file, but it has copies of everything he could get his hands on. And more. He even hired a private investigator to see what he could find."

"I've seen the official case file, read transcripts even though I was there through the trial," she said. "I don't see how a file your father maintained, even with notes from a private investigator, would help answer my questions about my mom."

"Time stamps."

"What?"

He turned the truck down the last curve. The family cabin loomed in the distance, two stories of thick log walls perched on the edge of one of the highest peaks in the Smoky Mountains west of Gatlinburg.

"Pictures," he said, as he urged his truck up the last fifty yards of steep grade. "Dad has tons and tons of pictures from the dance, the paths, the waterfalls and the barn. He had the PI buy copies of every single picture he could get from nearly everyone who was there that night. I imagine he has way more pictures than either the prosecutor or the defense ever had."

He pulled the truck to a stop in one of the parking spaces his parents had paved for their large family. "No one ever suspected your mom. Ever. There wasn't any reason to. So no one, to my knowledge, has ever tried to create a timeline from those pictures to prove where she was at different times that evening."

Peyton chewed her bottom lip, her hand tightening on his as she stared up at the cabin. "You really think enough of the pictures have dates and times on them to be of any use? I don't remember setting dates and times very often on my pictures when I was younger."

He squeezed her hand and let go so he could get out of the truck, but he hesitated after popping open the door.

"You underestimate the Mighty McKenzie. He had the PI print pictures from the actual photo cards in each camera, and write the dates and times from the metadata from those cards onto the back of each picture. That way, all of them have time stamps. And they should all be accurate."

For the first time in a long time, she gave him a smile that reached her eyes. "It will be such a relief to know, one way or the other. Thank you." Her gaze slid to the cabin. "It hasn't changed much over the years. It's still…huge."

He laughed. "I suppose it is. They needed a lot of space for four boys to run around. Mom had the kitchen renovated a few years ago, had new beams put in to carry the weight of the second story so she could have a wall knocked down. Open concept and all that. There might be a few new pieces of furniture here and there. But overall, it's pretty much the same."

He hopped down from the truck and headed around to her side. After opening the door, he reached in to help her down. Her soft hands gripped his shoulders like a lifeline. It was then that he saw the fear in her eyes and realized the depth of her concern over the reception she'd receive from his parents.

"It will be okay." He tried to reassure her. "I promise." She was so tiny compared to him. He couldn't help grinning when he lifted her down and set her on her feet.

She frowned up at him as if reading his mind. "No short jokes."

"No tall jokes."

She blinked, then laughed. "Deal."

He kept her hand tightly in his and led her to the door. It opened as soon as they got there, which told him his mother had been watching for them. She stood in the opening, smiling through her tears as she engulfed Peyton in a tight hug.

"Welcome home, daughter," she said, still holding Peyton in her arms. "We've missed you so much."

Tears were streaming down Peyton's face when Colin's mother finally let her go. Peyton gave him a helpless look, obviously not sure what to do. But his mother was already taking charge, grabbing Peyton's hand and tugging her into the house.

"Come along, Peyton. Dad's waiting in his office. Let's get all of that business stuff out of the way so we can chat about that lovely store of yours downtown. Peyton's Place, right? I was there yesterday. Just adorable. Love the croissants."

Colin imagined that Peyton wasn't looking forward to that conversation, to telling his mother that the store belonged to someone else now. His mother never slowed, pulling her through the family room toward the opposite end of the house. Peyton glanced at Colin over her shoulder, a bemused expression on her face.

He grinned and nodded his encouragement. The tears had stopped. And he'd be eternally grateful to his mother for her warm welcome of Peyton. It was exactly what she'd needed. But then, his mother always seemed to know what everyone needed.

She stopped at the open door to Colin's father's office, her arm around Peyton's shoulders. "William, get over here and welcome our daughter home."

"I'm coming, I'm coming," his father called out.

Colin stopped behind Peyton, not quite touching, but close enough so that he knew she'd be able to feel his warmth, know he was there for her no matter what.

He needn't have worried.

As soon as his father stopped in front of her and opened his arms, she let out a sob and stepped into his embrace.

Chapter Nineteen

Peyton couldn't help feeling intimidated sitting across the desk from Colin's distinguished-looking father, while Colin stood in front of the wall of bookshelves behind his dad, watching her with that intense gaze of his. Whether they realized it or not, the two of them presented a powerful united front that had her feeling defensive even though she knew they both only wanted to help. Maybe it was her usual Sterling family guilt that was making her feel that way.

She forced her attention back to the pictures she was flipping through, one of many stacks that had been taken from the dozens of folders spread out on the desk. The mass of information that McKenzie senior had accumulated on Brian's case made the official police file seem like an abridged summary.

There was a picture of her mom, wearing that awful forest-print dress Peyton had hated. She'd joked that her mother would blend in with the wood-paneled walls and no one would even see her. Her mom's feelings had been hurt—it was a brand-new dress and she'd loved it. Peyton had had to do a quick one-eighty and pretend she'd been kidding in order to appease her mom and make her smile again.

The dress really was hideous.

Another picture was one that she knew well. It had been the smoking gun at the trial, an out-of-focus snapshot of a figure fleeing into the woods, with the beginnings of flames barely visible in the lower window of the barn to his left. The figure's back was to the camera, but it was definitely a male. He had short dark hair, jeans and a tucked-in shirt—which described *most* of the boys at the dance. But *this figure* was holding a gas can.

The prosecution had argued that it proved Brian had set the fire. The defense argued that it proved someone else had set the fire. Peyton had stared at that shadowy figure for hours and still couldn't swear that it was, or wasn't, her brother. Of course, if it was, his argument to her at the high school was that he'd been taking that can out to *prevent* a fire. When she'd shared that information with Colin during the phone call on her drive to Memphis, he'd flat-out said he didn't believe it. She had to agree with him that it sounded weak, a desperate attempt to explain the unexplainable.

She flipped to the next picture, then the next and the next. She and Colin were in quite a few of them, her in a minidress that hugged every curve. Him looking sexier than humanly possible in jeans that hugged his lean hips and tight rear end, his collared shirt half tucked in as he swung her around the dance floor. She curled her fingers against the urge to trace the lines of his arms. That had been the last time she saw him in short sleeves.

She set the first stack of pictures aside and stared at the many more stacks she had yet to go through.

"Everything okay?" Colin asked.

She shrugged. "Real life cases sure aren't like TV, are they? All that CSI stuff, fingerprints, DNA. Brian's case has none of that. There's no black and white, only gray, and so many ways to look at what little evidence there is. I wouldn't have all the questions I have today if there was hard evidence to rely on. But his case is almost entirely circumstantial. It's just so frustrating."

His father waved toward the other side of the room,

where a row of cherrywood filing cabinets fit end to end beneath the wall of windows overlooking the mountains.

"Those cabinets hold my entire life's work, my personal notes on thousands of cases. Probably eighty percent are based almost *exclusively* on circumstantial evidence. Real life doesn't always come with videos, pictures, DNA and fingerprints. That's why we rely so heavily on old-fashioned police work—investigations, interviews and eyewitnesses."

"But eyewitnesses aren't reliable," she argued. "I'm no expert but even I've seen documentaries showing how two people can see the same thing from different vantage points and have completely different accountings of what happened."

Colin straightened away from the bookshelf behind him. "Which is exactly why law enforcement insists on having corroborating witnesses. In your brother's case, there were five people who agreed they saw Brian with that gas can near the barn. Including me. I knew your brother for years. Do you really think I'd swear under oath that I saw him if there was *any* doubt in my mind?"

She slowly shook her head. "No. I don't. But it was dark—"

"Not right by the barn where I saw him. Party lights were strung throughout the property, lighting up the paths and buildings. Remember? Brian ran out, and the barn went up in flames right after."

All three of them went silent, no doubt thinking about Colin running into that inferno to make sure no one was inside. He'd found two people already knocked unconscious by a burning, fallen timber. He hadn't hesitated to help them, regardless of the danger to himself.

Peyton cleared her throat and tried to get the conversation back on track. "I know that Brian claimed at the school over a week ago that he was indeed the one carrying that gas can—supposedly to prevent the fire. But since we're playing devil's advocate and trying to prove the truth, I'll argue that you can't swear it was him since you only saw him from the back. You saw a young man from behind, running away from you. It could have been anyone."

"I could see *you* from any angle, Peyton, and I'd know it was you."

Her face heated. She refused to look at his father. "I thought we were here to determine my mother's whereabouts during the dance, not rehash where Brian was."

Colin waved toward the other pictures and folders. "We are. But Dad and I both thought you might want to look at all of the evidence first, everything he has, to form a complete picture of what happened that night. If you go into a case with preconceived notions, you're likely to miss an important clue that could end up solving the entire puzzle. And as you just pointed out, Brian's recent version of events is the polar opposite of what he's claimed all these years. I don't think we can trust him."

"No arguments here." She rubbed her hands across her jeans.

His father pushed himself to standing. "How about I leave you two alone to go through all this without a federal judge looking over your shoulders?"

"You don't have to leave," Peyton said. "You're not making me feel uncomfortable."

He smiled. "I appreciate that. But I'm hankering for another one of those delicious croissants that Margaret picked up at your store yesterday. I'll check back later."

He left the room and closed the door.

Peyton chewed her bottom lip. "I suppose now isn't the time to tell him that Joan buys those croissants from another bakery across town and repackages them."

Colin grinned. "Probably not." He opened the top desk drawer and pulled out a small magnifying glass. "For the pictures, just in case. Sometimes little details escape the

naked eye and might be important." He sat down acros
from her. "How do you want to do this? I get the impres
sion that you're not interested in reviewing all the folders.

"Is it that obvious?"

"It *is* a lot to sort through. We can focus entirely on th
pictures for now, build a timeline off that and then deter
mine our next steps. Sound like a plan?"

"Sounds perfect. How do we start?"

He opened the drawer again, this time pulling out som
legal pads and pens and setting them in the middle of th
desk. "Divide and conquer. I suggest we separate any pic
tures of your mom to one stack, and pictures of Brian t
another. Any pictures of the scene itself—the barn befor
it burned down, and the immediate area surrounding it—
go in a third stack."

She nodded, then picked up the infamous smoking gu
picture. "Where would this one go? It's by the barn, bu
supposedly this is a picture of Brian."

"Fourth stack. Undecided. Once we have only the pic
tures we're most interested in, we use the time stamps o
the back of each one to put them in order."

"Timeline, right?"

He smiled. "Timeline."

They each took a stack of pictures and started sorting.

Even with the two of them culling through the pictures
it took over two hours to finish.

Peyton stood and crossed to the window, stretching he
aching back from being stooped over for so long. "Sorry
wasted your time. I should have known better than to ex
pect school kids to take enough pictures with the chaper
ones in them to do any good."

He joined her by the window and rested his hip agains
one of the filing cabinets. "It wasn't a waste of time. You
have to go down a lot of roads in an investigation to deter
mine whether they're worth going down. It had to be done.'

"What else is there? How else can we fill the gaps in the timeline?"

He scrubbed his jaw. "I hate to say it. But we're probably back to looking through Dad's entire file to find another thread to pull."

She groaned. "I don't think I'm up for that. It'll take a week to go through everything."

"Probably."

"How are you even working on this with me at this point? I'm not going to get you fired for missing work am I?"

He hesitated. "I'm not working this on my own time anymore. I'm officially assigned to Brian's case, have been since the day you went back to Memphis." He waved toward the desk. "This, reviewing the old case files, is all part of that."

"Oh. Well, then, that's good. I guess. But I thought there was a conflict of interest, that you couldn't work on this because…"

"Because of our past?"

She nodded.

"My boss finally had to accept that there was no way to keep me from looking into everything, whether I was on my own or not. He decided to make it official. Besides, since your encounter at the school, things have…heated up. Catching Brian has become job number one. Pretty much everyone in law enforcement around here is helping, one way or another."

"You said catching *Brian*. You meant catching Brian and the three other escapees, right?"

He hesitated. "Right."

She put her hands on her hips. "Is there something you're not telling me?"

He straightened. "There are always things in investigations that can't be shared with civilians."

"Civilians? I'm a part of this, not just a civilian."

"There's no difference in the eyes of law enforcement." He waved toward his father's desk, at the folders spread across the top. "You've already been given far more access to information than most people ever would. I'm walking a thin line here. I can't do more than I already have."

She crossed her arms. "Do you always have to be so logical and make perfect sense? You make it impossible for me to be mad at you."

He grinned. "And here I was expecting a big fight. You surprise me."

"I'll save the big fight for later. I'm sure you're bound to really tick me off at some point."

"No doubt." He chuckled. "I guess we're done here then. Do you want to stay and visit awhile or—"

"If I have a choice, I'd rather go back to your house. I'm just not ready to be social, you know? With everything going on. That is, if it won't upset your parents."

"They'll understand. Just give me a few minutes. I haven't seen them in a while and I'm sure they'll have a few more questions for me before we go." He strode out the door and disappeared down the hall.

She looked back at the desk, the messy piles of folders and pictures scattered everywhere. They looked so out of place in the otherwise pristine office. She headed to the desk and started straightening everything into logical piles. But since she wasn't sure which folders to put the various pictures in, she arranged all of them in neat stacks in front of the folders. The smoking gun picture ended up on top of one group. A picture of her mom in that awful forest-print dress sat on top of the grouping beside it.

She couldn't resist picking up the controversial picture one more time and staring at the fleeing figure with the gas can.

Is that you, Brian? Are you carrying that gas can be-

cause you started the fire, or were trying to prevent one? Have I been defending you all these years even though you're guilty? Is Colin right?

She glanced at the picture of her mom, then picked it up.

Or have you been the culprit all along, Mom? Are you responsible for hurting Colin? Did you let your son go to prison for your crime?

As usual, no answers came to her. Would she ever really know what had happened? She set the picture down, glancing from one to the other, her mom in the ugly dress to the figure with the gas can. She frowned and looked back at her mom again. Something wasn't quite right. Something was…off. She looked at the other picture, then back again, several times. She sucked in a breath, then grabbed both pictures and ran to the window. Tilting them up to the sunlight, she overlapped them a few inches.

Then she saw it.

The little detail she'd missed all these years, that everyone had missed, because the picture was so dark and blurry. There was no reason to think anything of it, and she probably never would have, if she hadn't seen it next to the other picture.

Laughter sounded from down the hall, followed by the clink of dishes. She could hear Colin's deep voice as he said something to his parents. His mom laughed again, probably at some joke he'd made or a funny memory he'd shared. Such a happy family, so *normal*. And she'd brought such turmoil into their lives. She'd been right before, when she'd said her whole life was a lie.

She studied the pictures again. It was such a tiny detail. Could she be wrong? She needed to be absolutely sure before telling Colin what she'd found. Because it changed everything. She crossed to the desk and had just picked up the small magnifying glass that Colin's father had set out when she heard footsteps coming down the hall toward the room. She whirled around, looking for her purse, then remembered she hadn't brought it. She turned her back to the door and shoved the small magnifying glass and two pictures down her cleavage into her bra.

The footsteps stopped. "Peyton? Ready to go?"

She fastened another button on her blouse, then forced a smile and turned around. "Ready."

Chapter Twenty

Peyton headed into the house with Colin, but paused in the back hallway instead of going into the main room.

She motioned toward his office door. "Do you mind if I borrow your office for a few minutes? I want to take another look at my albums while the pictures from your dad's files are still fresh in my mind." She crossed her fingers behind her back. Not that she was really lying. She did want to look at the albums again. But that wasn't the main reason she wanted a few minutes to herself.

"Sure, take all the time you need. But I'm hungry. How does a ham and cheese sandwich with lemonade sound?"

"It's only eleven. A bit early for lunch, isn't it?"

He rubbed his stomach. "Second breakfast."

She put her hands on her hips. "Second breakfast? Like the tiny hobbits have in *The Lord of the Rings*? I don't suppose that's another unsubtle attempt to tease me about my vertical stature?"

"I'm sure I don't know what you mean." He winked and strode past the stairs toward the kitchen.

"I like mustard and mayo on mine," she called out.

"You got it."

She smiled and pulled the pictures and magnifying glass out of her bra as she hurried into his office. After clicking on his desk lamp, she bent over and held both the pictures close to the light, studying them. It didn't take long to confirm that she hadn't been mistaken. She put the pictures down on top of a folder and slumped into the desk chair.

What next? What else was lurking in her family's deep dark closets? And how many more times would she have to stand in the firing line and take another cannon to her heart? She was vaguely surprised she wasn't crying her eyes out again. But the urge to cry just wasn't there. She'd gone numb at this point. Thank God for small favors.

She had to tell Colin. Might as well rip off the Band-Aid and get it over with. She picked up the pictures, then noticed the neat printing on the folder label beneath them: Autopsy Results—Corrected: Molly Sterling. Why would Colin have an autopsy report on her mother? Setting her two pictures aside, she was about to flip open the folder when the label on the one beneath it had her drawing a sharp breath: Autopsy Results and Ballistics: Benjamin Sterling. Her father's autopsy report. She'd never seen a copy before, had never even thought to ask for one. Why did Colin have it? How in the world were both of her parents' autopsies relevant to the research on Brian? To the search for him and his fellow escapees?

Her hands shook as she took both of the folders and headed to the office couch to read them.

COLIN HUMMED "Boulevard of Broken Dreams" as he inventoried everything he'd set out on the kitchen island. Bread, check. Although nothing as fresh and delicious as he knew Peyton could bake. Ham, check. Provolone cheese, check. He remembered she liked that. Mayo, check. Mustard, check. He didn't remember her mustard preference so he'd gone with spicy brown since that's what he liked. They'd always had a lot of the same likes and dislikes.

He'd promised lemonade, but the pitcher in the refrigerator was almost empty. He checked the pantry. There were fresh green apples, navel oranges, baking potatoes.

No lemons. A twelve-pack of lemon-lime soda caught his eye. A poor substitute for fresh-squeezed lemonade, but at least it was in the same flavor category. He grabbed a couple of cans and set them on the island before filling some glasses with ice.

Now, all he had to do was slap the sandwiches together and—

He straightened, a piece of cheese dangling between his fingers. Peyton was in his office. To look at her albums. The last time he'd been in the office was early this morning making folders and printing out copies of—

Oh, no. Please, please, no.

He tossed the cheese on one of the plates and sprinted to his office, catching himself against the door frame.

Peyton was sitting on the couch in front of the bookshelves, her hands resting on two closed folders in her lap. Her face was alarmingly pale. And when she finally looked up at him, her calm exterior was belied by the pain in her tortured gaze.

Colin swallowed against the tightness in his throat and knelt on the floor in front of her. "Peyton, sweetheart. I'm so sor—"

"When were you going to tell me that my mother might still be alive? And how long were you going to let me believe that you'd shot my father, when Brian's the one who killed him?"

PEYTON SAT CROSS-LEGGED on the couch facing Colin with both of the folders in her lap. He sat sideways on the other end, his right arm resting along the back of the couch, one leg drawn up, the other stretched out in front of him.

She held up the folder with her father's name on it. "Let's get the easy one over with first. This is dated the day after I went to Memphis. Why didn't you tell me that ballistics tests prove the bullet that killed my father came from the gun that I took from Brian at the high school?"

He opened his mouth to respond, but Peyton held up a hand to stop him. "And don't you dare say you just wanted to protect me."

He closed his mouth.

"Seriously?" she asked. "You were trying to protect me? Again?"

He held his hands out in a conciliatory gesture. "You love your brother. I didn't want to add this to the burden you're already bearing when it comes to him."

"You'd rather I just go on believing that *you* shot him?"

"What's the point in rehashing the event and making you relive that pain all over again?"

"That's just another way of saying you were trying to protect me."

His jaw tightened and he crossed his arms over his chest.

Peyton let out a long sigh. "Okay. Well. I know you did what you felt was right, even though I *completely* disagree with your decision. Knowing that my brother killed my father…" She ruthlessly tamped down her emotions before she could continue. "That's a pretty important thing to know. If he could do something like that, and lie to my face about it when we spoke at the high school, he's capable of anything. My eyes are wide open now when it comes to my brother."

"You're handling this a lot better than I probably would have in your position," he admitted.

She scoffed. "I think what you meant to say is that you're astonished that I'm not drowning in a puddle of tears right now."

"That's not what I—"

"It's okay. I get it. I've been a nervous wreck ever since Brian showed up in my kitchen. And I've been crying so much I should invest in a tissue company. But I'm stronger than I look, and way stronger than I've been acting lately." She held up the second folder. "And I'm going to do my level best to hold it together while you answer my questions about this. But it's a lot to take in, so no promises."

His gaze flicked to the second folder in her lap, his brows knitting with worry. But, to his credit, he didn't try once again to convince her to let it go and ignore what she'd read.

"A lot of this is medical jargon over my head, so I'm not sure I got it all. You said there was an issue with the coroner, that he didn't perform his due diligence when conducting the autopsy on my mother." She held the folder out toward him. "Explain it to me. Please."

His reluctance was obvious in his expression, but he leaned forward and took the folder from her. When he didn't open it, she fisted her hands in frustration.

"Are you really going to make me go to Chief Landry or another marshal to ask them to explain this to me?"

"No." He pitched the folder onto the couch between them. "But I don't need to look at the reports to answer your questions. I called the coroner initially because it didn't sit right that your mom's car caught on fire in the accident. That's rare. And as you'd already pointed out, fire seems to crop up a lot in relation to your mom, from the sorority house fire onward. What I discovered is that the coroner was overworked and had a backlog of cases. He made a judgment call that your mom's case didn't seem suspicious, that it was simply a tragic accident. He skipped steps. He didn't pull dental records or try to test DNA because there was only one person in the car, the vehicle was registered to your mom and the victim was wearing jewelry that your father identified as belonging to her. Her purse was also in the car, half burned, with credit cards and her driver's license inside."

She held her hands out. "Makes sense to me. Honestly, I'd assume it was her too."

"As the coroner, he can't assume anything. In a case like this especially, where the body was, forgive me, burned beyond recognition, it's his duty to perform medical tests to verify the victim's identity. After I spoke to him, I strongly encouraged him to pull the X-rays that he took during the autopsy and get dental records to compare—"

"Strongly encouraged?" She couldn't help smiling, if only a little. "I'll bet you had his career and future pension flashing in front of his eyes."

He returned her smile. "Possibly." His smile faded. "Peyton, the woman in the car wasn't your mother."

She'd read that in the report, but hearing it out loud seemed to suck the oxygen from the room. She wrapped her arms around her middle, nausea coiling in her stomach. If her mom hadn't been in the car, then another woman died in her place.

"Go on," she whispered, her throat so tight, she could barely speak. "Just say it. All of it."

His look of sympathy was almost her undoing. She clasped her hands in her lap and waited like a prisoner on death row watching the minutes tick away to midnight, hoping for the phone to ring but knowing that it won't.

"The coroner was able to get dental records overnight and did the comparison that he should have done originally. That proved the woman in the car wasn't your mother. But there aren't any missing persons cases in Memphis or the surrounding counties that seem like good candidates to be the victim. As for whether the car was tampered with to cause the accident, the car was crushed at a junkyard, so it can't be reexamined. However, the police did a thorough job of examining it the first time and I'm confident with their findings—that the car was in good working order before the crash. Based on that, and the lack of missing persons cases that I mentioned, I'm inclined to think the simplest scenario is the one that makes sense here. Someone robbed your mom and stole her car, then paid the ultimate price for their crimes."

He seemed to be waiting for her to say something, maybe to ask the next obvious question. But she didn't. She couldn't. Just holding herself together was taking all her energy.

"As for your mom," he continued, "that's open for speculation. The memorial service was over three months ago. If she's alive, one would expect that she'd have come forward, maybe to say she was carjacked or something. Since that hasn't happened, there are two logical possibilities. Either she was…murdered…by the person who took her car, or—"

"She's alive and wants people to think that she's dead," she managed to whisper.

"Yes."

"Is there…" She cleared her throat. "Is there any chance that if my mom really is alive, and hiding somewhere, for whatever reason, that the woman in her car…that my mom…" She couldn't say it, couldn't wrap her mind around it. But she had to know. She gave him a helpless look, hoping he'd understand what she was asking.

"You want to know whether your mom murdered the woman who was found in the car?"

She pursed her lips and nodded.

"The answer to that is complicated. There are extensive sketches and photographs from the police report that clearly indicate the car crashed into the tree and then caught on fire. And even though fire destroys evidence, the fire didn't completely consume the car. It was put out quickly enough to preserve enough clues for the police to piece together a few things. For example, there's no evidence that anyone besides the driver was in the car at the time of the accident. Also, the doors were jammed shut. And probably the most telling detail of all is that the driver had soot in her lungs at the time of the autopsy."

She covered her mouth. "Oh no."

He grimaced. "Yeah. I know. She was breathing when the car caught on fire. Hopefully she passed out and didn't suffer. Taking everything I just said into account, we know that she wasn't killed and placed in the car as part of some elaborate scheme. She was driving the car and wrecked it, and suffered horrible consequences as a result. Your mother probably had nothing to do with her death."

"Probably. I hope you're right. That would be one thing I could be thankful for. But that means either my mom was—" she twisted her hands together "—murdered, the victim of a carjacking. Or what? She decided when her car was taken that she'd take advantage of it? Use the opportunity to disappear? Why would she do that? She was dying of cancer. Given her prognosis, if she is alive and not undergoing treatment, she doesn't have much longer to live. So why fake her death?"

"I haven't been able to come up with any viable theories on that just yet. The only thing I can think of, and that's really thin, is that she wanted to spare her family the ordeal of watching her waste away from her disease. Maybe she thought it was a kinder way to say goodbye. A clean break. But regardless of the reason for disappearing, she'd still need money to live on. She'd need food, somewhere to stay, pain pills to help make her more comfortable."

"That wouldn't be a problem. Mom had her own money, separate from Dad, for as long as I can remember. It's just how they did things. Yes, she was helping pay Brian's legal fees. But she'd never give up all of her savings for him, or anyone else. I can totally see her stashing extra money away over the years, like from the grocery budget or clothing allowance, and building up a good nest egg. Plus, Dad had his faults, but being stingy wasn't one of them. Any time Mom asked for money, if he had it, he gave it to her." She shifted on the couch and rested her arm across the back like he was doing. "What happens next from a law-enforcement perspective, as far as my mom is concerned?"

"Quite a bit. The coroner has to revoke your mom's death certificate since the body in the car wasn't hers. Memphis police have already opened a missing persons report on your mom."

"Wow. Either you woke up a ton of people last night to get all of this rolling, or you were super busy this morning before I ever got out of bed."

He smiled. "A little of both. Memphis PD is also reopening the investigation around the crash to include the time-line leading up to it. The goal is to search for witnesses and to track your mother's movements to figure out where she was last seen. They've got a good team up there. I'm confident they'll do everything they can to figure out what happened to her."

"Thank you, Colin. I appreciate you explaining everything. I don't guess any of this helps with the search for Brian and his fellow escapees though."

His hand tensed against the back of the couch. If her hand hadn't been close to his, she wouldn't have even caught the movement.

"There's something else, isn't there?" she asked. "Something you're not telling me, about Brian? And the other fugitives?"

He scrubbed his jaw and straightened. "Our sandwiches. I left the lunch meat on the counter. I should put it away before it—"

"Colin. Please. No more surprises. Let's level with each other here and now and not hold anything else back."

He rested his forearms on his knees and turned his head To look at her. "Each other? There's something about the case that *you're* not telling *me*?"

She hesitated, then nodded. "It's the reason I came in here to begin with. I needed a few minutes to look at something, to be absolutely sure before I told you. But let's be clear. I was going to tell you." She smiled. "Unlike someone else I know around here." Her attempt at infusing a teasing tone into her gibe didn't even coax a smile out of him.

He stood and crossed to the window that looked over the backyard and the acres of green grass and trees that seemed to go on forever. She'd admired that same view many times from the windows off the kitchen since coming to his home. The longer he stood there, the more nervous and full of dread she became. She smoothed her hands on her jeans and crossed to the window, stopping a few feet behind him.

"I've been badgering you all morning," she said. "Time for me to woman up, I guess, and tell you what I've discovered." She moved to the desk to grab the pictures she'd left on top of one of the albums.

"Peyton."

His somber tone had her turning around. He had his hands in his pockets and was leaning against the windowsill, his long legs braced out in front of him. "We aren't searching for the three fugitives anymore who escaped with your brother. We found their bodies the same day you spoke to Brian at the high school."

"Bodies? You found their…bodies?"

"They were burned."

She pressed her hand to her throat. "Oh my God. To keep the police from knowing it was them? How did they die? Were they shot? Oh, Colin. Please don't tell me that Brian shot them right before meeting me, with the same gun that I took from him." She shuddered at the thought of touching the gun that had been used to kill her father and possibly three other men.

He slowly shook his head. "They weren't shot."

"I don't understand. You said the bodies were…" She

read the truth in his eyes, and shuddered. "Oh, dear Lord above. Who would... Brian? You're telling me he—"

"No. The timing wasn't right. He couldn't have set the fire. Someone else did, at the same time that he was being chased through the woods miles away by some marshals. We believe that Brian is working with someone else, and that second person is the one who killed the escapees. It could explain a lot. A partner could have arranged transportation, picked them up after they escaped the van, gave them money, had places picked out ahead of time where they could hide to evade the searchers. It can also explain where the gun came from that was used to shoot Jennings and your father."

"Wait. The gun I took from Brian didn't belong to Officer Jennings?"

"His gun was still in his holster when they found him. He never had a chance to draw."

"One more lie to chalk up to Brian. I should have known. You think this...partner...is the one who killed the fugitives?"

"I don't think one person could have kept them compliant to allow him to tie them up to a tree. Someone must have held a gun on them while someone else tied them up. Then the one with the gun left, and the partner...took care of loose ends."

"Brian was the one with the gun," she said, her voice hoarse.

"I believe so, yes."

She turned back toward the desk and slowly lowered herself into the chair. She picked up the two pictures that she'd taken from McKenzie senior's office and set them in front of her. "Who do you think his partner is?"

"I have a theory."

She let out a ragged breath. "Me too." She held the first photo up in the air. "If you take a fresh look at the smoking gun picture, you'll see the window in the barn isn't quite square. That's because the lower-left corner has a small piece of fabric behind it, inside the barn. It looks almost exactly like the wood on the barn itself, so it's nearly impossible to notice unless you're looking for it." She held up the second picture, the one of her mother wearing the forest-print dress. "That fabric exactly matches the pattern on the dress my mother was wearing the night of the dance." She smiled sadly. "I think we both know who started the barn fire now. And we have our answer about whether my mother is alive or dead."

Chapter Twenty-One

Several times throughout the day, Colin headed to the stairs, determined to talk Peyton into coming down from her room. But each time he put his foot on the bottom step, he stopped. She hadn't been angry at him when she'd left his office. She'd been sad, confused, overwhelmed. And she'd told him she needed some time to make sense of everything she'd learned, to figure out her next steps.

He wanted more than anything for her to figure out those next steps *with him*, to let him be there for her. But she wasn't ready to lean on him, to lessen her burdens by sharing them, to work through their hopes and fears together, like they'd once done. The idea that she might never be ready terrified him. Because the one constant in his life, the one thing he'd realized since she'd come back, was that he'd been fooling himself thinking he'd gotten over her. He could never get over her. He loved her more now than ever before. And he didn't know how he was going to survive if she walked out of his life again.

One thing was certain, he couldn't keep pacing the floor all day. He had to get out of here, work off some of this nervous energy. Take his mind off Peyton. Take his mind off an investigation that kept opening up wounds from the past but never seemed to lead to a resolution.

He strode through the family room, through the kitchen and out the door. Ignoring the stairs, he leaped off the back deck and took off at a run, not stopping until he reached the workshop building.

He unlocked the door and flung it open, then propped it back with a piece of wood to get some airflow inside. Even with shorts on because of the heat, he was already sweating. The long sleeves didn't help. And with Peyton upstairs and showing no sign of coming down, there was no reason to give himself heatstroke. He took off his shirt and flung it on a workbench. Then he headed straight to the broken tractor, determined to finally wrestle it into submission.

Several hours later, the beast was purring like a cat drunk on catnip. Not long after that, both ATVs had a fresh oil change and a new fuel filter, and were shined up and ready for future treks over the mountain to check on his newest acquisition, the tract of land he'd had his eye on for years but that had only come available a few months ago. But since he didn't want to be out of sight of the house just in case Brian—and his mother—decided to pay a visit, he spent the remaining daylight hours patching and painting over the bullet holes Brian's last visit had made in the siding on the workshop building.

The light sensor had the bug light behind the house flickering on when he set his dirty boots on the deck and headed inside. He used his shirt to wipe the sweat from his chest and arms as he strode through the house to his bedroom to take a much-needed shower. He stepped inside his bedroom, and froze. Peyton was standing in profile on the other side of the bed, looking out the window into the side yard.

"There you are," she said as she began to turn around. "I've been look—"

Her eyes widened and she pressed her hands to her throat, staring at his chest. "Oh, Colin. Oh no, *Colin.*"

He'd learned to expect this type of reaction from other people. He hadn't expected it from her, though, not after everything they'd been through the past few weeks. What a fool he'd been to think that she could love him enough to overlook the physical, love him for who he was, not the scarred shell he'd become.

The urge to cover himself was nearly overwhelming as her horrified gaze traveled over the ridges and dips that covered his chest and arms. But he wasn't about to cower and act ashamed. He'd saved two people's lives. It had cost him dearly. But given the choice, he'd do it all over again. Life was a precious gift, worth any sacrifice. Even if it meant sacrificing the love of his life.

"Colin," she choked out, still not looking up at his face.

He gritted his teeth. "If you're through staring in disgust at my scars, I need to take a shower."

Her gaze flew to his. "What? No, I didn't mean—"

"Excuse me." He strode past her into the master bathroom and considered it a victory that he managed to shut the door without slamming it.

PEYTON ZIPPED THE bag of freshly baked croissants closed and set them on the kitchen island. With Colin gone for several hours now, she'd filled the time baking, and had definitely gone with a chocolate theme. Three dozen chocolate fudge cookies sat in another bag. A devil's food cake took up the middle, resting on a plain dinner plate covered with plastic wrap since she couldn't find a cake keeper in Colin's kitchen. Yet another sheet of chocolate chip cookies, still too warm to put away, sat cooling on the opposite end of the island.

The oven beeped, letting her know it was preheated again for her next venture—a homemade Dutch apple pie. Well, almost homemade. She'd been forced to make the crust from a few cans of ready-made biscuit dough. But she'd almost wept when she'd seen the bag of fresh-picked apples sitting on a shelf in the pantry. Not because it meant she could make a decent pie. But because she remembered how much Colin had always loved apples, green not red. And how much fun they'd had together picking them at the same orchard every summer.

She slid the pie into the oven and set the timer. Then washed her hands in the sink.

"Someone's been busy. Again."

She whirled around. Colin stood in the opening to the family room. His expression was guarded, his gaze flitting over the food on top of the island. He was fully dressed, once again wearing jeans and a long-sleeved shirt that buttoned at his wrists. Only his feet were bare.

"I, ah, hope you don't mind that I took over your kitchen. I tend to bake when I'm—"

"Upset. I know." He leaned against the wall. "I'm sorry about earlier. I should have kept my shirt on when I came inside. I assumed you'd still be upstairs. I shouldn't have."

She blinked. "I don't…are you seriously apologizing to me?"

He moved into the kitchen. "Not everyone can handle it, seeing the scars. I should have been more careful." His hand hovered over one of the chocolate chip cookies cooling on the baking sheet. "Do you mind?"

"What? No, of course not. It's your food, after all. Please. Take whatever you want, I…" She swallowed as he took a bite of a cookie, then closed his eyes, a look of pleasure washing over his handsome face.

He opened his eyes. "That's probably the best chocolate chip cookie I've ever had. I'll bet it was a favorite at your store." He popped the rest of the cookie into his mouth and crossed to the sink.

She moved out of the way so he could wash his hands.

"Glad you liked it."

He dried his hands on the dish towel and leaned down to look in the oven. "Is that an apple pie?"

"I hope you don't mind. I used most of the apples in your pantry. Were you saving them for something?"

He hung the dish cloth on a hook by the sink, then rested his hip against the counter. "Not particularly. I've told you before, you're welcome to use anything in the kitchen. No exceptions."

"Thanks. Um, Colin. About before. I think you misunderstood. I wasn't—"

"Don't worry about it. I really should be used to that kind of reaction by now. Even my brothers give me a startled look if I take off my shirt while working outside." He smiled, but the smile didn't quite reach his eyes. "Forget it. Have you eaten dinner? I took a nap after my shower and woke up starving." He yanked open the refrigerator and peered inside. "I never did make those sandwiches earlier. I could still throw together some—"

"Stop it." She leaned past him and shut the refrigerator door. "We need to talk." She flattened a palm against his chest, feeling the ridges of scars beneath the material. "We need to talk about *this*." She tapped his shirt.

He plucked her hand off him, his eyes darkening. "Turns out I'm not as hungry as I thought." He moved past her and strode out of the kitchen.

She hurried after him. "Colin, please. Stop."

"Good night, Peyton." He passed the stairs, heading to his bedroom.

She spotted her book bag by the couch and grabbed it. Colin shoved his bedroom door open. In desperation, she lifted the bag into the air and flipped it upside down. The letters tumbled out, thumping against the coffee table and plunking onto the hardwood floor in a sea of white, like flat, rectangular snow.

He stopped and looked over his shoulder. His gaze traveled over envelope after envelope, his brow furrowed in confusion. "What are you doing?"

She tossed the now empty bag onto one of the couches. "They're from you, the letters you sent me after the fire. All sixty-two of them. Until my father's death, until I found these hidden in the attic, I never knew you'd tried to contact me after the fire. My father refused to let me call you. He took my phone away. And he swore you never once tried to even send me a text."

His face reddened as he turned to face her. "And you believed him?"

She felt her own face flushing with heat. "He was my *father*. I had no reason *not* to believe him."

"No reason except that I loved you. How could you think that I wouldn't try to contact you?" His hands fisted beside him. "I laid in the burn unit for weeks and all I thought about, other than the pain, was you. I prayed you'd come back, that I'd open my eyes one morning and see you bending over my bed, feel your hand brushing the hair out of my eyes. But you never came. Not once."

Her throat tightened. "Colin, I didn't—"

"I came to see you. Did you know that? In Memphis, after I built this stupid house for you."

She blinked. "You built this house for *me*?"

"Every board of the wraparound porch I knew you'd love, the swing you've always wanted, the ginormous kitchen. Did you think I cared about having state-of-the-art appliances and an island? I can barely cook." He waved his hands in the air, as if waving away his words. "Doesn't matter. None of it. I went to Memphis to tell you about the house, use it as a bribe to try to get you to come back. But you'd moved on with someone else."

She stared at him, shocked. "I'd moved on? What are you talking about?"

"Your marriage. Obviously, it didn't last. You're not wearing a wedding ring and you sure haven't mentioned a husband since coming back. But you had no problem finding someone else. Your father told me all about it."

She took a step toward him, shaking her head, anger over this latest example of her father's lies tempered only by her grief and dismay. "And you believed him?"

He stared at her, confusion crinkling his brow. "You never got married?"

She clutched her hands together, tears burning the backs of her eyes. "No. I didn't."

This time, he took a hesitant step toward her. "You didn't...find someone else?"

"How could I? No one I've ever met compares to you." She slowly moved closer, then stopped. There was still far too much space between them, literally and figuratively. "I don't know what was going through my father's mind when he lied to both of us. He told me your burns weren't that serious, that you were released from the hospital that same day. And he forbade me from contacting you, said it would jeopardize my brother's trial, that he could end up in prison and it would be my fault."

Colin stared at her, but didn't say anything.

"Looking back, it's easy to see that it was foolish of me to believe him. But I was young, and naive, and terrified that I could be the reason my brother's life was ruined. That's hard to understand, I know. But back then, it was our family against yours. We were trying to keep Brian out of prison. You were going to testify against him. That's probably why Daddy kept the letters secret. He wouldn't have wanted me to read them and be conflicted between working to help Brian and being by your side."

She swallowed, hard. "I'd like to think that he felt guilty, that he realized he'd done both of us wrong by hiding your letters. That's the only reason that makes sense for him saving them all this time."

She took another step toward him. His intent gaze followed her as she slowly crossed the room.

"I read them in Memphis before I came back, half a dozen times. You were in so much physical pain, far more than I ever imagined. I had no idea how badly you were burned. I didn't even know you'd ended up in a burn unit. I'm surprised it wasn't mentioned during the trial."

He squeezed his eyes shut. "I didn't want to pile it on, to make things any worse for your family than it had to be. If Brian went to prison, I wanted it to be because of the arson, and almost killing two people, not for what he did to me. So we asked the prosecutor to keep the information about the severity of my injuries out of the trial. But I still thought you'd at least ask about me." He opened his eyes, raw pain staring back at her. "You never did."

"Oh, Colin," she whispered, her throat tight.

Six feet away, five. She stopped directly in front of him, so close that she could feel his heat reaching out to her.

"What do you want, Peyton? Is there even a point to this, now? If you can't stand the sight of me, there's no way we could ever heal the mistakes of our past." His voice was flat, his expression blank. But there was no hiding the warring emotions in his stormy eyes. There was pain, so much pain. Frustration, anger. And something…else. It was the something else that gave her courage. And hope.

"What I want is to explain my earlier reaction to seeing you without a shirt on."

His jaw flexed. "That's not necessary." He started to turn away, but she grabbed his arm.

"Wait." She dropped her hand. "Please."

He faced the doorjamb a moment, before turning back. "What?"

"The earlier letters, the handwriting wasn't yours. Who wrote them?"

He blew out a breath. "Duncan most of the time. Adam

some of the time. Even Ian pitched in on one or two. My hands were bandaged. Everything was bandaged from my neck to my naval. I couldn't hold a pen."

Her heart squeezed in her chest. "You dictated the letters?"

He gave her a crisp nod and stared over the top of her head. "Is that all?"

"Later, the writing changed. It was messy, hard to read. That was you, wasn't it? In spite of the pain, the difficulty, you pushed through. Even though I never replied to your earlier letters. You kept writing."

"Oh for the love of…enough, Peyton. There's no reason to go through all of this. I was eighteen, nineteen by the time I was out of rehab and back home. Young, in love, in pain. But life goes on. Time passes. We grow up. Let's leave the past in the past."

"You still love me, Colin. That's not in the past."

He opened his mouth as if to protest, then closed it without saying anything.

"You love me," she repeated, knowing her heart would shatter if he denied it.

After an eternity, he finally replied. "Doesn't matter."

She let out a shaky relieved breath. "I love you too."

He stiffened, as if she'd hit him. "Doesn't. Matter."

"Why not?"

He laughed, but there was no humor to it. "We've both been fooling ourselves thinking that this, that you and I, could ever work out. Even if your brother didn't start the barn fire, he's guilty for the death of Officer Jennings. And I'm the one trying to put him back in prison. He's likely to face the death penalty. You'll never be able to forgive me for that, in spite of everything you've found out about him since coming back. And I couldn't blame you. I can't imagine being in your position. If something like that happened to one of my brothers, it would destroy me. So I'm okay with you not being able to forgive me. I understand. But it will always be there between us."

She shook her head. "There's nothing to forgive. Brian made his own choices. You're doing your job and what's right. I wouldn't be here trying to help you catch him if I didn't understand that."

He dropped his head to his chest before meeting her gaze once again. "The deck is stacked against us. I've been hoping, all this time, that I was wrong. That we could make this work. Somehow. But aside from everything I already mentioned, if my scars are a barrier between us, there's no hope. That's not something I can change. It's out of my hands."

"Oh, Colin. Sweet, wonderful Colin. That's what I've been trying to explain. You misunderstood, earlier. Disgust is *not* what I felt when I saw you without your shirt. And it isn't what I feel right now."

She stepped closer and pressed both of her palms against his chest. He flinched, but didn't pull away. She slid her fingers to the top button of his shirt. He grabbed her hands.

"Peyton, don't. Seeing the scars across a room is one thing. Up close is far worse."

She looked up at him. "Let me. Please." When he didn't move, she added, "Trust me."

His brow furrowed. But he slowly dropped his hands to his sides.

She went back to work on the button, beneath his wary gaze.

"I didn't feel disgust." She slid the button free and gently pulled his shirt open a few inches. "I wasn't horrified." She opened another button. His shirt gapped a good six inches now, revealing a crisscross of puckered scars over an otherwise incredibly well-defined chest that would have made most men envious, most women hot. She was no exception.

Another button freed. More scar-covered muscles bared to her hungry gaze.

And her touch.

She leaned forward and pressed her mouth against a particularly savage-looking scar, and kissed him.

He jerked at the contact. "Peyton." His ragged whisper was a mixture of confusion and wonder.

She kissed him again, while freeing the remaining buttons. His pulse leaped in his throat and his skin heated at her touch. Her own pulse rushed in her ears. She slowly pulled his shirt completely open, then watched his face as she reached up to slide the material down his arms.

Once again, he stopped her, his hands pressing hers down on his shoulders. "This is madness." His voice was husky. "When I carried those people out of the barn, their clothes had melted onto their bodies. They were burned far worse than me. That's how my chest was burned, from their clothes pressing against mine. But I was wearing a short-sleeved shirt, which gave me some protection. But not my arms. There wasn't anything between their melted clothes and the skin on my arms as I carried them. Do you understand what I'm saying?"

"The scars on your arms are much worse than on your chest. I understand, Colin. And it doesn't change anything. Let me do this. Please."

He searched her eyes, then slowly dropped his hands and turned around so she could pull his shirt off his shoulders, apparently giving her a chance to change her mind before seeing the worst of the damage the fire had done. She wasn't changing her mind.

She bunched the fabric, then pulled it off and let it drop to the floor. His back was smooth and well defined, even sexier than she'd remembered, with only a few small white lines on the sides showing where the burns extended from the front.

Then he turned around.

She drew a sharp breath. "Oh, Colin."

He stiffened. "I knew this was a mistake." He grabbed for his shirt, but she put her foot on top of it. He looked up at her, his hand still clutching the fabric.

"You don't need to cover up," she told him. "Haven't you been listening? When I spoke just now, it was out of guilt and regret. The only disgust I feel is for myself. There's sorrow too, of course. When I see the scars, I see your pain, think about how much you suffered. I wish I could have somehow saved you from that pain. That's what you see in my face. That's what you hear in my voice. Shock, yes. Because even after reading your letters, I still had no idea just how badly you'd suffered. Now, seeing it for myself..." She shook her head. "I'm so sorry, Colin. Regardless of who is responsible, I'm so sorry that you were hurt. And I'm so, so sorry that I wasn't there when you needed me."

She very deliberately leaned down and kissed a shiny, puckered scar on his right biceps.

His breath caught.

She placed both her hands on his upper arms, then feathered her fingers across his skin.

He slowly straightened, leaving his shirt on the floor. She straightened with him, keeping her hands on his arms, smoothing her fingers up and down, across the peaks and valleys of the angry marks that were the result of so much damage, had caused so much pain.

Then she slid her hands across his shoulders, down his chest, following the dark line she remembered in her mind, even though it was no longer there to guide her hand. She continued down, down to where his jeans sagged below his naval, hanging low on his lean hips.

His eyes blazed at her, his nostrils flaring as if he was struggling to breathe. She wasn't in much better shape. Her heart pounded in her chest. Every nerve in her body sizzled, and all she'd done was slide her hands over his chest and abs. There was more to explore. So much more.

She reached for the button on his jeans.

He grabbed her hands. "Don't."

She frowned. "Why? I love you. I want—"

He shuddered. "So do I. Believe me, I *want*. But if you go any further, I won't be able to stop. I want you too much."

"Then don't stop. I don't want you to." She tugged her hands free from his and reversed direction, sliding them up his body and linking her fingers together behind his neck. "If you doubt me, feel my heart. It's racing. For you, Colin. That's what you do to me. Still. After all this time. After everything that's happened. My body still yearns for yours. I yearn for *you*."

She slid her hands down and splayed them once again across the pads of his chest. "These scars are your battle scars. They're medals of honor. What you did, going into that burning building not once, but twice to save two people you didn't even know…" She shook her head. "That's incredible. And I assure you, seeing the proof of your character isn't a turnoff in any way. It's a turn *on*. Because of what it means. Touch me, Colin. Feel the truth of what I'm telling you."

She didn't wait for him to make a move. Instead, she lifted his right hand and molded it against her breast. He groaned low in his throat, his fingers flexing against her, caressing, stroking. Her entire body flushed with heat.

"You feel my heart racing?" she whispered. "It's never raced like that for anyone but you."

He shuddered again and raised his hands to cup her cheeks, gently stroke his thumb across her lower lip. "We can't do this."

She blinked, the fog of passion thinning. "What? Why not?"

"Because I can't protect you. When I said few people can see my scars without being repulsed, I meant it. *I don't have any protection*."

She frowned, not understanding. He stared at her, waiting. Then she got it, her eyes flying open wide. She almost whimpered with frustration. "You don't have any condoms? Please tell me you're joking."

He shook his head. "I wish I were. I don't have any…" He straightened. "Hold that thought." He headed into the bedroom.

She followed, pausing in the doorway to see him open the nightstand by his bed. He rummaged inside, then slammed it shut.

"Where the hell did I—" He ran into the closet.

Peyton wrapped her arms around her waist, beginning to feel depressed and a bit silly for initiating something both of them wanted so very much, but might not be able to finish.

He stepped back into the bedroom, holding a small box in his hand.

She blinked. "I thought you didn't have any? Now I'm wondering why you do." She put her hands on her hips, jealousy riding her hard and fast. She'd never thought of him with anyone else before. It had never occurred to her, which was dumb considering how wonderful he was. Any woman should be thrilled to be with him. Still, knowing that he'd been with someone else sent a jolt of pain straight to her heart.

He stopped in front of her and tossed the box onto the nightstand. "Stop looking at me like that, Peyton. I didn't buy those. Duncan did. For you."

"Duncan? For me? I thought he was engaged to someone else."

He frowned. "That's not what I meant. He bought them for me and you, not him and you."

She grinned and slid her hands down his chest toward the top of his jeans. "I'm teasing. Be sure to thank him the next time you see him. For me." She winked and unbuttoned his jeans. "But we don't need them quite yet."

She slowly, ever so slowly, unzipped his pants, her gaze locked on his. "I've missed you, Colin." She pushed his pants down his thighs.

"Peyton," he rasped, his body jerking against her hands.

"And I've really…" She closed her fingers around him and stroked.

He swore and jerked again.

She kissed the base of his throat, using both of her hands to caress and treasure the very essence of him. "I've really missed this." She grinned and slid down his body onto her knees.

Chapter Twenty-Two

Beeeep, beeeep, beeeep!

Peyton jerked awake beside Colin, both of them bolting upright in bed.

"What *is* that?" She covered her ears against the high-pitched shriek.

"Smoke alarm!" He threw the covers off and jumped from the bed, dragging on his jeans as he answered. Before Peyton could even blink the sleep from her eyes, he was shrugging into his shirt and racing out the door.

Her heart seemed to stutter in her chest. She jumped out of bed and yanked another of Colin's shirts from a hanger in his closet to cover her nakedness. Then she ran through the family room to the kitchen where the awful electronic shrieking was coming from. She stumbled to a halt by the island, realization dawning as Colin grabbed a smoking pan out of the oven and dumped it into the sink.

"Oh, no! My apple pie!"

She ran to the sink and turned the faucet on, running water over the stinking mess while he opened the back door. He swung it back and forth to draw fresh air into the room and try to clear the smoke out.

Peyton grabbed the dish towel off its hook and ran to the far corner of the room just below the shrieking smoke detector. She batted the towel at it, furiously trying to force the remaining smoke away.

"Give it to me, shorty." He winked to soften the insult as he yanked the dish towel from her and waved it back and forth beneath the alarm.

"I'll hold the door open." She ran to the door and mimicked Colin's earlier strategy, pulling the door back and forth to force air in and smoke out. The ceilings were high, compounding the problem of getting enough fresh air in to make the alarm stop even though most of the smoke had already cleared.

Finally, blessed silence reigned inside the house once again.

She looked back at him, wincing when his gaze met hers. "I completely forgot about the pie."

"That's okay." He grinned. "I thoroughly enjoyed making you forget."

Her face heated and he laughed.

He stepped to the sink, his nose wrinkling. "Give me a second. I'll toss this outside to get the smell out. I can bag it up in the morning if the wildlife doesn't take care of it by then." Using a couple of pot holders, he picked up the ruined pie pan and carried it to the door.

She moved backward, pushing the door open for him and stepping out to let him pass.

"Nice shirt. Definitely looks better on you than me." He winked, then froze, his gaze transfixed by something behind her. "My phone's on the nightstand by the bed. Call 911." He tossed the pie to the ground and grabbed his boots off the deck.

"What's wrong?" She whirled around, then covered her mouth in horror. The sky was glowing an eerie orange farther down the mountain. "The woods! They're on fire!"

He already had one boot on and yanked on the second. "Not the woods." His gaze met hers. "Your house. Go. Call 911."

She grabbed his arm. "Don't. It could be a trap."

"It probably is. But Landry has an officer stationed at your place to keep an eye on things. If Brian or your mom are there, the officer could be in serious trouble."

Her stomach lurched at the thought of the three escapees tied to a tree, burned alive. "Don't go. Please. It's too dangerous."

"I have to. Every second counts in a fire." He shrugged off her hand. "I'll use the ATV from my workshop. I can take a shortcut through the woods and get there faster than in my truck."

"What about your vest, your gun?"

"After what happened last time, I put backups of both in the workshop building. Go!" He leaped off the deck and took off.

Peyton ran inside the house, vaulted over the coffee table and practically flew toward the master bedroom.

This can't be happening. Not again. Dear Lord, please keep Colin safe! And please protect the officer at my house.

She was running so fast by the time she reached the bedroom that she couldn't stop. She fell against the bed then jerked upright and grabbed the phone, putting it on speaker mode so she could talk to the 911 operator as she yanked on her jeans and blouse. She rattled off the address while stuffing her feet into her sneakers.

Beeeep, beeeep, beeeep!

Peyton winced at the sound of the smoke alarm going off again. Had she forgotten to turn off the oven when she took out the ruined pie?

"Ma'am?" the 911 operator called out. "Are you still there? What's going on?"

Peyton blinked, her eyes burning. She couldn't see any smoke, but she could smell it. "I'm not sure. The smoke alarm is going off inside the house again."

"Again? Are there two houses on fire?"

That thought sent a cold chill down her spine. "I don't

know. Just tell the firemen to hurry, please, to the Sterling house," she said. "That's where Deputy US Marshal Colin McKenzie went. Send the police too. Brian Sterling, an escaped convict, may be in the area. He may…he may have set the fire. His mother, Molly Sterling, could be with him." She coughed and looked around. Was the air getting thicker or was it her imagination? "Both are arsonists and extremely dangerous."

Beeeep, beeeep, beeeep!

The alarm seemed much louder now. No, all of the alarms in the house were shrieking now, not just the one in the kitchen. What was going on?

"I've got police and fire rescue on the way, ma'am. Please stay on the line until they arrive. Check those alarms, Miss Sterling. You might have to evacuate the house. If you do, stay outside and wait for the police to give you further instructions."

Peyton let out a disgusted sound. "That's not happening." She tossed the phone onto the bed and wiped her tearing eyes. She located his pistol and two magazines in the nightstand. She shoved a magazine into the gun, snapped the holster onto her hip and pocketed the extra magazine.

She looked through the bedroom doorway. The house was definitely getting smoky. But it didn't seem thick enough for the house to be on fire. And she didn't see any flames. Could it be that smoke from the house fire down the mountain was blowing this way and seeping inside, setting off the alarms? Maybe that had been the plan all along. Brian, or her mom, had set the Sterling house on fire to draw Colin outside.

If so, their plan was working.

She was about to run out of the bedroom when Colin's parting words echoed in her mind. He'd said he had an extra Kevlar vest in the workshop. Which meant the one he normally used should be in his closet. She ran inside and saw it hanging on hooks on the back wall, next to a rifle. She was wicked good with a rifle. Much better than with a pistol. And it would give her the ability to shoot from farther away. She didn't want to get in close and interfere with whatever strategy Colin might use. But if she could do something to protect him from afar, she absolutely would.

Thankfully Colin didn't take the same precautions of locking up his gun and ammo in his bedroom as he'd done in the pantry, probably because he wouldn't expect any guests to rummage through his bedroom closet. There was a box of ammunition on the top shelf, out in the open.

Rifle in hand, she ran out of the bedroom, coughing against the smoke. Then she swore and ran back in for Colin's truck keys. She grabbed them and took off toward the garage.

The smoke was worse in the garage, probably because it wasn't as airtight as the main house. She pressed the button on the wall to start the door rolling up and ran to the truck. As soon as she threw open the driver's side door, she swore a blue streak. How was she going to climb up into the stupid thing? There was a sports car on the other side of the garage. But she'd looked in the window before and saw that it was a stick. She'd never learned to drive a manual transmission.

Colin needs you.

She gritted her teeth, grabbed the steering wheel and tried to lift her leg inside. The stupid vest was so big and stiff it pushed against her thigh, making it impossible. She coughed again, then tossed her rifle into the truck and tore off the vest. After pitching it inside, she grabbed the steering wheel again and slung her right leg up. There! She had her foot on the door threshold. Now all she had to do was—

The passenger door flew open and her brother stood in the opening, aiming a pistol at her. "Don't even think about going for your gun."

Chapter Twenty-Three

Colin ducked down beneath the thick curtain of smoke in the living room of the Sterling house, holding a wet dish towel over his mouth to help him breathe.

"Officer? It's Marshal McKenzie. Can you hear me? Where are you?"

The only sound he heard was the roar of the flames licking across the walls. The only thing not burning was the floor, and that wouldn't hold true much longer.

No one had been outside when he got there. He'd run to the front of the house, confirming there was a patrol car in the driveway. But he hadn't found the officer to go with it. Knowing Brian and Molly, if they'd set the fire as a trap for him, the officer was probably inside. But even knowing that might be their plan, to roast him alive, he had to go in and try to find the missing officer.

"Hello? Is anyone in here?"

Nothing. He took a few more steps into the inferno, dread coiling in his stomach when he saw the hallway that led to the bedrooms. It was completely engulfed. If the police officer was back there, Colin was already too late.

He took another step, then another, squinting against the dark smoke. Even crouching down with his nose and mouth covered, he could barely breathe. The heat and smoke were too intense. He had to get out of there. A blazing recliner forced him to move farther into the room and give it a wide berth so he could head back through the kitchen where he'd come in. He almost fell over the body that came into view. A uniformed officer was lying facedown.

He scooped the body up in his arms, the slight weight telling him it was likely a woman. But the smoke was so thick there was little else he could see. Eyes streaming tears, he threw her over his shoulder and sprinted toward the kitchen.

A loud crash sounded behind him as part of a wall caved in. He jumped to the side but a piece of wood slammed his shoulder, almost knocking him to the floor. He stumbled, using both hands now to clutch the officer while he held his breath. Whirling away from the burning cabinets in the kitchen, he ran out the door into the backyard.

He didn't stop running until he was far enough from the house not to feel the heat of the flames. Then he dropped to his knees and lowered his burden to the ground. Coughing and blinking against the sting of smoke, he used his shirtsleeves to wipe at his streaming eyes. When he could see clearly again, he bent over the officer to check on her. That's when he realized his mad dash into the house had been in vain. There was nothing he could do to help Officer Simmons. A bullet had blown away the back of her head.

He fisted his hands beside him and swore viciously. What a senseless loss of life. He lifted his head and scanned the woods behind the house. Where were the cowards who'd set this trap for him? Why weren't they laughing right now from the woods as Brian had done that night he'd cornered Colin by the workshop? Why weren't they shooting at him when they had him right where they wanted him?

Maybe they were behind him, waiting for him to turn around. He carefully drew his pistol, then jumped to his feet and whirled. Nothing. There was no one there. He turned in a slow circle. Then stopped. Orange flames danced against the distant night sky, right about where his house would be.

Right where he'd left Peyton while he raced down here to try to save someone else.

His heart lurched in his chest. He shoved his pistol into his holster and ran toward his ATV, parked twenty yards away.

Let her be okay. Please, God. Help me make it in time to save her.

He started the ATV, then took off up the mountain.

"I DON'T UNDERSTAND. Why are you doing this, Brian?"

Peyton stood outside of the workshop building watching Colin's dream house, their dream house, burn to the ground. Beside her, Brian stood watching the same thing. But where she was devastated, he was smiling, the flames from the house reflecting in his eyes, making him look every bit the devil that she now knew him to be.

"Brian? Where's Colin?"

He sighed and turned toward her, the pistol still in his hand, but pointing at the ground instead of her. She didn't kid herself into thinking it was because he didn't want to risk shooting her. He probably just didn't want to keep holding the heavy gun up in the air.

"I imagine he's at our house, the old Sterling homestead. He's too late though. It's a flaming mess by now. He won't be able to put it out."

"You imagine? Then you didn't hurt him?"

He gave her an aggravated look. "I've never killed anyone, Peyton, in spite of what your boyfriend has probably told you. He stole ten years off my life, would have stolen more if I hadn't escaped. All the other witnesses at the barn fire were kind of iffy, not a hundred percent certain it was me. They were easy to discredit. But McKenzie swore up and down he had zero doubt. It was his testimony that put me away. He ruined my life." He gestured toward the fire. "Now, I'm ruining his. Or, at least, as much as I can before

I disappear. This is my revenge. Maybe sometime down the road, after he rebuilds, I'll pay him another visit. But for now, this will have to do."

He holstered his pistol. "I know you don't believe me. But I didn't set that barn fire. I didn't kill that cop, the one in Memphis. This fire—" he motioned toward the inferno in front of them "—is my first real fire. I have to admit, it's cool. I doubt it'll be my last. But just like I made sure you and McKenzie were out before I lit this one, that's what I'll always do. I'm not the evil person you think I am."

She tried to follow his twisted logic, but none of it made sense to her. "Then, you're just walking away? You came here tonight to burn Colin's house down? And burned our family house down to get him out of the way?"

"Worked pretty good. There is one other thing." He pulled her to him and hugged her tight.

She stiffened and pushed against him.

He sighed and let her go, his eyes sad. "You were always there for me growing up. I told you at the high school that I'd never hurt you. I meant it. I'll never hurt you. Good-bye, sis."

He turned his back on her and started walking away. It was then that she noticed the ATV just past the corner of the workshop building, his getaway vehicle. She didn't try to stop him. She turned around and started jogging the other way, toward her old house. She had to get to Colin, to see if he really was okay. Or whether her brother was lying once again.

"Not so fast, Peyton."

She stumbled to a halt as two people stepped out of the woods across from her. Colin was in front, his clothes and face blackened with soot. The shirt he wore hung half open, some buttons torn off. He clearly wasn't wearing his Kevlar vest, and she didn't have to guess why. Her mother must have made him take it off. She was standing behind him, slightly off to the side and pointing a pistol.

"Mom?" she whispered, her voice breaking. Even though she'd already suspected that her mother might still be alive, seeing her had Peyton's whole body shaking. The woman looked twenty years older than she had almost four months ago. Her skin glowed a sickly yellow in the flickering light from the fire. Her once-blonde hair had turned almost white.

Part of Peyton wanted to run to her, to hug her and tell her how good it was to see her again. But the rest of her wanted to shake her mother and yank that gun out of her hand.

Colin's gaze was riveted on Peyton. He didn't seem to notice—or care—that his house was burning to the ground. He gave her a subtle nod, as if to let her know he was okay. Then he looked past her, off to the left, and his jaw tightened into a hard line.

She turned around to see her brother running up to them, a look of fury on his face. "Mom? What are you doing? You were supposed to let me handle this."

"Colin McKenzie is still alive," she said. "You haven't *handled* anything."

"I didn't come here to kill him. I did exactly what I wanted." He waved toward the house, which was crackling and roaring on the other side of the lawn. "We need to go before the firemen and cops get here."

"No. He destroyed your life, Brian. He deserves to be punished."

Peyton took a step forward. Colin frowned and shook his head, but she ignored him. She had to. She couldn't do nothing and risk her mother pulling the trigger. Somehow, Peyton had to turn the tables, get the advantage. She took another step, and her mother turned the gun. On Peyton.

"Oh, Mom," she whispered brokenly. "What are you

doing? Why did you fake your death? And why would you destroy Brian's life by breaking him out of prison when he could have been a free man in a handful of years? If anyone has ruined his life, it's you."

Molly Sterling narrowed her eyes. "I'm dying, daughter. I don't have much longer. And prison was killing your brother, not that you noticed. I told your father a few years ago during a visit with Brian that we needed to come up with a plan to get him out. That he wasn't going to make it to when his sentence was up. Your father called us both fools and refused to see his own son after that. So I had to take matters into my own hands."

Peyton took another step closer, then another. "How did faking your death help Brian? I don't understand."

Her mother rolled her eyes. "I was carjacked, back in Memphis." She snorted. "Can you imagine? Turned out to be a blessing. Some homeless-looking woman took my purse, my jewelry, then drove off in my car. She hadn't gone a block before the fool ran off the road into a tree." She laughed again, as if the woman's death was funny.

Peyton's stomach clenched with nausea.

"I was going to call the police, then stopped," her mother continued. "I realized what a boon this was. I could disappear and no one would come looking for me. The accident must have ruptured the fuel tank. The whole car reeked of gas. All I had to do was reach in the broken window and take my lighter from my purse, then…" She shrugged, a mad light dancing in her eyes.

"Oh Mom," Peyton whispered, nearly choking on her grief and disgust at what her mother had done.

"Disappearing allowed me to work on my plan to get Brian out. Your father was watching me too closely. He saw I was searching on the internet for information about prison transports and threatened to call the police if I didn't stop."

She smiled at Brian, who was staring at her a short distance from Peyton, his mouth open in horror. "I had to break my baby out. As soon as that stupid lawyer of his filed another one of his ridiculous motions to get Brian a break from prison, I made my move." She laughed. "A break. Ha. I broke him out, little old me. All it took was a bribe to an overworked, underpaid van driver to weaken the lock on the back of the van."

Brian stepped closer to Peyton. "Peyton's right, Mom. If you hadn't interfered, I'd have been out soon. But you had to shoot that cop. If they catch me now, I'm facing the death penalty just because I ran, because I chose to escape like the other guys. They'll never believe that I wasn't in on your plan, that I didn't know you'd be there, or that you'd shoot anyone. I'm guilty by association."

Peyton sucked in a breath. "Mom? You killed Officer Jennings?"

"A mother will do anything to save her son. Don't you see?" She looked at Brian, her eyes imploring him to understand. "You were wasting away behind bars. You know you wouldn't have made it until the end of your sentence. I had to get you out, see you freed before I died."

Colin suddenly spun around and yanked the pistol out of Peyton's mother's hand. He whirled back toward Brian just as Brian brought up his own gun and leveled it at Colin.

"Brian!" Peyton yelled. "Don't!"

Her mother stumbled back, then circled closer to Peyton's brother. "Shoot him, Brian. That's what we came here for. Shoot him."

"Like you shot Officer Simmons at the old Sterling homestead?" Colin asked. "You left the body inside to lure me into the inferno. Did you hope I'd be killed in the fire?"

Brian's eyes widened. "Mom? No. Please tell me you didn't do that."

Colin sidled toward Peyton, keeping his gun trained on

Brian. But he stopped several yards away, probably to keep Brian's gun from pointing anywhere near her.

"How many people have you killed, Mrs. Sterling? There's Officer Jennings in Memphis, Officer Simmons, the three fugitives who escaped with Brian—"

"What?" Brian's eyes had gone even wider, his face losing all its color. "We tied them up so we could escape on our own, Mom. What did you do after I left to talk to Peyton?"

"The same thing she's done all along," Colin said. "Eliminated anyone who was an inconvenience. I'm guessing it all started with the sorority-house fire at your college, isn't that right Mrs. Sterling? What happened? Did one of the girls steal your boyfriend or something? So you decided to kill her?"

"What…what's he talking about?" Brian sounded confused, lost. His gun was still pointing at Colin, but he kept glancing at his mother.

Peyton clenched her hands at her sides, panic making her pulse rush in her ears. She was desperate to help but not sure what to do that wouldn't make things worse or get someone killed.

"Mom?" Brian asked again, his voice turning angry. "Is Colin telling the truth? You killed those men?"

"They don't matter," she said. "None of that matters."

Brian swore.

Peyton pressed a hand to her mouth, hot tears coursing down her cheeks. How had she never realized how twisted and evil her mother was?

Sirens sounded from down the mountain, just barely loud enough to be heard over the crackling of the fire.

"Drop your gun, Brian," Colin told him. "It's your only chance of getting out of here alive. Soon the mountains will be swarming with cops."

"Shoot him and let's go, before the cops get here," his mother urged.

Brian's gun wobbled.

"Don't, Brian," Peyton said. "I can't let you hurt him."

Colin frowned at her. "Stop it, Peyton," he whispered harshly.

He wanted to protect her. He obviously didn't want her trying anything. But these two screwed-up people in front of them were her family. She couldn't stand silently by while they discussed whether or not to kill the man she loved. She had to do something.

"I know you didn't start the barn fire, Brian," she said.

His wild-eyed gaze flicked to hers. "You're just saying that because you don't want me to shoot McKenzie."

"I don't want you to shoot him. You're right. I love him, very much. But I love you too. And I'm not lying when I tell you that I know you didn't torch the barn. I have proof, a picture. It shows mom inside the barn with the flames licking at the windows."

He frowned. "No way. I would have seen that picture at the trial."

"It's that smoking gun picture. We all looked at it a thousand times. But I looked at it again just a few days ago. And that's when I saw that forest-print fabric from Mom's dress in the lower edge of the window, just as the flames started. She was inside while you were taking the gas can out, thinking you were helping. She let you go to prison for her crimes. She didn't break you out of prison to see you free before she died. She broke you out to assuage her own guilt for letting you take the blame all these years. She didn't want to die with that guilt on her conscience."

Brian slowly turned his gun on his mother. "Is that true?"

His voice sounded so young, so bewildered and lost that it broke Peyton's heart.

Colin kept his gun trained on Peyton's brother. "Drop it, Brian."

"Mom?" Brian's voice cracked. "Mom?"

Her face crumpled, as if she'd finally realized that she'd lost the battle. Or was it all part of an act? Yet another lie to get what she wanted? "I'm sorry. I didn't know anyone was inside. And I didn't know you had run out with that can. I must have gone back in right after you ran out. If I'd known, I wouldn't have lit the match. I'm so sorry."

He slowly lowered his gun, a stricken look on his face. "You let me go to prison. All this time, you let me sit there, rotting away, when you were the one who should have been there."

Her mother sobbed, covering her face with her hands.

Brian turned his tortured gaze to Colin, then Peyton. "I wasn't in the woods that night, here, at the shooting. It was Mom. She's the one who called Dad asking for money for both of us. I didn't know until later." He drew a ragged breath. "She gave me the gun for my protection in case the police were with you when I went to meet you at the school. It didn't bother her one bit that she handed her son the gun she'd used to kill his father." His tortured gaze met Peyton's. "She killed him. She killed Dad." He shook his head, tears streaming down his face.

Most of the sirens seemed to have stopped down the mountain, probably at the Sterling house. But one of them was still coming, probably a fire truck investigating the second set of flames lighting up the sky.

"Forgive me, baby," her mother pleaded, sidling closer to Brian. "You have to forgive me."

He ignored her, staring at Peyton. "I love you. I'm sorry, for all of this. But I can't go back to prison. I just can't."

She saw the intent in his eyes. "Brian, no!"

He jerked the gun up and shot himself. He dropped to the ground.

"Brian!" She started toward him.

"Peyton!" Colin yelled.

Everything seemed to happen as if in slow motion.

Her mother threw herself to the ground, grabbing for Brian's pistol.

Peyton looked back at Colin.

He leaped toward her.

She twisted around to see her mother bringing up Brian's pistol and pointing it at her.

Boom!

Peyton was thrown to the ground, landing hard, her chin snapping against the hard dirt. Colin had slammed into her, knocking her out of the way just as her mother had squeezed the trigger. She pushed herself up and looked back.

Colin was on the ground a few feet away where he'd landed and rolled, blood blooming on his side. His pistol had fallen out of his hand when he'd knocked Peyton down. She jerked her head up to see her mother smiling a sickening smile as she stared at Colin, Brian's gun still in her hands as she slowly aimed once more. This time, at Colin's head.

"Mom! Over here!" Peyton flailed her arms in the air.

Her mother jerked the gun toward Peyton.

Boom! Boom! Boom!

Her mother stared at her in shock, then slowly crumpled to the ground.

Peyton gasped, then whirled around. Colin lay on his side, his pistol in his hands where he'd snatched it up. Once again, he'd saved her. But at what cost? The dirt was soaked in blood beneath him. The pistol fell from his fingers and he collapsed onto his back.

"Colin!" She scrambled forward on her knees.

"Freeze! Don't move!" someone yelled behind her, and she realized the police had finally arrived.

She ignored them and hurried to Colin. He blinked up at her, as if having trouble focusing. The tears she'd thought had dried up flooded her eyes as she pressed her hand against his side, trying to staunch the flow of blood.

He gasped and gritted his teeth.

"I'm sorry. I'm sorry. I have to stop the bleeding. Damn it, Colin. You should have shot my mother before she got Brian's gun back. Then she couldn't have hurt you."

He blinked up at her. "She's your mother. Didn't want you to hate me. Didn't want to shoot her."

"Oh, Colin. I could never hate you."

Rough hands grabbed her from behind. "Ma'am, back off."

"No, let me go! I have to put pressure on the wound."

Police were swarming across the yard, running toward them.

"Leave her alone," Colin rasped. "She's not one of the shooters. Leave her alone."

The policeman let her go and she scrambled to Colin's side, once again pressing against his wound.

"Get an ambulance," she yelled over her shoulder. "Marshal McKenzie has been shot."

"We're here," some EMTs yelled, scrambling toward them with their kits in their hands.

"Over here," one of the policemen shouted, waving at the EMTs as he knelt beside her mother. "This one's still alive. She's in rough shape."

"We've got another one over here," another policeman yelled. "GSW to the head, but he's still with us."

Peyton blinked. "Brian?" She saw the EMTs change direction and veer toward her brother and her mom. "No!" She glared at the EMTs. "McKenzie first. Get over here. Now!"

Another pair of EMTs seemed to materialize out of thin air and knelt beside Colin.

"Ma'am, please. You need to move out of the way and let us help him."

"He's bleeding. I can't move my hand. He's bleeding." Her tears ran down her face, dripping off her chin.

"I know, ma'am. We're going to help him. You need to let go."

"Peyton?"

She blinked furiously at her tears and looked down. "Colin?"

He lifted his hand and wiped at her tears. "I'm okay. I'll be okay. Let them do their job, sweetheart."

She blinked, then moved back, letting the EMTs take over. She scrambled around to his other side and stroked his hair as they put an oxygen mask over his face.

He lifted it up. "Don't cry, Peyton. They're working on your family. They'll do everything they can. Don't cry."

She pushed his hand away and put the mask over his nose and mouth. "I'm not crying for them, you silly man. I'm crying for you. You're my family. You always have been, always will be. I'm crying for you."

Chapter Twenty-Four

Peyton barely paid attention to the beautiful mountains and acres of green grass and trees surrounding them. She was too busy keeping a close watch on Colin since he insisted on driving the ATV. Even at a snail's pace, she could tell it was jarring his side, causing him pain. He was infuriating, refusing to follow doctor's orders and take it easy.

"If you rip out your stitches again, I'm going to let you bleed to death. Maybe then you'll finally learn your lesson and do what the doctor tells you to do."

"If you let me bleed to death, I won't be around to learn my lesson."

"Technicalities. Seriously, Colin. This is insane. It's only been three weeks since the shooting. The most *recent* shooting. Good grief. You've been shot twice in less than two months. You should be home in bed instead of driving me halfway across the mountain." She grimaced. "I mean at your parents' home, since *The Evil Ones* destroyed your beautiful house."

He gave her an admonishing look and steered around a fallen tree. "You need to quit calling your mom and brother *The Evil Ones*. They aren't evil. They're…mentally unstable. They need our sympathy, not our scorn."

"Yes, well. You can give them sympathy. I'll give them scorn."

He smiled and shook his head. A few minutes later, he

finally stopped the ATV. "Come on, my little protector," he teased. "Help me off this thing."

She hopped down and untied his crutches from the back. "You're not even supposed to be walking. Who gave you these things anyway? I don't see how they really help when you've been shot in the side. You should—"

He cupped his hand over her mouth. "Maybe you should take up baking again when you're rattled. My ears could use a rest."

She handed him the crutches and then put her hands on her hips. "Not funny. And I'm pretty sure I'm never baking again. It reminds me too much of my mother."

He eased down from the driver's seat and leaned on his crutches. "I heard she's doing surprisingly well, recovering from her gunshot wounds and responding to chemo and radiation. And there's hope for Brian too. The bullet lodged in his skull but they've managed to control the swelling. It's a miracle, really, that both of them are recovering so well."

She walked beside him, bending down to move sticks and rocks out of his way as he slowly ambled across the grass. "I wouldn't know. I haven't seen either of them."

He stopped.

She looked up at him, her brow furrowed. "Are you okay? Do you need me to bring the ATV over here so you can sit?"

"Why haven't you visited them? The trials are a long way off. You should take advantage of this time while they're both in the hospital and you can see them every day if you want."

She shook her head. "I chose you, Colin. I'll never make that mistake again. I'll always choose you."

He sighed heavily. "That's what I was afraid you'd say."

She frowned. "I don't understand."

He smoothed the hair back from her face. "I was wrong

to ever say that to you, about choices. I was bitter, angry. I wanted you to put me first, before all others."

"I do. I will. I always should have."

He shook his head. "No. I mean, yes, we love each other. We should always look out for each other. But there's room in our lives for other people too. I never should have expected you to choose between me and your family. No matter what they'd done, no matter how sick or disturbed they may be, they're still your mother and brother. And I know that deep inside, you can't help but love them. I want you to know that it's okay to love them. And if you want to see them, I'm okay with it. I'll even go with you if you want."

Tears filled her eyes. "Dang it, Colin. You're making me cry again."

"I really do need to buy some stock in that tissue company you mentioned before."

She smiled through her tears. "You're such a good person. Far more forgiving than I think I'll ever be. But thank you. I'll think about it."

"That's all I ask. Now, I'd really appreciate it if you'd pay attention to your surroundings for a moment."

"I am."

He sighed and motioned with his head over her shoulder. "Not to me. To where we are. Turn around."

She did, then gasped. "Colin. It's…we're…oh my gosh. The beautiful meadow, and the mountains over there, and, oh, the waterfall. It's still pristine, so perfect. This is our secret spot, where we used to sneak off for hours in high school." She pointed to a spot near the waterfall. "That's where we first kissed."

"No. It isn't."

She frowned and turned back to him. "It isn't?"

He shook his head. "The first time we kissed was on the playground in second grade. You knocked me down and planted a big sloppy wet one right on my lips." He grinned. "That's the day I fell in love with you."

She blinked and wiped at a new flood of tears. "Oh, Colin. That's the sweetest thing. I didn't remember that."

"I remember every minute of my life with you."

"Tissues, dang it. I need a tissue." She swiped at her ears again.

"I'll kiss all your tears away in a minute. But there's one more thing you need to see. Turn around again. And this time, look down in the valley, on the other side of the waterfall."

She turned around. "What am I looking for, exactly?"

"Something orange."

"Orange? I don't…" She slowly turned back to face him. "Are those…property markers?"

"They're property stakes, yes. They mark the corners where the foundation of our new home is going to be built."

"Our new home?"

"I bought this land, our special place. And I want to build a future with you here, just like we always dreamed." He shifted one of his crutches and reached into his pocket, then held out a black velvet box toward her.

Her hands shook as she opened the lid. "That has to be the most beautiful thing I've ever seen."

"Not even close."

She glanced up at him in question.

"You," he said. "Nothing and no one is more beautiful than you."

She shook her head. "Those pain pills must be making you loopy. You're getting all mushy and silly."

"Then I must be doing this right." He shifted both crutches to one hand, and started to bend down.

She grabbed his arms, stopping him. "Don't you dare get down on one knee. I'll never be able to get you up again."

He grimaced and straightened. "You might be right. But I wanted this to be perfect for you."

She pulled the ring out of the box and handed it to him. "Just pop the question okay? That's all I need for this to be perfect."

He grinned. "Peyton Sterling, will you marry me?"

"Yes!" She was so excited she could barely hold still as he slid the ring onto her finger. She wiggled it in the sunlight, watching it sparkle. Then she threw her arms around his neck. "I love you, Colin McKenzie. More than you could ever know."

"And I love you, the future Mrs. McKenzie. Always have, always will."

"Would you just kiss me already?"

He was laughing as he pressed his lips to hers.

* * * * *

MISSING IN THE MOUNTAINS

JULIE ANNE LINDSEY

MISSING IN THE MOUNTAINS

JULIE ANNE LINDSEY

Chapter One

Chapter One

Emma Hart couldn't shake the unsettling notion that something was wrong. The sensation had pestered her all day, needling away at her calm. Though she hadn't said so, her sister and housemate, Sara, seemed to feel it too. Sara had hunched over her cell phone and a notebook most of the day, barely speaking or touching her dinner. It wasn't like Sara to be inside short of a blizzard, yet there she was. All day.

Emma had thrown herself into the tedium of housework and the exhaustion of new-mommy duties, hoping to keep her mind off the inexplicable feeling that trouble was afoot. Nothing had worked. The prickle over her skin that had raised the hair on her arms and itched in her mind since dawn refused to let up, even now as the gorgeous setting sun nestled low on the horizon between distant mountains. If there was a silver lining, it was that the peculiar day was finally nearing its end, and tomorrow was always better.

She crossed her ankles on the old back-porch swing and shifted her attention to the beautiful gold and apricot hues spilling over everything in sight, including her perfect baby boy, Henry. Emma hoisted him off her lap and wiggled him in the air until a wide toothless grin emerged. There was the thing she lived for. A smile spread over her lips as she brought him down to her chest. "Someday I'm going to teach you to rope and ride, the way your granddaddy taught Sara and me." It would have been nice if Henry's father was around to teach him those things the way her father had taught her, but it didn't do to dwell on what wasn't, not when the things that were tended to be so fleeting.

Henry's daddy was a soldier on leave when they'd met, but he'd been raised a cowboy. Brought up on a ranch like hers, not too far from there, but he'd been deployed before she'd known she was pregnant, and despite the voice message she'd left asking him to call her, he never had. Of course, that wasn't a surprise since the next time she'd tried to call him the number was no longer in service. The local news hadn't announced his death the way they often did when a local soldier was lost, so she could only assume he'd survived that "eight week" mission he'd gone on nearly a year ago and had simply chosen to avoid her after his return. Whenever she thought of how his selfishness would force Henry to grow up without a father, Emma was glad he hadn't died on that mission. This way, if she ever saw him again, she could kill him herself.

Emma forced down the bitter knot rising in her throat and worked a pleasant smile over her lips. "You will always be enough for me," she promised Henry, "and I will be enough for you. Whatever that means on any given day. Always." She nuzzled his sun-kissed cheek, then stretched onto her feet as the last orange fingers of the sunlight slid out of view, replaced with the tranquil blues of twilight. "What do you say about a warm bath and fuzzy jammies before your nighttime bottle?" she asked. Now she needed a distraction from the icky feeling that had followed her all day *and* from the frustration of a man who'd probably forgotten her name.

Emma jumped as the back door flew open, her knuckles colliding sharply with the handle. "What on earth!"

Sara stood on the threshold, one palm on the door, skin pale as the rising moon. "You need to come inside. Now," she gasped. "Hurry."

Emma obeyed, and Sara locked the door behind them, then checked the window locks and pulled the curtains. Without speaking again, she moved to the next room and did the same.

"What's going on?" Emma followed on her sister's heels, fear riding high in her gut. "Why are you doing that?" They only battened down the hatches if the news predicted heavy winds or rain. "It's a beautiful night. There's no storm coming."

"You're wrong about that," Sara mumbled.

Emma hurried around her sister, forcing herself into Sara's path. "Hey. What's that supposed to mean?"

Sara shot her a remorseful look, letting her gaze slide briefly to Henry, then back to her work. "I need you to listen to me and do as I say. We have to be quiet." Her hands trembled as she reached for the nearest light switch and flipped it off. Her face whipped back in Emma's direction a moment later. "Is your truck in the garage? Or the driveway?"

"Garage."

"Good." She nodded, her eyes frantic.

"Hey." Emma set her hand on Sara's. "Stop." Her sister never behaved this way. She was naturally calm to the extreme, cool in a crisis and found the positive in everything. Whatever had her so worked up was enough to make Emma want to pack a bag and move. "You're scaring me. Tell me what's going on."

Fat tears welled in Sara's eyes. "I can't."

"Sara," Emma demanded, using her most pointed tone without upsetting Henry, "you can tell me anything. You know that. I don't understand what's happened. You were fine at dinner."

Sara snorted, a derisive, ugly sound. "Was I?"

"Weren't you?" Emma grabbed hold of her sister's wrist, a lifelong stubborn streak piercing her forced calm.

Before she could answer, a set of headlights flashed over the front window, and Sara froze. "Don't make any noise," she said, looking half-ill. "We're not home."

Suddenly Sara's erratic behavior began making sense. "Is this the reason you're locking us up like Fort Knox?" Emma asked. "You knew someone was coming?" Someone who obviously terrified her. "Who?"

Sara jerked her arm free and went to peek through the living room curtain. "Hide," she seethed. "You're in danger. Henry's in danger. We all are. Now, go! Keep him quiet. Find his pacifier." Her rasping whisper cut through Emma's heart, and she pressed her back to the nearest wall, away from the front window.

"Not until you tell me what's going on," Emma shot back in a harsh whisper.

Heavy footfalls rumbled across the porch, and someone rapped against the door in loud, demanding strikes until Emma was sure the door would fall down.

"I'm calling the police," Emma said. "If you won't tell me what's going on, then you can tell them."

Henry started in her arms. He released a small whimper as the pounding continued.

Sara turned to them. Her eyes were wide, her face the

perfect mask of horror and resolve. "Hide first. Call the police after." She rubbed her palms against her jeans and stepped forward, toward the rattling door.

"Where are you going?"

Sara gave Emma a pleading look, then swallowed hard. "I'm going to answer the door before he breaks it down. If you hide, he'll assume I'm alone, and you'll be safe, but I won't give him what he wants."

Emma's stomach twisted and coiled with nausea. "What does he want?"

Sara took another step.

"I won't leave you."

Sara shot one determined glance over her shoulder. "Your job is to protect Henry. Mine is to protect you. Now, hide."

Terror gripped Emma, and she snagged the cordless phone handset from the wall, immediately dialing the local police department. She ducked around the edge of the living room wall, hiding just out of sight in the long hallway that led to the bedrooms. "Come on," she urged, impatient for the ringing call to connect.

The dead bolt snicked back in the next room. The door swung open on squeaky hinges.

"I've already called the police," Sara said coldly in lieu of a proper greeting.

A choking gasp cracked through the silence a moment later.

Emma sucked air. Horrific images of what could have caused such a sound raced through her head. There were no more words in the silent home. Just the low gurgling of someone desperate for air. Emma prayed the sound wasn't coming from Sara.

A tinny voice broke through the phone speaker at her ear. "Knox Ridge Police Department."

Emma inched toward the end of the hall, ignoring the woman on the line. Desperate to know her sister was okay, she counted silently to three, then peeked her head around the corner, chest tight with fear.

A man in head-to-toe black, a ski mask and leather gloves had one giant hand wrapped around Sara's throat while she clawed uselessly at his fingers. Her eyes were wild, bulging, her mouth gaping for air. The man raised a pistol in his free hand.

Hot tears rushed over Emma's eyes. She had the police on the phone, but couldn't speak. If the man heard her, he might use his gun on Sara. *Or on Henry.*

Hide. Sara's desperate voice echoed in Emma's addled mind. *Protect Henry.*

"Knox Ridge Police Department," the woman on the phone repeated. Her small voice suddenly sounded like a booming gong.

Henry bunched his face and opened his quivering lips, a scream poised to break.

Emma took one last too-risky look into the living room, needing assurance her sister hadn't been choked to death while she'd stood helplessly by and deliberated over what to do next.

The man tossed Sara onto the couch like a rag doll and climbed on top of her in a flash. He lowered his face to hers and growled through the mask. "Who did you tell?" He pinned her hands overhead and pressed them hard into the cushions until they vanished from sight.

"No one." Sara choked out the words, still coughing and gasping for air. "No one. I have no one to tell. I swear it."

Henry released a warning cry, and the man's face snapped in Emma's direction.

Emma rocked back on socked feet and took off like a bullet down the hallway. Henry bounced and jostled in her arms as she pressed him to her chest and gripped the phone between one ear and shoulder. She slid and scooted as adrenaline forced her legs faster than her feet could find purchase on the hard, slick floors.

"What was that?" the man asked, footsteps already falling through the living room, nearing the hall at a clip.

"Cat!" Sara yelped. "It was only the cat."

Emma snatched their mean old barn cat off the hallway windowsill on her way to the master bedroom, and she threw him into the space behind her. He'd surely bite her the next time he saw her, but she'd gladly choose to face off with him rather than whoever was attempting to murder Sara.

The cat screeched and hissed, claws skidding over the wide wooden planks as he slid in the direction of Sara and the masked lunatic.

The footfalls stopped.

Emma barreled into her closet and pulled the door shut behind her. Her heart hammered and her chest ached. She climbed through the clothes racks, over boxes and blankets and shoes, then curled herself around her son and shushed him out of a fast-approaching fit.

Several wild heartbeats later, the footfalls retreated back toward her sister, who she hoped had had the good sense to run.

"Who did you tell?" the man's voice came again, impossibly angrier.

Emma's heart fell. Sara hadn't run.

"Ma'am?" the voice asked through the phone. "Miss Hart? Caller ID shows this as the Hart residence?"

What was happening? *Why* was it happening?

"Miss Hart," the woman persisted.

"Yes," she whispered, finally finding her voice. She cringed with each terrorizing demand of the intruder in the next room. *Who did you tell?*

Sara screamed.

Her gut-wrenching wail ripped through the rafters, the drywall and Emma's soul. "Someone is hurting my sister," she whispered. "Please, hurry."

Emma's gaze darted through the dark space. If only she hadn't moved her daddy's rifles into a gun safe after Henry was born. If only Henry was sleeping in his crib, and she could trust him not to scream. If only she could help Sara.

A deafening crack stopped her ragged thoughts. The sound of skin on skin. A brain-jarring slap. Or jaw-breaking punch. Every sound was amplified in the impossibly still home. Emma heard the muted thud of a collapsing body.

Then no more screaming. No more demanding growls. Just silence.

Outside, the rumble of an engine drew hope to Emma's heart. The psychopath was leaving. Whatever condition Sara was in, at least she hadn't been shot, and the police were on the way. Sara would be okay, and she would tell them everything so the son of a gun who did this to her would pay.

Emma crept from her hiding spot and raced to her bedroom window, confirming the empty driveway before racing back down the hallway, heart in her throat and preparing to provide triage while they awaited the first responders.

On a deep intake of air, she shored her nerve at the end of the hallway, tucked Henry tight to her chest and dared a peek into her living room.

But all that remained of her sister was a thick smear of blood on the polished wooden floor.

Chapter Two

Sawyer Lance, former Army Ranger and cofounder of Fortress Security, reached reluctantly for the ringing phone. It was late and he was tired. Protecting civilians was harder than he'd predicted when opening the private sector security firm. Far more challenging than similar work overseas where he could at least shoot the bad guys. He tossed another pair of aspirin into his mouth before blindly raising the phone from his desk.

What would it be this time? Another punk ex-husband or boyfriend bullying the woman he claimed to love? An unhinged stranger stalking a woman who didn't know he existed beyond the fact he harassed her anonymously with creepy unwanted gifts and the occasional break-in? "Fortress," he answered, his voice little better than a bark. "This is Sawyer Lance."

The long pause that followed was nearly cause for him to hang up. Instead, he rubbed his forehead, knowing sometimes frightened folks needed time to gather their thoughts.

"Fortress," he repeated, becoming alert at the sound of soft breaths through the line. His muscles tensed. "If this is an emergency, you need to call 911 and get yourself to safety. Call me after. Police first."

He waited.

The quiet breathing continued.

"I can contact your local authorities if you're unable." Sawyer pulled the phone away from his ear and checked the caller ID. "Can you tell me your..." Two little words graced the screen and nearly ripped a hole through his chest. *Emma. Hart.* Sawyer's heart seized, and his lungs seemed to stop midexhale. "Emma?"

Emma Hart had been the only woman Sawyer ever imagined a future with, and a set of monsters overseas had stolen that from him. He'd been forced to say good-bye to her for the sake of a simple eight-week mission. That mission should have brought him right up to his last day in the service. Instead, it had gotten him captured and tortured. His team had gotten worse.

"You're alive," she said, a snare of accusation in her voice.

"Yeah." If she wanted to call it that. He'd fought six long months to get away from his captors and back to the secluded US military base. Another two months before he was debriefed and returned stateside. More weeks before the long-overdue discharge.

"Yet, you never called," she said.

Emma's message had been the last one left on his cell phone before the service was disconnected. The cell contract had ended while he was overseas, trapped for months past the contract's renewal date. He'd planned to get a new phone after the mission, after he'd returned stateside and been discharged. He'd even told himself Emma's number would be the first one he'd call. It was one of many plans his captivity had ruined.

"No," he answered finally, sadly.

He hadn't returned her call for multiple reasons. Part

of him knew he wasn't ready to do normal things again, like date, or pretend he didn't wake up in cold sweats most nights. The rest of him doubted Emma was in the market for a 180-pound sack of misplaced anger, jangled nerves and general distrust. He couldn't make her happy anymore. *She'd sounded so darn happy on that voice mail.* Unlike now, he realized.

Instinct stiffened Sawyer's spine. "What's wrong?" Something in her voice set him on edge. She might've been mad at him, but there was something else there too.

"Sara's gone," she said, her voice breaking on the second word.

"Gone?" he repeated. His mind scrambled to make sense of the word. "How? When?"

"Tonight," she said. "He just came in here and took her."

Sawyer was already on his feet, gathering his things, shoving a fresh magazine into his sidearm. "Who?"

"I don't know. She told me to hide."

He slowed, pressing a folding knife and wallet into his pocket. "So, Sara's alive? Just missing?"

"I don't know if she's alive," Emma snapped, "but she's not *just missing*. She was choked, overpowered, hit and dragged away. There's nothing *just* about it."

"Of course." Sawyer shook his head hard, moving faster toward the exit. "I meant no disrespect. I'm only gathering facts." He stooped to grab his go-bag and a duffel of supplies from the closet floor. "What did the police say?"

"They're looking into it."

Sawyer blew out a humorless half laugh. So, the police were chasing their tails and waiting for Sara to appear on their laps. "I'm glad you called. I can keep you safe." He swung his laptop bag over one shoulder on his way out the door.

"You always talked about your plans to open Fortress Security with Wyatt," Emma said. "I figured he'd answer the call. I hoped he'd remember me and be willing to help. I didn't know what else to do."

"You did the right thing," he assured her.

"I know the last thing you probably want to do is see me—" her voice was strangled and tight "—but I'm scared, and I need help."

"I'm already on the way," Sawyer said, tossing his bags into his pickup, then climbing behind the wheel. "Are you home?"

"Yeah."

He gunned the engine to life and jammed the shifter into Drive. "I'm heading your way from the office. I won't be an hour."

"Okay."

He listened keenly to a few more rattling breaths.

"Sawyer?"

The quaver in her voice was a punch through his gut. "Yeah."

"You should have called."

EMMA'S WORDS HAUNTED him as he made the trip to her family ranch at a record pace, nearly doubling the posted speed limits whenever possible. The desolate country roads were poorly lit but easily navigated. At times, long stretches between darkened fields made visibility clear for miles, and Sawyer took full advantage. The hillier, curvier portions got a good cussing.

He hit the gravel under the carved Hart Ranch sign with a deep crunch and grind. Stones pinged and bounced against the undercarriage of his pickup, flying out in a cloud of dust behind him.

A small silhouette paced the porch. Long hair drifting in the wind around her face, exactly like the ghost from his past that she was. She went still when he started his walk across the lawn.

Sawyer pulled the cowboy hat off his head and pressed it to his aching chest. "Emma." His lungs seemed to fill fully for the first time since answering her call.

She gave a small nod, running the pads of both thumbs beneath red puffy eyes and brushing shaky palms over flushed cheeks. "Hello, Sawyer."

He took a step closer, and she wrapped her arms around a new, curvier figure. Sawyer tried not to stare, but the change looked damn good on her. So did the spark of ferocity in her eyes. He didn't know what had sparked the fire, but whatever it was, the change suited her. And it would help her get through the tough days ahead. Unfortunately, civilian abductions weren't known for their happy endings.

She appraised him as he climbed the steps. Her smart blue eyes scrutinized the visible scars along his neck and forearms, pausing briefly at the angry, puckered skin above his left eye. Then swiftly moving on to the lines of black ink circling his biceps beneath one shirtsleeve. "Thank you for coming."

"Of course."

Behind her, the small sound of a crying baby drifted through the open door.

Emma's chin ticked up. She turned immediately. "Come in. I've been through all of Sara's things, and I have something I want you to look at."

Sawyer followed. His heart clenched as the baby's

cries grew more fervent. "Sara had a baby?" He tried to imagine it and failed. The willowy blonde had more interest in horses than men when he'd briefly known her.

"No." Emma grabbed the flashing baby monitor and shut it off as she passed through the dimly lit family room. "You can have a seat. I'll only be a minute."

"Are you babysitting?" he asked, ignoring her order and following her down the hall toward the bedrooms, unwilling to let her out of his sight and drawn by a strange tether to the infant's cry. "Was the baby here when Sara was taken?"

Emma opened her bedroom door and strode inside. A crib stood against the wall across from her bed. "No," she said, "and yes."

Sawyer paused at the end of the crib, puzzling over her unnecessary coyness. "You aren't babysitting?" he asked dumbly, watching as she raised the kicking blue bundle into her arms and slid a pacifier into the baby's mouth with practiced skill.

"No," she whispered, rocking the infant gently into sedation. "This is Henry." She turned a pride-filled smile in Sawyer's direction. "I named him after my father."

Sawyer's gut rolled against his spine. His jaw locked, and his fingers curled into fists at his sides. This was what had changed her. The carefree woman he'd known had been made into her own kind of soldier in his absence. Emma was a mother. "He's yours," Sawyer said, repeating the fact, trying to make it real for him. The words were bittersweet on his tongue. Any joy he might've felt for her was tainted selfishly with feelings of loss for himself. With regret. And thoughts of things that might have been. "You have a son."

"I do," she answered as Henry worked the pacifier in his tiny mouth. "And so do you."

EMMA HELD HER tongue as she waited for a response. She could practically see the wheels turning in Sawyer's head, adding up time, weeks, months. She ground her teeth against the need for an explanation. She hadn't been with anyone else since Sawyer. He'd barely left the States before she knew she was pregnant. If Henry's perfect olive skin and pale blue eyes weren't enough proof, then maybe Sawyer should look in a mirror.

"Mine?" His gaze jumped continually between her face and Henry's.

"Yes." She moved past him toward the hallway. "I need to sit down. You probably should too."

She led Sawyer back into the living room, giving a wide berth to the freshly bleached floorboards where Sara's blood had been spilled. She took a seat on the chair farthest from the couch where the monster had pinned her sister. It took effort to force the still-raw images from her mind.

Sawyer squatted on the floor in front of her chair, jeans pulled tight against his strong thighs, big hands dangling between his knees as he balanced, a look of shock and confusion etched on his brow. "Why didn't you tell me?"

Emma pursed her lips, culling the desire to scream. "I tried." She made each word stand on its own, tempted to recite all the one-sided arguments she'd practiced to perfection in the shower all these months since his "eight week" mission ended.

"I got a message from you," he said. "Did you know you were pregnant when you left the voice mail?"

The accusation in his tone ignited a fire in her belly. "That was why I called. I'd just confirmed with my doctor, and I was happy," she snapped.

"Then why didn't you tell me? Why would you keep something like this from me? I'm a father, Emma. A *father* and I had no idea."

"You could have returned my call," she said.

"You could've told me in the voice mail."

"I didn't want to tell you something this important in a voice mail. I wanted to tell you in person, and you were supposed to be home in two more weeks, and I spent every one of those last fourteen days deciding how I'd deliver the surprise. Maybe with some cutesy sign or a little custom-made onesie." She shook her head. "I can see it was stupid of me now, but I was *thrilled* to be having your baby, and you had your phone number changed."

"I didn't have my number changed." Sawyer ground the words through clenched teeth.

"Disconnected then," she conceded, "without the courtesy of letting me know first. You made it clear you didn't want to hear from me again, and you didn't want to call me either, or you would have."

"That isn't what happened."

Emma squinted her eyes, wishing she could scream and yell and lose control, but she refused to frighten Henry or give Sawyer the satisfaction of seeing her so rattled. Instead, she said, "I called your number every month after my prenatal appointment, and I listened to the notification that your number had been disconnected. I forced myself to remember you were done with me, even if my heart wasn't done with you, and you have no idea what that was like for me."

His frustrated expression fell slowly into a grimace. "I

wasn't home when you left that voice mail. I didn't even get it until last month."

"Then you should have called last month."

"How could I have known this?" he asked, extending a hand toward the baby in her arms. "It's been more than a year since we've spoken. I assumed you'd moved on."

Her eyebrows shot up. "I did. I'm fine. We're fine," she said, casting a gaze at her son. "I had to get my act together, with or without you, and I had to find peace for Henry's sake. So I stopped calling you, and I let us go."

He fixed a heated gaze on her, his face wrought with emotion. Hurt, frustration, regret. "What would've happened if Sara hadn't been taken today?" he asked. "I would've just gone on with my life having no idea I was a father?"

Emma glared back, wind sucked from her chest. She wanted to shove him hard and knock him onto his backside, but there wasn't time for that. "We can fight about this later. Right now I need to figure out what happened to Sara," she said. "I found a notebook full of numbers hidden in her room. Will you look at it for me and see if it makes any sense to you?"

"How old is he?" Sawyer asked, unmoved by her change of subject. His gaze was locked on Henry. "When was he born? What did he weigh?"

Emma steadied her nerves and wet her lips. Those were fair enough questions. "His name is Henry Sawyer Hart. He's four months old, born June 8 at 8:17 a.m. He weighed eight pounds, eleven ounces. He was twenty-one inches long."

"You gave him my name."

"Middle name. It seemed like the right thing to do."

Sawyer pressed the heels of his hands to his eyes and dug them in.

"Why didn't you call?" she asked again, needing to know once and for all what had happened between their last passionate night of love declarations and the dead silence that began afterward and never ended.

Sawyer dropped his hands from his eyes. He stretched onto his feet and braced broad hands over narrow hips. Warning flared in his eyes. There was a debate going on in that head of his, but his lips were sealed tight.

Maybe he didn't have a reason. Maybe he didn't want to admit their time together had been nothing more than a fling. Not real to him like it had been to her. It was easy to see he wasn't the same guy she'd fallen in love with. The man before her was hard and distant. Not the man who'd swept her into his arms and twirled her until she was breathless with laughter.

Maybe that guy had never been real.

Emma's throat tightened as the look on his face grew pained. "Never mind. You don't owe me an explanation." She lifted Sara's notebook from the end table beside her and extended it to Sawyer. "Here. Let's just move on. Maybe there's something in there that will help the police figure out who took her and why. She's been gone twenty-four hours already, and our odds of finding her diminish significantly after seventy-two."

Sawyer caught the narrow book in his fingertips and held her gaze. "My team and I were captured. They were killed."

Emma's mouth fell open. "What?"

"They died. I didn't. I've only been home a few weeks. My cell service plan wasn't renewed on time because I wasn't home, so it was canceled. I didn't change the number or disconnect the phone. I wasn't thinking about any of that. I was trying to survive, and I don't want to talk about what happened."

She worked her mouth shut. Her own harsh words crashed back to mind like a ton of bricks. She'd blamed him for not returning her calls without bothering to ask why he hadn't. She'd assumed the worst, that he'd avoided her intentionally, played her for a fool, never realizing that him avoiding her was hardly the worst thing that could have happened. Her gaze snapped back to the scars. Thick, raised marks across his skin that weren't there a year ago. On his neck and arms. What looked like the results of a serious burn above his left eye. "Sawyer."

He lifted a palm. "Don't."

Emma cradled Henry tighter, comforting the one piece of Sawyer that would allow it. She'd heard stories, saw movies and read books about men who'd been through similar things, losing their teams, being held against their wills. There was a common thread to every man's story. Their experiences had wrecked them.

"I know what your sister is going through," Sawyer said, "not the physical details, but emotionally. Mentally." His serious blue eyes rose to meet her gaze. "I'll help find her," he said. "And I will keep you and Henry safe while I do."

Emma nodded. "Thank you."

He carried the notebook to the couch where Sara had fought with her attacker, and collapsed onto the cushions. He spread the notebook open across his palms, but his gaze continually moved to Emma's before sliding back to Henry.

"What?" Emma finally asked, her heart warming

and softening toward the man she'd thought had tossed her away.

His eyes flashed dark and protective, but he didn't look away from his son. "You should've left that message."

Chapter Three

Sawyer didn't sleep. Emma had taken the barely manageable wreckage of his life and flipped it on its head. She might as well have flipped *him* on his head. He was a father.

The words had circled endlessly in his mind as he pored over the contents of Sara's notebook and made multiple trips down the hallway to check on Emma and Henry. *His son.*

A son he hadn't even known existed until a few hours ago. He might've never known about Henry at all if something horrible hadn't happened to Sara, forcing Emma to reach out for help. And Henry could've grown up thinking his father was the kind of man who would run out on a woman and his son.

It made him madder every time he thought about it.

He'd nearly missed the most important part of his life because pride had stopped him from returning Emma's call. And it sure wouldn't have killed her to add the life-changing detail to her message.

The glow of a pending sunrise hovered on the horizon when he finally put Sara's notebook on the kitchen table and went to make coffee. Down the hall, he heard the stirring sounds of Emma and his baby. Sawyer set the coffee to brew, then opened the refrigerator. By the time Emma and Henry emerged from their shared room, Sawyer had a simple breakfast prepared for two. "I hope you don't mind," he said. "Restless hands."

Emma stopped at the kitchen's edge, Henry on one hip. She'd dressed in nice-fitting blue jeans and a long-sleeved thermal shirt that hugged all her new curves in the nicest of ways. Her straight brown hair hung over her shoulders and feathered across her forehead.

Sawyer longed to run his fingers through the strands and pull her against him. He wanted to comfort her. To make promises for Sara's safety that he couldn't keep. He'd promised to find her, but if he didn't do that fast... His mind wandered to images of his fallen team.

"You didn't sleep," Emma said, fastening Henry into a high chair.

"Rarely do." He lifted a pan full of eggs from the stove and flicked the burner off, forcing his thoughts back to the present. "Hungry?"

"I don't know." She went to the counter to make a bottle for Henry. A moment later she took the seat beside the high chair and poised the bottle to Henry's lips. "I feel like none of this is real. Like I'm waiting to wake up from a nightmare."

Sawyer cleared his throat. "You should try to put a little something in your stomach."

Henry sucked greedily on the bottle, peering at Sawyer with big blue eyes. His denim overalls had little horses embroidered on the knees, and his tiny brown socks were printed to look like cowboy boots.

Sawyer's hands itched to hold him, but he divided the eggs onto two plates instead, then poured twin cups of coffee for Emma and himself. The idea of holding something as precious as Henry frightened him, and Sawyer was rarely afraid. He took a seat beside Emma at the table and wrapped calloused palms around the small white mug. His hands had done awful things in the name of freedom. His hands were meant for hard labor, for holding rifles and following orders.

Emma took a slice of plain toast from the pile he'd plated and set between them, and bit into the corner. "What did you think of Sara's notebook? It was hidden so it must be important, right?"

"Maybe." Sawyer dug a fork into his breakfast. "Sara works at a bank, right?"

"Credit union," Emma said. "She's an account specialist, and she had that notebook with her all day before she was taken. I found it hidden in a basket of dirty clothes. She must've put it there when she realized that man was coming for her."

Sawyer cleaned his plate and grabbed a second slice of toast. "I want to visit her office today. I wasted a ton of time overlooking the obvious. I was looking at the numbers like a soldier. Trying to solve them like a cipher. First, I assumed they were a code. When that didn't work, I imagined them as dates and times or map coordinates, addresses, you name it." He gave a humorless chuckle. "Eventually I remembered Sara works at the credit union. Those numbers are probably a list of accounts. She's just jammed them all together, probably to disguise them."

Emma finished her toast and took away the empty baby bottle. "What are you going to do at the credit union?"

"I want to find out if she was working on any special projects. If any accounts or customers might've been giving her trouble, and if she seemed like herself the last few times she was in. I'd also really like to get a look at her desk. See if she kept any more notebooks like that one." He tipped his head toward the book on the table.

Emma unbuckled Henry from the high chair. "The police will probably be asking the same things today. The staff will be leery and guarded after that. Everyone loves Sara, and they don't know you. I doubt anyone will be candid with a stranger given what's happened." She turned Henry against her chest and patted his back. "I'll go. They know me. I'll ask to see her desk and try to collect anything that might be of interest. Then we can go through it here in privacy. If we find anything that leads to more specific questions, we can go back after lunch and ask."

Sawyer frowned. "I think you'd better let me be the face of this for you. As it is, whoever took Sara doesn't seem interested in you, and I'd rather you not get involved. Her abductor didn't even search the house while he was here. His mission was pointed. Not at you, and I'd like to keep it that way."

Emma chewed her lip, cheeks flushed with distress. "I'm Sara's only sister and I live with her. How long do you really think it will take before he comes for me? For Henry? If she doesn't give up whatever it is that he wants from her?"

Sawyer locked his jaw. The abductor would be smart to use Sara's family as leverage if she gave him any trouble. Sawyer's captors had tried the same thing. Eliminating his men one by one, using their allegiances to one another to find the weakest link. But there had been no weak link, and they had died. One by one. "All the more reason for you to stay out of sight."

"But if Sara was keeping a secret book of account

numbers," Emma said, "then someone at the credit union might know something about her kidnapping, and I don't want to draw any attention that will keep me from getting a look at her desk. You—" she lifted a narrow finger at him "—draw attention."

Sawyer sucked his teeth. It wasn't the first time he'd heard it. His six-foot-two-inch frame had been thickened, hardened and cultivated during his time in the service. The added scars and tattoos only served to enhance his dangerous appearance. Slowly, he relaxed against the seat back. He didn't like it, but she had a point, and while he would have preferred to go in and throw some weight around, Emma's idea wasn't a bad one.

EMMA CLIMBED ONTO the curb across the street from the credit union, Henry on one hip, his empty diaper bag on her shoulder. "I won't be long," she told Sawyer, who made no pretense of agreeing with her decision to go in alone.

She shut the door and hurried along the crosswalk before the light changed. Traffic was tight on the normally quiet streets of downtown Knox Ridge. The sidewalks teemed with people enjoying a beautiful Saturday morning. The weekly farmers market was set up a few blocks away, and barricades closed the street to traffic at the next intersection, making parking a nightmare. They'd gotten lucky finding a space in view of the credit union, but it was just another thing Sawyer had complained about. He'd wanted to be closer. Preferably right in front of the door. As if Emma was somehow in danger on a busy sidewalk at ten in the morning.

An exiting customer saw Emma coming and held the door.

"Thank you," she said, slipping inside.

The credit union's interior was quiet. A line of people stood between rows of velvet ropes, awaiting their turn with a teller. The air smelled vaguely of aged paper and new carpet. And despite the fact it was barely October, instrumental holiday music drifted softly overhead.

Emma scanned the room for a familiar face that wasn't already with a customer.

Kate, the assistant manager, came swiftly into view. Her eyes widened when she caught sight of Emma, and she cut through the space in a flash. "Oh my goodness. How are you?" she asked. "The police were here this morning. They told me what happened. I can't believe it."

Emma swallowed a painful lump in her throat. She hadn't expected to get emotional at the mere mention of *what happened*. She'd had a hold on herself at home, but out in the world, knowing other people knew made Sara's abduction seem impossibly more real. "What did the police say?" Emma asked. "Do they have a suspect? Or a clue?" If so, no one had bothered to call Emma with the information.

"No. They were asking a lot of questions. None I could answer. I just saw Sara a few days ago and she was fine. She looked tired, maybe distracted, but not enough that I even thought to ask her about it. I mean, we're all tired, right?"

Emma certainly was. She took a breath and prepared her practiced line to get into Sara's desk. "Did the police go through her things? Would you mind if I did? I think she has the spare house key," Emma lied, "and now I'm paranoid someone will come walking in at night while I'm sleeping."

Kate paled. "Oh no. Of course. This way." She walked

Emma to a row of cubicles along the far wall and waved an arm toward Sara's desk. "There it is. Take a look. I wouldn't know where to start."

Emma gave Kate her most pitiful face as she lowered onto her sister's chair. "Sara did seem tired. I'd assumed it was work-related stress. She probably had a lot on her plate or an extra difficult account."

Kate puzzled. "We're all overworked, but she never mentioned a difficult account. She had about a metric ton of questions a few weeks back on how our banking system works, but I had no clue. I directed her to Mr. Harrison." She pointed to an open office door across the room. A bearded, middle-aged guy was on the phone and already watching them from his desk, brow furrowed.

"Do you want to talk to him?" Kate asked. "He can tell you more about whatever Sara was doing." Her bottom lip poked out. "You must be trying to get your mind around her last few days."

"They weren't her last days," Emma snapped, surprising herself with the force of her words.

Kate started. "I didn't mean that," she said. "Not like that."

Emma stared, biting her lip and collecting her calm. "Sorry. I'm on edge. You understand." She flicked her gaze to Mr. Harrison, a normally kind man who looked suddenly agitated inside his office. "I don't think I'm ready to talk to anyone else." It might've been her restless night, her emotional state or sheer paranoia, but the branch manager seemed to have fixed his angry eyes on her, despite the line of patrons moving between them. If Mr. Harrison had anything to do with what had happened to Sara, then Emma wasn't in a hurry to run in there and ask about it. Better to let the police or Sawyer do that.

She lowered her eyes to the tidy piles on Sara's desk. "Did the police go through her things?"

"They looked," Kate said, "but they didn't take anything. They were more interested in how she'd been acting lately or if anyone had come to see her here that potentially upset her. Angry ex-boyfriends, things like that."

Right, Emma thought, *because the police didn't have the notebook*. She'd only located it last night while waiting for Sawyer to arrive. The police didn't have a reason to wonder if someone at her work was involved when they'd visited. Maybe Emma didn't either. Maybe the notebook was something else completely, and Emma was reaching for threads, for some way to feel more useful, when in truth there was nothing to do but wait.

She'd get the notebook to the detective in charge as soon as possible. Let him take it from here.

A door slammed and Emma gasped. She and Kate swung in the direction of the sound.

Mr. Harrison's door was closed.

"Kate?" A teller waved from across the room.

Kate frowned. "Sorry. I'll only be a minute," she told Emma.

"I'll be fine." A minute was all Emma needed. She swiveled on her sister's chair and stared at the desk. "Drawers first," she told Henry. Then she opened his empty diaper bag on the floor and began dropping everything with Sara's handwriting into the bag. She took memory sticks from the middle desk drawer and the appointment book from the desktop. Anything remotely personal could be a clue, and maybe she'd see something in Sara's notes that the police hadn't. Then she might be able to give them a lead, in addition to the notebook, that would help identify Sara's abductor. Emma shuddered at the memory of the man's awful growling voice. *Who did you tell?* Her gaze jumped to Mr. Harrison's closed office door. Could he know who took her sister?

She blinked through another threat of tears.

A framed photo of Sara, Emma and their parents sat on the corner of her sister's desk. Their mom had been gone just over five years. Their dad had been gone much longer, but the holes their parents had left behind were permanent. Emma tucked the frame into her purse, unwilling to stow her parents' image with the hodgepodge of who-knew-what from Sara's desk.

Across the room Kate started back in her direction.

Emma kicked the bottom drawers shut on either side of her, then heaved the bulging diaper bag back onto her shoulder. She gave the middle drawer a shove with her free hand.

"Did you find your key?" Kate asked, coming to a stop at the cubicle's opening.

"No." Emma tipped her head and stroked Henry's fuzzy brown hair. "I guess it's lost."

"Have you checked her car?" Kate offered. "If she's anything like me, it's probably in a cup holder. I find everything from hair ties to business cards in there."

"Good idea." Emma pushed Sara's chair in when she rose, then made a show of fussing over Henry on her way out, hoping to keep Kate's eyes on her adorable baby boy instead of her suddenly crammed diaper bag.

She hurried back onto the sidewalk with a feeling of victory and rush of relief. The local marching band played their high school fight song a few blocks away, adding an excellent backdrop to her enthusiasm. They were probably entertaining at the farmer's market to raise money again, but it certainly felt personal. Emma smiled a little wider.

She arranged the too-heavy diaper bag in the crook of her arm, having nearly dislocated her shoulder with the number of note pads and notebooks she'd confiscated. "I'm going to call this a success," she told Henry, dropping a kiss onto his tiny forehead.

Heavy fingers clamped hard around her elbow. "Don't say a word, or your baby's going to take a mighty fall." A man's low voice growled in her ear. He moved into her periphery, pulling her against his side and keeping pace there.

Ice slid through Emma's veins. It was *the* voice. *Who did you tell?*

She scanned the street for Sawyer, but the man's head turned at the eruption of a bass drumline. His thick arms crossed over his chest as the marching band carried their tune to a crescendo.

A moment later, the man tugged her around the building's edge and into a small alley.

"Don't hurt him," she pleaded.

"Give the bag to me." The man moved into her view; his face was covered in a black scarf from his chin to his nose. The dark hood of his jacket hung low over his forehead.

"No." Emma needed the things in that bag. The fact he wanted the bag was a sure sign that she finally had what she needed to find Sara. "Where's my sister?"

His hand moved from her elbow to the back of her neck, compressing and squeezing until shooting pain raced up the back of her head and she cried out for him to stop. "I wasn't making a request."

He released her with a shove. "Hand over the bag, or I squeeze your baby's head next."

Emma stumbled forward, twisting at the waist to put more distance between the lunatic and her son.

Henry screamed.

The man curled meaty fingers around the straps of Henry's diaper bag and jerked hard enough to leave material burns along her forearm as it slid. Before he separated it from her completely, Emma clenched a fist around one strap. "No!" she screamed.

"Stop!" Sawyer's voice blasted through the white noise of the street beyond the alley. A heartbeat later his livid face came into view across the crowded road. "Stop!" His eyes were fierce, and his voice boomed with authority. "Help her!" he yelled, motioning to Emma in the alley.

A few confused faces turned in her direction, gawking from the safety of the sidewalk just a few yards away.

Emma tried to hold on, tried to stall her attacker ten more seconds, just long enough for Sawyer to reach her, but the man's expression turned lethal. He reached a giant hand forward for her baby, eyes narrowed and darkening.

"No!" Emma screamed. She jerked left, spinning Henry farther away as a massive fist crashed into her cheekbone with a deafening thud. Her head snapped back and her vision blurred. Emma's knees buckled, and her back hit the brick wall of the credit union behind her. Air expelled from her lungs as she slid onto the filthy broken asphalt, Henry screaming in her arms.

The bag flew from her useless, flaccid fingers, and the man was in motion, beating a path down the alley, away from the crowd, away from Sawyer and away from Emma.

Henry wailed into her ear, arching his back in distress as Sawyer skidded to a stop at her side.

"Emma!"

She felt her strength giving way. Her arms knew to hold on, but her thoughts slipped into nothing. "Sawyer," she started, but the darkness rushed in to take her.

Chapter Four

Sawyer watched in horror as the man in black pulled back his fist and shot it forward at Emma and her baby. At *Sawyer's* baby. Fury burned in his veins, propelling him faster, erasing the final distance between them as Emma's body began to wobble and fall. She uttered Sawyer's name as his feet reached the curb only a yard from her side. The desperate, heartbreaking sound was nearly enough to land him on his knees.

Time seemed to stand still as her eyelids drooped shut, extinguishing the final glimmer of her awareness. Sawyer dove for them, catching Emma's body in a hug as it went limp and pressing both her and Henry to his chest. "Call 911!" he demanded, turning to fix a pointed look on the gathered bystanders.

Sawyer gritted his teeth as the assailant pushed through a throng of pedestrians at the alley's opposite end and escaped his wrath, for now, with Emma's bag.

The soft whir of emergency sirens spun to life in the distance, barely audible over Henry's cries.

Sawyer focused on the lives he held in his arms. He repositioned them, allowing Emma's arms to fall to her sides, and getting a more comforting hold on Henry. "Shh," he whispered to his son. The seething anger he felt for Emma's attacker would have to wait. "I've got you, and you're going to be okay," he vowed, kissing the child's head on instinct, cuddling him tighter. And he would return the man's assaulting punch at the first opportunity.

Emma's lids fluttered open. "Henry."

"I've got him, and help is on the way for you." Sawyer took a moment to evaluate the rising bruise on her cheekbone. Her assailant's fist had been large enough to mark her from jaw to temple, and Sawyer felt his fingers curl once more with the need to return the hit. "The police and ambulance are almost here," he assured her.

The sirens were loud now. Emergency vehicles would arrive at any moment.

Then Sawyer could plot his revenge on the man who'd done this to his family.

A SLOW AND GENTLE jostling roused Emma once more. The low murmur of a crowd and distant sounds of traffic pricked her ears. A cool and hearty breeze roused her with a snap. Suddenly, Emma's muddled thoughts pulled together in a sharp and deeply horrific memory. A man had attacked her and Henry outside the credit union. He'd taken all of Sara's things. Stolen the diaper bag from her hands. *And hit her.* "Henry!" Her eyes jerked wide.

"He's here," Sawyer answered. He appeared at her side, baby tucked safely in the crook of his arm. "He's okay."

Henry worked the small blue pacifier in his mouth. A broad grin stretched beneath the little soother when he caught her in his sight.

Emma sighed in relief. "Thank you," she whispered, fighting tears and taking inventory of the changes in her situation. The assailant was gone. Sawyer was here, and she was strapped to a gurney. An EMT pressed cool, probing fingers to her wrist. "Did he get away?" she asked Sawyer, craning her neck for signs of a policeman with the lunatic in handcuffs.

"Yeah," Sawyer answered. "I'm sorry."

She shook her head. "You saved Henry."

The muscle pulsed in Sawyer's jaw. His eyes were hard and cold. "The man who hurt you got away."

Sawyer's voice raised goose bumps over her skin. His calculating expression didn't help.

"Your cheek will be tender for a while," the EMT said. He explored the red-hot ache with a gentle touch. "Skin didn't break," he said. "There's no need for a bandage or stitches, but I recommend ice for swelling and aspirin as needed for pain." He flashed a blinding light into her eyes, and she winced. "Blurry vision?" he asked.

"No."

"Memory loss?"

"No." She frowned. That wasn't completely true. "I don't remember you arriving," she said, "but I remember being cornered, robbed and assaulted by a man in head-to-toe black. He wore a scarf across the bottom half of his face."

The EMT nodded, a small frown on his lips. "I'm sorry that happened to you and your baby." He pocketed the light. "If you develop any nausea or unusual neck pain, go to the ER. Tell them about this."

"Okay," she agreed, eager to get off the gurney and avoid an ambulance ride she absolutely couldn't afford. "I can go?"

He raised his attention to Sawyer, already moving

into position so he could help her down. "You'll drive her?" he asked.

Sawyer reached for Emma's hand. "Yes."

"Not so fast," a vaguely familiar voice interrupted. The detective who'd come to her home to take the report of Sara's abduction moved into view, pen and paper in hand. "I have a few questions, if you don't mind. I've spoken to several witnesses, and I'd like to get your statement as well before the details become murky from time."

Sawyer stepped between the detective and the gurney. His pale blue eyes locked onto hers. "You don't have to do this now if you don't want to. He can come by later, or I can take you to the station when you're feeling better."

Emma took a deep, settling breath and lifted her chin. "I can do it now," she said, and then she slowly relived the second-worst experience of her life in vivid detail.

When it was over, she told Detective Rosen about Sara's hidden notebook, and he promised to pick it up personally, after he'd finished with the current crime scene.

At home, she showered until her skin pruned up, attempting and failing to wash the feel of the man's hands off her. Then, with Henry dozing in his crib, she cried herself to sleep in the middle of the afternoon.

She woke to an empty crib at her bedside and the tangy scent of barbecue in the air.

She was on her feet instantly in search of her son. The scents of her grill suggested all was well, that Sawyer was grilling, but she wasn't sure she liked him nabbing Henry without letting her know. She crept down the hallway toward the kitchen warring with herself. Henry was his son, but surely common courtesy dictated that he at least let her know before taking him like that. No one else in her world would have dared. Maybe Sara. The thought clogged her throat.

Emma found Sawyer on the back porch, manning the grill as suspected.

He turned before she spoke, as if he'd somehow sensed her arrival. "Hey," he said, his gaze lingering on her cheek. "Did we wake you?"

"No," Emma said flatly, "but I wish you would have. Instead, I woke to find an empty crib. I didn't like it." Across from the grill, aligned with the porch swing she loved, Henry swung cheerfully from a red-and-yellow baby swing fastened to the rafters of the porch roof. "You put up the swing," she said, unsure if she was doubly frustrated that Sawyer had helped himself to that too, or warmed by the gesture.

Sawyer opened the lid to her steaming grill and flipped a line of burgers with practiced skill. "I found it in the garage while I was double-checking the perimeter. I think I woke the little guy with your power drill, but he let me off the hook when I suggested he give the swing a try." Pride tugged Sawyer's lips, and Emma wondered if it was his handiwork or Henry that caused it. "If you don't want the swing there, I can move it," he said, brows dipping into a V. "Whatever you want."

"It's fine," Emma said, drifting toward her son. "He clearly loves it." She stroked Henry's soft brown hair and kissed his head, inhaling the soft scents of sunshine and baby shampoo. She'd come so close to seeing him hurt today. Her fingers found the aching skin of her cheek on instinct, recalling the moment of impact with perfect, bone-rattling clarity. Then she'd been rescued by the man of her dreams. A man she'd long ago assumed had walked out of her life permanently, only to turn up and move in with her on the night of their strange reunion.

Last night.

Her stomach churned with the weight of all that had happened these last twenty-four hours. Nearly forty-eight, if she started counting from the moment her sister had been torn from their home. Her heart raced, and her mouth dried. It was just too much.

Sawyer closed the grill lid and watched her for a long beat before speaking. "Do you want to sit down?" He poured her a glass of ice water from the pitcher sitting on the little table she normally shared with Sara. "I planned to check in on you when the burgers were done. It's been a long day. I thought you might want to eat."

Emma curled one arm around her middle, attempting feebly to hold herself together. "You didn't have to do this," she said.

Sawyer gave his spatula a little spin. "It's just burgers," he said smoothly, as if that was true.

But it wasn't *just burgers*. It was the attentiveness and compassion. The protection and security. It was all the things she'd missed so deeply when Sawyer had left, and it was like peeling the scab off a wound she'd worked very hard to heal.

Emma straightened her spine. "I meant you don't have to watch Henry so I can sleep or hang swings or cook for me." The gestures were clearly meant to be helpful and not intrusive, she decided, and she couldn't be mad that he'd taken Henry from the crib when he woke. It was a fatherly thing to do. The swing. The burgers. All acts of kindness. But Emma's gut still churned with anger. She didn't need Sawyer's help with those things. She'd been fine on her own all these months. Why should he get to walk back in and pretend he'd been here all along?

Sawyer narrowed his eyes. "It's the least I can do, don't you think?"

"No," she said honestly. "I called Fortress Security because I needed help keeping Henry safe and finding Sara. You saved us from that lunatic today. That's what I need from you. That and help finding my sister."

Sawyer's eyes went cold at the mention of the man in the alley. It was a new look on him. One she wasn't sure she'd ever get used to. "How are you feeling?" he asked.

"My face hurts," she said. "I'm mad in general. I'm also thankful Henry wasn't hurt."

Sawyer took a step in her direction, hand raised as if he might touch her swollen cheek. He stopped short, clearly thinking better of it, and lowered his arm. He raised his attention from the bruise to her eyes. "I'm going to find the man who did this."

"Good, because I think he was the same man who took Sara," she said through a tightening throat, "and that man is a monster."

"What?" Sawyer's already aggravated expression darkened. "Are you sure?"

She nodded. "I recognized his voice. So, I can tell you from experience that Henry and I were lucky. I stood by and listened as he strangled Sara with his bare hands, held her down, made her bleed, then dragged her away." The memory of mopping her sister's blood off the living room floor rushed back to mind, and she stood, ready to run. She didn't want to have an emotional breakdown in front of Henry. Or Sawyer. The day had been too difficult already. "Excuse me."

Sawyer was on his feet instantly. "Hey." He caught her

in his arms and pulled her against his chest. The strong, familiar embrace felt so much like home, so much like everything she'd been missing for far too long. "I know I wasn't here for you before," he said, "but I'm here now, and I'm not going anywhere. You're not alone, Emma." He stroked her hair, and her heart gave a heavy thump.

She tried not to read into his promise. He wasn't going anywhere *for now*, but he'd be gone again when Sara came home. He would stay in Henry's life after that, but not in hers. Not really. Not the way her twisting heart wanted. Tears pricked her eyes, and her chest grew heavy with the need to cry.

"Excuse me," she blurted, bobbing free of him and running back inside.

Tears streamed over her cheeks with every footstep down the long hall to her room.

SAWYER KNOCKED ON Emma's door a few minutes later, then swung it open. The en suite bathroom door was ajar. "Emma?" he called. "Everything okay?"

She stepped out of the bathroom with red-rimmed eyes and blotchy skin. "Sorry. I needed a minute."

Sawyer set Henry in the crib beside her bed, a fresh cocktail of anger and regret mixing in his gut. "Feeling better?"

"No." She blew out a shaky breath, checking the corners of her mouth with her fingertips. "Not much. How's Henry?"

Sawyer gave his son a quick look. "He conked out in the swing. I wasn't sure it was good for him to sleep with his head tipped the way it was."

"Thanks." She moved toward the crib, toward Henry, and the urge to pull her against him was nearly too much.

He shoved his hands into his pockets. "You know that what happened to Sara isn't your fault," he said. "You couldn't have fought that guy and protected Henry at the same time. You did the only thing you could do. You were smart, quick thinking and brave."

"I don't feel like any of those things," she said, dragging her gaze from Henry to Sawyer.

He understood. Better than she could know. "Well, do you feel like a burger?"

Emma nodded, and Sawyer led her to the kitchen, where he'd set the table in her absence. She took a seat and downed the glass of ice water he'd poured for her. "How'd everything look when you checked the property?"

"Could be better," he said, hoping to sound less frustrated than he had been at the sight of the inadequate security measures protecting two single women and a baby. "Your locks are old. The windows are old. There are no security cameras. No alarm." He ran a heavy hand over his head and gripped the back of his neck. "I'll replace the locks and see what I can do to better secure the windows."

Emma set her empty glass aside and frowned. "I'd hoped to raise Henry on a farm, not inside a fortress."

"We all hope for a lot of things," Sawyer said stiffly. "But we have to adapt to the situations at hand, and right now, you need a fortress."

Emma placed a burger on her plate and covered it in mushrooms and onions, going through the motions, he assumed, but forgoing the bun.

Sawyer made his burger and bit into it, keeping one eye on her. He'd grilled burgers for her a dozen times during their monthlong whirlwind romance. In fact, some of his favorite memories with Emma had a grill in the background.

He'd been given a thirty-day leave last year after a particularly intense and dangerous mission, and he'd only expected to sleep in and veg out. Instead, he'd met Emma at a bonfire near a lake where he'd been fishing. He'd marched over to her, introduced himself. They'd hit it off, and he begged for her number when it was time for her to leave. He called her as she walked away. Invited her to fireworks in the park the next night. They'd spent nearly every day together from there. Until he had to go back.

Emma pushed the veggies around with her fork. "What if we don't find her?" she asked, pulling his thoughts back to the present.

Sawyer paused, the burger partway to his lips. "We'll find her."

"How do you know?"

"Because it's what I do. I search and rescue. I find people who don't want to be found, and I bring folks who are desperate to be found home." Images of his last mission flashed into mind. He'd taken his men on a rescue mission with bad intel. He'd assessed the risk, and he'd been dead wrong. He walked them into a trap, and that had cost five good men their lives. It darn near cost Sawyer his sanity.

"What if we find her and it's too late when we do?" The quaver in Emma's voice opened Sawyer's eyes. He hadn't realized he'd shut them.

Sawyer put the burger down. "We're going to find Sara, and she's going to be okay when we do," he promised. "Meanwhile, I'll be here to make sure no one gets near you or Henry again while we figure out what was going on. Okay?"

Emma shook her head, looking half-ill and pursing her lips.

"What?" he asked. They'd just covered her safety, Henry's safety and Sara's safe return. What else could make her look that way?

"I let go of the bag," she said. "I had everything from Sara's desk in that bag, and I let him have it."

"You didn't let him have anything," Sawyer argued. "I watched you fight him for it while holding a baby."

Emma shook her head. "Now he has what he wanted, and he doesn't have a reason to keep her alive anymore. Letting go of that bag might've killed my sister."

"Whoa." Sawyer raised his hands into a T for a time-out. "Look. You don't know any of that. Not his motivation. Not his endgame. You don't even know if what he wanted was in that bag. If he wanted the notebook with the numbers, the joke is on him because we had that and Detective Rosen picked it up an hour ago as promised."

Emma lifted hopeful eyes to his. "Yeah."

"Yeah," he said.

She nodded, steadying herself. "You're right." She forked a stack of mushrooms, studying them, her thoughts clearly somewhere else.

"Spill it," Sawyer said, wiping his mouth and then pressing the napkin to the table. "I've been gone awhile, but I know that face. You've got something to say. So, say it. It's better to clear the air than try to work through the smoke. Heaven knows we've got little fires burning everywhere."

She leaned forward, elbows on the table. "How did you get through the things you went through overseas? I know you're trained. You're smart. You're tough. That's not what I mean."

Sawyer bit into his burger, locked in her gaze and wishing she knew it was memories of her that had gotten him through the worst things imaginable. "Hope."

Emma pushed a forkful of mushrooms into her mouth and watched him curiously. She nodded. "I can do that." She chewed, swallowed, had some water, still scrutinizing Sawyer until he itched to get up and move. Her gaze shifted quickly away before returning to meet his. "I spent a lot of time over the past year wondering if you ever thought of me," she said, cheeks reddening.

He could see the honesty cost her. So, he would be honest right back. "I did. Often. I used to think of the things we'd done together. Now I'm just thinking about all the things I've missed." He clamped his mouth shut and did his best to look less vulnerable than he suddenly felt. Things were complicated enough between him and Emma without him getting emotional. This wasn't the time for heart-to-hearts and personal confessions.

The mission was to find Sara and protect Emma and Henry at all costs. He took another angrier bite of burger.

Emma stood and left.

Sawyer groaned. He used to be a people person. He made people comfortable, at ease, even happy. Lately, he could clear a room with a look and a greeting. He hadn't particularly minded the change until now.

Emma returned several minutes later with a scrapbook. She set it on the table beside his plate. "Sara made this for me."

She returned to her seat and lifted her fork to finish dinner.

Sawyer examined the big blue book. Henry's name and newborn photo were glued to the cover and framed with red ribbon. A photo of Emma in a ponytail and "baby on board" T-shirt was positioned just below the first. Her beautifully round belly was tough to look away from, and it hit him again. She'd been pregnant. Delivered their child. Brought him home. Got to know him. Learned to care for him, and Sawyer had missed it all.

He opened the book and turned the pages with reverence, poring over every detail. Every photo. Every inscription. He admired the proud smile on Emma's face in each photo.

"What's wrong?" Emma asked, resting back in her chair. "You look furious."

"No." He closed the book. A swell of pride and gratitude expanded his chest. "Thank you," he said softly.

She quirked a brow. "You can't keep that. Sara made it for me."

"No." He laughed. "Not for the book. For Henry."

Emma's cheeks reddened again. "It's not like I made him on my own."

"No, but you did everything else on your own," he said. "I can't imagine how frightening it was to learn you were going to have a baby. Especially one whose father was literally MIA." He thought again of the monsters who'd taken those months and his men from him, but forced the images aside. He curled his fingers around the book's edge, grounding himself to the present. "You could've chosen so many other ways to deal with your pregnancy, and I swear I never would've judged you, whatever you'd decided, but—" he cleared his thickening throat "—but because you made these choices—" he lifted the scrapbook in a white-knuckle grip "—I'm a father, and whatever you think of me now, I am irrevocably indebted to you for this."

Emma's mouth fell open, then was slowly pulled shut. "You're welcome."

Sawyer's aching heart warmed at her acceptance of his apology. It was a step in the right direction. "What was it like?" he asked.

"Scary at first, then pretty amazing," she said, forking a bite of bunless burger into her mouth. "I got really fat."

Sawyer let his gaze trail over her, indulging himself in the admiration of her new curves. "Agree to disagree."

"I'm working on getting back in shape now," she assured him. "It feels good but getting chubby with a purpose was fun too." Her lips twitched, nearly accomplishing a smile.

By the time dinner was done, and Sawyer had cleared the table, some of the smoky air between them had cleared, as well. Emma joined him at the sink in companionable silence as they washed and dried dishes by hand before putting them away. It was dangerously easy to be with Emma when she wasn't looking at him as if *he* might be the one in need of protection *from her*. Easy to let himself think there could a future for them, that he could somehow make up for his absence when it had counted most.

But Sawyer couldn't afford to think that way. Couldn't afford to get distracted until he brought Sara home safely as promised. Only after he'd proved himself worthy of Emma's trust would he allow himself to dream of more. Until then, he had work to do.

Chapter Five

Sawyer's eyes snapped open, his senses on alert. According to the clock on Emma's living room wall, it was approaching 3:00 a.m., meaning he'd slept for four straight hours. It was the longest stretch he'd managed since returning stateside, and he felt unnervingly vulnerable for it.

Normally he woke to the screams of his fallen teammates or the pain of his own torture, but not this time. So, what had woken him?

He tuned in to the quiet home, suddenly acutely aware that it was his gut that had jerked him into the moment. *Instinct.* His pulse quickened as he listened. For what? He wasn't sure. Sawyer straightened, planted his feet silently on the floor.

The baby monitor on the coffee table caught his eye. He waited for an indication that Henry had stirred and woken Sawyer, but there was only the slow and steady breaths of a sleeping child.

"Sawyer?" Emma whispered, struggling upright on the couch, where she'd fallen asleep midsentence during the retelling of a pregnancy story. He'd been wholly engrossed in the details, but her words had turned to soft snores before she'd finished, and he hadn't had the heart to wake her or the guts to try to move her. He certainly had no right to touch her.

She frowned in the dark. "What's wrong?"

He considered telling her everything was fine, but he hadn't had time to confirm that yet, and the distinct creak of floorboards removed the possibility it was true.

Her eyes stretched wide. "Someone's in the house?" She flicked her gaze to the baby monitor, and panic drained the blood from her face.

Sawyer lifted a finger to his lips, then reached for his sidearm, tucked carefully between the cushion and over-stuffed arm of Emma's chair where he'd rested. Then he reached for her. Much as he didn't want to bring her into harm's way, he couldn't afford to leave her alone either.

Emma followed closely on his heels, her small hands at his waist as they crept down the hall toward the sound.

Each bedroom door was open as they passed. Each light off. The laundry room. The guest bedroom, where Sawyer's things were stashed. Emma's room, where Henry slept soundly, unaware of the intruder or his parents' fears.

At her bedroom door, Emma released Sawyer and stepped over the threshold. She shot a pleading gaze at him, and he nodded before pulling the door shut with her inside.

He waited for the soft snick of the lock before moving on.

The bathroom door was open also. A night-light illuminated the narrow space, projecting the silhouette of a duck onto one wall.

When Sawyer reached Sara's room, the door was closed.

A beam of light flashed along the floor inside, leaking

into the hallway at his feet. A sly grin slid over Sawyer's mouth. He hadn't imagined an opportunity to return the man's punch so soon, but he was glad for it, and unlike Emma, this guy wouldn't be waking up so soon after the hit.

Sawyer cast a look over his shoulder, confirming he was still alone, and he hoped Emma had taken Henry to hide wherever they'd gone the night Sara was taken. Someplace she could call the police and wait safely until help arrived.

He struck a defensive position behind the closed door and turned the doorknob carefully. The soldier in him rose instinctively and unbidden. His mind and muscles falling instantly on their training.

The door swung on noisy hinges, and the creaking of floorboards turned quickly into the loud groan and rattle of an aged wooden window frame forced upward faster than it was prepared to go.

"Not on my watch," Sawyer said, flipping the light on and aiming his gun toward the window. "Stop right there."

A man in all black looked at him from the bedroom window, one half of his body still inside the room as he straddled the casing, a black duffel bag over his shoulder.

"Release the bag and climb back inside slowly," Sawyer demanded, hyperaware that only one of the intruder's hands was visible from this angle.

The man shifted the duffel from his shoulder to his palm and stretched it into the room toward Sawyer.

"Drop it," Sawyer barked. "Now, show me your other hand."

The man dipped his chin slowly. His opposite hand came into view with a gun poised to shoot.

"Put your weapon down." Sawyer's voice slid into the deep authoritative timbre that forced most folks to obey his commands. This man didn't budge.

"I *will* shoot you," Sawyer warned. "I'm willing to bet my aim is better than yours." He let his mouth curve into a sinister smile, enjoying the weight and feel of his SIG Sauer against his palm and the flash of indecision on the man's face.

Henry's scream broke the silent standoff and Sawyer's concentration. A million terrifying scenarios thundered through his brain like a punch to his gut. Was there a second intruder? Had Sawyer overlooked him? Was Henry hurt? Was Emma?

The intruder's gun went off with a deafening bang!

Sawyer jumped back into the hall, pressing himself to the wall and cursing inwardly at the moment of distraction. "Emma!" he called.

Henry cried again, but Emma didn't answer.

Sawyer swore. He spun silently back into Sara's bedroom, already aiming for the window. He pulled his trigger as the muffled thud of the duffel bag hit the ground outside. The man took a second wild shot at Sawyer, then toppled out the open window, smearing blood over the frame and Sara's wall beneath.

Sawyer's attention stuck to the hole in the drywall a few feet away from his head. The intruder's final shot had missed him by several feet, but the hole had punched through a wall shared with Sara's room. A wall shared by Henry and his crib.

EMMA'S PULSE BEAT in her ears as she burrowed deeper into the walk-in closet that had been her refuge just two nights before. She could only pray it would be enough to protect her again. She shushed her fussing baby and tried desperately not to imagine Sawyer being injured while she hid. She couldn't live knowing another loved one had been taken from her while she sat idly by, but what could she do? She couldn't leave Henry, and she wouldn't risk making him an orphan, so she was stuck. Hiding and waiting. And praying. Again.

The dispatch officer insisted on staying on the line with her until the police arrived. "Can you see anything from your location?" she asked.

"No," Emma whispered. "Please hurry."

"What can you hear?" the dispatcher asked. "Can you tell me the number of intruders based on voices?"

Emma shook her head, unsure she could make another sound even if she wanted. Even if she wasn't terrified her voice would give away her hiding spot and put her baby in danger.

"Ma'am," the dispatcher began again, but a sudden gunshot reverberated through the silent home, stopping her midinterrogation.

Emma's heart seized and her chest constricted.

"Was that gunfire?" the dispatch officer asked abruptly, concern in her voice.

"I—" Emma nodded. "Yes." She stroked Henry's hair as he began to scream once more. "Help us," she breathed. "Please."

The blast that erupted next poured tears onto her cheeks.

Henry's eyes were wide in the glow from her phone. His lips pulled low into a full pout, startled to silence by the sound but ready to wail at any moment.

"Was anyone hurt? Do you need an ambulance?" the dispatcher demanded.

"I don't know." She covered her mouth with one palm to stifle a building sob.

The door to her room banged open, and she screamed. The door ricocheted against the wall, rattling the closet where she hid. "Henry!" Sawyer yelled. "Emma!"

A wave of relief pressed the air from her lungs. "Here," she croaked. "We're here." She inched forward as the closet door opened, balancing a crying Henry in her arms and the phone against her shoulder.

Sawyer dropped to his knees and pulled them into his arms. "Thank goodness." He took Henry from her, then offered a hand to pull her to her feet. "Call 911," he instructed. "I shot the intruder, but he got away with a duffel bag. I don't know what was in it."

Emma lifted the phone from her shoulder. "They're on the way."

He closed his eyes for a long beat, then reopened them to kiss Henry's hair and round cheeks a dozen times before kissing Emma's forehead and pulling her close. "May I?" he asked, sliding a hand up to take the phone. He spoke heatedly with Dispatch for several moments while Emma stepped away.

Her insides fluttered and her limbs quaked with excess adrenaline as she tried to follow Sawyer's explanation of what had happened inside Sara's room.

"I definitely hit him. There's blood. He'll need a hospital," Sawyer said.

A dark spot on the wall caught Emma's attention, and she moved across her room to inspect it through the bars of Henry's crib. A hole in the drywall. Inches from the place where Henry laid his head at night. She touched the hole with shaking fingers, and nausea rolled in her stomach. "He could be dead," she whispered.

Sawyer opened a pocketknife and dug the casing from the wall with his handkerchief. "I've got the brass," he said. "This might be all we need to track him. We can match the gun if it's registered. Match the print if he's in the system."

Flashers lit the world outside her bedroom window.

"Cavalry's here," he told Dispatch, pulling the curtain back for a look into the driveway.

Sawyer returned the phone to Emma, then headed for the front door with Henry to greet the emergency responders.

Emma tried not to look too long or hard at the crib or the bullet hole in the wall at its side. She doubted she'd ever be able to lay Henry there again, and she was sure she wouldn't sleep if she did.

She followed them to the living room, Henry lodged tightly against Sawyer's chest, silent and calm. Shocking because Henry wasn't good with strangers. Though Sawyer wasn't really a stranger, she thought. Sawyer was his father.

She took Henry from him as he greeted the line of police officers, crime scene officials and the detective she'd spoken to earlier that day. She didn't have it in her to speak without crying, and tears would help nothing. Coffee, on the other hand, cured a multitude of things, and she could make a pot to be useful.

She moved to the kitchen as men and women in uniforms canvassed her home. There wouldn't be any more sleeping for her tonight, but honestly, she wasn't sure how she'd ever sleep again.

Sawyer paused outside the kitchen as a pair of uniforms passed by. "You okay?" he asked, concern and compassion plain in the words and his expression.

"Mmm-hmm." She nodded, pushing her attention back to the chore at hand.

Tonight's gunshots had punctured more than the drywall. The possibility she'd lost Sawyer again had wrenched her heart in agony and eradicated her carefully constructed walls of emotional protection. The realization that he was safe but would leave once Sara was home, made her chest pinch and ache in the extreme. She wasn't sure what that meant, but she was nearly positive it wouldn't end well for her raw and aching heart.

Chapter Six

Emma set Henry in his high chair once he'd calmed from the scare and offered him his favorite teether. At just over four months, his coordination wasn't great, but once he got the rubber cactus to his mouth, he normally chewed happily. Tonight was no different, and Emma marveled at the resilience of her son. If only she could suck it up so easily and move on to the moment at hand.

She turned to the counter and rubbed trembling palms down the legs of her jeans. Brewing the coffee and setting out the cups, cream and sugar would give her an outlet for the energy surplus buzzing around inside her.

Sawyer appeared a moment later, leaning against the jamb. "How are you holding up?"

"Not as well as Henry," she said, "but I suppose I should expect as much from your son." She poured a mug of coffee and extended it in Sawyer's direction. "Coffee?"

Sawyer accepted the mug. He took a long pull on the steaming drink, eyes focused on her. "You did great tonight," he said. "With everything going on, I forgot to say that sooner, but it's true. Henry's a lucky kid."

Emma nodded woodenly. What had she done besides hide? *Again.* She was sick of being caught off guard and forced to react to all the villainous encounters. She wanted to *do* something that would stop them. Not hide until the situations passed. "We need to find out what he was looking for," she said. "It was a good sign. If whatever he wanted wasn't in the bag of things I took from her office, then Sara might still be alive."

Sawyer gave one stiff dip of his chin.

"If he found whatever he'd been after in her room tonight, then we don't have much time," she said. "We have to do something."

Detective Rosen arrived in the kitchen behind Sawyer. "Do I smell coffee?"

Sawyer nodded. "Help yourself."

The detective poured a cup, then offered Emma his hand. "I'm sorry to be back so soon, Miss Hart. I understand you were able to contact Dispatch while staying out of danger's path and protecting your son to boot. Nice work."

"Any word on Sara's whereabouts?" Emma asked, ignoring the comment about her spectacular abilities to hide and use a telephone.

"I'm sorry," Rosen said. "Not yet. We're running down every lead, but we don't have anything to share at the moment."

"Well, which is it?" she asked, working to control her tone and not upset Henry again. "Is there nothing to share or just nothing you're willing to share?"

The detective looked at Sawyer, who returned his level gaze. "Nothing worth sharing," he said.

"Try me," Emma dared. "You'd be surprised how little it would take to reassure me right now."

Detective Rosen rocked back on his heels and cleared his throat. "Well, we're working on the theory that this had something to do with her position at the credit union," he began. "We're unclear how her job and the abduction are related, but we believe they are."

Emma's hopes sank. She'd hoped the leads he'd mentioned were significant. Maybe even inside tips of some sort. Instead, it sounded like the police didn't have anything more than she'd come up with on her own.

Sawyer moved to her side, silently sharing his strength with her. "Any luck on deciphering the notebook's contents?"

"Not yet." Detective Rosen set his empty mug aside and fixed Emma with a patient look. "Mr. Lance said the intruder took a duffel bag with him. Do you think you might be able to walk through the room and tell me what's missing?"

Emma stepped away from Sawyer and pulled Henry from his high chair with a kiss. "I didn't spend much time in Sara's room," she said, moving into the hall behind the detective. "I'm not sure I'd notice if anything was missing besides the furniture, but I'll try."

A handful of men in various uniforms filled the space inside her sister's room, dusting the window frame for prints, taking photos and collecting blood from the floor.

Emma inched inside. Her pulse quickened and her breaths grew shallow. Seeing the policemen and crime scene people picking through Sara's things was like losing her all over again. The blood on the wall and windowsill reminded her of the broad smear she'd cleaned off the living room floor.

"Hey." Sawyer moved in front of her, the toes of his shoes bumping hers. "Take your time."

She snuggled Henry tighter and forced her gaze around the room. The items on Sara's vanity, bookcase and nightstand were scattered. The floor was covered with the contents of her closet. Her mattress was askew from the box spring. "Maybe if I clean up," she said. "It's too messy right now. I don't know where to look."

"All right," the detective said. "We're almost done. You can let us know once you've had time to reorganize." He handed Sawyer a business card, then drifted back down the hallway.

More than an hour later, the house was finally, eerily still.

Sawyer double-checked the door lock, then turned to face her. "What do you want to do?" he asked.

She shook her head, heartbroken and mystified. "I have no idea."

He pulled a set of keys from his pocket and raised them beside his handsome face. "Why don't we get out of here?"

HE DIDN'T HAVE to ask Emma twice. When he'd offered to take her and Henry to his place for a while, she'd packed two bags without hesitation. Inside the cab of his truck, Emma watched her family ranch until it was swallowed by distance and darkness.

"What are you thinking?" he asked when the curiosity became too much.

"I don't know where you live," she said with a small laugh. "I was thinking that two days ago I would never have agreed to go home with someone without asking where they lived."

Sawyer locked his jaw against the complaint that he wasn't just someone. He was Henry's father, a man she'd called in to protect her and someone she'd once claimed to have loved.

She fiddled with the hem of her shirt. "I suppose you don't still live on base with four other rangers."

"No," he said. "They tend to cut off our housing once we're discharged." He glanced her way across the dimly lit cab. "I bought a place in the next county. We won't be more than an hour away if the police call with new information and you want to get back."

Emma turned curious eyes on him. "Where in the next county?"

"Lake Anna," he said, nearly crushed by a wave of nostalgia.

She swiveled in her seat, eyes wide with interest. They'd met at Lake Anna, and Emma had loved visiting the lake when they'd dated. She told him once that she wanted to live there someday, and he'd promised to buy her a home with a dock and lots of privacy so they could make love under the stars anytime they wanted. Sawyer assumed the rising color in her cheeks meant that she hadn't forgotten that conversation either.

He checked the rearview mirror as they moved along the desolate highway, one of only a few dozen cars traveling just before dawn. He passed his exit and got off on an unlit, extremely rural ramp instead, checking again for signs they'd been followed. By the time he backtracked several miles and made a few unnecessary turns to confirm they were still alone, the sun was rising.

Emma straightened and rubbed her eyes as they bounced down the pitted gravel lane to his simple A-frame cottage. The motion light snapped on as he settled the vehicle outside, welcoming him home. The lawn was still dark, shaded by the surrounding forest, but the lake before them was the color of fire, reflecting the sunrise over its glassy surface.

Sawyer bypassed the wide parking area near his back porch in favor of a smaller, narrower patch of gravel near the home's side entrance. He used this door as his front door, because the actual front of his home faced the lake.

Sawyer climbed out and grabbed Emma's things from the back, then met her on the passenger side. He took Henry's bulbous car seat carrier from her hands. "You'll be safe here," he promised, stepping onto the wide wraparound porch. "We weren't followed, and I've barely moved in, so even if the man I shot managed to get my name somehow, the only people who know where I live are my teammates in Lexington. The home is technically owned by the company, for privacy reasons, so it will take some time and know-how to track us here."

He unlocked the door and hit the light switch inside, then motioned for Emma to pass. Sawyer keyed in the code to the silent alarm system, then caught Emma's eye as she took the place in.

She folded her arms and made a circuit around the living room, stopping to look at the photos on his mantel, then out the stretch of windows facing the lake.

Sawyer set Henry's car seat near the couch and went to join her. "What do you think?"

"It's beautiful," she said.

"Thanks." He gave the space a critical exam. Packed boxes filled the corners. Stacks of paint cans and piles of new fixtures lined the walls and nearly every flat surface. He'd gotten the place at a steal, planning to use it as a safe house for Fortress until he fell in love with it. Unable to separate the cabin and its location from his memories with Emma, he'd decided to move in. That decision had led to a lot of unexpected work and added costs. Like updating *everything* and getting the place a mailbox and address. For the past fifty or so years, it had been little more than a cabin in the woods. Someplace someone had built to spend weekends, but never intended as a home. "It needs a lot of work, but they say it's all about location, right?"

"That's what they say," she said softly, still focused on the lake and rising sun. "I can't believe you've been this close and I had no idea."

Sawyer had thought the same thing the moment she'd told him he had a son. He was just one county line away, and he'd still missed the kid's entire life so far.

"How's Cade?" she asked his reflection in the glass. "I've been so wrapped up in my messes that I haven't even thought to ask you about your little brother."

Sawyer smiled at their reflections, side by side in his new home. "Cade's good. He's finishing up with the Marines soon, and he'll join Fortress when he gets out."

"Sounds like your security firm has become the family business." She nodded appreciatively, a note of pride in her voice. "You had your doubts about going big right out of the army, but I knew," she said. "I've always known you could do anything."

Sawyer stepped closer and put his hands back into his pockets to stop them from reaching for her. "Wyatt put everything in motion." Sawyer had been scheduled for discharge with Wyatt, his closest friend and brother in arms, but his captivity had kept him from it and forced Wyatt to do everything on his own. Another case of Sawyer leaving loved ones to fend for themselves.

Wyatt, like Emma, had done a fine job without him.

Emma erased the final few inches between them, bringing her foot and leg flush with his. She linked her arm through his and tipped her head against his shoulder.

Sawyer raised the opposite arm across his chest and set his hand over hers on his arm.

Soon the sun gleamed orange and was well above the horizon, looking as if it might have risen from the fiery water's depths. Sawyer couldn't resist it any longer. He slid the patio door open and ushered Emma outside. She gave their sleeping son a glance before moving onto the deck, where Sawyer had spent every early morning since he'd moved in. If there was an upside to insomnia, it was that he never missed a sunrise.

"Where are all the other lake houses?" Emma asked, scanning the scene in both directions. "I remember there being so many."

"Those are closer to town. We're on a finger of the lake, tucked between a privately owned hundred-acre property and the national forest."

"Wow." She pushed a strand of windblown hair behind her ear and surveyed the scene again, this time with a look of remarkable appreciation. Pride swelled nonsensically in Sawyer's chest once more. Her approval of his home probably meant more to him than it should, but he didn't care, he liked it.

Emma turned to him; there seemed to be a question in her eyes, but she didn't ask it. "I should set up Henry's crib," she said. "I hate to see him sleeping in the car seat." She headed back inside and lifted the portable crib off the floor where Sawyer had left it. "Where do you want us?"

Sawyer bit his tongue against the truth, that he wanted her and Henry right there, with him permanently, but he knew that wasn't what she'd meant, and it was much too soon, not to mention unfair, to spring something like that on her. What he needed to do was find Sara. Complete the mission. Prove himself.

He showed Emma to the spare room across the hall from his, and watched as she expertly unpacked and set up the portable crib, then changed Henry and got him back to sleep with only the smallest cry of protest. She really was great at being a mother. His son was a lucky boy.

Sawyer's father had been a real son of a gun, and Sawyer had sworn long ago to never repeat any of his varied and extensive mistakes. *If* he ever had a family of his own. He'd already started off on the wrong foot by not returning Emma's calls. Even if he thought he was doing her a favor. He should've let her make that decision for herself. Now he could only hope that she'd forgive him. She might understand logically why he hadn't called, but the pain of feeling rejected and unwanted was a lot to overcome, and there was nothing logical about the process.

"Sawyer?" Emma asked, pulling him from his reverie. "Are you going to lie down awhile?"

"No." He bristled at the thought. He had far too much to protect under his roof now, and too much work to be done in the meanwhile. "I'm going to have another look at Sara's notebook."

Emma crossed her arms and frowned. "I thought you gave it to Detective Rosen."

He nodded. "I did. Right after I photographed the pages."

She smiled. "Okay. I'm not sure I'll be able to sleep, but I'm going to try. Once Henry wakes, he'll need me."

"Of course." Sawyer moved toward the door, longing to tell her she wasn't alone. She didn't have to carry the weight of single parenthood anymore. He could make bottles, change diapers, shake rattles. He was hardly a professional at those things, but he was a quick study and he wanted to learn. Instead, he settled for "I'll be here if you need me."

Emma curled her small hand over his on the doorknob. "Thank you," she said softly.

Sawyer's body stiffened at her touch, with the urge to pull her against him and kiss her the way he'd dreamed of doing for a year. "For what?"

"For coming to my rescue the other night. For protecting us now." She removed her hand from his and slid her palm up the length of his arm and over his shoulder. When her fingers reached the back of his neck, a firestorm of electricity coursed through him.

She rocked onto her toes and kissed his cheek. "Good night."

Sawyer nodded once, then pulled the bedroom door shut between them while he could still bring himself to walk away.

EMMA WOKE HOURS later to the sound of Henry's laughter.

Her bedroom door was open and his portable crib was empty, but his laugh was brightening her day even before her feet had hit the floor. According to her phone, it was nearly lunchtime. She'd had more sleep than she'd expected, given the circumstances, and she felt almost hopeful as she padded down the hall of Sawyer's lake house toward the living area.

The sliding patio doors were open, and Sawyer was on the porch swing with Henry, a near repeat of a similar situation yesterday. Funny the difference a day made. Emma couldn't find it in her to be irritated now. A cool breeze blew off the lake, tousling her hair as she emerged onto the wide wooden planks and joined them. "Sounds like you guys are having a good time."

"We are," Sawyer answered. "We've already been down to the dock to feed the ducks and fish," he said. "Henry had a bottle and is on his third diaper. It's been a busy morning."

Emma stroked her son's cheek. "When did you learn to make bottles and change diapers?" she asked, enjoying the warm, easy smile on Sawyer's face. He looked at ease, even peaceful, holding Henry to his chest.

"YouTube," he said. "I considered asking you for instructions, but I didn't want to wake you."

"Well, that was one way to do it." Emma smiled at the sunlight winking across the water. She'd always wanted a place just like this one, and Sawyer had found one, complete with a boat dock and canoe. Now here they were, in the place they'd wanted to be, but time and circumstance had changed everything. Was there a way back for them, after all they'd been through? The electricity continually zinging in the air between them suggested there was, but was chemistry enough? She had Henry to think about now.

"I made coffee if you need a pick-me-up," Sawyer said. "Creamer's in the refrigerator if you want it."

"Thanks." She turned for the house, suddenly desperate for the caffeine.

Sawyer stood with Henry. "Why don't we make lunch and watch the twelve o'clock news? Maybe there will be coverage of Sara's disappearance. Cops can be tight lipped, but reporters rarely are."

Emma nodded. "Good idea."

Sawyer beat her to the refrigerator and passed her the creamer. "How about BLTs?"

"Sounds good." She poured the coffee while Sawyer made the sandwiches and Henry bobbed in his por table high chair, attached to the side of Sawyer's table. She scanned the utilitarian space and smiled. Sawyer's decorating style was a clear reflection of himself. The only valuable items in sight were above the fireplace. In the event of a robbery, the television was the best a thief would do here. In case of a fire, Sawyer would go straight for the line of framed photos below the flat screen. She pulled her purse off the back of the chair and dug inside for another priceless photo and carried it to the mantel. "Do you mind?" she asked, setting the picture of her parents with her and Sara in line beside Sawyer's photos. "I took it from Sara's desk and put it in my purse for safe-keeping. Luckily, that psychopath didn't get it when he took the diaper bag."

Sawyer moved into the space behind her and powered on the television. The heat from his torso warmed her chest as he reached around her. "You can put anything of yours anywhere you like around here."

She let herself lean back and rest against him a moment before returning to the kitchen. She had to stay focused. Had to remember what was at stake. Sara was missing, and that was why Sawyer was there, not to fulfill some long-suffering fantasy of Emma's. Her heart was already a mess of tattered shreds without giving in to a desire that would only leave her hollow and ruined.

Sawyer set the table, and they settled in to a quiet meal of chips and sandwiches when the local news began.

"Do you think they'll mention the break-in at my place last night?" she asked. "Or my mugging outside the credit union?" Did the whole town know what she was going through?

A woman in a gray pantsuit stood before the camera.

"Here at the scene of an early-morning hit-and-run on Main Street," she began.

"A hit-and-run," Emma groaned. "What is going on in our town lately? Has everyone gone mad?"

Sawyer's eyes narrowed, but he didn't move his attention from the television. He lifted the remote and pumped the volume up to ten. "That looks like Sara's credit union in the background."

"What?" Emma set her sandwich aside and peered more closely at the flat screen over the fireplace.

"According to authorities," the reporter continued, "assistant branch manager Kate Brisbane was on her way to work this morning when a white sedan struck and threw her, leaving Kate with extensive injuries. She was taken by ambulance to Mercy General Hospital, where doctors have admitted her to the ICU for treatment and observation."

Emma covered her mouth with both hands. She'd just spoken to Kate yesterday before she was cornered outside the credit union, mugged and hit. Kate's accident couldn't have been a coincidence. Could it? She turned her gaze to Sawyer, who was still glaring at the television.

"Kate Brisbane is the one you spoke with yesterday before you were assaulted?" he asked.

"Yes."

He pushed to his feet, plate in hand. "You want to go to the hospital?" he asked. "Pretend to be family so we can talk to Kate and see if she remembers anything more than the color of the car that hit her?"

"Absolutely."

Chapter Seven

Emma fought her surging emotions all the way to the hospital. The last few days were taking a toll on her both mentally and physically. Any one of the things she was experiencing would normally have been enough to keep her busy overthinking for weeks. Piling them up day after day without a moment to breath or process was making her half-ill, jittery and desperate for a break.

Sawyer watched his mirrors diligently, his gaze making a continual circuit from rearview, to sideview, to the road, then back again. She presumed the exercise was to be sure they weren't being followed, and for roughly the thousandth time since Sawyer's arrival, she was struck with overwhelming gratitude to have him there with her.

He followed the hospital signs to visitor parking without a word, then helped her out of the truck before reaching for Henry's car seat. "Are you ready for this?" he asked.

"Not really," she admitted. She hadn't been ready for any of it, but here she was. She took Sawyer's arm as he beeped the doors locked on the truck and turned for the hospital entrance. She tried not to imagine they were a real family as passersby smiled at them. Though it was certainly a nice thought.

She let her mind slip past the reminder that this was only temporary as she stepped through the hospital's automatic doors, and she refocused on the reason they were there. Someone had tried to kill Kate this morning, and anything Kate could remember might be the key to finding Sara.

Sawyer hit the elevator button, and the doors parted. He scanned the partial list of floors and wards as Emma boarded ahead of him. She hit the number six when he stepped in behind her.

"How do you know which floor the ICU is on?" he asked.

"It's the same as Labor and Delivery," she said. "Opposite wings."

The doors parted a moment later, and Sawyer stepped out with their son. "I should have been here with you. I didn't even know."

Emma sucked down a shaky breath as they moved along the brightly lit corridor toward the ICU. "It's okay," she promised, "because now you do."

Memories of waddling down that same hallway a few short months ago rushed back to her. Water broken, doubled over in pain. It was the most beautiful and terrifying night of Emma's life. Sara had been a total mess, completely freaked-out, running ahead of Emma to clear the path and waving her arms like she was hailing a taxi. They'd both been sure that Emma might deliver Henry at any moment. They'd read all the books and still knew nothing. It had been another twelve hours before Henry made his big debut. Emma slept more than Sara that night, thanks to the blessed epidural. Sara sat vigil, reading the tabloids and retelling funny stories from their childhood when Emma had woken. She'd held Emma's hand through every contraction, been the perfect coach, a dedicated aunt and a devoted sister.

And Emma wanted her back.

She gritted her teeth against the urge to cry. She'd already cried enough these last two days to fulfill her quota for a lifetime. Instead, she hiked her chin up an inch and approached the desk with resolve. "Hello, I'm Emma Hart. I'm here to see Kate Brisbane."

The nurse gave her and Sawyer a long look. "Are you family?"

"Yes," she lied.

"Well, as I've explained to her other family members—" the nurse motioned to a waiting room full of people behind them "—Kate is still unconscious, and we're only allowing immediate family five-minute sessions. You can take a seat with your relatives, and when she's ready for another visitor, you can decide among yourselves who it will be."

Emma's cheeks warmed. She hadn't thought of all the real family members who might be there for Kate. "Thank you," she said, taking Sawyer's hand and moving into the waiting room. "Well, that didn't go the way I wanted."

Sawyer gave her fingers a squeeze.

A dozen heads turned their way. She recognized one as Detective Rosen.

The detective stood and shook the hands of the couple he'd been speaking with, then came to meet Emma and Sawyer near the doorway. "I guess you saw the morning news."

Emma raised her eyebrows. "I guess so. Were you going to contact me if I hadn't?"

"We didn't see a reason to reach out to you just yet,"

the detective hedged. "We're looking into Kate's accident to determine if there's a connection."

Emma barked a humorless laugh. "*If* there's a connection? There's no way this was a coincidence," she said, crossing her arms over her chest. "This happened because Sara worked with Kate, and someone probably saw me talking with her yesterday."

The detective opened his arms and stepped forward, corralling them into the hallway, away from Kate's family. "We don't know that," he whispered.

"You do know that," she countered. "First, some psychopath walks right into my home and tears Sara away, then I'm attacked outside the credit union where she works. Our home is broken into that night, and this morning Sara's assistant manager is hit by a car. You don't have to have a signed confession to know these things are all part of a bigger picture."

Sawyer angled himself in on the detective, voice low. "Have you at least matched the fingerprints or blood in Sara's room to someone yet?"

"No," Detective Rosen said flatly. "Those things take time, and as for the signed confession, it would be nice because I can't assume anything. The investigation must be based on facts for it to hold up in court, and we can't afford to play catch and release with murderers. They tend to not play nice upon release."

Emma pressed the heels of her hands to her eyes.

"What about you?" Detective Rosen asked. "Were you able to think of anything else that might help us catch whoever was in your home? Did you notice anything missing when you straightened up your sister's room?"

Emma shook her head and dropped her hands to her sides. "Not yet," she said, suddenly ashamed to admit she'd left the home right after he did. "Maybe they were looking for the notebook." She lifted her thumb to her mouth and bit into the skin along her thumbnail. "When will you hear back from your lab?"

"A few days to a couple weeks," he said, lifting a hand to stop her complaint before she had time to voice it. "Knox County doesn't have a lab. We have to send our work out, then it has to get in line behind the work of every other district in our situation." He pulled a phone from the inside pocket of his jacket. "Excuse me."

Emma frowned as the detective walked away. She turned to Sawyer, frustration stinging her nose and throat. "Can you believe this?"

He headed back for the elevator. "Let's take another look at Sara's notebook. It's the only real lead we have, and it'll keep us busy. I've sent photos of the pages to my team at Fortress. Wyatt is good with puzzles like this. Maybe we can at least figure out if the notebook is relevant."

"Okay," she agreed. She'd nearly forgotten about the notebook with everything else going on. Maybe it was nothing, but if it was something that would bring Sara home, she needed to get copies to anyone who could help.

SAWYER MATCHED HIS pace to Emma's as they moved across the parking lot to his truck. She was clearly upset, and he understood why. Investigations didn't move as swiftly as they should, nothing like what was portrayed on television, and the truth was that finding Sara the old-fashioned way would be much quicker than waiting for feedback from a lab in the next county. Lucky for them, he had the men of Fortress Security at his disposal.

He beeped his truck doors unlocked, then secured a

sleeping Henry inside. As much as Sawyer missed the kid's smiling face, he was glad someone could still rest. He certainly couldn't.

He slid behind the wheel, powered the windows down and waited while Emma buckled up. The warm autumn breeze fluttered her hair, sending her sweet scent over him. He gripped the wheel a little tighter in response.

"Why do you think someone tried to kill Kate?" Emma asked, gathering her hair over one shoulder.

"I don't know," he admitted. "Maybe she knew more than she let on when the two of you spoke."

Sawyer scanned the lot for signs of anyone who'd taken an interest in them. A man on a motorcycle in the next row caught his attention. His bike faced away from their truck, but he dropped his cigarette and ground it out with his boot when Sawyer started the engine.

Emma turned a guilty expression in Sawyer's direction. "Is it awful that this hit-and-run gives me hope for Sara?"

He settled back in his seat, watching to see what the motorcyclist did next. "How so?"

"Maybe the fact these horrible things keep happening is an indication that whoever took Sara is still trying to get all the evidence she has on him. I think he'll keep her alive until he's sure he's covered his tracks and collected everything against him. The night he took her, he kept asking who she'd told. 'Who did you tell? Who did you tell?'" Emma lowered her voice to something fairly menacing as she repeated the question. She rubbed her palms over the gooseflesh on her arms as she spoke. "And Kate's attack tells us something else. The man who took Sara has a partner or a team or something. You shot someone last night, and there was a lot of blood left behind for a flesh wound. I can't imagine anyone pulling off a hit-and-run only a few hours after taking a bullet like that." She looked over her shoulder at the hospital. "So there are at least two men. The one who took Sara and mugged me, and the guy who broke in last night. Do you think Detective Rosen thought to ask the hospital staff if anyone was admitted with a gunshot wound last night?"

"Yeah," Sawyer said, shifting into Drive as the motorcycle cruised out of the parking lot. "He would've reached out to them right away, and even if he didn't, hospitals have to report knife and gunshot wounds. It's the law."

Emma settled back in her seat. "Right. Good."

Sawyer took the next left and headed in the opposite direction as the motorcycle. Something about the man had put his instincts on edge, and there was little Sawyer could do about it with Emma and Henry in tow. For all he knew, the driver had intended to get his attention and draw him down a certain path where trouble awaited. On his own, Sawyer would have loved the opportunity for engagement, but for now, he needed to keep Emma and Henry safe.

"I can't stop wondering why someone would have hit Kate," Emma said. "You were right when you said she might've known more than she let on, but in what way? Was she part of the scheme all along, whatever it is? Did she become a loose end? Or did Sara confide in Kate when she hadn't confided in me? And why?"

"Maybe it wasn't like that," Sawyer suggested. "Maybe Sara stumbled across an issue at work and asked Kate about it. You said Kate told you Sara had questions. Maybe just knowing Sara's concerns was enough for the criminal to want to shut her up."

Emma pulled her lips to the side. "Maybe. I didn't ask

her what Sara's questions were. I only asked how Sara had seemed the last few days, and Kate said Sara had been fine. Maybe a little tired, but she hadn't noticed anything significant or helpful."

Sawyer glanced her way. "Could she have been lying? If Sara had confided in her, then been abducted, it would make sense for her to hide what she knew. She could have reasoned that she would be taken too."

Emma bit into the skin along her thumbnail. "I should have asked her more questions."

Sawyer followed signs for the scenic byway. They could take the road through the national forest all the way back to his place without ever getting on the highway. The speed limits were much lower, but less traffic would make it easier to know if they were being followed.

His phone rang in his cup holder, and he recognized Wyatt's number immediately. He poked the speaker button to answer. "Hey," he said. "You've got me and Emma on speaker. We're in the truck headed back to the lake house now. What do you have?"

"Hey, Emma," Wyatt said, taking a minute to be cordial. "I'm real sorry you and your sister are going through all this."

Her eyes glossed with instant tears. "Thank you."

"We'll get her back," he said. "I'm working on these numbers now, and Sawyer's a force to be reckoned with on search and rescue."

Sawyer's gut wrenched at his friend's high praise. Sawyer's last search and rescue mission had gotten his team killed. "What have you learned about the numbers?" he asked.

"They're accounts, like you said, locals attached to overseas partners, I think. I want to call your cousin,

Blake, at the FBI on this. He can dig deeper than I can—legally anyway—if he takes an interest, and I think he will."

"Blake's card is on my desk. If you can't find it, call his brother West. He's the sheriff over in Cade County, Kentucky."

"On it," Wyatt said. "And, Emma…congratulations on the baby. Sawyer sent me some pictures. He's handsome as a derby stallion."

Emma smiled. "Thanks." She slid her eyes Sawyer's way. "You'll have to meet him someday."

"Plan to," Wyatt said. "I'll be in touch about these numbers."

Sawyer disconnected and turned his attention back to the road. "I sent a few pictures of Henry to the team when I sent the notebook scans."

Emma's smile grew. "Good."

The road through the national forest was winding and peaceful, a stark contrast to their lives. Lush foliage on either side masked the brilliant blue sky overhead, but shafts of determined sunlight filtered between the leaves and branches to create a marvelous display on the black-top stretching uphill before them. Sawyer had been to a lot of places around the world, but there was no place more beautiful than this. Tennessee had always had everything he needed. *At the moment,* he thought, glancing through his cab, he had everything he needed right there in his truck.

Henry fussed, and Emma twisted in her seat to reassure him.

"Sawyer?" she said softly, turning forward as the truck floated around another downhill curve. "Did you notice the motorcycle at the hospital?"

"Yes," he said. "Why?" His gaze flicked to his rear-view mirror and found the answer. A black motorcycle with a rider in matching helmet and gear blinked into view, then vanished behind the curve of the mountain as the winding road carried them steeply down.

"It's him, isn't it?" she asked.

Sawyer didn't answer. He couldn't be sure at that distance, but his gut said it was the same man. "I'll let him pass on the next straight stretch," he said. "We'll get the number on the license plate and contact Detective Rosen." Even if the rider's reappearance was nothing, it was worth a phone call to be sure.

Sawyer pressed the brake gently, reducing his speed around the next sweeping curve. The pedal was softer than before, working, but not quite right.

The motorcycle drew nearer, its pint-size Alabama plate clearly visible now.

The road straightened before them, and Sawyer powered his window down, reaching an arm out and waving the man around as he continued to slow.

The motorcycle fell back.

"What's he doing?" Emma asked, voice quaking.

"I don't know." Sawyer stepped on the gas as they headed up the next hill. "Give Detective Rosen a call. Maybe they can run the plate. Tell him we'll get turned around and head over to the station. I don't like this."

Emma dug her phone from her pocket.

Sawyer crested the next hill and began the sharp decline on the other side. There was a wide lookout and parking lot with multiple trailheads at the base of the hill. It would be a good place to turn and head back before their tail figured out they were staying in the next county and not just out to enjoy the scenic drive. It would also give Sawyer a chance to look at his spongy brakes.

"That's right," Emma said, describing the situation into her phone. She unfastened her seat belt and turned onto her knees to stare through the back window. "Sawyer, slow down a little more. I can't read the numbers on his plate."

Sawyer added pressure to the pedal, and it slid easily down. Alarm shot through his system and a curse slipped between his lips. The brakes were out. The motorcycle wasn't tailing them. He was monitoring them. He'd probably cut the brake lines at the hospital and was watching to see the efforts pay off.

"Emma," he said, eyes widening as a huge camper trailer headed up the mountain in their direction, barely between the narrow curving lines. "Turn around." He hugged the mountain on his right, looking for a way to slow them down, even as the grade of the road seemed to steepen.

Henry gave a small cry in complaint, and Sawyer's heart constricted further. "Emma," he growled this time. "Turn around," he ordered. "Buckle up."

"I can almost read the plate," she said.

Sawyer took the next bend at nearly fifty miles per hour. The sign had suggested thirty-five.

Emma fell against the door, thrown off balance by the speed of the turn. "Slow down," she snapped, fumbling for her seat belt.

"I can't." Sawyer ground the words out. He adjusted his white-knuckle grip on the steering wheel and pressed the limp brake pedal into the floorboards. "My brakes are out."

"What? How?"

He pulled the shifter down from Drive, dropping it into a lower gear. The engine growled in protest. "I think someone punctured the line at the hospital. The brakes were fine when we left, but every time I've depressed the pedal since then, I've been pumping brake fluid onto the ground. Now we're out."

She covered her mouth with one hand, and Sawyer knew she understood what they were facing. She relayed the situation to Detective Rosen in sharp gasps, voice cracking and breaking on each desperate word.

The road plateaued slightly before taking another downward turn. Sawyer pulled the shifter again, moving it into the lowest gear. The engine revved and groaned, shooting the rpm gauge into the red.

Before them, a line of cars plugged away behind a slow-moving school bus. *Beep! Beep! Beep!* He jammed his thumb against his emergency flashers and continued a battering assault on his horn. Silently swearing and begging the drivers to get the message. His truck was out of control, and if they didn't move, he was going to take them all out with him.

The cars veered sharply, one by one, skidding into the soft shoulder against the hillside on the right as Sawyer's truck barreled past. A thick plume of dust lifted into the air as the vehicles skidded to a stop.

The school bus continued on.

Henry cried in the seat behind Sawyer, probably startled half to death by the blaring horn. His protests grew steadily more fervent as the truck closed in on the school bus. Tiny horrified faces came into view, staring back at him through the dusty emergency exit.

The road curved again, and the bus's brake lights came on.

Sawyer yanked the emergency brake and the truck made a horrendous sound. Dark, acrid smoke clouded the air outside his window, filtering through his vents and causing Emma to cough, but the truck didn't stop.

With no other choice to make, Sawyer gritted his teeth and resolved to leave the road at any cost. Whatever he hit, short of a hiker, would be better than the bus full of children or careening over the mountainside. He held his position between the lines as he took the plunging curve around the mountain, seeking the first semilevel place to exit and slow his runaway vehicle.

At first sight of a trailhead around the bend, he pulled hard on the wheel. The truck slipped beside the school bus and over the rough, rocky berm with a deep guttural roar. The school bus swerved over the yellow line, and the pickup tore off-road completely, cutting a wild path through the miniature parking lot at the trailhead and taking a wooden sign with the location's official name down with it. The windshield cracked as the wood splintered and deflected off it.

Beside him, Emma threw her hands out as if the windshield might burst, and she screamed loud enough to chill Sawyer's blood.

Outside, people screamed and ran. They yanked babies from strollers and lifted children from the grass, launching their families against the tree-covered hillside. A mass of children in matching T-shirts fled a pavilion beyond the lot, and Sawyer directed his truck toward the newly emptied structure, hoping the slight uphill grade and a series of small collisions could safely slow the vehicle.

One by one, the picnic tables exploded under the impact of his truck's grille. One by one, the damage less-

ened until the little table and the hill brought his truck
to a whiplashing stop.

In the parking lot behind them, a black motorcycle
cruised calmly past.

Chapter Eight

Sawyer met the police and paramedics in the parking lot and directed them to where Emma and Henry sat on the grass. The path of destruction from the main road to the grassy bank opposite the pavilion was broad and littered with the fragments of state-donated picnic seating. Miraculously, no one had been killed, unless Sawyer counted the trailhead sign, row of picnic tables and his truck.

Detective Rosen joined them several minutes later, having stopped to speak with a number of witnesses and onlookers. "Are you all okay?" he asked, turning his eyes to the paramedic as he walked away.

"Yes, just shaken," Emma said, speaking for them all. "What did you learn?" She tipped her head to indicate the crowd behind them while Henry slept soundly in her arms.

"The Alabama plate was bogus," Detective Rosen said. "A bystander caught the motorcycle on video while taping your out-of-control truck. My guys ran the numbers, but that plate hasn't been in use in a decade. Probably thrown out and picked up by someone."

Sawyer lowered himself onto the grass beside Emma and looped a protective arm across her back.

She leaned against him, deflated, and said, "So even with a license plate number, a description of the vehicle and a hundred witnesses, we still don't know who did this?"

"Sadly, no."

Sawyer gave her a gentle squeeze. "What else do you know?"

"We know the truck's brakes were definitely tampered with," Detective Rosen said.

Emma huffed a disgusted sigh, then pushed onto her feet with Henry in her arms. "I need a minute," she said, walking away.

Sawyer raised a brow at the detective. He stood and dusted his palms against his pants. "You need to figure this out," he said. "Half those kids probably caught the whole thing on video with their cell phones."

"They did," Detective Rosen said, "and we'll review every frame, but the motorcyclist was in head-to-toe black. No one knows what he looks like under the gear, and we don't have a plate for the vehicle. We're doing what we can with what we have to work with, which isn't much."

"What about the hospital parking lot?" Sawyer asked. "My brakes were fine when I left. Then they got spongy and went out before I realized what was happening. The guy on the bike was there when we left. I think he might've punctured the lines while we were inside, so I wouldn't know what happened until it was too late. If you review the security feed from the cameras in that lot, you'll find him."

"We can try," he said, pulling a cell phone from his pocket. "But you should know the cameras outside the credit union, which would have been useful in identifying Emma's mugger or the hit-and-run driver, were out. I don't think it's a coincidence."

Sawyer tipped his head back and shut his eyes for a moment. "That's because it's not. These crimes were all planned. It's not good news for the police, or the victims."

"Mr. Lance?"

Sawyer opened his eyes. The tow truck operator lumbered in his direction. "Where do you want the truck taken?"

Sawyer eyeballed the extended cab of the logoed vehicle. "Wherever you recommend," he said. "Would you mind taking us to a local car rental company on the way?"

Two hours later Sawyer steered a rented SUV home from the police station, using the flattest and most low-trafficked route possible between counties. He'd rented the new vehicle under his company's name and given Fortress Security's address in case anyone tried to track him through the rental.

Sawyer's rustic A-frame house came into view through the trees, and he felt his shoulders relax.

He went straight to the kitchen for two glasses of ice water, and Emma curled onto the couch with Henry on her lap. She accepted the ice water with deep, thirsty gulps, but the fear and uncertainty in her eyes broke Sawyer's heart. He'd vowed to protect her and their son at all costs, but they'd nearly died at his hand today.

Sawyer brought up the photos of Sara's notebook on his phone as he made his way to the living room. He needed to put a name to their assailant before someone came at them again. He had a duty to protect Henry and Emma, *his son and his...* The thought twisted into a painful knot. Henry was his son, but Emma wasn't *his* anything anymore.

He hated that truth nearly as much as he hated the man who kept trying to hurt her.

Emma pulled her feet beneath her on the couch and turned wide blue eyes on Sawyer. "If the motorcyclist knew your truck, then he must know your name."

"Not necessarily," Sawyer said, determined to keep his cool.

"If he knows your name, he can find your address," she said. "He can find Henry."

Sawyer shook his head and offered her his hand. "It won't be easy," he said. "My truck, like my house, is registered to the company."

"But the company has a website," she said. "The website has a list of the Fortress team members' names. *Your name*," she said.

"I will protect you," he said. "This looks dire now, but it will be okay. I'm sure of it." And he intended to do anything he could to keep that promise.

The fire in Emma's eyes dimmed, and she shook her head in a look of resignation. "He'll find us again, Sawyer. He won't stop, and it's only a matter of time."

Sawyer took a seat at her side. He wanted to encourage and reassure her, but he was having trouble believing she was wrong. Instead, he held his phone between them, a photo from Sara's notebook on the screen. "Then we'd better find him before he finds us."

EMMA ANALYZED THE notebook pages late into the night, but nothing had changed. The numbers were still too long to be account numbers from Sara's credit union. Emma had already compared her fourteen-digit account number to the massive thirty-digit ones in the notebook. There was definitely more to the number-cluttered pages than just account numbers. She only wished she had a guess about what that might be.

Emma padded softly into the kitchen for another glass of water. Henry was fast asleep in his portable crib, and she'd already showered and changed into her favorite cotton shorts and tank top after dinner. If things went well for a change, Emma might get comfortable enough to fall asleep soon. The stress was taking a toll, and she needed the break. As it was, there was no way to release the ever-mounting tension, but a little rest could go a long way to taking the edge off, and that was what she needed most. She'd considered a jog along the lake earlier, or even a swim, but knowing a psychopath could pop up anywhere at any time had kept her close to her baby. Sadly, there would be no burning off steam for Emma until the nightmare was over. Assuming she survived at all.

The soft snick of an opening door put Emma's senses on alert. She stepped away from the countertop and leaned around the kitchen doorway for a look down the short hall. Scents of shampoo and body wash wafted out of the open bathroom door on a cloud of steamy air.

Emma's body tensed for new reasons as Sawyer moved into view. He pulled a black Fortress Security T-shirt over damp, rosy skin, still hot and beaded with water from the shower. His wet hair dripped over his temples and onto his broad, muscled shoulders.

She forced her mouth closed with effort.

"Sorry it took so long," he said, a look of profound guilt on his handsome face. "I was trying to decide if I should shave." He ran a broad palm over the dark two-day stubble, and Emma's knees went soft with an on-slaught of memories. She'd intimately enjoyed Sawyer's stubble in the past. She knew firsthand about the rash it left on the tender flesh of her breasts and inner thighs when rubbed just right.

"I like the stubble," she said a bit breathlessly.

Sawyer's brows rose, and a sly grin slid over his handsome face. "That so?"

"Mmm-hmm." She cleared her throat and pressed a palm over her racing heart to calm the climbing beat.

Sawyer kept smiling.

"What?" she asked, pressing the glass of ice water to her lips before she lost control and kissed him again, the way she had the night before. *No*, she thought. She wouldn't kiss him like that again. That had been a chaste kiss on the cheek. Not even close to the way she longed to kiss or touch him. Emma swallowed hard and set the drink aside before she dropped it.

"You know," Sawyer began, closing in on her with intense brooding eyes, "we never really talked about the fact you kissed me last night."

Heat rose in her chest and cheeks at the reminder. Her gaze lingered on his lips. "It was a friendly, appropriate, completely innocent gesture," she said, hating the quaver in her voice.

"Why'd you do it?" he asked.

Emma struggled to swallow. Her chin hitched upward. "What do you mean?" She crossed her arms over her chest to protect her heart.

Sawyer took another step in her direction and reached for her, unfolding her arms and resting his broad palms against the curves of her waist. "Why'd you do it?" he asked again, widening his stance to plant one foot on either side of hers, pinning her against the countertop with his stare and the weight of his body.

Emma gripped his arms for balance, enjoying the

heat and strength of him. "I missed kissing you," she whispered, unable to catch her breath. "I miss *you* and it makes it hard not to touch you."

Sawyer raised his hands slowly up her sides, grazing her ribs with his fingers, the sides of her breasts with his thumbs, then cradling her face between his palms, careful to avoid the darkening bruise along her cheek. "I missed you too," he whispered. The clean scents of toothpaste and mouthwash teased her senses for a heartbeat before Sawyer took her mouth with practiced skill.

He kissed her as perfectly as he had a thousand times before, and she curled herself around him in response. The taste of him on her lips pulled a greedy, exhilarating moan from her core, and she drank him in, enjoying the release much more than any evening jog.

She ignored the little voice in her head reminding her that a jog wouldn't break her heart when it was over.

Chapter Nine

Emma watched the sunrise over the lake, her legs draped over Sawyer's lap on his back-porch swing. They'd kissed until she was sure the burning need for more would turn her brain to ash, then she'd slipped away to gather her wits. The kiss had been enough for now, considering the excruciatingly complicated circumstances.

He'd found her on the porch swing, kissed her head and settled in at her side, pulling her legs over his and resting her feet on the cushion beside him.

"I think we should talk to the branch manager," she told Sawyer as the fiery sun finally lifted into the sky. "When I was at the credit union gathering the things from Sara's desk, Kate told me Sara had a bunch of questions for Mr. Harrison. Maybe her questions were related to whatever's going on here. Maybe he's part of this."

Sawyer stroked the backs of his fingers down her arm. "I'll give Detective Rosen a call."

"No." She pulled her legs away and planted her feet on the floor. "We can call Detective Rosen afterward, especially if Mr. Harrison says anything useful, but I want to talk to him without the detective there. Besides, the police have already questioned the credit union staff. Maybe he'll be less on guard speaking to someone without a badge. He knows me, and maybe he knows something that can help me find Sara."

Sawyer frowned. "I understand why you want to go. I just wish you wouldn't."

Emma pursed her lips, prepared to fight as long and hard as necessary to get her way on this. "It wasn't a request for permission."

His lips quirked, apparently tempted to smile but thinking better of it. "Two women at that credit union have already been hurt. If it was up to me, I'd keep you in my pocket until the danger passed. Or book us a room at one of those all-inclusive resorts under assumed identities so we could sleep with both eyes closed for a night or two."

Emma's heart sputtered. "I can't leave Sara," she said. "I won't."

Sawyer tucked flyaway hair behind her ear. "I know. I was just enjoying a daydream where I know you're safe."

She smiled. "Then you'll take me to the credit union when it opens?"

He tipped his head over one shoulder and released a heavy sigh. "The manager is a significant link between Kate and Sara, so it's worth a conversation. I just don't know if it's a good idea to cross his path. Like you said, he might know something, or he might be the one behind all this."

"That's exactly why we need to talk to him."

TRAFFIC WAS LIGHT on the way to the credit union. At nine fifteen, the school buses had already delivered the students, most office workers were at their desks and lunch hour was another two hours away. Sawyer parked the rented SUV across the street at the end of the block, and went to join Emma on her side of the vehicle.

Henry was bright-eyed and smiling as she tucked him snugly into a thick circle of fabric hung over one shoulder and across her body. He looked like a purse with a pacifier, and it made Sawyer smile.

"Are you sure you don't need to hold on to him?" he asked.

Emma shot him a sharp look.

He raised his palms.

A few moments later he opened the credit union door for her, still eyeballing the strange circle of fabric. "Will that thing fit me?"

"I doubt it," she said. "A lady at church measured me for it, but Henry's also got a backpack he enjoys. That's one size fits all."

"You put him in a backpack?" Sawyer frowned. "Whatever happened to just carrying your kid?"

"Baby slings and backpacks keep your hands free," she answered softly. "Not everyone has someone to help carry the baby *and* haul their groceries or unlock the car door or pay the cashier."

The words tightened Sawyer's core. Emma had needed help with those things, and help hadn't been there. *He* hadn't been there.

"Emma," a maternal voice cooed. A woman with a round face and salt-and-pepper hair motioned them to the transaction counter. "Come on over here and let me see that little man," she said.

Emma obliged with a smile. "How are you, Gladys?"

"Better than you, it seems." She frowned at the angry bruise on Emma's pretty face. "I heard about your mugging, the break-in. Sara, then poor Kate. It's a darn shame. Things are all but sideways around here lately. If there's anything I can do to help you, just ask. I can cook, clean, babysit. Whatever you need. I've already been praying night and day."

"Thank you," Emma said, wrapping her arms around Henry, something Sawyer had noticed her doing anytime she looked uneasy or afraid.

Henry kicked and stretched, discontent at standing still, Sawyer suspected.

"Here." Sawyer reached for his son. "I can take him. You can visit."

Gladys watched, wide-eyed, as Emma passed the baby to him. "Well, now I think you've forgotten to introduce me to someone important here. You never let anyone hold that baby."

Sawyer gathered his son high on his chest and kissed his cheeks.

"Gladys," Emma said, "this is Sawyer Lance."

Gladys sucked air. "The daddy."

Sawyer extended a hand in her direction. "Yes, ma'am."

Her smile grew as they shook. "I've been praying for you too," she said. "These two have needed you something fierce."

"I've needed them too," he said, releasing Gladys's hand and pulling Emma against his side.

Gladys pressed her hands to her chest.

An elderly couple came to stand in line behind Sawyer.

"Well," Emma said, "we'd better get out of your way so you can work. Is Mr. Harrison in his office?"

Gladys dipped her head and lowered her voice. "No. He didn't come in today, and as far as I know he didn't call off. Instead, we've got that one." She pointed to the office where a vaguely familiar face sat behind the desk, staring at the computer. "His name is Christopher something or other from our corporate office."

Sawyer moved out of the way, and Emma followed.

"Thank you," Emma told Gladys before turning her back to the woman and trapping Sawyer in her sharp gaze. "Why do you think Mr. Harrison isn't here?" she asked. "And where do you think he is?"

Those were very good questions. "Let's see if Christopher from corporate knows," he suggested.

The tall blond man at the manager's desk stood when he noticed their approach. He met them outside the office and pulled the door shut behind him. "Good morning," he said. "What can I do for such a fine-looking family this morning?" His name tag proclaimed the words *Christopher Lawson*, and his clothes said he knew how to pick them. All quality, neat as a pin and fashionable down to his tassel-topped loafers.

Emma offered him a polite smile. "We were just looking for Mr. Harrison," she said. "We always say hello when we're in the neighborhood."

Christopher crossed long arms over a narrow chest and widened his lanky stance. "Well, I'm happy to pass the message on, but Mr. Harrison's not in today."

"Shame," Emma said, dropping the smile. "Is he ill?"

Christopher shrugged, curious blue eyes twinkling. "Hard to say. Is there anything I can help you with?"

"No." Emma slid her hand into Sawyer's. "I guess we'll have to stop back the next time we're in the area." She swung Sawyer toward the door and nearly dragged him outside.

They crossed the street at the corner before speaking. Sawyer repositioned Henry in his arms and unlocked the

SUV doors. "What do you think?" he asked. "Is Mr. Harrison sick or halfway to Aruba?"

Emma frowned. "Maybe, but if he's the one who took Sara and he's leaving the country, then what happens to my sister?"

Sawyer didn't want to answer that. He buckled Henry into his car seat, then went around to climb behind the wheel. "What did you think of Christopher?"

"I don't know," she said. "He was strangely familiar, but I don't think we'd ever met, if that makes any sense."

Sawyer buckled up and checked his mirrors before pulling into traffic. "Any idea where Mr. Harrison lives? Maybe the best way to find out why he's not at work is to ask him ourselves."

Emma tapped the screen of her phone. "I might have his address," she said. "The office Christmas party was at his house a couple years ago, and the invitation was digital." She paused to look at Sawyer. "Maybe that's how I recognize Christopher. There were a few folks from corporate at the party."

"Which way?" Sawyer asked.

Emma called out the turns through town as Sawyer manned the wheel. Thirty minutes later they arrived at an upscale parklike neighborhood, befitting a middle-aged banker. "I think his house is the brick one-story at the end of the road," she said. "I remember parking in the back. There's a big concrete area outside a giant garage and a pool."

"Here?" Sawyer asked as they motored slowly toward the brick home. A cluster of people stood on the sidewalk across the street as Sawyer turned the corner toward the rear parking area Emma had described. Emergency vehicles came into view.

"What on earth?" Emma sat forward. "That's Detective Rosen's car. Do you think the manager has been keeping Sara here all along? Could they have found her? Why wouldn't the police have contacted me?"

Sawyer shifted into Park, and Emma leaped out. He unfastened a sleeping Henry from the seat behind his and took his time following Emma through the crowd.

A pair of older women smiled at Henry, and Sawyer slowed to let them admire the baby.

"Hello," he said cordially. "Do you have any idea what's going on here? We were just on our way over for a visit."

"Oh, dear," the woman on the right said softly. "I'm so sorry."

Sawyer raised his brows. "About?"

"I was walking Mr. Bootsy after breakfast, and I heard a terrible calamity coming from inside the house," she said. "I didn't want to seem as if I was being nosy, so we crossed the street, but then there was a loud blast, like a gunshot. I ran right home and called the police after that."

"Sawyer." Emma's voice turned his head in her direction. The horror in her eyes set his feet into a jog.

Beside her, a pair of EMTs guided a gurney toward the home, a folded body bag on top.

Chapter Ten

Sawyer cut through the crowd to Emma's side. He wrapped his arm around her and pulled her against his chest, practically reading her mind. "The bag's not for Sara," he said, leaning his mouth to Emma's ear. "It's most likely for Mr. Harrison."

Emma swallowed hard as she looked up at him, her breaths coming far too shallowly. She looked to Henry, and Sawyer passed the baby into her arms. Emma snuggled him to her chest and nuzzled him tenderly. Her gaze trailed the gurney with the body bag on its path to the house. "How can you be sure?"

Sawyer took Emma's trembling hand. "Come on," he said, giving her fingers a tug. He pulled her away from the crowd and through the front yard instead. "Neighbors heard a commotion this morning." He caught Emma's eye as they approached Mr. Harrison's porch. Sawyer climbed the steps, silently towing Emma along with him. "My guess is that Mr. Harrison figured out what Sara was onto with all those questions before her abduction, and he asked the wrong person about it. That or the man who took her found out she'd taken her concerns to Mr. Harrison. Either way, I'm sure he was the fatality here."

"We don't know he's dead," Emma said.

Sawyer tipped his head briefly to each shoulder. "This is his house, and we saw the body bag."

Emma sighed. "We should talk to Detective Rosen."

Sawyer peered through one of the front windows before moving onto the next. "I'm looking for him." He tried the door and a second window, then went back down the steps and around the opposite side of the house with Emma in his wake.

A row of flowering trees and bushes cast long shadows over the side yard, making their movement across the lawn less noticeable to traffic and onlookers. "Here," he whispered, motioning her closer. "Listen."

The curtains were drawn on the next window, but a number of male voices warbled inside. Sawyer adjusted his position for a look through the slight part in heavy linen panels. From his new vantage, he could see the reason for the crowd and emergency responders as well as the body bag.

Mr. Harrison was splayed over a desk in what appeared to be a home office, a handgun near his limp hand and a bullet wound at his temple.

Sawyer stepped back to make room for Emma, who slid into the small space before him.

She rose to her toes to see above the sill, then fell back with a gasp. "He killed himself," she whispered. "Why would he do that?"

Sawyer braced his palms on her waist, steadying her, then took her hand and finished the circle around Mr. Harrison's home. They crossed the small courtyard by the swimming pool and emergency vehicles, and let themselves into the kitchen.

Detective Rosen stood inside, rubbing his chin with one hand and speaking quietly to an EMT. He started at

Sawyer and Emma's appearance. "What are you doing here?" he asked, skipping the pleasantries.

"Door was open," Sawyer said. "What about you?" He moved farther into the room, getting a better look at the crime scene. It took only a minute to know his gut was right. Mr. Harrison hadn't committed suicide.

The detective frowned. "I'm a cop. I belong here. It's your appearance I'm concerned about."

Emma moved between them, positioning her back to the open office door where Mr. Harrison lay. "We were at the credit union this morning, and the man taking Mr. Harrison's place said he hadn't shown up or called off today."

"So you rushed right over?" the detective asked dryly.

Emma swallowed long and loud. "I thought his absence might have something to do with Sara's disappearance."

"Murder would also explain his failure to call off or show up," Sawyer said.

Detective Rosen lifted his brow. "Murder?"

Sawyer stepped forward. "That's why you're here, isn't it?" He turned to face the office. "First responders probably noticed the angle of the wound is wrong for a suicide. Whoever held the gun before leaving it on the desk beside the victim's hand was standing over him. Mr. Harrison was shot at close range, but there are no muzzle burns around the wound. Most suicide victims press the barrel to their skin to ensure they get the job done." Sawyer had seen it firsthand, and more often than he cared to recall during his time in service. "Furthermore, the gun is beside his right hand, but his desk phone, mouse, pens and coffee mug are on his left, suggesting Mr. Harrison was left-handed."

Detective Rosen sucked his teeth but didn't argue. "There are no signs of forced entry," he said, casting a look at the kitchen door, where Emma stood with Henry, looking more than ready to leave.

Sawyer nodded. He'd noticed that too. "He knew the killer, or he had another reason to open the door to him. Someone posing as a utility worker, salesman, new neighbor…looking for a lost dog, could've been anything."

Detective Rosen rubbed his chin again. "The crime scene team is coming to check for prints." He opened his arms the way he had at the hospital and stepped toward the door, herding Sawyer back to Emma, then outside.

"Wait," Emma said, stepping out into the sun. "Could Sara have been here?"

"No." Detective Rosen shook his head. "There are no signs that anyone other than Mr. Harrison had been living here. Now, kindly remove yourselves from the property. Civilians aren't permitted at a crime scene."

EMMA'S SKIN CRAWLED with tension and grief as they moved away from the home. Back through the shaded yard and past the window where she'd seen Mr. Harrison's body. The image of him slumped over his desk would never be completely erased from her mind.

"Hey." Sawyer's palm found the small of her back.

A thick bout of nausea and panic rose through her core to her throat. "Take Henry," she said, fighting the terrible sensation and passing the baby to his father.

Sawyer pulled Henry to his chest, and Emma bent forward at the waist, huffing for air and hoping not to be sick on Mr. Harrison's lawn. She counted slowly, forcing her lungs to take bigger and deeper gulps of air despite the burn in her constricted throat with each pull.

Sawyer leaned her against him and rubbed her back. "It's okay. Take your time."

A few moments later her knees were weak, but the black dots in her vision had cleared. She straightened her spine and squared her shoulders with feeble resolve. "Sorry."

"Don't be," Sawyer said.

Emma pursed her lips. A thousand horrific thoughts cluttered her frightened mind. "What if we find Sara like that soon?"

"No," he said. "Sara's smart. She's cautious, and she's a fighter. I'm sure that whoever has her is no competition for her will to get back to you. We just have to figure out where she is."

Emma hoped he was right. Sara was strong, but maybe her captor was stronger. Maybe her physical injuries had weakened her mental ability to stay focused and fight. "I've been praying that she'll escape," Emma said, stepping back into the sunlight of the front yard, "but she was in bad shape. You should've seen the blood on our living room floor. The way he choked her and climbed on her. The sound when he hit her." Emma's teeth began to chatter despite the morning's heat.

Sawyer helped her into the SUV and fastened her seat belt for her before shutting the door.

She watched as he did the same for Henry, then climbed behind the wheel.

"What?" he asked, reaching for the ignition and checking his mirrors.

Emma unbuckled and slid across the bench to him. She pulled herself against his side and buried her face in the warm curve of his neck. She gripped the strong muscles of his shoulder and breathed him in until her racing heartbeat slowed to the steady confident pace of his. "This lunatic hit Kate with a car and shot Mr. Harrison. What's he going to do to Sara?"

Sawyer pulled her onto his lap and cradled her in his arms, sliding the seat back gently to make room. "Sara's going to be okay," he whispered into her hair, "and so are you."

It had been a long time since Emma let someone else carry her burdens for her. Not since losing her parents had she truly let her guard down, and even then she shared the pain with Sara. Sitting there now, curled in Sawyer's arms made her dream of a life where she could trade off the work of being strong from time to time. Sawyer had been gone for a year, but he was back now. He was there with her and Henry, and maybe she couldn't make him stay, but she could make sure he knew that was what she wanted. That her heart had been torn open all over again at the sight of him, and only his enduring presence would heal her.

Sawyer's rough palm brushed the soft skin of her cheek. He tucked strong fingers beneath her chin and searched her face with soulful blue eyes. "What are you thinking?"

"I don't know what I'd do without you," she whispered.

Sawyer lowered his mouth to hers and kissed her gently before resting his cheek against the top of her head. "I hope you'll never again find out."

Emma agreed, and tonight she'd make sure Sawyer understood just how much she wanted him to stay.

Chapter Eleven

Sawyer held Emma's hand as they drove back through town. He stroked her fingers with the pad of his thumb and imagined a life where the three of them—Emma, Henry and himself—could spend days together doing whatever they wanted and getting to know one another, not haunting crime scenes in search of stolen loved ones and debating murder versus suicide. He struggled to keep his eyes on the road and off the people inside the SUV. He needed to protect them at all costs and find Emma's sister, but he wasn't sure what to do next. His team members were on other assignments, and already working the numbers from Sara's notebook in their spare time. Sawyer was supposed to be the man on call. The extra hands. But he'd gotten this call, and everything had changed. His jaw tightened and his grip on the wheel intensified. Keeping Emma and Henry safe made it impossible to go out on his own, and while there were some situations where a young family moved inconspicuously, the places he wanted to go would be dangerous for him alone, and he refused to be the reason Emma was ever frightened again.

If it was up to him, Sawyer would lock up Emma and Henry safely somewhere, maybe even back at Fortress Security with a few armed and trained bodyguards, then Sawyer would return to Emma's town. He'd start at the local pool halls and bars, asking anyone who'd had enough alcohol to loosen their lips if they'd heard about the missing woman or the hit-and-run. Surely in a community as small as Emma's all the thugs and lowlifes knew one another. Someone had surely bragged about the money they were going to come into. Someone would buy one too many rounds on him. There was jealousy among thieves, and Sawyer was sure he could find a lead the police couldn't if only he could divide himself in two to get to it. He gave Emma another long look, then glanced at Henry's sleeping face in the rearview mirror. They weren't officially his family yet, but he was willing to do anything in his power to make it that way, if Emma would have him.

She turned to face him at the stoplight, as if she'd somehow heard her name in his mind. "Can we stop at my place before we go back to yours?" she asked. "I'd like to pack some more of my things and what's left of Henry's. Maybe even bring his crib." The words were music to Sawyer's ears, but he hated the uncertainty he heard in them. Had he given her some reason to think he wouldn't be thrilled at the suggestion? Had their late-night make-out session not conveyed the fact that he wanted nothing more than to be with her, and with Henry, every day?

She watched him with an uplifted brow.

"All right," he said finally, simply. But he needed to do better. He needed to make his intentions crystal clear so there would be no room for misunderstanding. *Sooner rather than later*, he thought, *before anything else can go wrong*. There were already enough complications between them. "Why don't we stop by the outlets and buy a crib for my place?" Sawyer suggested. "There's no sense in hauling one back and forth when I need one now too."

"What?" Her narrow brows hunkered low between her eyes. "Why?"

"I want to spend as much time with Henry as possible now that I know he exists. It makes sense for him to have a room at my place too."

Emma's expression went flat, and she turned forward once more. "Okay."

"What?" Sawyer asked, taking the next right toward Emma's home. Clearly they weren't going shopping.

She bit into the skin along her thumbnail. "Nothing, it's fine."

Sawyer gave a dark chuckle. He hadn't been gone nearly long enough to have forgotten what *fine* meant. It meant she was mad, and for no good reason as far as he could tell.

She made a little fist and tucked her bitten thumb inside it, still forcing her attention outside as they took the final turn onto her long rural street.

He worked his jaw, determined to let her be mad about nothing. Except, she shouldn't be mad. She should be glad he wanted to be with his son as much as possible. Shouldn't she? Wasn't that the good, honorable and *right* thing to want? He squinted across the seat at her. "What's wrong?"

"Nothing."

Sawyer cut the engine in her driveway and turned toward her, throwing one arm over the seat back beside him. "Nope."

Emma's cheeks reddened. "Yep," she said, sliding out onto the gravel and shutting the door behind her. Hard.

Sawyer climbed out and met her at Henry's door,

where she unlatched his car seat from the base. He considered taking the heavy carrier from her or at least offering to carry it, but Emma was upset, and he'd learned quickly that she kept Henry close at times like these. *Even if she was mad about nothing.*

He followed them to the front door and outstretched a hand, offering to hold the carrier while she dug for her key.

She hooked the seat in the crook of her arm and handled everything herself. A moment later she pointed her key at the lock and froze. She backed up a step and looked at Sawyer. "It's unlocked."

The frustration he'd felt toward her unexplained attitude bled away, and every instinct he had steeled him to defend her. He motioned Emma behind him as he turned the knob. She hurriedly obeyed.

The door swung easily inward, and Sawyer cursed. She was right. Someone had been there, and the house screamed with the evidence. He pulled his weapon and reached for Emma with his free hand, pulling her and Henry close behind him.

The house was in utter disarray. Every item in sight had been turned upside down. Someone was desperate to find something. *The thing that he had broken into Sara's room to find*, Sawyer thought. A good sign that whatever Sara had on this guy was still in play. A good sign because her life likely depended on that.

Sawyer ached to prowl through the upended room and shoot today's intruder the way he'd shot the last, but his legs locked and his muscles froze before he reached the center of the living room. He couldn't take his family one step farther into a potential ambush, and he couldn't send them out of his sight to wait. He stepped back, urging

Emma onto the porch, then rushing her down the steps beside him to the SUV, where he locked them all inside and started the engine in case they needed to make a fast retreat.

His muscles ached to pounce on the man who'd done this, but that would have to wait. Right now, he had his family to think of.

THE POLICE ARRIVED within minutes of Emma's call to Detective Rosen. He came later, having been caught up at Mr. Harrison's murder scene. Comparatively, she supposed Mr. Harrison's situation had probably seemed more pressing, but she disagreed. She and Henry were still alive, still in danger, and finding out who kept coming at them seemed paramount to finding out who'd killed a man after the fact. Maybe if the police got to the bottom of her situation now, she and Henry would never end up like... Emma's stomach coiled at the thought of Mr. Harrison's fate becoming Henry's.

Emma took Henry to the rocker in the living room as men and women in uniforms began showing up in pairs. It was both profoundly tragic and strangely reassuring that the faces were becoming familiar to her. She'd seen them all at least once these last few days, some after Sara's abduction, others after her own mugging, the first break-in or the runaway truck scenario. The small-town police force was only so big, and now she'd met them all, or at least it seemed that way. Thankfully, they all knew that this was part of a complex ongoing investigation, and Emma hadn't had to repeat any information for them. She wasn't sure she could without bringing on an emotional breakdown, and there was no time for that.

She kept Henry close, singing softly and stroking his

hair and cheek until he grew tired of watching the crowd and he dozed in her arms. Henry was her life now, and keeping him close to her heart seemed to be the only thing keeping her from losing her mind. As long as Henry was safe, everything else would be too.

Even if her mother's dishes were shattered and the bookshelves her father had made her on her tenth birthday were ruined. Even if every sweet memory she'd made before her parents' deaths were slowly being chipped away and ruined by one murderous psychopath...

If Henry was okay, Emma would be okay too.

Emma tried not to think about the scene before her. She didn't let her gaze or mind settle on the woman dusting her door for prints or the photographer snapping shots of her destroyed things. They were just *things*. But her stomach clenched at the sight of her framed photos scattered on the ground, some torn from the frames. Photos of her parents. Photos of Henry. Images of her and Sara through the years. How could she go on in a life without Sara? Emma wasn't even sure who she was without her for context. They were best friends. Confidantes. *Sisters.*

Sawyer walked into the room, instantly pulling her jangled nerves together. Something about his presence had a way of doing that. Calming her. He'd stuck to Detective Rosen's side after his arrival, talking, listening and occasionally making calls. She admired Sawyer's unwavering confidence under fire. Ironically, of all the terrible things they'd encountered together these last few days, she'd seen him rattled only once, and that was in the SUV earlier when he'd offered to buy a second crib for Henry and she'd abandoned the conversation.

Her spine stiffened with the memory. He wanted to get his own crib for Henry instead of sharing the crib

Emma wiped her mouth and set the napkin aside. "Can we talk?"

"Yes." Sawyer frowned, prepared to vehemently plead his case. No, he hadn't returned her message when he'd gotten home, and he understood now that he should have, but he was trying to do the right thing by letting her go. He thought she'd moved on, and he had no right to barge back in, in search of something that was no longer there. Of course, he didn't know about Henry then, but now that he did, he'd never walk away from his son.

Sawyer didn't want to walk away from Emma either.

She flopped back in her chair, the hem of her shirt knotted around her fingers. "We need to talk about the crib situation and my behavior earlier."

Sawyer dragged his chair around the table and captured her fidgeting hands in his, overcome with the need to stop her from saying the words that would break him. "Me first," he said, swallowing his pride. He couldn't let her push him back out of her life until she knew how he felt. If she still wanted out after he'd spilled his guts, he couldn't stop her, but at least she would have all the facts before making a huge decision. "I should have called," he said.

Her mouth opened, then slowly shut without a protest.

"I was trying to do the right thing, but I can see now how wrong it was." He lifted her hands in his and pressed them to his lips. "Emma, you are the only reason I'm even here today. Thoughts of you were what got me through my darkest times. The memories we made together kept me fighting when I wanted to give up." He squeezed her hands. "I needed to get back here to you like I'd promised I would. Now here I am. I'm home. A civilian and a father."

Emma blinked. "And? What are you saying, Sawyer?"

"I'm saying that I don't know what kind of arrangement you have in mind for us with Henry in the future, but I'll accept whatever terms you give as long as I can be with him as often as possible. I've already missed too much. I don't want to miss another thing. Not his first word or first step. Not his first baseball game or fishing derby or car or college…"

Emma sniffled. "Sawyer."

"Wait." He steeled himself for the finish. He was only halfway there, and he needed to finish before some other calamity kept him from it. "Once I'd made it back on base, away from the insurgents who'd held me all those months, I thought things would get better, but they didn't. Being physically safe seemed to shift the stress. Once I was no longer in survival mode, I had time to think. And it's all I did, but then I had a hard time concentrating on anything other than what I'd been through. I couldn't eat or sleep. I retreated into my head with the memories I didn't want. It was like falling into a black hole every day. By the time I made it back stateside and was discharged, I was spinning out of control. My team at Fortress helped. They kept my head on straight. Gave me renewed purpose. New missions to save lives. My guys checked on me, made sure I toed the line and wasn't slipping back into the darkness, and it made all the difference. I was only beginning to feel human again when I took your call the other night, but I hadn't felt like myself in a year before that. It was like I'd been lost at sea and you were the lighthouse. I saw your face, and everything changed."

Emma blinked fat tears over her cheeks. She lifted her hands to her mouth and released a small sigh.

Shame racked Sawyer. He never wanted to be the reason for her tears, and he certainly hadn't meant to burden her with his troubles, only to open up to her so that she could understand. "I want you to be happy, you and Henry, even if that's not with me. Just…be happy."

Her expression hardened, and she folded her arms. "Why wouldn't I be happy with you?"

He frowned. "Didn't you hear me? I'm a mess. A barely recovered nightmare who just promised to protect you a few days ago and has failed repeatedly."

"That's not true," she said, setting her jaw and shifting her weight.

His gaze slid to the angry purple-and-brown bruise across her cheekbone.

"I was mugged outside a credit union," she said, apparently knowing where his thoughts had gone. "No one could have predicted that. *No one.*"

He opened his mouth to tell her that was his job. To troubleshoot, to think ahead of the danger and keep her away from it, not stand across the street while she was assaulted and pretend it could have happened to anyone. He'd been lax, and it had cost her.

She raised a palm to stop the interruption. "You've done nothing but protect me every minute since you got here, so don't try to tell yourself or me otherwise, because I'm not buying it."

Sawyer's mouth snapped shut. He watched the hard line of her narrow jaw clench, and despite himself, a pinch of misplaced pride swept through him. He loved that fire in her. The spark for justice when she thought something wasn't fair or right. The internal defender. Emma was kindness and honor, love and determination. She was all the things he aspired to be, and seeing her so ready to defend him sent a wave of warmth and hope through his chest.

"You haven't failed me," she said. "Not once. Not even when you got home and decided not to return my message. I can be hurt that you didn't call, but it won't change the fact that I would've done the same thing in your position. I would've tried to protect you from me too, and I would've done exactly what you did."

Sawyer's heart clenched. "What?"

"I think you are a brave and honorable man, Sawyer Lance. I don't want you to ever think any differently. I'm proud to know you, and I'm proud that you are my son's father. I was only upset about the crib earlier because I didn't like the idea of dividing Henry between us. It sounded like you wanted to split custody, but I don't want that."

Sawyer raised his palms to cup her beautiful face. A reed of hope rearing in him. "What do you want?"

She fixed emotion-filled eyes on his. "You."

Sawyer closed his mouth over hers, unable to contain himself any longer.

He kissed her slowly, deliberately, until she was breathless and unsteady in his arms, then he carried her inside.

Chapter Thirteen

The next two days went quietly. Too quietly. No news. No new leads. The few times Detective Rosen called with updates, the information had changed nothing. Security footage of the hit-and-run outside the credit union confirmed the vehicle was a rental registered to Mr. Harrison, but there was no clear shot of the driver. Kate had regained consciousness and was doing much better, but she hadn't gotten a look at the driver either. Sawyer suspected it hadn't been Harrison behind the wheel, but considering the bank manager had been murdered, there was no way to know for sure now.

Detective Rosen had also let them know a hospital in the next town had reported a male gunshot victim. The man's wound was consistent with one delivered by the gun Sawyer had used on the intruder sneaking through Sara's window. Unfortunately, the shot had been a through and through, and there was no way to definitively connect that man's injury to Sawyer's gun. Since Sawyer never saw his face, and couldn't identify him anyway, the man was released after providing a bogus story. The local detective was supposed to follow up with him. His blood was being sent to a lab where it would eventually be tested against the blood collected from Sara's windowsill.

None of this got them one step closer to finding Sara, and time was marching on. Six days had passed since she'd been dragged from her home, and Sawyer still had no idea who could have done it, or where she could be. Worse, Emma had been right that first night when she'd said the odds of finding her sister would diminish significantly after the first seventy-two hours.

He reached for Emma in the dark bedroom. He'd fallen asleep with her in his arms again, feeling happier and lighter than he had in a year. He could get used to what they had going, and he was determined to ask her to stay with him once he'd returned her sister safely. Sawyer knew that rescuing Sara wouldn't bring his fallen teammates back, but it would be a great step in regaining his peace.

Emma rolled against him, her long hair splayed over his pillow and her warm breasts pressed to his chest. He longed to take her again, but that was no surprise. He never stopped wanting her. He'd always thought the month he'd had with her when they met was perfect, but he'd been wrong. Hearing Emma tell him that she wanted him and that she was proud he was her son's father, *that* was perfect.

Sawyer stroked her hair and kissed her forehead before settling back onto his pillow, smiling and thoroughly content.

Moonlight streamed across the ceiling, and he was immeasurably thankful for the rest he'd gotten these last two nights with Emma. Though he wasn't sure what had woken him this time. Another nightmare? He didn't think so. He couldn't recall dreaming. Henry? Sawyer set his senses on alert and listened hard in the darkness. His son's breaths came deep and steady through the monitor. Henry was fast asleep, but instinct tugged at Sawyer's chest the way it had when someone had been in Emma's house with them that night.

Sawyer rose onto his elbows and forearms, a sense of dread erasing the peace he'd had only moments before. A heartbeat later he heard it. The low growling of a small engine. Maybe even an ATV like the intruder at Emma's house had escaped on.

Sawyer slid out of bed and dressed quickly in the darkness, listening closely to every creak, breath and heartbeat within his walls. The growl drew closer, and he cursed as an unfortunate realization struck. He hadn't heard an ATV. He'd heard at least three.

"Emma," he whispered, nudging her shoulder. "Wake up."

She jolted upright, eyes glazed with fatigue. "Henry?"

"No," Sawyer said. This was much worse. "We've got company."

Emma scrambled out of bed and pulled one of his T-shirts over her head, making an instant dress that stopped midthigh. "What's happening?"

Sawyer slid steady fingers between the panels of his bedroom curtain and peered into the night. Emma slid in front of him. Four single headlights cut through the dense and distant forest. All were headed toward Sawyer's home. "Call the police." Sawyer gripped Emma's shoulders and turned her to face him. "Get Henry and hide," he said. He snagged his sidearm from the nightstand and tucked it into his waistband, then pulled another from a drawer and kept it in his right hand.

Emma dialed and pressed the phone to her ear. "I don't

know where to hide," she said, moving toward Henry's crib. "I don't know what to do."

Sawyer dropped the curtain back into place. She had a good question. He'd never had to hide before, certainly not on his own property, and he had no idea what to tell her.

"Hello," she said into the receiver, "this is Emma Hart, and I need help." She rattled off an overview of the last few days with mention of the four ATVs headed their way.

Sawyer handed her the keys to the rented SUV. "Get to the truck and drive to the police station."

"What about you?" she asked, gathering her sleeping baby and his blankets into her arms, the cell phone clenched between her shoulder and cheek.

"I can handle four men, but not while keeping an eye on the two of you. You need to stay safe. Protect Henry. I'll focus on the intruders."

"I'm so sick of running," she said, frowning fiercely.

The debate was cut short when the ATVs went silent outside.

Sawyer parted the curtains again. The headlights were out, and the world was silent. They'd abandoned their vehicles. "They're moving forward on foot," he said, turning back to Emma once more.

She slid into her shoes and disconnected the phone call. "Local police are on the way," she said. "Dispatch is calling Detective Rosen for us. They'll fill him in on what's happening now."

"Good work." Sawyer ushered Emma down the hall toward his back door and pressed his back to the wall. Emma followed his example. Together, they watched a foursome of armed silhouettes drift across the lawn in the moonlight, heading for the front porch. Sawyer gave Emma a reassuring look. "I'll take care of them. You and Henry head for the SUV," Sawyer whispered. "Get in and drive. Don't stop until you reach the local police precinct."

Emma gripped his arm, unfathomable fear in her big blue eyes.

He set his hand over hers. "It's going to be okay. Get yourself and Henry to safety." Sawyer squeezed her fingers, then slid into the night, hating himself for leaving her behind, but it was for the best. Sawyer was well trained, but there was only one of him, and he had no idea who these men were. They could be former military or even mercenaries for all he knew. To be safe, Henry and Emma needed to get as far away as possible. The intruders had come via ATVs, which they'd left a significant distance away from the house. Even when they heard the SUV spark to life, there would be little they could do to stop it.

Sawyer jumped over the handrail at the side of the porch, steering clear of the motion sensing light, then crept around the side of his home, gun drawn.

Frogs and crickets sang in the grasses and near the lake. A sky full of stars arched overhead. The same stars he'd watched through the corner of a filthy window during the nights of his captivity. He pushed the memory aside and listened for the gentle stir of the SUV engine.

He stilled to listen as whispered voices rose to his ears. "You get the girl and the baby," one man said. "I'll take out the bodyguard."

Sawyer's jaw locked. *No one* was getting his girl or his baby. He lowered into a crouch and cut through the shadows like a lion after its prey, determined to stop them, incapacitate them, hold them until the police arrived, whatever the cost.

A brilliant, silvery moon came and went behind a mass of fast-moving clouds overhead. Memories of his last night-strike forced their way into his head. His pace slowed as the earth shifted beneath him. The scene morphed and changed before his eyes. Suddenly he was in uniform, outside an enemy stronghold in dangerous territory with his team behind him. He felt the drip of sweat slip from beneath his helmet and ride over his temple to his jaw. Saw the guards up ahead. Militants. Two at the door. One on the roof. One on patrol. He hadn't known about that one before. Sawyer stumbled to a stop. He blinked and rubbed his eyes, willing the images to clear, willing his heart rate to settle, his concentration to return. He sipped cool night air and cursed himself inwardly. He thought he'd put these episodes behind him. Thought his mind was on the mend.

One of the four trespassers came into view, keeping watch along the home's edge. The others had gone ahead. This was their lookout, and Sawyer had the element of surprise on his side. He could drop the man with a single shot. Not a kill shot, but one that would put him down and keep him there. The sound would pull the others from the home, and if it went well, Sawyer could lie in wait, hidden in the shadows, plucking them off one by one until he had a pile of bleeding criminals awaiting the arrival of local law enforcement. If it went poorly and they split up before coming outside, Sawyer could find himself surrounded.

He sighted his handgun, choosing the least lethal, most effective shot. But the memories returned, and his weapon grew unsteady in his outstretched hands. His finger grazed the trigger, then pulled back. Touched, then relented. During his last mission, it had been the sound of his fire that had given away their approach. He had gotten them captured. Gotten his team killed.

Sawyer's tongue seemed to swell, his throat tightened. He lowered the gun and shook his head hard, as if he might be able to clear his thoughts physically. He had to move. Had to do something. The others were surely inside by now, and Sawyer still hadn't heard the SUV's engine ignite. He had to act. He couldn't afford not to. His breaths were quick and shallow as he crept through the night, closing in on the nearest target.

The distinct sound of the back door caused his heart to sprint. The normally soft metallic click was like an explosion in the night.

The man before him turned. His curious eyes went wide at the sight of Sawyer a mere foot away.

Sawyer's gun was up on instinct, stopping the man from raising his, but Sawyer couldn't force his finger back to the trigger. He couldn't feel his fingers or toes. Fear had wrapped him like a wet, heavy blanket, and the knowledge he wasn't in complete control was enough to make him want to run.

But soldiers don't run.

He braced himself. Forced down the fear. Even as the dark world shimmied and brightened around him.

A sinister grin curled the man's lips, and he lunged.

"Dammit," Sawyer whispered, opening his stance and accepting the weight of the wild, untrained attack.

Three quick moves later, the thud of the man's falling body brought Sawyer back to the moment, and images of that long-ago night were shoved away. *One down and three to go.*

EMMA HELD HENRY close and listened to the night. She had the SUV keys in one palm and her shoulder pressed against the back door of Sawyer's home, preparing to run. All she had to do was find the courage.

The SUV was parked in the gravel drive twenty feet away. It would be simple, under normal conditions, to cross the small porch, hop down the short flight of stairs and be at the vehicle in seconds, even carrying Henry.

But these weren't normal conditions, and Emma's heart was seizing with panic at the thought of making a run for it now. She'd seen the silhouettes of the trespassers as they'd approached, and they were armed. She couldn't dodge or outrun a bullet, and she couldn't bring herself to risk Henry's life by trying. Her mind urged her to hide, not run. Hiding had saved Henry on the night of Sara's abduction and again on the night the intruder had broken into Sara's room. Hiding worked for them.

Running was a dangerous unknown.

Behind her, the front door opened with a heavy creak. Soft footfalls spread through the house, forcing her onto the back porch.

Help is on the way, she reminded herself. *The local police are coming.*

She released the screen door behind her, eyes focused on her goal. The SUV. She dared a small step forward, but something held her back. The tail of Sawyer's over-size shirt was caught in the door. Emma bit her lip and willed herself to remain calm. The moment she let panic take over, she'd make messy, potentially deadly decisions.

Henry squirmed in her arms, his small features bunching.

"Shh, shh, shh," she cooed.

The footfalls inside drew closer, headed her way.

Emma jerked forward, freeing herself from the door with a quiet thwap! She flew down the back porch stairs on silent feet. The motion light flashed on as she reached the base of the steps. The short distance to the SUV warped and stretched before her like a dream where the hallway never ended and no matter how hard or fast she ran for the door, she wouldn't arrive.

Move, she begged herself. *Run.*

The back door opened, and Emma scurried into the shadows against the house. It was too late to make a run for the SUV in the bath of security lighting. She'd missed her moment. Running now would only put a massive target on her back *and Henry's*.

She crouched alongside the porch, careful to keep her head low, and she scanned her dark surroundings.

"Where are they?" a man growled.

"I don't know," another man answered. "The car's here. They couldn't have gone far."

Emma listened to the footfalls as they paced the porch. She ducked deeper out of sight as the men approached the railing at her side.

"Check the house again," the first man said. "Where are your brothers?"

There was a long pause. "I don't know," the second lower voice said.

"Well, find them!"

One set of footsteps headed back into the house and out of earshot. The other man lingered. Waiting. Maybe even sensing she was near.

Emma watched as he leaned over the railing's edge and scanned the darkness. He was dressed in head-to-toe black riding gear, like the man who'd cut the brake lines on Sawyer's truck and chased them through the national forest. This man didn't have a helmet, but she still didn't recognize his face.

A chilly autumn breeze whipped through the air, and Henry made a small discontented sound.

Emma jumped back, jamming her bare legs into the thorns and briars of bushes along Sawyer's home. She bit her tongue against the stings of instant bruises and cuts and pressed a steadying kiss to Henry's once again crumpled expression.

Her baby's eyes fluttered shut and pinched tight as he tried to hold on to sleep.

The porch boards creaked.

The man was coming.

Emma broke into a sprint through the night, clutching Henry to her chest to absorb the impact of her flight. He squirmed but didn't cry.

She paused at the front of the house. Where could she go? Not onto the deck, dock or lake. She peered at the dark forest across the field. The men had come from the forest on the opposite side of the home. Was this tree line safe? Or was it possible more bad men lurked there, as well? How many were there? *Where were they?* she wondered, nearly frozen with fear once more.

"Did you find them?" an angry voice asked. The sound echoed in the night, near the opposite end of the house now, but any one of the four men could be on her in a second.

"No," another low male voice answered. "No sign of the lady, the baby or the guy. I didn't find my brothers either."

"Come on," the other voice said. "We'll split up and circle the place. You go that way. I'll go this way. We'll meet in the middle."

Emma sucked in a hard breath. She had to move. If she ran for the trees, they'd spot her crossing the field. The SUV was far away now, on the opposite end of the house. Behind her, near the voices.

A new fear breached her thoughts. Where was Sawyer? Where were the man's brothers? Did Sawyer have them, or did they have Sawyer?

She pushed the thoughts aside. One problem at a time. Right now, she was on her own to save Henry, and that started by staying hidden and alive until the local police could arrive. She scanned her options once more, looked into Henry's precious face, and made her decision.

"I love you," she whispered against Henry's soft hair. "You stay still, and I'll do everything I can to protect you."

As if in acceptance of their deal, Henry gave a soft snore.

Emma counted down from three, then she hurried across the short lawn toward the water. She slowed at the sandy bank, choosing her footing carefully so there wouldn't be footprints to follow. She took easy steps into the cold water. Fall's shorter days and colder nights had taken hold of the lake, despite unseasonably warm days. She sucked air as she waded deeper, to her thighs, her bottom. Then she carried Henry toward the dock and pulled a large red-and-white cooler from the weathered boards. She took it with her beneath the dock.

Carefully, she placed Henry and his mass of blankets into the cooler, onto the sand-and-dirt-lined bottom.

Satisfied the makeshift boat would hold up, she ducked beneath the dock, sinking to her shoulders in the frigid water, and floated Henry along with her.

Ripples moved across the previously serene surface, a hundred neon signs pointing out their escape route.

Emma held as still as possible and anchored the cooler in place before her. She closed her eyes, hoping the ripples would stop before the men came to examine the lake.

A frog jumped nearby, making a little splash. Henry squirmed in the cooler.

"Shh, shh, shh," she soothed, holding the little vessel as it rocked on the ripples ebbing around her.

His tiny lips formed an angry frown, though his eyes were determinedly closed.

"Did you hear that?" a man asked. The harsh whisper startled Emma with its nearness. "I think I heard something near the water."

Emma gripped the cooler, hating herself for choosing the worst hiding place in the world. If they spotted her, she couldn't even run. She hadn't saved Henry and herself. She'd made them easy targets.

Two sets of feet pounded onto the deck above them.

Emma cringed. Her heart raced, and her stomach lurched. She lifted a desperate prayer as her fingertips nudged the soft rubber tip of Henry's pacifier caught in the blanket folds. She plugged it into his twisted mouth and stiffened every muscle in her body, willing her baby to be silent and the ripples to stop announcing her presence.

"No boat," one of the men said, taking a few steps closer.

The second man paced overhead. "I'm sure I heard something."

"Fish," his partner muttered, "ducks, bats, frogs. Who cares? We've got to keep looking."

The weight of their combined retreat rattled the

boards, shaking dirt onto Emma's head. She stretched a palm over Henry's slowly wrinkling expression.

"Achoo!" Henry sneezed in a tiny puff of air.

The men froze. "What the hell was that?"

"What?"

Emma could see their faces through the space between boards now. She could read their murderous expressions and see their hands on their guns. All they had to do was look down, and her life was over. *Henry's* was over. His little boat couldn't save him from a bullet.

Her limbs and lips began to tremble. Her teeth rattled hard in her head. Tears welled in her eyes.

Bang! Bang! Bang!

A trio of gunshots erupted in the distance.

And Emma's heart thunked hard and heavy.

She'd already lost her parents and possibly Sara. Had she just lost Sawyer, as well?

Chapter Fourteen

The men on the dock lurched into desperate sprints, arms
and knees pumping, guns drawn as they raced toward
the sound of gunfire.

Henry flailed in his little boat, then broke into tears.
The violent cries were masked by a shoot-out. Emma
inched through the water, away from the dock, away
from the muzzle flashes and gunshots on the west side
of Sawyer's home, the same side where the intruders had
left their ATVs. A rush of unexpected pleasure drove
through her as she realized a gunfight meant Sawyer was
still alive and conscious out there somewhere.

The jolt of happiness propelled her to action. She
moved more quickly through the water, towing Henry
carefully back to shore.

His temper quieted slightly as she pulled him into her
arms and left the cooler in the water to sink. His little
breaths came hard and fast, and his bottom lip trembled,
puffing in and out with each raspy gasp, but for the moment, the wails had stopped.

Emma ran in sopping, squeaking sneakers toward the
woods on the opposite side of Sawyer's house, away from
the national forest, the intruders and the gunshots. Hot
tears stung her icy cheeks as she flew through the night,

stumbling on frozen legs, her wet skin screaming from the chill of blowing wind. Could Sawyer hold off four armed men on his own? For how long? How much ammo did he have on him? How much had he already expelled?

Where were the local cops?

Her hand went to the phone tucked into her bra, intending to call 911 and check on the cavalry, but the icy feel of her shirt slid through her heart. Her phone was gone. Likely lost forever at the bottom of Lake Anna.

The night was suddenly still. Quiet. No more shots fired. No sounds of a struggle.

Nothing.

Emma sent up a prayer and kept moving.

Soon, the low and distant cries of emergency vehicles and first responders pricked her ears. A moment later a much nearer sound wound to life. The familiar growl of ATV engines fading quickly into the night.

She stopped. Turned back. What did the sounds mean? Had the shooting stopped because the intruders heard the sirens and fled?

Or had the shooting stopped because they'd killed Sawyer and would come for her again the moment the police left her unattended?

Her heart ached with the possibility he could be gone. "Sawyer," she whispered. Surely it couldn't be true. She stepped back toward the house, drawn by the need to know he was okay.

She didn't want to know a world, or a life, without him in it. It wasn't fair. It wasn't right.

A hot tear fell from her eye to Henry's forehead. Startled, his arms jerked wide. His lips curved down in the perfect angry frown.

"Sorry, baby," she whispered through a growing lump in her throat.

"Emma!"

Her name boomed through the night.

She lifted her gaze to the house, senses heightened. "Sawyer?" she asked the darkness.

"Emma!" he hollered again, this time closer, his voice intent and demanding. "Emma! Come out. It's clear." The silhouette of a man appeared beneath the cone of the security light as he passed the back porch.

"Sawyer!" Emma gasped. "Here! We're here." She started back across the field at a jog. *He was okay.*

Sawyer ran at her, arms wide. "Emma," he croaked. "I thought I'd lost you." He stroked her hair and kissed her face.

She bawled ugly tears of joy.

Henry screamed. He'd had enough of this night. He was outside after bedtime. He'd been floated in the water. Put inside a cooler. Had his little eardrums tested by a gunfight.

"The gunfight," she said, teeth beginning to chatter. "What h-happened?"

Sawyer pulled back with a questioning frown. "You thought I'd lose a gunfight?"

"There were four of them," she said. "I h-heard dozens of sh-shots."

"I only shot four times," Sawyer said. "I missed twice. It's tougher than you'd think to hit a man dressed in black who's running through the night." He wrapped his arms around her and rubbed her frozen skin for friction. "I hit one in the leg before he got to his vehicle, and I hit the other's ATV before he drove away. The rest of the shots you heard were all theirs missing me. I took down the first two men hand to hand. They're out cold where I dropped them. The other pair fled."

Emergency lights cut through the night as a line of first responders rolled along the gravel drive to Sawyer's home.

Henry, Sawyer and Emma were safe again for now.

Sawyer pulled Henry into his arms and held him tight, then looked carefully at Emma for the first time. "Did you fall in the water?" He glanced back at Henry, who was completely dry.

"N-n-no." She considered where to start the story, then told it as quickly as possible while trying not to bite her tongue or break her teeth from all the shivers and chattering.

SAWYER FELT HIS blood boil as he listened to Emma retell the events that had forced her into frigid waters with their infant son. He pulled her a little tighter, wishing that he'd been there for her instead of across the property, letting two trespassers get away.

The side yard teemed with activity when they rounded the corner. Two cruisers and two ambulances were parked behind an unmarked SUV, presumably the detective on duty. Sawyer led Emma toward the ambulance.

"Oh, sweetie." An older heavyset woman rushed to meet them outside the open ambulance bay doors. Her sweet spirit and nurturing nature were evident in her kind eyes and audible in her gentle tone. Sawyer relaxed by a fraction. The woman reached for Emma, ushering her to the ambulance. "You look like you're freezing. Come here. Let's get you warm." She caught a blanket by its corners and stretched it in Emma's direction, opened wide to wrap around her patient's trembling shoulders.

"That's a start," she said, motioning Emma toward the vehicle. "Hop in so I can fix you up," she said.

Emma's teeth chattered. "H-H-Henry,"

The woman's expression faltered. Her warm brown eyes snapped in Sawyer's direction, hyperfocused on the blanket in his arms. "Was the baby hurt?"

"No," Sawyer said with confidence. If he had been, it would've been the first thing she said.

Emma shook her head. "He's just t-tired and sc-scared."

Sawyer rubbed the blanket covering her back. "Let her look you over. I've got Henry," he promised. "We're fine."

The older woman tipped her head and refreshed her smile. "I've got heated blankets and dry scrubs in the bus."

Emma nodded woodenly, pressing her lips into a thin white line.

Sawyer kissed her head, then helped her into the ambulance.

"We'll only be a moment," the woman said before pulling the bay doors shut.

Sawyer leaned in, listening through the panels.

"Here you are. Go ahead and change out of that wet shirt, then I'll get your vitals."

Sawyer breathed easier. Emma was in good hands. Now he'd find out who the four trespassers had been. He'd knocked two of them out cold. Maybe at least one of them would talk. He frowned at the spot on the lawn where he'd left the first man unconscious. Hopefully, he'd been collected by the local officers and put in cuffs somewhere for safekeeping.

"Mr. Lance?" A man in jeans, a T-shirt and ball cap called from his porch.

Sawyer changed directions.

The man was Sawyer's age give or take a few years. His boots were unlaced and there were creases on his cheeks, signs he hadn't been on duty when he'd gotten the call to come tonight. The sleep marks were also indicative of a deep sleep recently interrupted. Sawyer couldn't help envying a man who was able to sleep so deeply that the sheets had left marks that were still visible. Sawyer had only truly slept soundly a few times in the better part of a year, each of those times had been this week, always with Emma in his arms.

Sawyer shook the man's hand. "Sawyer Lance."

"Detective Steven Miller," the man said. "I spoke with Detective Rosen on my drive over, and he brought me up to speed. Were you or Miss Hart harmed tonight?"

"No."

His gaze slid to the blue bundle in Sawyer's arms. "Was your son?"

"No," Sawyer said, feeling his protective hold on Henry tighten. Was this the way Emma felt all those times he'd noticed her pulling Henry a little closer? "Emma's with the EMT right now."

The detective's mouth turned down. "How many trespassers were here tonight?"

"Four," Sawyer said, turning his attention toward the spot in the yard where the first man he'd knocked out had landed. "I left one right over there, and another in the hallway outside my bathroom. Two got away on the ATVs they rode in on." He raised a hand in the direction where the vehicles had been. "I hit one vehicle and one driver. A superficial leg wound. I'd aimed for the tires, but the trees are thick, and they were moving fast."

"And it's the middle of the night," Detective Miller said. "How far away were you?"

"About thirty yards."

The detective gave an appreciative whistle. "I'd say you did all right."

"What happened to the man I left outside?" Sawyer asked, avoiding the detective's next logical question. *Where did Sawyer train to shoot like that?* It wasn't a deviation in topic he wanted to take right now. Right now, he wanted facts and answers.

"Outside?" Miller shook his head. "We only found one man. Inside."

Sawyer opened his mouth to swear, then shut it. His gaze dropping to the infant in his arms. He'd never been one to take issue with cursing, but it just felt wrong to be the one introducing his baby to the words. "I guess he got away." Though he wasn't sure when. Sawyer hadn't seen a third headlight when the other two men fled, and he hadn't heard another engine rev to life after the other had run off. "I don't suppose you recognize the man you found in here?" he asked.

"I do," Miller said.

Sawyer felt his brow raise. "Is that right?"

Emma jogged in their direction and up the steps to Sawyer's side, dressed in pale blue scrubs that dragged the ground and sagged off her shoulders. She wound her arms around his middle and pressed a cold cheek to his chest. "I'm fine," she said, rolling her eyes up to his. "Shaken up and cold, but well. How's Henry?"

"Perfect," Sawyer answered. "This is Detective Steven Miller. Detective Rosen filled him in on the case."

The detective extended a hand in her direction and they shook.

Emma gave him a slow and careful look, stopping to examine the badge on Miller's belt. "I didn't mean to interrupt. You said you recognized one of the men?"

A uniformed officer appeared, tugging a man in cuffs along at his side.

"Yep." The detective raised a palm, halting the cop and criminal. "Miss Hart, Mr. Lance, this is David Finn, an occasional visitor at the local police department. Petty crimes mostly."

Sawyer ground his teeth, aching to knock David Finn back into unconsciousness for about a week.

"Your last name is Finn?" Emma asked, releasing Sawyer and squinting up at the scowling man and his big black eye.

"Yeah? So?" he snapped.

Emma chewed her bottom lip. "I just wanted to hear him talk," she said. "This isn't the man who mugged me or took my sister. His voice is all wrong, and it's not the man who broke into Sara's room. Sawyer shot that guy."

David Finn slid his gaze to Sawyer, and Sawyer smiled.

He reached for Emma, bringing her back against his side.

Detective Miller gave Finn an appraising look. "So, what's your big important role in this mess, Finn? How do you fit into the business of terrifying this nice family? You're certainly not the muscle," he said with a wicked grin, circling a finger in the direction of the man's swollen eye. "And I'm still trying to figure out when you graduated from graffitiing the corner store to the attempted murder of a new mother and her infant."

"Man," Finn drawled, "I didn't attempt murder on nobody. I didn't even touch that woman or her baby, and I ain't talking to you until I talk to a lawyer."

Miller motioned the uniform to take Finn away.

As they passed, Emma pressed closer to Sawyer, a small tremor playing in her hand on his back. "I heard his voice when I was hiding," she said. "He was looking for his brother or brothers. David had family here tonight. Why?"

David craned his neck for a look back as the officer hauled him down the steps. He didn't speak, but the fear was plain in his eyes. David knew Emma knew about his brothers, and they weren't getting away like he'd thought. That truth gave Sawyer a measure of satisfaction.

It also worried him to know that by failing the mission, the sloppy foursome had turned their target into a witness.

Emma rubbed her palms against her arms, still fighting the cold.

"Why don't we go inside?" Sawyer said. "You're probably chilled to the bone, and Henry will be more comfortable in his crib, away from the wind."

Emma nodded. She looked to Miller. "Can you stay for coffee or tea, Detective?"

He took a long look at the scene beyond the porch. The ambulances and cruisers were packing up and pulling out, leaving his unmarked SUV alone beside Sawyer's rental. "Why not?" he said. "I'll be hanging around until the crime scene crew gets here to collect empty casings from the shoot-out. I might as well warm up while I wait."

"Great," Emma said, her spirits seeming to lift a bit.

Sawyer held the door for Emma and Miller, then followed them inside. "Is there anything I can do to help tonight?" he asked. "Finding the casings, identifying the tread marks or tracking the escape route?"

"Nothing tonight," Miller said. "I'd like to have you both speak with a sketch artist tomorrow if you're willing. Anything you can remember about the fourth man's face. I have photos of the Finn boys you can use to identify which ones were here tonight."

Emma nodded. "Okay." She led the way into the kitchen and stared at the counter. "Tea or coffee?" she asked.

"Coffee," Miller said. "Black."

Sawyer stopped to admire the limited number of scratches on the front door's dead bolt. "One of those men knew how to use a lock pick."

"Yep," Miller responded. "Probably the one you saw leaving in handcuffs. Petty theft is his idea of a good time."

Sawyer stared at the lock, hating what an easy mark he'd made Emma and Henry. He'd assumed the fact that his home was registered to the company, in another county and had only recently become a place with an address would be enough to keep them safe for a few days. He ran a freaking private protection company, and he'd failed to lock down his own home.

Sawyer excused himself to put Henry in his crib, then headed back to the kitchen. When the sun rose, his place was getting a security overhaul that would be worthy of his company name.

Emma lined mugs on the counter where his old coffee machine puffed and grunted against the backsplash. "Will Detective Rosen be out tonight?" she asked Miller.

"No." The detective scanned Sawyer's home casually as he spoke. "Rosen said he's got his hands full back in

Knox County. Seems the sudden crime spree over there has taxed their force to the limits, and he's barely treading water."

"How much did he tell you about my situation?" she asked.

Miller tipped his head over each shoulder briefly. "He says your sister found and documented evidence of an embezzlement scheme at her credit union. Someone was pulling hundreds of thousands of dollars a year out of the accounts by manipulating the computer system."

Emma shot Sawyer a pointed look. "That's a lot of money."

"Did he say how they were doing it?" she asked, filling three mugs with coffee and ferrying them to the table in a tight triangle between her palms.

"Computers," he said. "Someone manipulated the program that determines the interest owed on folks' accounts. The system began directing a small portion of the interest earned into an offshore account. The interest owed on most accounts is only about one-and-a-half percent, and the portion diverted from each account was minuscule at best. Most people didn't notice a few extra dollars or cents gone. Most probably didn't bother to do the math on it, just trusted the bank to add their one-and-a-half percent every quarter. In the event someone noticed and called the credit union on it, a correction was made immediately, and those accounts were credited fifty dollars as restitution for the error. Then that account was removed from the list of accounts being attacked."

"Then Sara noticed what was happening," Emma guessed.

Miller took another long pull on the steamy black coffee. "According to Rosen, she started looking at every account. One by one."

Sawyer smiled, watching Emma's face light up at the mention of her sister. "That's Sara," she said, "and it explains the mass amount of numbers in her notebook."

Detective Miller sat back in his seat. "Your sister tracked every error and the date the error was made for the past twelve months, logged the details, built a case to show the credit union's interest program had a flaw. Then, somehow, she managed to get her hands on the matching offshore account numbers, and Rosen thinks that was when things changed. Probably, whoever she looked to for help was high enough up the food chain to have been part of the scheme she'd uncovered. She sounds like a smart, determined, resourceful woman."

"She is," Emma said. "I wish Detective Rosen would have told us all this. He knows I want to be kept in the loop, but he rarely calls. It's infuriating."

Miller finished his coffee and set the mug aside. "It's a lot of information, but none of it brings you any closer to your sister, and I think Rosen's hoping to call with news that matters. Men like Rosen and me got into this for the people. I'm guessing he doesn't give two flips about bank interest. He's working to get Sara home." He offered a small smile. "I wish I was officially on that case because it sounds a world more interesting than the junk I deal with over here in Tennessee's most rural county."

Sawyer rubbed a palm against the stubble covering his cheek. He lived in Tennessee's most rural county, on a finger of a lake sandwiched between two forests. "How do you think these guys found us out here tonight?" It had taken emergency responders at least ten minutes to arrive, and they knew exactly where to go. The remoteness, Sawyer realized, was great until he needed the authorities, then he'd have to be prepared to wait.

Miller cast a look at Emma, then back to Sawyer. "Rosen's men have been searching Miss Hart's land, looking for the bullet that went through the man you shot earlier this week. If they find it and match it to their suspect, they can arrest him. They haven't found the bullet yet, but they did find a listening device late this afternoon. You'll be hearing from him tomorrow about a sweep of the home's interior for additional devices."

Sawyer moaned. "The man with the duffel bag came to plant bugs while he snooped."

"Seems like."

Emma paled. "We talked about Sawyer's home while we cleaned. The lake. Our time here."

Detective Miller frowned and pushed to his feet. "I'd better get out there. See if I can find some of the casings from tonight's showdown. Match the bullets to the guns. Guns to their owners."

Sawyer followed Miller to the door. "Before you go, what can you tell us about David Finn and his brothers?"

"Not a lot. The Finns are a big family, and they keep to themselves. Dad's a mechanic. Mom stays home with all the kids. They're strapped for cash most of the time like a lot of folks around here. Some of the older boys have been in trouble from time to time, vandalism, shoplifting, petty theft. Nothing like this."

Sawyer mulled that over. "When you say the Finns are strapped for cash, how strapped are you talking? They don't have enough money to take the whole gang out for ice cream after T-ball, or they don't even have enough money for the kids to play T-ball?"

"More like the church delivers gifts every year so the kids have something to open on Christmas morning."

A whoosh of air left Emma's chest as she appeared at Sawyer's side. There was sudden and profound sadness in her eyes. "So, David and his brothers were likely the hired henchmen," she said. "Coerced into participation by their need to assist the family."

Detective Miller cocked his head. "It's nice of you to jump to that conclusion. I'm not sure most would in your position."

Sawyer smiled. Emma's kind heart and compassion were two of his favorite things about her.

Emma looked at Sawyer. "What?" Her brows knit together. "Most people are good," she said with finality. "What wouldn't you do to feed your family?"

Sawyer considered ticking off a list. *Murder. Theft. Kidnapping.* But he wasn't sure. Wouldn't he steal to feed his son? Wouldn't he kill to protect his wife? Mother? Brother? The honest answer was that it would depend on the circumstances. That he honestly didn't know. He'd never, thankfully, been in the dire straits Miller described. He'd never been in the Finns' shoes, so he couldn't judge, but he'd like to think that he'd always side with the law.

Detective Miller's cheek kicked up in a lazy half smile as he watched the exchange between Emma and Sawyer.

Emma's shoulders drooped. "I'm not trying to make excuses for criminals," she said. "At the risk of sounding awful, David Finn didn't look, sound or carry himself like someone with a lot of education, motivation or discipline. So, I doubt he's the criminal mastermind behind all this. Couple that with his family's financial situation, and it's more likely that he's made a bad decision for what he sees as a good reason."

Miller slid his gaze to Sawyer and smiled. "She's observant."

Sawyer laughed. "Yes, she is. I also noticed that the leather riding gear they wore was high-end, and those ATVs were new."

"So, either this wasn't the Finn brothers' first job," Emma said, "or the one in charge bought new bikes for his crew."

Sawyer gave her hand a squeeze. "That's my guess."

"New bikes?" Miller asked. "Did you get a make and model?"

"Yeah." Sawyer grabbed a pen and paper, then jotted down a description of the vehicles. He stopped suddenly, a smile spreading over his face. "Emma and I saw four headlights in the trees when the men arrived. Four bikes. Four men."

Emma smiled. "David didn't leave on his ATV."

It was still out there.

Miller swung the door open. "Nice work." He tipped two fingers to the brim of his ball cap. "I think I'll go see about that vehicle. I should be able to find the owner through the registration or purchase order. Thank you for the coffee."

"Detective Miller," Emma said, rushing to catch him before he slipped back into the night. "Wait."

Miller stopped on the threshold and raised his brows.

"Did Detective Rosen say if there has been a new lead on my sister?"

The detective took his time answering, but Sawyer saw the slight sag in his shoulders, the downward curve of his mouth. No news. "No, ma'am, I'm sorry," he said finally.

Emma blew out a soft breath. "Okay, well…" She looked at the floor, at her hands, scrambling for something more. "Is there any chance that the Finns have her? Could they be keeping her somewhere?" she asked. "Maybe hiding Sara has been their role in this until now. If they were being paid to keep her hidden, the payoff might've been enough money to buy the ATVs and riding gear."

Sawyer slid an arm around her back, eyes locked on Miller. Was it possible? "Is there someplace on the Finns' land where that could be possible? There were three brothers here tonight. That's more than enough muscle to contain one injured woman."

Detective Miller paused. He scooped the ball cap off his head and ran his fingers through messy hair. "It's a big property," he said. "Family land. I haven't been there personally, but I hear it's landlocked. Good for hunting and not much else."

"No neighbors, then," Emma said. "Secluded."

Miller rubbed his chin. "I suppose much of it is. I'd need a warrant to go poking through the home or property."

Emma stiffened against Sawyer's side. "Does that mean you think I could be right? Do you have enough evidence to get a warrant?"

He tugged the cap back on, swiveled it just right. "Not yet, but I'll call the station, see if the officers were able to get David to talk, and I'll take a look at the ATV left in the forest. If I can get a confession or link the Finns to the embezzlement scheme or something else connected to your sister, I'll have enough to wake up a judge." He smiled and stood a little taller. "I'll see what I can do."

Emma grabbed onto his hand as he turned to leave. "Thank you," she breathed.

Sawyer folded Emma into his arms and kissed her head. What she'd asked of the detective was a long shot, but it was something.

Chapter Fifteen

Sawyer curled Emma against his chest. She'd showered until her skin was hot and pink, then dressed in sweatpants and a sweatshirt and crawled into bed fighting a tremor. He'd kissed her head and shoulders and wrapped her in his arms until her rigid muscles relaxed. When he'd felt her soft, easy breaths on his arm, he knew she'd finally found sleep.

She jumped around 3:00 a.m. when the sound of crunching gravel announced that Miller and the crime scene crew had finished searching the forest for clues and were on their way out. One officer stayed behind, keeping watch indefinitely at Miller's request.

"It's okay," Sawyer whispered. He stroked her cheek with the back of his fingers, careful to avoid the yellowing bruise from her mugging, and he snuggled her a little tighter. "I've got you."

Emma shimmied in his arms, rolling to face him with sleepy blue eyes. "Do you think Detective Miller will be able to get the warrant?"

"I hope so," Sawyer said.

He kissed her forehead and gave her a warm smile, but he hated that the first idea they'd had about where Sara might be was just a guess. It was the first hope they'd had, and after all the bad things that had already happened, he worried about how Emma would handle it if this theory didn't pan out.

Emma didn't speak again for a long while. She drew patterns on his chest with her fingertips, leaving heated trails over the fabric of his shirt. "The judge might not think there's enough cause to issue a warrant."

Honestly, Sawyer didn't either. Not yet. "I know." Sara could be with the man who took her and not with the Finns, or she could be at a site not directly related to any of the people they knew were involved. She could be anywhere.

Emma rolled back an inch and looked up at him in the darkness. "What if you and I take Henry to see the Finns in the morning?"

Alarm struck through Sawyer at the thought of Emma going within a mile of that family. "I don't think that's a great idea."

"Why not?" she asked. "If Detective Miller can't get enough together to justify a warrant, maybe we can. We can stop by and introduce ourselves to the parents, let them know we're the family their sons broke in on last night, and that my sister's missing. We can tell them we're worried about her, and we're only there to see if they have any idea who their sons have been spending time with lately. Not to accuse them of anything. Maybe they'll talk to us. They might be defensive toward policemen, but mother to mother, Mrs. Finn should understand my fear and want to help me if she can."

Sawyer rose onto his elbow and rested his cheek in his hand. "I wouldn't want to do anything that could tip the other boys off," he said. "They know David was caught tonight, but they might not know that we know they were here with him, or that we're considering the possibility that Sara is being kept on their land. Knocking on their door and introducing ourselves could set off all the alarms, and if she is there, our appearance could be enough to make them move her. Personally, I don't like a plan with that much risk," he said. "Not with Sara's safety on the line. Not to mention, we don't want to muck up whatever Miller and Rosen are doing."

Emma dropped her head in frustration. She rolled back over and settled against him before falling asleep once more.

Despite her nearness and the steady sounds of Henry's breaths in the crib beside his bed, Sawyer didn't sleep. He wouldn't sleep until his home was secure and all the men involved in the break-in were behind bars. Instead, he spent the hours until dawn devising a way to keep Emma safe while getting a look at the Finns' land without upsetting the case authorities were building.

THE NEXT DAY was long and quiet. Sawyer arranged an early-morning delivery of enough security equipment to thoroughly lock down the cozy A-frame home. He upgraded the ruined security system and added a feature that would cause flashing lights and an earsplitting alarm in the event of tampering. The chaos would confuse an intruder long enough for Sawyer to drop him. He'd learned the hard way that a system that only alerted the police wouldn't be enough. His home was simply too far from the nearest police station.

After lunch he changed the locks and dead bolts on the doors, and reinforced the jambs to protect against an intruder intent on kicking his way in. Emma stopped him from putting bars on the windows, so he ordered bulletproof glass to be delivered in three to five business days. In the meantime, he set up cameras and a silent alarm system along the property's perimeter that reported to his main computer inside.

Emma spent the day playing, cuddling and napping with Henry. She'd eaten all her meals with Sawyer, but hadn't had much to say, except when Detective Miller had arrived with a sketch artist, eliminating their need to make a run to the station. Miller walked the property while Sawyer and Emma did their best to describe the men they'd seen last night. Afterward, Miller had brought her a surprise. Her cell phone was in the bushes along the house, dropped in her escape from the trespassers, instead of in the lake, where she thought it had gone.

Once Miller and the artist left, there was only endless silence. Whoever said no news was good news had clearly never had to wait on something.

When Emma slipped into the shower after dinner, Sawyer moved onto the back porch to call the detectives. He started with Detective Miller.

Sawyer gave the trees around his property another long exam. He doubted he'd ever forget the mess they'd been through last night, and he knew Emma wouldn't. Maybe it was time to return the A-frame to the company and look for a place to put down roots with her and Henry. A place where they could make happy memories. Someplace near parks and good schools. Maybe Emma would help him find the perfect spot to raise their son together, if he didn't screw everything up.

"Miller," the detective answered.

Sawyer made a quick pass through the formalities before getting down to business. "Anything new since you left this afternoon? Were you able to get David Finn to talk, or have you traced the ATV to its owner?" Ice fingers dug into the hair at the base of his neck, then slid down his spine. Sawyer rolled his shoulders and stretched his neck, throwing a cautious eye toward the trees.

"Nah," Miller said. "Finn's not talking, but I located the store that sold the ATV."

"Great," Sawyer said, standing straighter.

"You'd think." Miller grunted. "The purchase order says the buyer paid cash for the bike left in the trees last night. The camera over the register is a dummy, and the teenage sales clerk doesn't remember what the customer looked like because that was the night her boyfriend broke up with her and she vowed to never notice another man again. She only answered the few questions she did because I had a badge."

Sawyer dragged a hand over the back of his neck and gritted his teeth.

"The sales receipt recorded the date and time of the pickup, so I've requested security footage from nearby businesses around that time. We might get lucky and catch a glimpse of the truck hauling the ATV away. If I can get a plate on the truck, I can follow the registration back to the owner."

Sawyer crossed his arms and scanned the distance again. "Any chance you got that warrant?"

"Based on what I've got?" he asked. "No. I don't have anything to link Mr. and Mrs. Finn to Sara's abduction. David might be their son, but he doesn't live with them."

"Where does he live?"

"Ratty apartment downtown. No signs of Sara," Miller said. "I checked last night."

Sawyer said his goodbyes, then dialed Rosen.

Rosen was equally unhelpful, but he confirmed the

listening device Miller said had been found on Emma's property. He thanked Sawyer for the message Emma had left earlier providing verbal permission to sweep the house for additional bugs, along with directions to find the hidden key kept in their greenhouse. He had a team out there now.

Sawyer wandered back down the hall to his room, a little defeated, and waited for Emma to finish in the shower.

"Goodness!" Emma gasped upon sight of him on the floor with Henry. "What are you doing?" She pressed a palm to her chest as she lowered herself beside them.

"We're playing airplane," Sawyer said, passing their son her way with some enthusiastic jet sounds. "You look beautiful," he said, dropping a kiss on her nose. "How are you feeling?"

She shrugged. "Hopeful, I think. I'm almost glad those guys came for us here because now we have the power of two county law enforcement groups helping us look for Sara."

Sawyer scooted closer. "I had an idea. Now that I've got this place locked down, except for the window bars." He narrowed his eyes at her.

She bumped her arm against his. "That was a ridiculous suggestion."

"It wasn't a suggestion. The bars are in the closet now."

Emma smiled, her head shaking. "Go on with your new idea, please."

"I think the men who were here last night are probably regrouping and planning their next move. One was definitely shot, and I don't know how big this crew is, but that makes two with a GSW inside three nights, so now might be a good time for us to make a move."

Emma settled Henry on her lap and fixed a curious look on Sawyer. "What do you have in mind?"

Sawyer filled her in on the calls he'd made while she showered, then he suggested what he'd been weighing all day. "I want to gear up and head over to the Finn property at dusk, alone."

Emma squinted. "What does that mean?"

"I don't want to knock on their door. I don't want to give them the chance to say no. I want to enter the Finn property at its most remote access point, walk the land, look for outbuildings, abandoned mine shafts, anywhere big enough to hold Sara. I want you to wait here with Henry. You'll be safe if you stay inside, and Miller's got a lawman stationed on the property in case you need him."

Emma cuddled Henry close. "You're going on a rescue mission."

"Yes." The idea of Sara being held against her will had weighed on him more heavily every day. He knew that pain and understood those complicated feelings too well. The heartbreaking belief that no one was coming. The guilt and remorse. Sawyer's decision to shoot the night guard had alerted other unseen enemies, ultimately leading to the capture, torture and murder of his teammates. Sara, no doubt, blamed herself for pursuing the issue at her credit union. "If I find her, I can bring her home. The police can't even look."

Emma set her hand against his cheek and pressed her forehead to his. She sucked in an audible breath.

"I won't go if you don't feel one hundred percent safe here without me. You and Henry are my top priority."

Emma sniffled softly, then pressed her lips to his, drawing a deep, involuntary groan from him before she pulled away. "Go," she said with a smile. "Find Sara. We'll be right here waiting when you get back."

Sawyer got to work immediately, dressing in black and gathering his weapons and ammo. A sidearm in his belt holster. A spare at his ankle. A duffel bag with night-vision goggles, smoke bombs, wire cutters and anything else he thought might help him on his mission. "I might be a while," he said. "Could be past dawn. I pulled the topography map off the county auditor's website, and there's a lot of ground to cover."

She gripped his wrists in her small hands, a fervent look on her beautiful face. "Just come back to me," she said. "I love you, Sawyer Lance, and I don't want to spend another day without you in my life or in Henry's. We're your teammates now."

Sawyer's heart swelled. "I will come home to you," he vowed, "and if Sara's anywhere on those hundred or so acres of Finn land, I'm going to find her, and I'm bringing her home." He slid his arms around her and delivered a deep and assuring kiss before stepping onto the porch. "I'll wait while you set the alarm."

Emma nodded. She punched in the code, and the little activation light flashed red. *Armed.*

Sawyer let the officer patrolling his property know he'd be gone awhile, then he jogged to the rented SUV and climbed behind the wheel. Twilight was upon him, but he had a map and a twofold plan: search and recover. Return home to his new team.

NIGHT FELL SLOWLY over Emma's temporary home. She put Henry to bed around ten and knew he'd stay there dreaming contentedly until dawn. She, on the other hand, doubted she'd be able to sleep until she saw Sawyer's face again. There were so many things she should have told him. Her heart was full and warm with the knowledge that while she'd retreated into her head for the day, and he'd locked the house down like Fort Knox, he'd also been plotting a way to help her sister.

By two thirty in the morning, her nerves had gotten the best of her, and she set a kettle on the stove for tea. The pot whistled, and Emma went to pour herself a little chamomile tea. She tried hard to keep her mind off the possibility that Sara would come home tonight, but hope was stubborn, and she'd thought of little else since Sawyer had gone to look for her.

She filled a cup and inhaled the sweetly scented steam as she raised it to her lips.

Poised to sip, the lights flickered.

Emma braced herself against the counter and waited, listening to the wind whistle around the windows.

A moment later the lights flickered again.

Moving to the door, phone in hand, she dared a look outside for the officer on guard duty. When she didn't see him in his car, she dialed the number he'd given her when he'd arrived for his shift.

The officer didn't answer.

Her heart rate kicked into double time.

Sawyer had secured the home today. He'd barred the door. Installed a high-tech alarm system that would contact the police if the power lines were cut or anyone broke in while the alarm was set, which it was. He'd made every provision short of window bars or bulletproof glass, she reminded herself She was safe as long as she didn't go outside.

She stared hard into the night, willing the patrolling officer to appear. Maybe he'd dropped his phone without realizing or had left it in his cruiser while making a sweep of the perimeter.

The tall grassy field beyond the glass waved to her in the moonlight. Trees arched and stretched. Fallen leaves spun in tiny tornadoes around the yard, but there were no signs of intruders. No growling ATVs. No telltale headlights or silhouettes of armed men. *Just the wind.*

She dialed the officer again. Maybe he'd just missed the call.

The lights blinked out before the call connected, leaving her in the dark as the call went to voice mail once more.

"We're safe," she whispered. "This is fine. Only a brewing storm." She turned from the window, determined to stay calm. Sawyer had worked on the home's wiring all day, replacing the security system, installing new lights and sirens. The wind had probably just knocked something loose.

But she couldn't explain away the missing cop.

She brought up 911 on her phone and debated.

A loud pop turned her toward the hallway. The sound was loud and strange. Like nothing she'd heard before and very close. The newly installed security lights began to flash in the hallway and living area. An alarm blared in short, sharp blasts. Gnarled fingers of fear curled around her heart and squeezed.

Henry!

Emma ran down the hallway to the bedroom, slightly disoriented by the intense, repetitive bursts of light and sound. Her phone's flashlight beam streaked the walls and floor ahead of her as she gripped the room's door-jamb and propelled herself inside.

Light from her phone fell over an empty crib.

"No." Air rushed from Emma's lungs in a painful whoosh. Her mouth dried. The muscles of her stomach gripped. *This couldn't be happening. It wasn't possible.*

"Henry!" She swung the beam around the room. There were no security lights in the bedrooms, and the continuous flash from the hallway only added to her fear and unease.

The picture window beside the bed was shattered, cracked into a thousand individual crystals, most of which were now on the floor, glittering under the beam of her light. *This was the sound she heard.* Someone had broken the glass, and taken Henry.

"Henry!" she screamed, flashing the phone's light wildly through the space. She ran to the window in search of someone taking off with her son outside.

Instead, she found the missing officer. Facedown and unmoving in the grass.

"Henry!" Her scream became a sob. Sawyer had taken the only vehicle. She was trapped. Alone. Helpless.

Emma turned the phone over in her palm and hit Send on the call she'd had at the ready.

"Nine-one-one, what's your emergency?" A tinny voice echoed across the line.

"Someone kidnapped my son," she said, working to calm her labored breaths. She couldn't report the crime if she had a panic attack, went into shock or passed out.

"What is your name?" the dispatcher asked. "And where are you now? I'll send someone immediately."

Henry's cries broke through the intermittent blares, and Emma spun back toward the hallway. "I don't think I'm alone," she whispered.

"Are you saying there's an intruder in your home?" the voice asked. "Ma'am? Where are you?"

A sudden scream sent Emma into the dark hallway, sprinting frantically toward the sound of her son.

"Ma'am?" the voice asked. "I need your name and location."

"My name is Emma Hart," she rasped. "I'm at a cabin on Lake Anna off of Pinehurst by the national forest." She slid to a wild stop on socked feet at the end of the brightly flashing hall.

Before her, a large man blocked the way. Tall and lean, he towered over her, making the baby in his arms seem impossibly more fragile.

"Henry," she whispered.

"Hang up," the man said. "Now."

Emma disconnected the call.

The man stepped closer. He wore the black leather riding gear she'd come to know and loathe. He also wore a ski mask. "Put the phone down." The eerie calm in his voice was familiar and impossibly scarier than any sound she'd ever heard. This was the man who'd taken Sara.

Henry kicked and arched his back in a fit of fear and anger.

Emma dropped the phone where she stood, outstretching her arms. "Please. Give him to me." Her voice quaked. Her eyes burned and blurred with tears. She couldn't allow this monster to have her son. "I'll do whatever you want. Just don't hurt him."

The man motioned her toward the door. "I'd hoped you'd say that." The sinister curl of his lips was visible through the ski mask. He liked her fear, she realized. This was an elaborate game to him.

And he would kill her when he finished playing. Her. Sara. And Henry.

"Now, turn off your alarm."

Emma pried her dry, pasty mouth open and willed her words to be level and calm. "The alarm is wired to all points of entry. Windows included. When you broke it, you caused an alarm. Someone is probably already on their way."

He pulled a handgun from behind him and pointed it at the number pad, easily balancing her baby in one hand and the firearm in the other. "Shut it off."

Emma's windpipe narrowed. She obeyed, praying the emergency call she'd made, coupled with the broken window, would bring help fast. She pressed the numbers on the keypad carefully until the red light flashed green. "It's off," she said, turning back to the man, arms outstretched once more. "Please," she begged.

"Outside." He pointed to the door.

Her stomach coiled, and her mind raced. She needed to get her hands on Henry. Needed to make a run for the woods or the road, get away and hide until help could arrive.

"Out," he repeated, this time with venom.

Henry screamed again, a loud, maddening demand nearly as loud as the siren she'd recently silenced. It was pure fear. Pure agony, and Emma felt each new cry in her soul.

"Okay." She choked. "Okay." She slid her feet into sneakers by the door and pulled back the security bar, flipped a line of new dead bolts, then moved into the windy night.

On the living room floor behind them, her cell phone began to ring.

"Go." Her abductor pressed the hard barrel of his gun against her spine and forced her ahead.

"To the trees," he growled. "And don't try anything

stupid, or I could get confused and drop this squirming kid. I might even step on him while I'm trying to get my hands on you."

Emma lifted her palms. "I won't," she whimpered. "Just, please, don't hurt him."

"Move."

"Where are we going?" she asked. "Are you taking us into the forest to kill us?"

He sniffed a laugh. "I could've killed you in your house," he said.

"Why didn't you?" She moved as slowly as possible with the gun against her back. The pressure of it bruising her spine. If she wasted enough time, maybe help would arrive.

Emma watched the horizon for a sweep of blue and white lights against the darkness, desperate to hear the racing sirens.

The weeds grew taller with every step away from Sawyer's neatly manicured lawn. Sticks and weeds brushed against her legs and clung to her shoes. Bristles and briars tore at her skin.

Beyond the first rows of trees, a black ATV waited with a rifle attached to a gun rack on the back. "Get on," he said.

"I don't know how to drive," she cried, confused and desperate. "There's nowhere for Henry."

The man moved in close. "Get on the bike, and you'll get your baby."

Emma scrambled onto the seat, arms reaching, tears falling.

As promised, he placed her son into her arms. She pulled Henry against her. His small body was cold from the blasting wind. He was dressed in one-piece terry cloth pajamas, no coat, no hat. The psychopath who took him hadn't even taken his blanket from the crib to warm him. Emma hugged and shushed and kissed Henry before turning back to the man with the gun. "I can't hold him and drive. He can't ride on this. It's not safe."

The man fastened the strap of a helmet under his chin, then gripped Henry's thin arm in one black gloved hand. "Fine, we'll leave him here."

"No!" Emma screeched, panic racking her chest at the thought of leaving her infant on the forest floor. What was wrong with this man? Who could be so cold and damaged?

"Move forward," he demanded, shoving her with his free hand.

"What?" Emma rearranged Henry in her arms, nuzzling his cold face against her warm neck and trying, uselessly, to shield him from the gusting wind. She looked at the narrowing seat and gas tank between her and the handlebars. "Where?"

The man swung one long leg over the padded area behind her, and she instinctively scooted up.

Her thighs gripped the icy metal of the tank.

The man leaned against her back, reaching around her for the handlebars and doubling her over in the process, his chest against her back, Henry clutched precariously to her torso. The engine revved to life, and the man kicked the beast into gear.

Henry gave a pained scream as the vehicle jolted into the night, his protests swallowed by the roaring engine beneath them.

The ATV slid around curves, throwing earth into the air as it bounded over hills and flew along paths nearly invisible to Emma. She clutched Henry to her, willing him to be safe, whatever happened next.

She couldn't imagine where they were being taken, or what the man's plan was for them once they got there, but Emma knew it wasn't good. Her tears fell hard and fast, blown from her eyes by the raging, frigid wind as they tore through the darkness, one slender beam of light to guide the way.

Chapter Sixteen

Emma lost track of time, clinging to the bike for her life and to her son for his. Her face, arms and legs were numb from the biting wind, and Henry shook wildly in her arms. She kept her eyes and mouth closed as much as possible, fighting against the fear and nausea, trying to keep herself together for when they stopped. Whenever that might be. She peeked, occasionally, in search of something she could use to orient herself. A landmark for location or a ranger's office for help when she was able to get free.

The only thing she saw were trees.

Eventually, the ATV slowed. The engine quieted to a purr, and the force of raging wind became something more endurable. Henry's screams were audible once more.

The driver climbed off the machine, chilling her back instantly where his body heat had warmed her. She struggled to straighten, thankful for the coldness that meant he was away from her, and she could arrange Henry more comfortably in her arms. The moon was bigger, brighter where they were now. On a mountain devoid of objects to block or filter the light.

Before them, the headlight illuminated a large ramshackle shed. There was nothing else in sight except trees and the collapsed remains of a home long ago given back to the forest. A thick metal chain and padlock hung strong and new around the shed's aged door handles, and another powerful round of fear pricked Emma's skin. Someone was storing something of great value.

Sara.

"Get up," the driver barked as he approached the barn. "This is the end of the road for you."

Emma swallowed hard. She climbed awkwardly off the bike and stood on numb, trembling legs.

Her captor turned to the building. His attention shifted to the lock.

This was Emma's chance to run. She twisted at the waist in search of an escape path. The forest was dense around her, and the slopes were steep in every direction, covered in rocks, leaves, twigs, a thousand things to trip on, fall over in the night. The path behind them was relatively clear, but her abductor had an ATV to give chase. Even without the bike, he was undoubtedly stronger, likely faster, and unlike her, he'd dressed for the weather. Even if she managed to stay out of his reach, she couldn't hide. Not while carrying a screaming baby.

"Let's go," the man snapped as the lock gave way. "Inside."

Emma swallowed hard. She couldn't move. The dilapidated shed suddenly looked more like a tomb. The fine hairs on her arms and neck rose to attention. She was certain that going inside meant never coming out, and she refused to sign her son's death warrant.

He wrenched the heavy lock off the loosened chain and thrust the door wide. "Inside," he repeated. "Now."

Emma shook her head, arms tight on Henry, lips trembling. She'd made things bad enough by getting on that bike. She couldn't keep obliging this criminal. The bully. The killer.

He turned on her. "I said…"

Emma ran.

Her feet pounded the earth, flying wildly over the path the ATV had taken, away from the shed and the man who'd forced her out of Sawyer's home at gunpoint. Heart pounding, mind reeling, she searched the darkness for a way off the path and into the trees without falling over the sharp cliff on one side or trying to climb the hill on the other.

Bang! A shot rang out, echoing through the hills and evacuating a thousand bats from nearby trees. Henry screamed.

Emma slowed, raising one palm like a criminal in surrender while holding Henry tightly with the other.

A heavy hand clamped over her shoulder and spun her around, shoving her back in the direction of the shed. The armed man stayed behind her. His thick angry fingers dug into the back of her neck and the flesh of her shoulder. He swore vehemently as he steered her to the open door.

She dug her heels into the earth as her baby cried and flailed in her arms. Terrified of what she'd find inside.

The man gave her another shove, and Emma stumbled forward.

She recognized the shadowy form on the filthy wooden floor immediately. "Sara."

Sara shifted, raising her face to squint at Emma. Her arms and legs were bound, her face bloodied. Clothes ruined. What had he done to her? "Emma! No!" Sara cried. "No." She slung a line of thoroughly emasculating swears at her captor, then spit at his feet.

He dealt Emma another powerful shove, and she lurched forward, across the threshold and onto her knees.

She released Henry with one hand to brace them against the fall, and her wrist gave a gut-wrenching crack upon impact. Shards of blinding light shot through her vision as the pain spread like a heat wave over her body.

Beside her, moonlight shone through a hole in the roof, lending an eerie glow to the horrific scene before her. Sara sobbed and begged their captor for Emma and Henry's safety. She was a thin and fractured mess. Bruised and battered, filthy and frail.

The man unzipped his jacket and reached inside.

Emma scrambled back, angling Henry away from the man and placing herself in front of Sara. "No!" she screamed, imagining the gun already pulled. "Don't!"

He produced a cell phone with one hand, then unfastened the chin strap on his helmet with the other. He removed the helmet and ski mask as he walked back through the door.

Emma held her breath, watching intently as he tucked the helmet under one arm and pressed the cell phone between his ear and shoulder. She shushed Henry and cradled her probably broken wrist, avoiding eye contact as the man turned back to close the door. His face flashed into view a heartbeat before the barrier slammed shut, and Emma's blood ran cold.

Christopher. The man who'd stood in for Mr. Harrison at the credit union on the morning the police had found Mr. Harrison's body. Christopher had probably murdered him, then rolled in for a day of work like nothing was out of the ordinary. He'd been cool, calm and collected when they'd spoken at nine thirty that morning. Her stomach lurched at the memory of his easy smile. It went beyond unhinged to something more like completely deranged.

Sara sobbed against the rough wooden floorboards, apparently half-out of her mind with fear and pain. Her face was battered and caked with dried blood. Her wrists and ankles were raw from the ropes used to bind them.

Emma crawled to her sister's side and gently laid Henry on the floor with her. "It's going to be okay," she whispered, low enough to keep the hope between sisters. "I'm here. We're together now, and we're going to be okay." Emma wasn't sure she believed the words, but they had always been true before. She was counting on them to be true now.

Sara shook her head, frantic. "He'll kill you. You aren't bound yet. You have to run."

Emma hooked her fingers into the ropes at Sara's wrists and tugged with her good hand. Her left hand. Her weak and uncoordinated hand. Nothing happened.

"Stop," Sara said, tears spilling over too-pale cheeks. "You've got to find a way out of here."

Emma relented. Sara was right. Christopher could return at any minute. "Okay."

Outside, the ATV engine kicked to life and slowly moved away.

Emma checked the door. Locked. She examined the hole in the roof. Too high. Nothing to climb on.

"I'm so sorry," Sara gasped. "It's my fault you're here. It's my fault you're hurt. That Henry's hurt. I tried to protect you from all this."

Emma gave Henry a long look. "I don't think Henry's hurt. He's just scared. Cold. Mad." She backed up to get a better look at her sister and their jail cell, then levered

Henry into her arms to comfort him. Her wrist screamed from the motion.

"I should have told you what I'd been up to," Sara said. "Then you could have told the police everything right away."

Emma shook her head and gently shushed her baby. "I would have done the same thing."

"I found discrepancies at the credit union," Sara said. "I thought the system was miscalculating interest, but it wasn't an accident. Christopher was stealing."

"I know," Emma said, circling the small room. She needed to find a way out of the shed before Christopher returned. No windows. One chained door. One hole in the ceiling out of reach.

"The accounts weren't just being shorted a portion of their interest. The missing interest was actually being diverted to an offshore account."

"I know," Emma repeated. "I gave your notebook to the police. We figured out what was happening, but no one knew who was behind it or where to look for you." She cuddled Henry closer, and his cries begin to soften. "Now I know it was Christopher."

Sara nodded. "Christopher works in IT at corporate. He wrote the program that stole the money. Harrison helped me figure out what was happening when I brought my notebook to him. We downloaded all the evidence we needed to contact the police, and I saved it on a thumb drive hidden in the picture frame on my desk at work, behind the photo of us with Mom and Dad." She blinked back another round of tears. "I wanted to keep you out of this to protect you, but all I did was put you and Henry in danger."

Emma pressed an ear to the wall and listened. Silence.

"I have that photo," she told Sara with a grin. "It's on the mantel at Sawyer's house. The evidence is safe." And best of all, the lunatic who mugged her for the diaper bag of Sara's things hadn't gotten it.

Sara stilled. Her eyes went wide. "Sawyer Lance?" She slid her gaze to Henry. "*The* Sawyer Lance?"

"Yeah." She pressed her good hand to the door and moved clockwise around the room in search of a weak link. In a cabin older than time, complete with chunks of missing roof, there had to be a board somewhere weaker than her. "I'll catch you up as soon as we get out of here." She pressed the toe of her shoe against the base of every wall board where it met the floor, testing the integrity of each dark spot for signs of rot. "Come on," she whispered.

Sara wriggled upright on the floor, calming like Henry and beginning to regain herself. Her tears were gone, and a fresh fire burned in her eyes. "You have the evidence," she said. "That means we can put Christopher in jail for a long time for embezzlement after we get out of here. Harrison will testify."

Emma sighed. "Harrison was murdered."

"Murdered?" Sara's lips parted in horror. "How?"

"Gunshot. Someone tried to make it look like a suicide, but they failed. I assume it was Christopher, but he has a crew of goons working with him now."

"The Finns," Sara whispered. "They bring me food and water."

"Yeah. I think there are others too. In the week that you've been gone, Christopher has added a lot to the embezzlement, including multiple counts of breaking and entering, a hit-and-run, tampering with brake lines, three counts of abduction, a mugging and assault." She thought it over. "The brake line thing might qualify as attempted murder, same with the hit-and-run."

Sara gasped, "What has been happening out there?"

"Nothing good," Emma said, reconsidering immediately. She'd been reunited with Sawyer. Henry with his father. She was in love. Those were all good things. And the thought of Sawyer sparked a new idea in her head. "Do you know if we're on Finn land?"

Sara nodded. "I think so."

Emma smiled. "Sawyer left at twilight to come here and search for you. He hasn't found you yet, which means he's still on his way." And that was very good news. "He must've covered a lot of ground by now. It's only a matter of time before he finds this shed."

She gave the next board a kick, and her foot broke through. "Here!" Emma kicked again. Then again. The wood crumbled and splintered under the force. Slowly the initial shoe-size hole expanded into something big enough to slide Henry through. Soon, they would be able to run.

"Keep going," Sara said, scooting in Emma's direction. "When it's big enough for you to get out, go. Get help."

Emma turned her attention on Sara as she continued to kick and press the decrepit board. "I don't want to leave you."

"I can't go," Sara said. "I can't run. My feet are bound."

"Maybe we can find a way to cut your ropes."

"No," Sara snapped. "I can't go, but you can. We always put Henry first. That's the rule, and we never break it. So, you'll take him and go. Come back with help."

Outside, the low rumble of an ATV returned, growing louder with each passing second.

Emma's gaze darted around the room in search of something sharp to work on Sara's binds, but she was right. There was only dirt and wood. Her next kick wrenched the board loose with a crack, and Emma lowered quickly to the floor. She planted both feet against the edges of crumbled wood and pushed. The planks snapped and groaned under pressure. Hunks of the wall fell into the grass outside, and Emma's feet were suddenly beyond the cabin. Her hips and shoulders would fit through, as well.

"You did it!" Sara said. "You did it! Go! Take Henry and run!"

Emma pulled her feet back and hurried to Sara's side. She threw her arm around her sister's back and hugged her tight, not knowing if it would be the last time she'd ever see her. The painful tightening of her chest, lungs and heart was nearly enough to make her stay. "I love you," she whispered. "You are my best friend. My sister. My hero. Always have been. Always will be."

The ATV arrived, and the engine was silenced.

Sara batted tears. "You be the hero tonight, okay?"

Emma nodded. "Okay." She kissed her sister, then turned for the newly made escape hatch.

Before she could cross the small space to safety, the chains rattled and the shed door swung open.

Chapter Seventeen

Christopher ignited a flashlight, briefly illuminating his angry face. His helmet and ski mask were off, his hair messy from the aftereffects of both. He swung the beam of light over the floor in search of his captives. Shock tore through his scowl as the beam stopped on the generous hole Emma had recently kicked in the wall.

"What the hell?" he snarled, storming inside the dank and musty shed, fists balled. "Did you do that? How the hell did you do that?"

Emma stiffened, scooted back, but didn't speak. A tremor rocked over her limbs and coiled her nerves into a spring. She'd been hit by him once, outside the credit union, and she'd seen him strangle Sara. She knew what he was capable of, and she hated herself for not being faster on the escape. She'd been so close. Another minute, and she and Henry would've been hidden in the shadows, on their way to find help.

Christopher squatted for a closer look at the hole, then turned to Emma with his signature sinister smile.

She swallowed hard, scrambling for an explanation, contemplating a run for the door. Though running from him hadn't gone her way the last time.

He jerked to his feet, and Emma angled away, blocking her battered sister from his view. "Let us go, and we won't tell anyone what you've done," she begged. The plea was little more than a whisper on her sticky, swollen tongue, her mouth dry and pasty with fear.

Christopher barked an ugly, humorless laugh. He pulled his phone from one pocket and stared at the illuminated screen. "In case you haven't noticed, I don't make deals," he said. "I give orders and I call the shots."

She imagined his inflated ego swelling until it lifted right through the hole in the ceiling. "Then what do you want from us?" she asked. "What's the point? Why did you bring us here?"

He stepped purposefully in Emma's direction, and she winced.

He smiled wider.

Emma widened her stance and prepared to dodge him if he reached for her, or duck if he swung. She breathed easier when he stopped moving and checked his phone. Still, she had no idea why he'd taken the three of them and delivered them to the godforsaken shed. If not to kill them, which he could have already done, then why?

Christopher returned the phone to his pocket, looking satisfied with whatever message he'd received. He leaned at the waist, cold blue eyes searching for Sara around Emma's side. "I worked on this for years, then you just jumped right in and ruined it. You couldn't let it go. You had to pursue it. Relentlessly. Even after you called corporate to report the problem, and I told you I'd handle it. You just couldn't let it go!" His tone grew louder and more hostile with every word.

Emma glanced at her sister's equally red face.

Sara glared past Emma to Christopher. "You're tech support. I called you for help with what I thought was a system glitch. I had no idea I'd contacted the person who'd created the problem," she said, "at least, not until the problem never cleared up."

"You weren't supposed to follow up! That's not your job!"

"You're just tech support?" Emma asked, recalling Christopher at the credit union in a suit and a smile.

"I'm not *just* anything. Except smart, rich and fed up," he snapped. "Harrison wouldn't confess to his part in the ongoing amateur investigation with your sister, even under threat of death, and you saw how that went for him. I used my corporate ID badge to pass as the stand-in manager because I needed access to Harrison's office computer to remove any evidence he kept there. I got that job done, but there's still the issue with Sara. She told me she has enough data to ruin me, but she won't tell me where it is or who she's told. Funny, because she had a real big mouth when it came to shouting the problem from the rooftops."

"I was trying to help people," Sara cried.

Henry gave a grunt and squeal of complaint against the angry voices.

Christopher blew out a breath of exasperation. "This could have all ended with you. I asked you who you told, and you lied. Now all these deaths are on your head."

Who did you tell?

The vicious whisper from Emma's memories rocked her back on her heels. She swallowed another lump of hate and remorse. "I was there," she said. "When you came into our home and tore her away. I heard you hit her. Choke her. Saw you slam her onto our couch and climb on top of her, bullying, intimidating. You wanted to know who she'd told, but she'd never told anyone except Harrison. Then you screwed up. You took her from me, and you shouldn't have done that."

Henry stiffened his limbs and released a scream that seemed to come all the way from his toes.

Christopher's eyes flashed hot. The hard set of his lips and rigidity of his stance warned her to tread carefully, but Emma stormed ahead.

"You're going to jail," she said, bouncing Henry gently in her arms. "It's only a matter of time now."

He shot Sara a fevered look, then fisted his hands into his messy hair. "You," he seethed, glaring at the woman he'd clearly abused for a week.

"You," she yelled back, angry and suddenly looking utterly unafraid. "You stole hundreds of thousands of dollars from local families who were already struggling to pay their bills and buy groceries. You helped yourself to a portion of the interest they'd earned. You've killed to keep it. To cover your tracks. You're a criminal. A monster and a thief."

Christopher narrowed his eyes. "And you made me a killer."

"Greed made you a killer!"

He tipped his head back and laughed. "Now, we're going to play a game," he said, turning his attention back to Emma. "I'd originally hoped that with enough persuasion, Sara would tell me where she put the files and evidence she's collected against me, but she hasn't been very accommodating. I tried hurting her. That didn't work. I tried isolating her. That didn't work. Food deprivation didn't work. Now the police have one of my men in custody, and he's sure to squeal on me to save his idiot brothers, so I need to get out of town fast. I can't go without those files. I didn't work this hard to become a fugitive living on the run."

"What kind of game?" Emma asked, circling back to what mattered and not caring if Christopher had to live in a cave in Tombouctou.

He fixed her with a warning stare, then sidestepped until he had a clear view of Sara on the floor behind her. "The game goes like this—Sara either tells me where the evidence is, or Sara watches while her baby sister and tiny nephew die slow, ugly deaths."

Emma moved back another step, putting more space between Henry and Christopher. "What about the Finn boys?" she asked. "You said you're in a hurry because they're going to turn on you. Will you kill them too? All of them?" She wrinkled her nose in challenge. "Seems like you might get one or two, but whoever's left will either get the best of you or get away and turn you in."

"You're forgetting that accidents happen, and those guys go everywhere together," Christopher said.

"Another case of cut brake lines?" she asked. Emma struggled not to be sick. He spoke about killing three brothers as coolly as if he were talking about the weather.

The building sound of an ATV engine turned Christopher to the door. "Excellent. He's here." He clapped his palms together. "That game we talked about starts now. You have three minutes to give me what I want or choose who dies first."

"You'll kill us all anyway," Sara said. "Why would I give you anything?"

Christopher smiled and pressed the door wide. "Three minutes," he said, shooting his gun into the air for emphasis before letting the barrier slam shut behind him.

SAWYER HAD LOST count of the number of acres he'd covered when he heard the gunshot. He'd been at it for hours and not found any trace of Sara or anyone else, and at just before dawn, the single gunshot seemed all kinds of wrong.

He'd left Emma and Henry inside a heavily secured home, protected by a state-of-the-art system, but instinct had his hand inside his pocket, seeking his cell phone anyway.

He frowned at the pitiful single bar of service, then dialed Emma, thankful to have any reception so deep in the forest. No answer.

He redialed and squinted at the slowly lightening sky while he waited. The sun would rise soon, and he'd be able to see farther, move faster, finish his mission and return to his family. That was how he thought of them now, he realized. *As his family.* His new team.

He dialed again, and the call went to voice mail. Sawyer's intuition flared. He dialed the number of the officer posted outside his home instead.

That call went to voice mail, as well.

Sawyer broke into a sprint, running full speed in the direction of his vehicle. This time, he dialed Detective Miller.

"This is Sawyer Lance," he stated without waiting for the customary hello when the call connected. "Have you heard from your man outside my home?"

"No," Miller answered hesitantly. "Where are you?"

"Looking for Sara, but Emma's not answering, and neither is her security patrol. I've just heard a gunshot. I think someone's taken her and Henry like they took Sara, and I think they're somewhere on Finn land with her now."

"Whoa," Detective Miller cautioned. "Slow down and start over. Where are you?" he asked again.

"Detective," Sawyer said through gritted teeth, feeling his temper flare, "check on my family. Call me when it's done. I'll fill you in after." He disconnected. His mind spun with calculations as he ran. The amount of time it would take him to return home. The amount of time it would take him to reach the Finns' home. The amount of time it would take to find the location of the gunshot based on the echo and his best guess.

His phone vibrated in his palm as he slid behind the wheel of his rented SUV. "Lance," he answered.

There was a long beat of silence before the detective spoke. "Emma made a 911 call late last night, when responders arrived, the home was empty. Your bedroom window was broken. Our man was down."

Sawyer beat his empty palm against the steering wheel and floored the gas pedal. He reversed down the long dirt road at the edge of the Finn property with abandon. Dirt flew in a cloud around him. "They were home when I left," Sawyer said. "I have the car, so where the hell are they?" He thought for a moment about the situation. "Did you say she called 911?" He pulled the phone away to check the screen. He'd missed four calls. Two from a number he recognized as belonging to the new security system. Two from Detective Miller. His teeth gnashed as he swung the vehicle around at the end of the lane. "You called," he said. "It never rang." Cell service wasn't any good on the mountain. Nothing but trees and wildlife for miles. No signs of civilization.

Sawyer swallowed past a growing lump in his throat as numerous horrific images cluttered his mind. "Were there signs of a struggle?" he asked, unable to bring himself to ask the bigger question. Was there blood?

"Just the broken window," Miller said. "Someone shut off the alarm using the code, but no one answered when the contact number was called."

"It didn't ring," Sawyer said. He spun the SUV at the end of the lane and shifted hard into Drive. There wasn't anything to be done at his place. Emma and Henry were already gone. The cops would slow him down with questions for their reports, and time was already wasting. He needed a new plan. "I'm going to the Finn house."

"You are not," Detective Miller ordered, his voice thick with authority.

"I am," Sawyer corrected. "If you don't want me there, I suggest you try to stop me."

A siren coughed to life on the other end of the line. Challenge accepted. "You've got no business—" Miller began.

Sawyer cut him off. Miller didn't get to decide what was or was not Sawyer's business, and Emma and Henry absolutely were. "I've been on the Finn property all night," Sawyer interjected. "Walking. Looking."

"Trespassing," Miller countered, the siren on his vehicle complaining in the background.

"Looking for places Sara might've been held. I didn't hurt anything. Didn't touch anything."

"Did you find anything?"

"No, but there's a lot more ground to cover, and I heard a gunshot. It was near, but not near enough that I could say where it came from specifically, and I don't have time to mess around trying not to infringe on other folks' rights when my rights and the rights of my family have been trodden over daily for a week. So, like I said, I'm going to talk to the Finns. If you don't want me there or you're just eager to charge me with trespassing, then you'd better come haul me in." He disconnected and dropped the phone onto his passenger seat, then depressed the gas pedal and tore up the quiet country road getting to the Finns' house.

He took his time pulling into the driveway, careful not to roll into an ambush. He parked several yards from the front porch and climbed out as the sun crested the horizon. Senses on alert, and one hand on the butt of his gun, Sawyer opened the driver's door.

The home's front door swung open a moment later. A man in bib-style Carhartt overalls walked out. His clothes were covered in old grease stains. His boots and ball cap looked equally well-worn. "Who's there?" he called, stepping onto the top porch step.

Sawyer remained partially behind the open door. "Sawyer Lance, Fortress Security," he announced. "I'm hoping you have a minute to talk."

"I have a minute," he said, "but the missus is making breakfast, and I try not to miss a meal. Can I ask what this is about?" Mr. Finn was pushing fifty, tall and lean with a mess of crow's-feet at the corner of each eye.

"Are you Mr. Finn?" Sawyer asked.

"That's right. I'm Mark Finn." He hooked his thumbs in the straps of his bibs, both hands visible.

Sawyer relaxed and shut the car door. "Mr. Finn, I'm here because my…" He paused, stuck for the word. His *what*? His girlfriend? The term felt far too juvenile for what Emma was to him. She was everything to him. She and Henry. He rolled his shoulders and began again, reminding himself that time was speeding ahead while he floundered in a stranger's driveway, worried about semantics and courtesies. "My baby and his mama were abducted last night, and there was a gunshot out this way not long ago. I'm worried she might be on your property somewhere and hurt." *Or worse*, he thought. But there had only been one gunshot. There were two of them. A mama and a son.

"I heard that shot," Mr. Finn said, trading his easy smile for a frown. "Could be anything. Everyone's got a rifle out here. Could be someone saw a snake. Maybe had target practice or whatnot."

"No," Sawyer interrupted. "It wasn't target practice. There was only one shot, Mr. Finn." He felt the tension in the air, saw the man's shoulders square, his chin rise. "I'm not here to accuse you of anything. I'm looking for your help."

Mr. Finn crossed his arms and whistled. "I think you should go."

A moment later a dog the size of Texas tore into view, shaggy, caked in mud and rocketing to a seat at Finn's side.

Sawyer divided his attention, wishing he'd left the door open between himself and the massive mutt. "One of your sons was arrested last night," Sawyer said flatly. "I know because he and his crew came into my home in search of my family. I held them off. Shot one. The others got away clean. David was arrested. I think the others came back while I was out today, and I'm afraid that shot was meant for either my baby or his mama."

Mr. Finn's face went pale. "My boys wouldn't do anything like that. You're mistaken and out of line for coming here like this, and you'd do best to go."

"No, sir," Sawyer said. "I can't do that. See, I need you to tell me where a woman could be held on your property without being noticed for a week. Maybe two women now and my baby. Then I want to look for them."

Mr. Finn's sheet-white skin paled further, leaning on a shade of green. "No."

The half bark of a police siren shut Sawyer's mouth, already open for a rebuttal.

Behind him, Detective Miller bounced his black truck over the pitted gravel drive, bubble light flashing on top of his vehicle.

The door to the home opened again. This time a woman in jeans and a button-down rushed out. She had silver in her dark ponytail and a kid on one hip. A boy half her height trailed after her. "What's this about, Mark?" she called. "I'm just about to serve breakfast."

Mark let his eyes shut slowly, then turned to repeat Sawyer's story with a gentler touch than Sawyer had delivered it.

Detective Miller slammed his truck door, then hastened up the drive to where they stood. He pressed his palms to his hips and glared at Sawyer. "Have you said your piece?"

Sawyer nodded. "I have."

"Good. Like I told you before, we can't legally access their land without a warrant. So, you need to leave or be arrested for trespassing."

"I'm not leaving," Sawyer said. He turned desperate, pleading eyes on Mrs. Finn. "Please, ma'am," he pressed. "My four-month-old son and his mama are missing. I believe they're both in grave danger, and I think someone is holding them on your property. All I want is the chance to look for them. If they're not here, I'll leave, apologize, refine my search. But I'm asking you—what would you do if you thought your spouse and one of your babies was being held on my property? What if I said you weren't allowed to look for them?"

Mrs. Finn shifted the kid on her hip and traded a look with her husband. She turned a serious gaze on Sawyer. "You got something of theirs with you?"

Sawyer scrambled to make sense of the question. "What?"

"A shirt, a blanket, a hair tie," she said. "It don't matter." She tucked her fingers in her mouth and whistled. A mess of kids came running. "These ain't all ours, but they'll help if they want breakfast, and you know they do. Blue will help too, if you've got something he can use to track." She nodded at the dog.

"Yes." Sawyer spun around, wrenching the SUV door open and digging behind the seats for something belonging to Emma or Henry. "Thank you," he said, fighting a punch of emotion. He came up with a blue blanket of Henry's and a hoodie of Emma's.

Blue gave the items a long sniff, then took off in search of more of those same scents.

The Finns, Detective Miller and a slew of kids from age five to fifteen fanned out across the backyard, headed into the woods.

"We've got a number of barns and outbuildings," Mr. Finn said as they crossed the wide, flat space behind the house. "The kids and I have built blinds, forts, tree houses, all that and more on this land over the years." He slowed as his family and neighbor kids slipped out of sight, no more than silhouettes against a brilliant morning sky.

Sawyer ached to run after Blue, who was long gone, but waited, anticipated what Mr. Finn had to say. The way he'd paled at the mention of his other sons had meant something. Sawyer hoped it meant he had a good idea where Emma and Henry might be.

Finn swung a worried gaze from Sawyer to Detective Miller and halted in his tracks.

Miller cocked a hip. "You got something on your mind, Mark?"

Mr. Finn scanned the trees. "When my oldest boy was in high school, he'd throw wild parties at a spot we call The Point. It's just a small plot of flat land where my great-granddad's house stood about a hundred and fifty years back, but the last time I was out that way, there was a shed still standing." He pointed in the direction opposite of where the others had gone. "There's an access road a couple miles from here that cuts back this way. Down near Pine Creek Road."

"I know it," Detective Miller said, pulling keys from his pocket. "I drove past it getting here." He smiled at Sawyer. "I can be there in about ten minutes. You coming, Lance?"

"No." Sawyer shook Finn's hand with gusto, then broke into a sprint. "I can be there in seven."

Chapter Eighteen

"Go!" Sara whispered frantically to Emma. "Please." She struggled to hold back the silent sobs racking her battered body.

Emma fought the urge to lose control right along with her sister, but that was a luxury Emma didn't have. She was unharmed and unbound. It was up to her to get them all out of there. Alive.

Henry squirmed in her arms. He'd screamed himself to sleep during the argument with Christopher, but he was restless. Ready to wake. To scream again. Ready for a bottle. A new diaper. All the things Emma couldn't provide for him.

"Go," Sara continued.

"No." Emma tilted forward, locking determined eyes on her sister. "I'm not leaving you here to be murdered."

"Think of Henry," Sara sobbed. "If you're still here when that door opens again, someone's going to die."

"He's going to kill us all regardless," Emma said. "The minute you tell him what he wants to know, you'll no longer be useful and we'll no longer have leverage. We'll all be dead the next second. So pull it together and help me think."

"You have to try to get away," Sara begged. "You

have no idea what he's capable of." Tears rolled over her bruised cheeks, through the squint of her swollen black eye. She pulled her knees to her chest, and the ideas of what Sara might have been through came at Emma like a tidal wave.

"If he comes back and we're gone, he'll kill you," Emma explained. "Henry will hear the shot and scream, giving away our position, then Christopher will kill us. That's if Henry doesn't start crying the minute I lay him down to slide through the hole. Once I get out—if I get out—I can't even hide in the shadows anymore. The sun is up."

Sara pulled in a sharp breath; her cries quieted. She blinked at the warm rays of orange and amber light cutting through the shed's ceiling. "Another day," she said, mesmerized. "Every night I think I won't see another day."

Emma paced the small room with Henry in her good arm, forcing her thoughts away from the pain of her broken wrist. Outside, the sound of an approaching engine grew louder, closer, before the silence. "We need a plan, or you're right—there won't be another day. Not for any of us."

"Maybe we can hold the door shut somehow," Sara suggested.

Emma shook her head. "If we try to stop him from coming in, he'll just shoot through the door and hit us both. Besides, I can hear a second voice. There are two men now, and we aren't stronger than two men. I think my wrist is broken, and you look like you haven't eaten in a week."

"I've tried," Sara whispered. "When they bring it, I try."

Emma leaned her forehead to the wall and angled for

a look at the new arrival between cracks in the rickety wooden boards.

"Who is it?" Sara asked.

"I think it's one of the Finn boys," she said. Though she hadn't gotten a clear look at him in the dark, she thought he might have been one of the two men on the dock while she'd hidden in the water. If she was right, then he'd already come to abduct and kill her once. Considering that she was currently abducted, it was an easy jump to the reason he was there now.

The newcomer climbed off his ATV with a gun on his hip. His shaggy red hair was unkempt, and his eyes were wild. His gaze jumped from the shed to Christopher. "I was thinking," he said nervously. "I think we can get this done another way. There's no one at either house now. We can leave them here, and while everyone's out hunting for them, we can go through both places, take another look. Find what we missed."

"No time," Christopher said. "I need to go, which means they need to go. You got that? If I come back here on my way out of town and find any of them alive, I'm coming for your family. All of them. Maybe I'll build a nice middle-of-the-night fire to take care of all those young siblings. Maybe a brutal car accident for your woman and your baby. While you're grieving over their twisted carnage, you'll know it was your fault. All because you couldn't do this one simple task. You want that?"

"No, man," Finn said. "I didn't want anyone to die." He scraped a heavy hand over his cheek. "I never agreed to this. You never said anything about kidnapping and murder."

"I just did." Christopher climbed onto his vehicle and

started the engine. "I've got to get this ride scrubbed down in case her or that kid drooled on it. They'll check it for DNA when they find it, and I don't need any other fingers pointed my way. I gave Sara three minutes to tell you where she hid the evidence. If she doesn't, then you've got to make her choose who to shoot first. Don't make me a liar."

"What if she tells me what you want to know?"

Christopher drew a finger across his neck. "Kill them anyway. No loose ends. Understand?"

"What about the baby?" Finn asked. "You said I could take it to a fire station. Give it a chance at a life."

"I'm going home to pack," Christopher said, ignoring Finn's question. "There's a hole in the back wall big enough for them to fit through. If you take too long going in, they'll force you to chase them. It's awful damn early for that, trust me." He stuffed the helmet onto his head and flipped the visor up. "I want to see three bodies when I come back, so do. Your. Job." He delivered the final three words with deliberate menace, then revved his engine to life.

Emma's heart leaped and twisted in her throat. "Sit up," she told Sara. "Scoot back, sit up. Hurry."

Sara obeyed. Bending her knees, she planted her bound feet on the floor and pressed her back to the wall, settling her bound wrists in front of her.

Emma set Henry on Sara's lap, fitting him into the sharp curve of her sister's body for balance, then she dragged them both against the wall beside the door.

Next, Emma ran for the hole. "Don't let him fall."

Sara gripped Henry's legs in her hands. "What are you doing?" Sara gasped. "You can't leave him with me. I can't protect him."

"I'm not leaving," Emma said, crouching to grab the edge of a broken board in her good hand. She braced her feet against the floor and leaned back, throwing her weight into the movement, arm straining, legs burning. "Come on," she whispered. Nothing happened.

She inched forward, rearranged her grip on the wood and tried again.

"What are you doing?" Sara repeated. "Get out and take Henry."

"I'm not leaving. I've only got one arm to hold Henry while I run through the forest in broad daylight with him screaming. We'll be dead inside five minutes." Her grip slid. She reset her efforts and tried again. "He'll give chase. He'll hunt us."

The board made a moaning creak.

"So what?" Sara asked. "You have to try. Why are you making the hole bigger if not to run?"

The board gave way with a sudden, shockingly loud crack, showering the floor in shards of rotted wood and sending Emma onto her backside with a thump. A smile broke over her lips. "I can't run, but I can fight."

Outside, a man swore, and the door rattled.

Emma grabbed her newly freed slat of weak, aged wood and ran to hide beside the door with Sara and Henry. And wait.

SAWYER'S CHEST THROBBED with the effort of an all-out run up an uneven, rocky grade toward the mountaintop where Mark Finn had suggested Emma and Henry might be held. Maybe Sara too. His leg muscles burned. His worried heart hammered from effort and fear. It had been too long since he'd heard that single gunshot. *A kill shot*, he thought. And even if she hadn't died immediately, she'd have bled out by now, with all the time he'd wasted asking Finn's permission to look. Then again, without Finn's input, he would have had no idea where to go. Now he knew there was a shed, and Emma might be there with Henry. The thought pushed him harder, faster.

Maybe Emma had gotten away. Maybe the shot had missed her, and she'd hidden.

Maybe she had made the shot.

Sawyer slowed at the low groan of an ATV and walked silently in the sound's direction. Through the dense growth of ancient trees, a black ATV rumbled downhill with only a driver on board.

EMMA WIDENED HER STANCE, raised the board onto her shoulder like a baseball bat and waited as the door wiggled, then opened.

And she swung.

The wood connected with the man's face in a gush of blood and curses. Her weapon split down the center in response, one long ragged crack, splinters of rot flying over the both of them. He stumbled back, blood pouring from his nose and mouth, eyes blinking, ready to fall. The man's arms flailed, hands reached out for balance and caught the doorjamb with a thud.

The gun in his hand went off.

Sara screamed. Emma gasped.

Searing pain scorched through Emma's side and her hand lowered to the spot on instinct. Her palm slid against a strange, slick warmth, and the world tilted, but the man didn't fall.

Not good.

She needed to knock him out, steal his ATV and race her son and sister to safety.

"You shot her!" Sara screamed. "Emma!"

Emma looked at her side, then her palms, confused and swimming in adrenaline. Blood seeped through her shirt. The eye-crossing, relentless pain came next. She locked her teeth and swung the wood again, heart in her mouth, pulse beating like thunder through her head.

This time, the man's hand shot out and caught the busted board. He wrenched it from her grip and threw it out the door behind him. "You broke my nose!" he wailed. Blood trailed over his lips, teeth and chin. The skin along the ridge of his nose was red, broken and quickly swelling. His eyes flamed hot.

Emma stumbled back, pressing both palms to her side, where blood flowed freely around and between her fingers now. Her broken wrist no longer ached, but her knees wobbled. Her head spun, and the pain of the gunshot chewed its way straight through her. The unconscionable burn radiated across her gut and up her chest until it ate through her vision, and the filthy, aged floorboards rushed up to meet her.

A SECOND GUNSHOT. Sawyer pulled his phone and his gun, double-timing his pace up the mountain toward the peak, where he hoped to find a shed, and Emma, Henry and Sara alive.

"Miller," the detective answered.

"Another shot," Sawyer said flatly, forcing his mind and body to stay tuned to the task. "Hear it?"

"I heard it. Got an ambulance coming."

Sawyer's shoulders relaxed by a fraction. "Did you get the ATV?"

"Yes, I did. Stopped him at the crossroad. Says he

didn't see the no-trespassing signs and was just out for a morning drive."

Sawyer cursed. Rage burst through him like shrapnel. "You let him go?"

"No," Miller said. "He was trespassing, carrying a concealed weapon without a license, and his vehicle fits the description of an ATV seen leaving the site of multiple recent crimes. My deputy is on his way to pick him up."

"Who is he?" Sawyer fumed. "A Finn boy?"

"No. ID says Christopher Lawson."

Lawson. "He was at the credit union, standing in for the dead manager on the day that guy was murdered." Sawyer pushed himself harder, faster, his breaths coming quick and a smile forming on his lips. "I think you've gone and captured the ringleader. Don't let that one go."

"No intent of the sort," Miller said in an easy, casual drawl.

Hope rose in his chest as the next plateau came into view, and the cries of his son rose on the wind. "I've got eyes on the shed. I can hear my son crying." And there was another shiny black ATV sitting out front. If the victim of that last gunshot wasn't the driver of this ATV, then he was likely to be the next one shot. "You'd better order up another ambulance."

THE SOUNDS OF Henry's and Sara's cries warbled through Emma's fuzzy head, and she pushed to her hands and knees on autopilot. "You don't have to do this," she said, adding immediately to the pleas of her sister.

The gun shook in Finn's hand. His gaze darted around the dank, rotten, earth-scented shed. He muttered behind the other palm, which he'd clamped to his mouth.

Emma forced herself back on her haunches, deliberating, watching Finn and gauging what he might do next. Desperation drove people to do awful things, and Finn seemed as desperate as any man Emma had ever seen. "Please," she tried again. "I'm already shot, but you can save my baby and my sister. Get them away from here and tell Christopher you buried their bodies or threw them in the river. Anything. Not this for them." She lifted a bloodied palm. Fresh crimson drops painted a thick path down her forearm. "They're all the family I've got."

His face contorted with indecision. He looked at his gun, at Sara and Henry on the floor, at Emma, bleeding and weak.

"You would want to protect your family if you could, wouldn't you?" Emma asked softly, hoping that big family of his had taught him to respect and honor a genetic bond.

Finn swung in her direction, a belligerent look on his youthful face. "I have family too. He'll kill them if I don't kill you."

"He's going to kill you anyway," Emma said. "He's going to kill all of us so he can keep his stolen money and his secret, but you don't have to do this. I can see this isn't who you are, and it's not what you want." She hoped she was right.

"This was supposed to be easy money," he said. "My lady just had another baby, and we don't have money for food or diapers. My folks can't help. They're strapped raising my brothers and sisters. I can't find work without leaving town. I can't look outside town for work without a car. Can't buy a car without money." He raised his hands and pressed them to his head, pointing the gun at the ceiling. "I was going to be the muscle. A bodyguard for

Christopher, a lookout when he needed me. I was going to earn enough to keep food, formula and diapers in the house until I got real work. Then he got his hands on my younger brothers, promising them everything. Buying them fancy ATVs and riding gear. He reeled them in and had them doing his dirty work before I even knew it was happening. Then he used them as leverage with me. If I walked out on him, he'd turn them in for the crimes he had them commit. The next thing I know, we're all doing terrible things and we're stuck."

"Now your brother David has been arrested," Emma said. "Christopher thinks he'll turn on him to keep you out of jail, so Christopher plans to kill you after you kill us."

Finn didn't blink. It was the second time she'd told him Christopher's plans, and the second time he'd taken the information in stride.

"You already know," Emma said, letting the truth settle in. "You know, but you're still willing to become a murderer for him. Why?"

Finn paced. "It buys me and my family time."

"No, it doesn't," Emma said. "And you can't take your whole family on the run with you. Your girl and your kids, maybe, but what about your folks and all those siblings? Have you made enough money from Christopher to relocate all of them? To keep running if he looks for you?"

"He won't look for us," Finn said. "He'll be busy running from the law too."

"And if he gets caught? Turns you in to make a deal for himself?"

Finn's breaths came more quickly. A line of sweat

raised on his forehead and lip. He pressed his palms to his temples. "Shut up so I can think."

Henry's cries grew desperate again, as if he was in pain. Hunger, Emma thought. When was the last time he'd eaten? Before bed last night. It was also the last time he'd been changed. Tears pricked her eyes. Her baby was hungry, and she couldn't feed him. Scared and she couldn't hold him.

Finn dropped his hands and looked from Emma to Sara. "Enough. Turn around. Both of you." He pressed his thumb to the hammer on his gun and pulled it back with a soft click that rolled Emma's stomach. "I just want this to be over," he said, exhausted. "Turn around. I'll make it quick. Three shots. Three seconds. You'll never know it happened, and it'll be over."

"Please," Sara cried. "Don't."

Finn scooped Henry into his arms and set him against the wall, near the hole Emma had made. He dragged Sara back against the far wall, opposite the door, and he motioned Emma into the space between her son and sister. Lining them up like bottles for target practice. "Close your eyes."

Emma gripped her side and reached for her baby.

Finn groaned. "Stop."

Emma couldn't stop. It wasn't in her. Henry was alone, crying, scared. He wouldn't die alone like that. She didn't care what Finn or anyone else said. "Mama's here," she called, working her voice into something less soaked in pain, less mired in grief. "Shh," she cooed.

"I said stop!" Finn raged, his boot connecting with her torso, spinning her into a hard roll that ended with a collision against the side wall, away from Henry and the escape hole. The impact stole her breath, knocked the wind from her lungs. She searched wildly through spotted vision for Henry when she stilled.

"Henry," she choked.

His cries were there, but he wasn't. Her gaze darted across the floor. Had he flailed and kicked himself through the hole? Had he fallen to the ground?

Emma's heart and stomach lurched.

Finn stormed forward, peering through the hole. "What the...?" He stood upright as Henry's cries grew distant and muffled. Panic colored his bloody face. "I should've just killed you all the minute I walked in here," he said, storming for the door. "I let you talk to me and get into my head, now..."

A blast of gunfire cut Finn's rant short. The sudden burst rang in Emma's ears and vibrated in her chest. Finn flew backward, arms waving, feet twisting, until he landed in a lifeless heap beside Sara.

The door swung open and Sara screamed.

A pair of men marched inside.

Emma's mind reeled. What had happened? Who had arrived? Who had shot Finn? Christopher?

The first man kicked the gun away from Finn, then lowered to check his neck for a pulse.

"Emma." Sawyer's voice broke through her muddled thoughts. His face swam into view, marred with fear and concern. He crouched before her, Henry crying in his arms. He pressed his forehead to hers, then kissed her lips with firm reassurance. "Sorry I'm late."

Detective Miller stood, stepped away from Finn's body. "He's gone," he said sadly, then moved to Sara's side and cut easily through her ropes with a pocketknife. Once she was freed, he hoisted her into his arms and carried her straight outside and into the day.

Sawyer's expression fell. His eyes stretched wide as he lifted a bloodied palm between them. "Emma?" His gaze trailed over her torso, over the smears of her blood on Henry's pajamas between them. "You've been shot."

Emma opened her mouth to tell him she was okay, that she loved him, but the words didn't come. She felt the strength of his arms around her. Smelled the sweet scent of Henry's baby shampoo as her head rolled back. Her thoughts fell into darkness.

Chapter Nineteen

Sawyer kissed Emma lightly under the canopy of lights outside her home. A lot had changed in the eight months since he'd ridden with her, breathless and terrified, to the hospital following her mountaintop rescue. His pulse still raced whenever he thought of that day. He still dreamed every manner of horrific scenarios where things went another way. Sometimes he arrived five minutes later. Too late to save her. He hated those dreams most. But when the nightmares of losing her woke him now, the way nightmares of losing his team had woken him before, he simply reached for her in the darkness and pulled her near. Then everything was right in the world.

"I love you," she whispered against his crisp white dress shirt, playfully flipping the end of his tie.

He kissed her again, at a complete loss for words.

Seeing her so healthy and beautiful under the endless rows of twinkle lights, surrounded by family and friends, it was hard to believe that he'd nearly lost her completely. She'd gone limp in his arms, and he'd felt the punch of it in his gut as clear and strong as if it would kill him too.

Eight months since he'd stood sentinel at her bedside following her surgery. Eight months since he'd prayed around the clock to see her beautiful blue eyes once more.

Eight months since he'd fallen to his knees the moment she'd spoken his name and begged her to be his wife. He hadn't gotten halfway through the rambling proposal before she'd said yes. It was her first word after three long days of silence, and it had the power to change his life.

She cradled his cheek in her palm as she smiled.

Two hundred guests and she only had eyes for him. His chest puffed in pride and satisfaction.

"What?" she asked.

"Just thinking about how lucky I am. How thankful," he said. It was a reminder he gave her often. "The hospital staff wasn't sure you'd make it." They'd said she lost a lot of blood on that mountain, too much for good odds.

"But you knew I would," she said.

"Yes, I did," he agreed. "They didn't know you like I do." They didn't know what Emma would do, what she'd endure or survive for the chance to raise her son.

Sawyer knew, and he'd waited patiently at her bedside with Henry and Sara until one day, Emma simply opened her eyes.

"Well, that makes us two lucky, thankful people," she said, sliding her palms gently against his chest.

Sawyer lifted her left hand and kissed the knuckles beside her engagement ring. The ring had been her mother's, but Sara had insisted Emma wear it after the engagement. Sawyer had a custom wedding band in the works to go with her mother's ring. She'd wear that soon too. For now, they'd settled on an open house–style engagement party where friends, families and neighbors could get a look at the girls they'd read about in newspapers and gossip columns straight through Christmas. The community had followed Emma's and Sara's recoveries like their own lives depended on it.

"Enough of that," a familiar voice boomed nearby. Detective Miller approached with Sara on his arm. Their flirting had started at the hospital, both checking in on Emma, and it continued to the present. Sawyer thought it was nice. Emma was more cautious, expectedly protective of her big sister, despite the fact that, to Sawyer's opinion, Miller had been a perfect gentleman every step of the way. "Save it for the ceremony," Miller said with a broad grin.

Sawyer gave Miller's hand a hearty shake. He owed the detective more than he could ever repay. Thanks to his dogged follow-up work, Christopher Lawson was in jail and going to stay there for a very long time. The expected charges of murder, attempted murder, embezzlement, kidnapping and a half dozen of others were just the tip of the iceberg once Miller got started. He'd combed through Christopher's personal computer as if it held the secrets of the universe, and he'd uncovered a treasure trove of evidence against Christopher in the process. Miller linked him and his accomplices to a bevy of other criminal offenses within the month. As a bonus, and as no surprise to the detective, David Finn had confessed everything he knew in trade for leniency on his brothers. Christopher turned on everyone in the hopes of reducing his sentence, but the FBI had been particularly interested in the money laundering and fraud. And they weren't interested in giving breaks.

Sawyer released his hand. "Sorry, man, I just can't seem to keep my hands off of her."

"So I've heard" was Miller's quick response. It earned him an elbow from Sara and a grin from Emma.

She pulled Sara into a hug. "Thank you for doing all

this," she said. "Everything is absolutely beautiful, completely over-the-top for an engagement party."

Sara stroked Emma's arm as she stepped back. "Consider this a test run for the big day."

Emma smiled into the apricot-hued horizon, lifting her chin to the warm setting sun. "I still can't believe I'm getting married on our land. Just like Mom and Dad."

"They'd be really happy," Sara said, tearing up. "I'm still just really glad you're alive."

Sawyer worked to swallow the brick of emotion that presented at the slightest reminder.

"Back at ya," Emma said.

Thankfully, Emma's broken wrist had healed as nicely as her gunshot wound. Both under constant watch and care from Sawyer and Sara, not to mention an endless string of casseroles and pies hand delivered by community members, a testimony and staple of courtesy in the South.

Sara leaned against her new beau's side, her gaze floating across the sea of people on her lawn. "I'd started thinking of Emma and I as alone in the world after Mom and Dad died, but there are nearly two hundred people here tonight, and we're expecting a hundred more for the wedding in September." She eyeballed Sawyer. "Though I think half these guests belong to you."

He smiled. "Probably so." The group near the stables, for example, now roaring with laughter as Henry toddled after a barn cat. He recognized every face from his team at Fortress Security, plus Wyatt's new wife and baby. The rest of that crowd was blood-related and soon to be Emma and Sara's family, as well. Most of them were Garretts. Cousins from Kentucky that seemed to have *protect and serve* in their blood.

For a pair of sisters so accustomed to being alone, Emma and Sara were in for a major adjustment. Henry would never know a day without someone to play with.

Sawyer's partner, Wyatt, caught him staring and led half the pack in Sawyer's direction. Wyatt's new wife laughed along behind them, leading Henry by one hand. His cousins' wives herded everyone else in his direction.

"Well, here comes a crowd," Sawyer muttered to his little circle, a smile already spreading on his lips. "What do you suppose they're up to?"

Wyatt pulled Sawyer in for a strong one-armed hug, then kissed Emma's and Sara's cheeks and shook Miller's hand. "We were just talking about the happy couple," he said, looking from Emma to Sawyer, then back.

Sawyer's senses went on alert. "What are you up to?"

Others from the lawn began a sweep in their direction, whispering and pointing as they moved.

Wyatt pressed a palm to his heart, feigning innocence. Poorly. "Henry was just telling us the story of how two quiet sisters single-handedly took down a psychopathic murderer, escaped abduction and ended a mass of fraud and embezzlement operations, armed only with wood from the dilapidated shed where they were held."

Emma laughed as Henry made a stumbling run for her calves. "Is that right?" she asked. "I know his vocabulary is up to fifteen words now, but I'm not sure he's mastered *dilapidated* or *psychopathic murderer* just yet."

"You'd be surprised," Wyatt said.

Sawyer hoisted Henry into his arms, awed as usual by the sensation of looking into a mirror or at a living photo from his youth. He kissed his son and felt the familiar tug of pride.

"What are you thinking?" Emma asked, smiling again, her skin aglow in the slowly setting sun.

"I'm just all kinds of happy," he said.

Emma beamed, all eyes on her as the crowd grew silent. "Well, I'm glad," she said, digging into the pocket of her pale pink sundress. "Because I have an early wedding present for you." She opened her palm to him, revealing a small scroll in the center. The little paper was tied with two thin white ribbons.

Sawyer dipped his head, unsure. "Is this a bride thing?" he asked, taking the scroll between his thumb and first finger for examination.

Emma smiled. "Open it."

He frowned, especially cautious with any surprise that his entire family and group of friends seemed to be in on. "You said it's a wedding gift?" he asked, removing and pocketing the white ribbons, then unfurling the white paper with his thumbs while Henry did his best to grab it from him.

"More like—" Emma paused and grinned impossibly wider "—Christmas gifts."

"Christmas gifts? It's the middle of summer." Sawyer made a sour face and kept unrolling. That clue didn't help him at all. Finally, he turned the paper over in his fingers. One heavy black square occupied the center of the slick white paper. A grayish semicircle centered in that. In the semicircle were two white peanut shapes. Some sparse text rode along the top. The date. *Yesterday.* His last name. *Lance.* The name of the hospital where Emma had been treated last fall. *Mercy General Hospital.* The word *female.* Written twice. "What is this?" He lifted his eyes to the group, who looked collectively disappointed in him.

He knew what he thought it was, but he didn't dare jump to conclusions that might bring him unnecessarily to tears in front of two hundred people.

"Here." Emma slid in close and pulled Henry onto her hip. She pointed to the first peanut. "This is your daughter." She slid her finger to the next peanut. "And this is also your daughter." She stepped back and watched him, one hand set protectively on her stomach.

"What?" He'd been right? Babies? He stared at the little paper through quickly blurring eyes. "You're really pregnant?"

She nodded, eyes glistening. "That's right, Sawyer Lance," she said. "In a few weeks, we'll marry and become an official family of three. But by the end of the year we'll be a family of five."

"Pregnant," Sawyer's gaze slid to her middle. He'd missed all this the first time. He'd longed for an opportunity to see her glow and bloom again one day. A day when he could be there for her. For anything she needed. That day was already here.

"Yes." She smiled.

"Twins?"

"Girls," she answered.

And like the day she'd opened her eyes in that hospital room, Sawyer knelt before her. This time, he kissed her belly through the soft fabric of her sundress, then rose to kiss her nose, her forehead, her cheeks and her mouth as the crowd burst into whoops and applause.

* * * * *

COMING SOON!

We really hope you enjoyed reading this book. If you're looking for more romance, be sure to head to the shops when new books are available on

Thursday 6th March

To see which titles are coming soon, please visit

millsandboon.co.uk/nextmonth

LET'S TALK
Romance

For exclusive extracts, competitions
and special offers, find us online:

f facebook.com/millsandboon

y @MillsandBoon

◉ @MillsandBoonUK

Get in touch on 01413 063232

For all the latest titles coming soon, visit
millsandboon.co.uk/nextmonth

MILLS & BOON

THE HEART OF ROMANCE

A ROMANCE FOR EVERY KIND OF READER

MODERN

Prepare to be swept off your feet by sophisticated, sexy and seductive heroes, in some of the world's most glamourous and romantic locations, where power and passion collide.
8 stories per month.

HISTORICAL

Escape with historical heroes from time gone by. Whether your passion is for wicked Regency Rakes, muscled Vikings or rugged Highlanders, awaken the romance of the past.
6 stories per month.

MEDICAL

Set your pulse racing with dedicated, delectable doctors in the high-pressure world of medicine, where emotions run high and passion, comfort and love are the best medicine.
6 stories per month.

True Love

Celebrate true love with tender stories of heartfelt romance, from the rush of falling in love to the joy a new baby can bring, and a focus on the emotional heart of a relationship.
8 stories per month.

Desire

Indulge in secrets and scandal, intense drama and plenty of sizzling hot action with powerful and passionate heroes who have it all: wealth, status, good looks…everything but the right woman.
6 stories per month.

HEROES

Experience all the excitement of a gripping thriller, with an intense romance at its heart. Resourceful, true-to-life women and strong, fearless men face danger and desire - a killer combination!
8 stories per month.

DARE

Sensual love stories featuring smart, sassy heroines you'd want as a best friend, and compelling intense heroes who are worthy of them.
4 stories per month.

To see which titles are coming soon, please visit

millsandboon.co.uk/nextmonth

MILLS & BOON

MODERN

Power and Passion

Prepare to be swept off your feet by sophisticated, sexy and seductive heroes, in some of the world's most glamourous and romantic locations, where power and passion collide.

Julia James
Heiress's
PREGNANCY SCANDAL
MILLS & BOON
MODERN

Jennie Lucas
Chosen as the
SHEIKH'S ROYAL BRIDE
MILLS & BOON
MODERN

Kim Lawrence
A WEDDING
at the
ITALIAN'S DEMAND
MILLS & BOON

Sharon Kendrick
The
SHEIKH'S SECRET BABY
MILLS & BOON
MODERN

Eight Modern stories published every month, find them at

millsandboon.co.uk/Modern